HAPPY ACCIDENT

Evan Tyler

Lisa and Michelle,
My saviors!
Love you soooo much!
Evan Tyler

Lisa and Murielle,

My saviors!

Have you soccer much!

Ever, Tyler

A HAPPY ACCIDENT

Printing History/October 2012

ISBN: 978-0-9884465-0-2

PRINTED IN THE UNITED STATES OF AMERICA

Acknowledgments:

To the two people who have always supported the dream,
Thank you for everything

To Aunt V,
Thanks for a second set of eyes and a boost of confidence

To every phenomenal musician of the 60's and 70's,
Without you, this would be impossible

To my number one,
You are the First and the Last

Prologue

Future Time: 1988

Choice was seven years old when she discovered her mother lying on the kitchen floor in a pool of blood. Crimson streams flowed from her flared nostrils and gaping mouth, meeting in a puddle that outlined her profile like a shadow. Left cheek pressed hard against the white linoleum, knees bent, and arms crisscrossed at her front, she was the image of a woman who had found rest in the middle of a fitful night's sleep.

Minutes earlier, Choice had skulked from her bedroom in search of a late snack, scrabbling her way through the black halls to the staircase that led to the kitchen. She wrapped her right hand around the banister and bound together the hem of her pink nightgown with her left as she took softly each step. Upon reaching the bottom of the staircase, she spotted her mother's figure on the right side of the kitchen, beside the stove. A shaft of steel moonlight beamed through the kitchen window, reflecting the sideward image of her face onto the pool of blood.

Choice crept forward, rubbing her hands up and down her bare arms. As she closed in, her mother's condition became entirely glaring—the glitter of her open eyes as lambent as diamonds, the scent of her blood like rusted metal.

Choice knelt down, dipping her knees into the pool of blood, soaking it up onto her nightgown. "Mummy, what happened?' she whispered eagerly, poking her mother's cheek. The chill of her skin generated unalloyed terror, causing Choice to tumble backward with a shriek.

Regaining her balance, Choice began pushing at her mother's midsection. Her languid shoulder flapped back, shaking the ground beneath Choice's bare feet. While she tried over and over to rock her mother to life, the kitchen lights suddenly flickered on around her. Over her shoulder, Choice saw her grandfather standing at the edge of the kitchen. His blue robe swirled around him as he charged to her side. He pressed his ear against her mother's chest, peering back up at Choice, doe-eyed, his bottom lip sagging feebly. The panic on her grandfather's face was the last sight Choice would see for the rest of her life.

From that moment forward, there was only darkness in front of her eyes, as though a black veil had been placed over her head. Months later, her grandfather would tell her that her sudden blindness was her mind's way of protecting her from the harrowing sight.

Yet, Choice's other senses hadn't protected her. She could still smell the metallic blood. She could still feel the air conditioner blowing ruthlessly against her bare arms. She could taste the salt of tears tumbling down her lips. She could hear her grandfather sputtering their address to an emergency operator.

Choice could hear her own screeching as she cried over and over again, "What is it? What is it? No. No. No!" unable to find any other words.

When Choice thought back on the scene as an adult, she imagined herself having some kind of out-of-body experience, the only available sight for the blind. From a bird's eye view, she had seen the passing images of herself. She had seen herself curled up like a limp fetus, her head pressed against the floor as the paramedics rushed the room. She had watched as her grandfather grabbed her up swiftly and swaddled her in his arms while she continued to wail. At the hospital, she had watched herself kicking and jerking as a doctor tried to examine her.

Unable to contain her inexorable fight, the nurse pressed Choice's shoulders against the bed while the doctor injected a sedative. Immediately, she slumped over, her head falling against her shoulder, and slept like a newborn until the drugs wore off. She did not scream when she opened her eyes, but lay still in the hospital room, unaware of whether morning had come.

Choice cried softly, hot tears stinging her cheeks. Her stomach quaked so violently that she was sure she would vomit. She leaned over the bed, a long trail of saliva dripping from her mouth to the floor.

Where was her grandfather? Where was a doctor? She needed more of the injection—anything to put her back to sleep. In her sleep, she could find a way out of this nightmare.

Choice knew that only one person could restore her slumber naturally. Only one.

"Come here, Choicey," her mother would say when Choice entered her room exhausted yet wired by a nightmare. "Your mummy will get you to sleep."

She would nestle Choice in her lap and sing until her eyelids grew heavy and her breathing became as slow and rhythmic as a grandfather clock. She'd sing that same imitation of a James Taylor lullaby that had put Choice to sleep for as long as she could remember:

So close those eyes
You can your eyes
We'll be fine
I don't have a love song
But I won't sing the blues anymore
Oh, but I can hear this song
And you will know this song
When I'm gone

Winter

What is better than a winter kiss?
A signal to a New Year's start
Caress me with your cool lips
Revive my bones, refresh my heart

Chapter One

Kindle didn't consider Real anything exceptional at first sight. He was tall and willowy, his long arms hanging from his short-sleeved T-shirt like winter branches. His features were neither hideous nor remarkable—his nose thin at the bridge but round at the tip, his lips pale rose like the center of his cheeks. The bright stage lights cast an iridescent halo behind his black hair and bleached his Jasmine skin vanilla. A slight cleft in his chin made masculine his bare face. Kindle didn't make out the color of his eyes until he moved his long bangs out of his face for the first time that evening.

Real slid his bangs behind his ears with the last strum of his guitar and a "thank you." Green—his eyes were a shimmering green, two drops of olive oil on a white pallet. When he and his band leapt off the stage into the crowd, he made his way to the bar where Kindle stood talking to the bartender. So, it was true. Real had been staring at her through his long bangs during the entire performance.

Grabbing a handful of drinks, Kindle pushed her way through the whistling crowd to the other side of the room. Pink and blue lights glazed the black floor. The walls boasted of a gothic painter's obsession with carcasses, bones and star-lit skies. Hardly impressed by punk art (or anything punk), she thought of the pictures as high-priced graffiti.

Kindle could ignore the lights and the music. She could almost ignore the people, if she pretended that they were extras on the set of her own movie. However, she could not ignore Real. He shadowed her the rest of the evening, one step behind her as she worked, withdrawing only a couple steps when the tip of his tennis shoe touched the heel of her ballerina flat.

He followed her as she served the jiggling crowd. He followed her through the whirls of smoke and the puddles of alcohol. He followed her through a maze of long-haired guys in tattered jeans and pale-faced girls in fishnets. He followed her faithfully, offering his salutation with a genteel cough, repeating his band's name, detailing his reason for being in England and his hope to go back to America really, really famous. Perhaps at a loss for anything else, he inquired about the cut beneath her bandaged index finger. Kindle continued working, impassive, sometimes steadying four bottles in each hand.

An hour after the band left the stage, the energy in the pub went from a roaring bustle to a purring hum as a steady flow of patrons trickled out onto Floyd Street. By one in the morning, Kindle also made her exit. She pulled her trench coat from the rack by the door and made her way out of the club onto the sidewalk, lights from passing cars and orange street lanterns making clear her path. Real walked behind her.

"Will you marry me?" he asked, pushing his hair out of his eyes when she suddenly turned to face him. His eyes were amber-flecked, his lashes sparse but long. Kindle considered that maybe he wasn't like the other grimy punk boys—the ones with the sewage green sludge beneath their fingernails, the ones making loud, stuttering demands for more beer.

The wind struck them brashly. Real tried pushing back his long hair as it whirled around his face. Kindle held her arms over her chest tightly, attempting to resist the gusts that flailed through her coat.

"Marry me," he said once more, sniffling. His nose had frosted to pink. White cold flowed from his mouth, his teeth glistening. "You must think I'm crazy or something. But the first time I saw you—" he glanced down at his black rubber watch, "—maybe it was, like, a week ago, you know, when we first performed—I knew that you were the one for me. I was sure of that."

Kindle folded in her lips to repress a smile. His approach was benign, his drawl stale and plain, as though he had come from the middle of Nowhere, America. Hers was clear, rich, utterly English when she responded, "Well, now I myself am sure of one thing."

"What's that?" He smiled.

"You're barmy."

He wrinkled his brows. "I'm what?

"You're crazy. Or maybe you're just a fool. I have no way of knowing. Perhaps I don't want to know."

Kindle marched ahead. He caught up to her and strolled beside her gingerly, turning his collar up and burrowing his hands in his pocket. They passed a row of small white and gold pubs and shops. The businesses were closed for the evening, but their tall windows gave a glimpse of object shadows in the darkness. It was a city falling asleep.

And yet, they were wide awake. Real was wide-eyed, searching her face curiously. His eagerness made her stomach flip-flop.

"What's your name?" he asked.

"You haven't even told me yours," Kindle returned.

"Well, my name is Bobby Carter."

"I thought it was Real."

He looked down at his T-shirt. It was black with white letters that spelled REAL. He smiled—a soft and quiet gesture, lines curving around his mouth like a pair of parenthesis. "It's just a T-shirt," he said. "My name is Bobby, but my stage name is Ricky Stallion. You know, like a horse or whatever."

"Like a horse, eh? Well, that's just clever, isn't it?" She stopped and grinned at him. "So very, very clever."

Bobby beamed, his skin awakening to gold. She wondered if his eagerness gave him some kind of immunity to the cold.

"So you like it? I mean, you like the name 'Ricky'? Does it sound like a rock star's name?"

"Not so much."

Bobby continued smiling but dropped his gaze to the sidewalk. "Brutally honest type?"

"I wouldn't consider myself a 'type.'" She smiled. "But you yourself are a star-type, aren't you? Suppose it doesn't matter if this little barmaid disapproves of your stage name."

He lifted his brows and grinned brighter, seemingly recharged by her compliment. "You think we're gonna be stars?"

Kindle turned the corner. The lane was dimmer, offering only a few streetlights and occasionally the glow of car headlights. She considered how scenes like these—ones with women walking next to strangers in black alleys—were the makings of cautionary tales. This evening, curiosity subdued sense.

Bobby kept in step with her, idly wagging his shoulders back and forth. They walked in between two columns of shabby, brown brick flats that were separated by a narrow, brown-paved road.

He brushed her shoulder with his arm and stepped off the sidewalk onto the road. "So you see star potential?" he tried again.

"I think you're a star already. That band of yours is just waiting to catch up."

"The Dare—that's the band's name," he replied, wiping the back of his hand over his mouth to clear a smile. "Our name."

"Well, that's a name this little barmaid approves of."

Bobby smirked, biting his lip coyly. "A good band name and a beautiful woman's approval—it's a sign from God; we've come to the right place. Guess we'll be in Manchester for a while."

"I'm glad to be a sign for you." She glanced up at him. "Perhaps more glad to know that my approval could determine the length of your tour stops."

"Well, uh, we're not really a touring band. Not yet anyway. Just came here to see if we could, you know, find more opportunities, get a change of scenery or whatever." He rubbed his hands together. "Definitely needed a change."

"How has the change been?"

He coughed, seemingly shy. "Well, we've been in England a few months now, but we just got to Manchester a couple days ago. It's been pretty righteous so far. Not like anything we've known."

"Glad to know you're enjoying it. We wouldn't want you to leave any time soon." Kindle sucked in her cheeks, overtly eluding a smile. "We Mancunians, anyway."

Bobby peered at her, smiling so broadly that the corner of his eyes wrinkled and smile lines deepened.

She was a little embarrassed for him, for the way he expressed his joy so openly; he seemed unable to control his facial expressions. Obviously, he didn't see the problem with flipping over all the cards at the beginning of the game. She imagined that he was one of those hippie boys who enjoyed lounging around his house naked, unafraid of surprise company. Did he not know the value of mystique?

Kindle pulled the collar of her coat up around her neck.

"So, uh, when am I gonna, like, learn your name?" he asked. "Do I have to guess at it?"

She grinned. "I'm sure I'd enjoy that."

"Okay. Well, alright then. For your enjoyment..." He squeezed his eyes shut and lifted one eyebrow, exaggeratedly thoughtful. "Is it Penelope?"

She nudged his arm playfully. "Penelope? Do I look like a Penelope?"

"I guess it depends."

"On?"

"Whether you like it or not," he said. "I mean, whether it'll make you like me more or not."

"If you guess my name right, I will like you more, no doubt. Maybe I'll even accept your proposal."

"Well, can I have a clue at least?" Lightly, he poked her arm. "Just one clue."

"I suppose that's only fair. So, here's your clue: my name is a real word in the English language."

"Ok." He nodded slowly, running his tongue over his back teeth. "I think I have it. Your name is Butterfly."

"Butterfly?" she responded, dropping her mouth affectedly. "I resemble a flying insect to you?"

"No, no. Not at all," he chuckled. "Honestly, you look like a princess to me. So is that it? Is your name Princess?"

"I should only wish." Kindle held her hands over the sides of her face, smoldering the heat beneath her blushing cheeks.

"I guess I give up then. I don't know what to say."

"My name's Kindle," she replied, extending her hand to him. "Like a fire, not a horse."

He laughed, grasping her bare hand with his wool-gloved hand. "Kindle what?"

"You would say Kindle Carter, wouldn't you?"

He laughed again.

When they stopped at the rusted metal gate, a stone's throw away from the steps leading up to her duplex unit, Bobby picked up her other hand and sandwiched it between his. He rubbed his hands together over hers to warm them before bringing them to his lips, blowing on them with mildly warm breath.

"So we're at your place," he said somewhat absently, releasing her hands and staring at the ground.

"Yes. I do reside here. For the time being."

"For the time being?" he reflected. "Well, where do you want to go? You ever been to the U.S.?"

"No. I've not been many places outside of the country." She paused. "But I've got no qualms with England, really."

"So where do you want to go?"

"I think I'll move to London one day."

"Yeah? What for?" he asked.

"Maybe you're not the only one who wants the bright lights."

Bobby stood with one foot on the bar at the bottom of the gate, rocking back and forth. She blinked her eyes at him once and walked through the gate, up to the top of the steps. He had not stopped smiling. She imagined now that he was a lot simpler than she had first thought.

"I'm trying to say that I want to be an actress one day," said Kindle. "I want to do musicals. Maybe I'll be a star one day, just like you."

"I'm not a star. Not really." He smiled faintly. "So, you wanna do musicals? That's pretty cool. Radical. Kinda surprising."

"Surprising? I'm sure you don't know me well enough to be surprised, Mr. Stallion."

"But I'd really like to. I mean, really, really, *really* like to."

Kindle glanced over her shoulder at the door to her apartment. "You absolutely cannot come in, Bobby, in case you were wondering."

"I wasn't wondering," he returned, shrugging and smirking. He must have reveled in what tiny bit of mystery he gave off. Maybe he knew a little something about mystique.

"Then what were you thinking?"

"I don't know if I should tell you."

Kindle half-smiled and looked him over from top to bottom before she turned toward the door.

"I was thinking how, like, incredibly beautiful you are. And that you probably don't wear a lot of makeup, do you?"

She turned back around. "I don't wear makeup at all."

"Well, that's even better. I don't know any girls who don't wear makeup."

"Thank you." She studied his ardent face. He was far more handsome under street lights than what she could appraise beneath the pub's foggy lights. "Thank you very much, Stallion. I should go now though. Have a lovely evening. That's well-wishing from your friendly Moss Side barmaid, Penelope Butterfly Princess."

He laughed, crinkle-eyed. "Can I come in to at least use the bathroom?"

Kindle turned back toward the door, holding in a laugh. She knew he feared extinguishing that little spark that kept them both warm in spite of the cold. But for the sake of preserving her magic, she mouthed, "Goodnight, Bobby."

Kindle reached behind herself and turned the doorknob, walking backward into her flat. He stood in place staring up at her as she pushed the door closed.

When Kindle lay down to sleep, the image of Bobby's smiling face hung under her eyelids like a banner. She sat up, shaking her head. There was no place for sleep, but certainly, there was time for dreams. Kindle pulled up the memory of each moment of their walk, as though she were editing a movie reel. She recalled his face. She imagined how her own face had looked. She re-scripted her words. She invented his thoughts.

Kindle considered that now, maybe, she had acquired that mystique that was so rare in the Moss Side neighborhood, where women couldn't afford time or energy for elusiveness. To top it off, she had created a little memory that she could stretch and twist and bend to entertain herself, to convince herself that she had some importance in the world—even if just to one person for a few moments.

****

Kindle dressed quickly for her day job. She had slept only two hours before her alarm clock rattled her. Even so, thoughts of Bobby had felt like rest, like a reprieve from real life.

She took the short walk to work, entering the hotel a half hour early, before the sun surfaced from behind the clouds. Inside the lobby, a few glass tables lined the walls. Two gold-trimmed chairs sat at each table, like a pair of regal old women. The check-in desk was settled at the rear center of the lobby.

Mr. Holster stood still behind the desk, chin raised, eyes roaming. If not the image of a trimmer Santa Claus with his snow-white hair and ruddy cheeks, he was certainly the picture of a Queen's guard. Kindle imagined that he measured his posture with a wooden ruler every morning as part of his daily routine. His reticence gave her the urge to tackle and tickle him each time she saw him. She imagined that, on her last day of work at the hotel, she would.

Kindle made her way to the front of the desk and placed her hands on top of it.

"Kindle Hyrum," Mr. Holster said, sounding more like a God voice-over than Santa Claus. "You're early."

"There's no such thing as early, right?" Kindle said. "Only late." She sighed, breathing out pure joy.

"I haven't heard those words since—" Holster dropped his head, adjusting his cuff links. "I haven't heard those words in a long time."

Kindle picked at her fingernails. "I haven't either."

She turned her back to him, hoping to alleviate the awkwardness. Like an apparition, Bobby Carter appeared at her left, floating toward her in a white T-shirt and star-spangled pajama pants. She turned back toward Mr. Holster.

Bobby stopped at her side, his hands behind his back. "Kindle," he smiled.

Quickly, she glanced up at Mr. Holster. He was ever sedate.

"What are you doing here?" Bobby asked. He pushed his hair behind his ear, enunciating the squareness of his jaw and the shadow of a beard that sprouted overnight.

Kindle drew her hands along her uniform, turning to face him. "Yes, well, your little barmaid is a hotel maid as well."

"So, you've got two jobs? That's totally rad."

"What a way to put it, Mr. Carter."

Bobby smiled. "You remembered my last name?"

"I did." She gave a single, stately nod.

"Killer. I mean, I'm really glad." He glanced down quickly, as though conferring with the floor for his next words. "We're, like, in room three hundred something or whatever. I forgot which exactly. We haven't been that long, I guess." He crossed his arms over his chest and hunched toward her to whisper, "I'm just taking a walk. Didn't sleep a lot last night. Are you good? You look good."

She put on an embellished smirk. "As good as to be expected with the many jobs that I work."

"Is that, like, sarcasm?" Bobby swung his arms back and forth, smiling.

"Absolutely," she replied. "That's, *like*, sarcasm."

He rubbed his eye like a sleepy child. "I hope I haven't offended you."

"Oh, no. No worries. I don't get offended. Ever."

"Wh—"

Leaving Bobby's half-syllable response lingering, Kindle treaded off. She made her way to the supply closet, mechanically selecting her tools, listening for the sound of his fading footsteps. Re-emerging from the closet, Kindle took a quick scan of the lobby before beginning her work. She moved from room to room, quietly dumping trash, making beds, scrubbing tubs...scolding herself.

Ill-preparation. Ill-preparation was to blame for this loss of her fragile, newly-acquired mystique. Sophisticated women balanced sweetness over confidence, like a tiara over their pretty little heads. Kindle had been outright rude, an annoying reflex of her shame.

Ill-preparation. There was no such thing as luck, only preparation for chance. If Kindle had prepared something to say in the possibility that she would see Bobby again, she wouldn't have fumbled so terribly. Instead, she had entertained herself with dreams of him. Dreams amounted to nothing.

Kindle continued scolding herself as she pulled her heavy cart down the halls. She stopped at one door, knocking furiously over the sound of raucous laughter that escaped from beneath the door.

Bobby swung open the door, his hair fluttering around his face. His three band mates sat on twin beds behind him. They turned their faces toward her—soldiers at attention.

Fully relapsed, Kindle centered her breath in the middle of her chest and brushed past Bobby, pulling her cart of cleaning supplies behind her. She entered the bathroom, browsing absently through an array of spray bottles. She breathed in short spurts.

"You're really gonna do that?" Bobby said, stepping into the bathroom and securing the door behind him.

His band mates quieted.

"I don't know what you're talking about," Kindle said evenly, selecting a spray bottle.

"You're gonna clean our tub?"

"It's a job. This is what work looks like."

"Well, I know," he said. "I mean, I work too."

"What is it that you do exactly?" she asked. She knelt down and began scrubbing the tub erratically.

"Well, I do music," Bobby replied.

Kindle snorted. "That's hardly work, Mr. Carter."

"Mr. Carter? You make me sound like a big stiff."

"Do you prefer Mr. Ricky Stallion? I probably won't call you that again." She shook her head, hoping to shake off the insolence that clung to her like a parasite. "I thought you were in a three hundred room. That's what you said. This is room 205."

"Yeah, I know. We just got here. I guess I was confused or whatever." He crossed his arms and shrugged his shoulders. "You can call me Bobby. I like that better."

"Delighted to hear that, Mr. Carter." Kindle began polishing the tub in uniform circles.

"Before, I wasn't trying to be offensive or anything like that."

"Of course not. It comes naturally for some people." She turned around, sitting before him on her knees. "Which one of those little boys out there do you sleep with?"

Bobby's eyes widened. "What?" He shook his head and laughed. "No, no. None of them. I sleep on the floor."

Kindle resumed her aimless scrubbing, sensing his stare on her back as beaming as a laser. Resolving to take control of the situation, she crafted a script in her head before rising to face him. When their eyes met, she immediately darted her gaze, dropping her lines. If only she could have shielded her face with her hands, like a frightened kitten. She wondered if a little makeup would have offered some confidence.

Bobby rubbed his hands together, smirking. "Well, um, I have rad news. We won't be performing at your bar anymore. I mean, Rory's."

She smoothed down the edges of her hair. "Why is that?"

"Well, Fred—he's our manager or whatever—he said that enough word has gotten out about us that we'll have to do bigger venues. Can you believe that? He says our audience would be too big to hold in anything as small as Rory's. I guess you were right, Kindle. We might be on our way to the stars."

"Excellent, Mr. Carter. Just superb." She shrugged, struggling to grasp a semblance of grace. "And just to think that I was considering becoming your wife. But now you've moved beyond me, haven't you?"

Bobby smiled—that slow-spreading, closed-mouth smile he had smiled last evening. It must have been his staple. "You've been thinking about it?" I mean, since last night?" His eyes shone. "That's great. I mean, I can dig it. This is just great.

I mean, this is sick, isn't it? The Dare's gonna be selling out
shows."

"You are manic, aren't you?"

He pushed back his hair and grinned. "I'm manic about
you."

She could have laughed. He must have thought he was a
Seventies Shakespeare.

"I mean, I'm crazy about you," he continued. "*Barmy*
about you. That's what you'd say, right?"

The corners of her mouth twitched. With a broad smile ,
she cooed, "Oh, come on, Bobby. Even your little mates will
think you're crazy now if they hear you say that to me."

"I guess I don't really care if they hear. I'm pretty sure
that they know that you're—what's the word?—you're...one in
a billion. Is that a good phrase? " Bobby leaned back against the
door, casually inspecting his fingernails.

"You're so strange." She glided her tongue over her
teeth, thoughtful. "It's very humble of you to sleep on a floor."

"Well, uh, I guess."

Kindle gripped the cart handle.

Bobby reached out to touch her wrist. She had expected
his long, thin fingers to be moist. Instead, they were warm, soft,
dry—a peculiar comfort. "I like you," he said. "It might even be
love-at-first-sight. Do you believe in that kind of thing?"

She breathed a short laugh. "Who are you, really?"

He laughed also, sniffling and rubbing his chin. "I don't
know, really. But maybe I'll find out when I get to know my
other half."

"Song line," she replied straightaway.

"Huh?"

"Put that line in a song," Kindle over-enunciated, as if
talking to a foreigner. She smiled and steered her cart toward
him, gesturing for him to make room for her departure.

Chapter Two

Bobby, not so much Ricky Stallion, made the line into a song. He named it "My Other Half," and it became The Dare's biggest crowd pleaser yet. Having taken him all of one hour to write on his acoustic guitar, it was the song that would ultimately move the band from crowds of one hundred to crowds of one thousand. After eleven months of playing it at every show—in both the acoustic and electric version—Epic Records finally got word of them and was ready to give them a shot. It would be twenty years later that the music commentators on VH1 would all agree that "My Other Half" was technically the first emo song, even before the term was officially coined in 1985.

Ricky Stallion would one day claim that the song idea came down to him on angel wings Christmas Day 1979. In actuality, it was December 29, 1979 that Kindle made the suggestion and December 30th when Bobby actually took her advice.

On New Year's Eve, Bobby skipped out immediately after the band's performance of the song at Sideshow. They had planned to celebrate their last performance of the year together, but Bobby insisted on taking a walk by himself. The end of the year called for time alone to reflect. Or whatever…

Bobby did less reflecting than hunting. He had to see her. He found his way to the street he had taken previously to get to her duplex. He walked the ragged sidewalk beside a pitted black street. On the other side, cars lined up next to a series of brick storefronts. Most of the letters on top of the building were white, though some had missing letters as conspicuous as missing teeth. One business advertised discount three-piece suits while another's red and yellow sign advertised liquor. Tall street lights lined both sides of the street—some orange and glowing, others dim and yet others refusing to give any light. Bobby realized that the old stores were standing in the middle of a neighborhood. The sooty, broken gingerbread houses, with their cracked windows and barred doors, actually belonged to families. Yellow light glowed from open windows and wild, gravelly laughter poured out of the screen doors. Bobby shook his head, suddenly awakened to the fact that this city was a mirror of the cities he had only seen in a blur when his father sped through them to get to their final destination. He wondered why he hadn't noticed it the night before. Maybe that's what love-at-first-sight did to a man—blinded him to everything else.

When he reached the gate of her duplex, he yelled her name at her window. Tree branches crackled in response.

"Kindle Carter," he yelled once more, aware that he hadn't yet picked up her last name. His voice echoed through the streets, announcing that he was all alone.

He sighed. Hunting was hard. And it was unbearably cold outside. He decided he would return to Sideshow, disappointed but sure the band could keep him entertained well enough.

No sooner than he had turned his back to the gate to begin his walk, he heard Kindle's voice.

"Color me surprised," she said, her voice raised to gather his attention.

Bobby turned back, smiling. She stood at the top step of the duplex, leaning against the stairs' wooden rail, her long waves streaming over her chest, creating a picture of Rapunzel.

He wrapped his hands around the gate's metal bars. "May I?" he asked.

She nodded once.

Bobby pushed himself up and jumped over the fence, landing hard on his feet, sending up a wave of dry dirt in the air. When he reached the bottom of the steps, Kindle came down to meet him, sitting on the last step. He sat beside her, immediately taking in her scent. It was some kind of buttercream fragrance. Maybe the smell of her soap. Undoubtedly, she had recently stepped out of the shower, her hair still slick and sparkling with water. With hardly a first thought, he slipped his knitted cap off his head and placed it on her head, tucking her bundle of wet hair inside. With her hair pulled up, he could fully gauge her beauty. Her face shined like a wax statue, all of her features exceptional. Broad, dark eyes like Diana Ross. Carly Simon lips—full and moist. Debbie Harry's sharp cheekbones.

She smiled. "A dapper young gentleman, you are," she said, looking down at their feet.

"Thank you," he responded. "Not that young though, I guess." He patted his leg. "Not in music years, anyway."

"What exactly are music years? Is that some odd time signature I've never heard of? Perhaps a calculation like dog years?"

"Nah," he said, rubbing his hands over her frosting cheeks. "Just an industry expectation, I guess. It's sorta now or never for me and the band."

"Well then, I suppose I'm not that young for an aspiring actress either."

"How old are you?"

She touched his shoulder with hers. "You can't ask a woman that, you know."

"Sorry." Bobby rubbed his index finger over his smirking lips. "So, uh, am I allowed to ask what year you were born?"

"What year I was born?" Kindle repeated, seemingly perplexed at first. She grinned. "What year were *you* born?"

"Fifty-six," he said. "November fourth."

Her face brightened. "Guess when I was born."

"I don't know." Bobby smiled, shaking his head.

"Fifty-nine. November twenty-fifth. We're children of November."

"You're only nineteen," he said. "So I'm, like, four years older than you. Wow. You're so young, younger than I thought."

"You've got a musician's mind," she said.

"What do you mean?"

"You're arithmetic is all wrong."

Bobby laughed, despite himself. "Probably should've gone to college, huh?" He rubbed the bridge of his nose, acutely aware of the gawkiness of his speech.

"Why didn't you?"

"Why didn't I what? Go to college?" He reflected. "I guess I just always wanted to do music. Pretty much." He placed his hand over her thigh, feeling that he had gained permission by the way she smiled. "What's that sound?"

Kindle looked up toward the door of her apartment, following the sound of the loud buzzing that had begun. "My New Year's alarm. It's midnight." She beamed. "Welcome to nineteen-eighty."

"Happy new years, Penelope Princess," he said, grabbing hold of her wrist as she started for her door. "Don't go. I can stand the noise." Right then, he was positive he could stand just about anything to keep her in sight.

She settled back down on the step, stretching his hat down over her ears, then extending her arms to stretch.

"So, um, there's no one in there to shut off the alarm? Mom? Dad?" His voice dropped. "Boyfriend? Husband?"

"E. None of the above." She smiled, leaning her head toward her shoulder. "None of those are actually life necessities. I'm what you would call a minimalist. "

"Well, who do you have to take care of you?" Bobby asked, this time twining his fingers through the tiny wet hairs at the nape of her neck.

"I take care of myself."

"That's pretty decent. I can dig it."

Kindle clapped her hands together, concluding that segment of the conversation. "So now that you've thoroughly explored my life, what about you? Who takes care of you?"

"I've got an apartment back home with my cousin Kyle. He's in the band. He's the, uh, the bass player. We look out for each other. You know, like brothers."

She nodded. "Any other details? Famous parents? Crooked siblings? Magic pets?"

Bobby tittered. "Nothing that interesting." He tilted his head to the sky. "I don't know what to say. I'm from Canton. In Michigan. Not Ohio. Born and raised. I'm pretty much an only child, so my parents are really, like, *interested* in everything I do. Mom wants me to do whatever I dig and dad wants me to go to school or pick up a trade or something."

"I could tell you were an only-child."

"How do you figure?"

"You're a little out of it. You don't worry about a thing, do you? Single children are usually that way."

"Well, you know, Elvis was an only-child. Jesus, too."

She laughed.

"You didn't say you had brothers or sisters," he said. "That would make you an only-child."

"I'm not a child anymore, Bobby." She shrugged.

Bobby stared at her lips. They had deepened to ruby red from the cold and were even more dazzling under moonlight. He brought forward his face to hers, on a silent quest for her mouth. She looked at him wordless, gaping, her cold breath mingling with his like white smoke swirls.

Yet, before their mouths met, she interjected, "Do you still want to use my toilet?"

Bobby chuckled, backing away from her face. He rubbed his chin with his palm, contorting his lips and eyebrows, as if in serious thought. "I don't know about that, Kindle. You know, if I come in I may never want to leave."

"Oh, but you would certainly have to leave. I couldn't be one of your punk groupies."

"There aren't any groupies here, I don't think." Bobby pulled up his coat sleeve and scratched his inner wrist. "So, um, what happens if I never see you again?"

"You're so desperate," she laughed.

"But you kinda like my desperation, right?" Bobby rested his forehead against hers. "So what do you say? Will you marry me now? Or do you want me to, like, wait?"

"Even if I ever wanted to marry you, it could never work," she said, retreating her face from his.

"How do you know?"

Kindle met his eyes and lifted an eyebrow. "It's very obvious."

"It's the eighties now. A lot of things have changed."

"And a lot of things are ever the same, Bobby. Besides, you don't know me. More importantly, I don't know you."

"But we can get to know each other."

"That's not what marriage is for."

"Who ever said that?"

Kindle looked up at the sky, her eyes a pendulum between the stars. "Common sense dictates."

He followed her eyes. "My mom says that being married means you've gotta, like, learn stuff about your spouse all the time. Like forever. And my parents have been married thirty years or something. They're experts."

"There's no such thing as a love expert."

Bobby reached into his coat pocket and pulled out a miniature writing pad.

And thus, he began to write The Dare's next song. "Love Expert" would eventually become Ricky Stallion and The Dare's third number one single, though it didn't fare quite as well as "My Other Half." It was a hit no less—a song that any Dare fan knew by heart, containing those colorful lyrics that Bobby Carter scribbled down on the little writing pad as Kindle stared at him.

"What are you writing?" Kindle interrupted.

Bobby shoved the writing pad back in his pocket. "You could be my inspiration or something. I mean, it's like every word you say is a song."

"So you're pinching my sayings to make yourself rich?" She raised her eyebrows. "Well, I want a quarter of your earnings."

"You can have it all if you marry me."

"Oh, you see now, money talks. So when do you propose doing this?"

"You know Manchester better than I do. Pick a day."

"Well," she mused, placing her index finger on her bottom lip. She hummed loudly, then brought her eyes quickly to his face. "January fifth. At the Registry. That should do. I'm sure we'll have a fine time—maybe we can have our reception at the pub. You could sing and play for our first dance. That will really exhibit your talents. You could immediately land a record deal."

Bobby bit his lip. "I guess you're not taking me seriously."

"Of course I'm taking you seriously," she said, standing. "Be here at nine on the fifth and allow me to show you how seriously I take you."

Bobby said nothing but nodded. Sober-faced, he stared at her for a full minute until she broke out into another grin. He stood and walked backward toward the gate, watching her as she entered her apartment.

****

Kindle's mother wouldn't have found any amusement in this kind of ambiguous chatter. "Don't let your mouth write checks that your arse can't cash," her mother used to say when she felt Kindle was becoming too much of a clown. It was her mother's overstated opinion that women should be clear in speech, that they had no time for being jokey little monkeys. But for Kindle, who dreamed all too often of being able to say anything and everything that she wanted, there was bound to be quite a bit of play when she was left un-chaperoned for good. Her mother died when she had just formally reached adulthood; yet, even at twenty years old, there was very little grown up about Kindle. Maybe adults did make dates by joking about marriage. How was Kindle to know? She'd never been on a date before. In the case that there would be a date on the fifth, she would be prepared.

When Bobby showed up at her apartment at seven-thirty the morning of the fifth, Kindle was ready for whatever the day was intended to be. She wore a pair of diamond earrings her mother had left her, deciding that for her first date, she should shine. As they began their walk, Bobby pulled out folded papers and a pen from the inside of his jacket.

After inspecting the papers, Kindle squinted her eyes at him. "I guess you've taken this marriage idea quite literally."

"I guess you haven't."

Kindle batted her eyes. "Of course, I have. Bend down."

Bobby hunched over and she used his back as a writing pad when she signed the papers. Excited at the prospect that she had found someone as quirky as she and as play-pretend as the movies, she laughed out loud.

As they continued walking, the wind beat against their faces. The sun was just beginning to break through the clouds. They turned onto Canal Street, marching beside its shoddy brick warehouses. The Rochdale Canal's swamp green water flickered, moving up and down in short waves.

A step behind, Bobby tapped Kindle's shoulder. "So, guess what, Kindle?"

"What is that, Bobby?"

"I hear that to be, like, legally married, we have to have two witnesses. At least."

"Is that so?" she said, skipping now, hoping he'd find her graceful exuberance appealing.

"Yep. So what do you say we do?"

Kindle stopped to face him. "I think we should ask someone to witness this blessed event."

She walked ahead of him, straight to a blonde woman in black leggings and a grey sweater dress. The woman leaned against the wall of the brick flat. She took a long drag of her cigarette, her eyes closed as if she were in ecstasy.

Bobby stood at Kindle's side, covering his mouth with his hand, concealing a smirk. The woman opened her eyes. "Yeah?" she asked brashly. She took another short drag.

"Please forgive my bothering you," Kindle started politely, "but there will be an amazing event taking place here shortly. And my fiancé and I need two witnesses."

The woman looked up at Bobby and pointed at him with her middle finger. "I know you from somewhere. You're one of the students at—oh, what's the school's name? "

Bobby shook his head.

"Well, who are you then?" She looked him over with disdain. "What are you doing?"

"We're, uh, we're getting married," said Bobby.

The woman curled her bottom lip up to keep the cigarette seated in her mouth. "Oh, blow me. You're eloping, aren't you?" She drew the cigarette from her mouth with her thumb and index finger. "How long will this take?"

"Not a long time, I don't think," Bobby said. "I'm Bobby. What's your name?"

"Do you really need my name?" She wrinkled her nose.

"No," Kindle interjected, seizing the papers from Bobby. She held them up flat with both hands in front of the woman's face. "But you will have to sign these."

The woman flicked her cigarette into the wind, her eyes squinted and forehead wrinkled. "Hannah. That's my name. And I guess your names are Young and Dumb."

Bobby and Kindle exchanged glances.

Hannah laughed briefly, hoarsely. "You know, I've been with my man five years and he hasn't spoken a word of marriage. Cringes at it. We both do. He more than I, I suppose." She shook her head. "Well, if you need my help, then you have it. If you're going to take the leap of death, it's a good thing that you're both willing parties."

Bobby looked at Hannah wholly perplexed, like a child discovering the nonexistence of Santa Claus. Kindle laughed, pushing him onward down Canal Street. Hannah walked behind them.

Bobby spotted and solicited the next person, a heavy grey-haired man in a worn pea coat and brown slacks. After the man accepted, the four walked two blocks together. Kindle laughed and winked at Bobby.

Upon entering the Registry, Bobby found the officiant, a young man with neat brown hair and frosty skin. He conversed with the man shortly while Kindle sat in the back, exchanging silent glances with Hannah and the grey-haired man. She exhaled and smiled when Bobby waved her over.

The Registry room was no larger than the hotel lobby. Bobby and Kindle stood on either side of a glossy wooden pulpit, holding hands and laughing intermittently as the officiant gathered papers. Hannah frequently and conspicuously stared at the clock at the top of the wall.

Bobby was an image of punk, his black hair coordinating with his black-and-white striped shirt. His straight black jeans were noticeably worn, tattered to grey at the knees. Kindle wore a white t-shirt and flimsy linen skirt that skimmed her feet. Both of them wore their hair in a ponytail, hers spiraling down her back and his sticking out an inch from his hair tie. She was wearing lipstick again. It was fuchsia this time, the same color as the old, clumpy nail polish she had applied at four-thirty that morning.

The officiant made his way to them and held up a paper before his eyes. "Robert Daniel Carter, do you take Kindle Janet Hyrum…"

"That's pronounced *Jeanette*," she said, removing her hand from her mouth as she finished yawning.

"Jeanette? Hyrum? Really?" Bobby inquired, grasping her hands tighter.

"Yes."

"I could call you KJ."

Kindle raised an eyebrow. "No."

The officiant coughed. "Robert, will you take Kindle here present for your lawful wedded wife, according to the rite of our Holy Mother, the Catholic Church?"

"What in all of earth and creation?" Kindle whispered.

"Catholic vows. I told him to do it like that. I'm Catholic," Bobby said, smiling and then looking back at the officiant.

"I'm Protestant. I think."

"So, we have Jesus in common, right?"

The officiant wrinkled his brows. "Robert, will you take Kindle here present for your lawful wedded wife, according to the rite of our Holy Mother, the Catholic Church?"

"Yes. I do. I mean, I will."

"Repeat after me. I, Robert, take you, Kindle, for my wife, to have and to hold, from this day forward, for better, for worse, for richer, for poorer, in sickness and in health, until death do us part."

Bobby repeated the vows slowly, in beats. He did not stumble, fixing his attention on the ceiling.

The officiant read Kindle the vows.

"I Kindle, take you, Bobby—"

"That's Robert," the officiant interrupted.

Kindle dropped Bobby's hands, rubbed her own hands together and huffed, her chest heaving melodramatically. "Okay. I, Kindle, take you, Robert, for my husband, to, um..." She looked at the ceiling. "Love and cherish," she guessed. She laughed boisterously.

"To have and to hold," Bobby whispered, laughter in his crinkled eyes.

"Yes. To have and to hold," she said. "From today onward, for..."

"Better, for worse," the officiant prompted.

"Better," Kindle said quickly, as if answering a question.

"Maybe you should just repeat what he says," Bobby said, laughter now in his voice.

"Okay. For Better, for worse. Sickness health, etcetera, etcetera."

The officiant shook his head. "Till death do you part."

"Till death do us part." She looked down, twisting her feet back and forth on her heels.

"Now for the exchanging of the rings."

"No rings," said Kindle.

"Can't afford them," Bobby added. "But it's okay." He tangled her fingers with his and brought them to his chest. "You've got my heart. And that's all that matters." His eyes became glassy. He dropped her hands and patted his pockets. "Oh, man," he said.

"Trifles, Bobby. You can write the song later," Kindle said grabbing back his hands.

He scrunched his face, pressing his teeth against his top lip. "Yeah. Sure. Of course. You're right."

"Is everyone now ready?" The officiant swept back an errant strand of hair from his forehead. The room was silent with expectation. "Well," the officiant continued, "by the power vested in me, I now—"

Kindle looked up at Bobby.

"—pronounce you—"

Bobby stood motionless, watching the officiant.

"—husband and wife."

Kindle clamped Bobby's hands. He didn't flinch. She considered that he might really be insane.

He grinned, his eyes shining, perhaps in anticipation of the sensation of her lips over his.

"Please, kiss your bride," the officiant said.

Bobby pressed his hand gently against her back to draw her closer. He bent down and set his lips in front of hers. She stared at his mouth, partially mesmerized by its lushness. Truly, he possessed a mouth worthy of a sweltering kiss, but his intentions weren't as appreciable.

"No," Kindle hissed.

"But we're married." Bobby laughed, as if staggered by the sound of the words from his own mouth. "I mean, it's just a tradition, you know, to kiss the bride." He looked her in the eyes and dropped his hand from her back. "But, I mean, it's okay if you don't want to. I can…" He paused. "*We* can wait." Bobby turned to the officiant. "We're just gonna wait."

The officiant lowered his eyebrows and pursed his lips. "Well, of course, every couple makes their own decision. And that's what you two have to look forward to—a life full of decisions made together."

When Kindle looked at Bobby once more, he was wearing the smile of a naughty little boy. She decided then that he wasn't crazy. Rather, he was on a joy ride in England, taking advantage of his ability to return to The States without any record of his escapades. Kindle had once heard her mum say that visitors to Manchester were usually searching for some outlandish adventure. They were looking to find trouble from which they could be quickly absolved. Manchester was a city of art's free enterprise. It was a place where people took bizarre chances, learning by trial and error. Manchester became her father's home when he moved there from London. Back then, he was sixteen and free as a bird.

Kindle stormed out of the room. Accompanied by the sound of Bobby's footsteps trailing behind her, she heard Hannah announcing loudly, "I know who you are. You're the man from that band. My man and I saw your show once. You made believers out of us."

****

Bobby grappled for Kindle's wrist as she burst through the Registry doors into the late morning sun. When she crossed her arms, he timorously shawled her stiff shoulders with his jacket, attempting to keep her warm. The sun shone imperiously in the sapphire sky, but the cold diminished its efforts.

"What just happened? Why did you just let that happen?" she stammered as they passed the row of office buildings.

"Listen—"

Kindle peered up at him, open-mouthed. She trekked faster. "I thought you were going to renege. I thought you knew that this was a joke. I thought you were being silly. I thought this was…your flirtation or something. Who in the hell are you?"

"Just—"

"Everything in me told me to say no," she interjected, "but I trusted that you would intervene because this was *your* jokey little plan. But just so you know, you won't get anything from me. I don't have money and I certainly don't give away my body in the pseudo-sanctity of a make-shift marriage." Abruptly, her countenance was lifted, like the sun splitting through storm clouds. She shook her head, laughing at the sidewalk. "But this can be fixed," she said. "We're not really married until we submit those papers. Doesn't mean a thing until then."

Bobby fixed his eyes upon the sky. He figured this moment would come. Sensible Kindle undoubtedly had to surface. Sensible Kindle—the one who alone took care of herself—couldn't handle something this extreme. Bobby preferred Unrehearsed Kindle—the one who had allowed him to walk her home in the dark, the one waiting to bud into a stage star, the one who didn't wear makeup. Unrehearsed Kindle was up for anything. She could understand the imminence of love. The imminence of love was very real for Bobby from the first night he saw her.

The first night The Dare played at her pub, Bobby spotted Kindle huddled in the back corner next to the bar, fanning herself languidly with an order pad. The perspiration on her cheeks caused her face to shine like a diamond. The whites of her eyes flashed as she looked around through the bar. After a moment, she stood straight up and returned to work, walking to the bar to converse shortly with the bartender. In his head, she moved to the tune of The Beatles, of George Harrison. Something in the way she moved attracted him like no other lover...he was wooed.

By the time The Dare finished their set and vaulted off the stage, Bobby had resolved to make his way to her. She wasn't difficult to find. Although she was dressed in all black like the rest of the crowd, her skin glistened like melting caramel.

She weaved through the crowd gracefully, her body curving and snaking to avoid colliding with anyone as she distributed drinks. On his trek to her, Bobby stopped several times to receive the praises of the crowd. When he stood within a yard of her, she lost balance of the drinks in her hands and they crashed to the ground. The people around her quickly scattered, leaving her and the broken glass in a lonely circle. To Bobby, the accident seemed as premeditated as a movie scene. It was his time to enter as the gallant lead.

As she bent down on her knees to collect the shards, Bobby noticed that her hair was more sable than black. It was in a loose bun on top of her head, some of the frizzy tendrils falling against her temple. She was a princess and a ballerina. He could be a prince and a knight.

Before Bobby could cut through the two guys in front of him, his cousin Kyle appeared at Kindle's side. Bobby had not expected Kyle to notice her. Not Kyle. But there he was, kneeling down to help her.

"No," she said, pushing Kyle's hand away from the glass. "Don't injure yourself. It was my own clumsiness."

Kyle twisted his eyebrows and stood. "Whatever. Do whatever you want," he yelled over the music, his indignation louder than his voice.

Her hands nested on her thighs, Kindle watched Kyle walk away. She raised her face toward the ceiling and shut her eyes. He thought she might be praying before she opened them and looked around at the mess once more. She picked up each piece of glass, one by one, and placed them in her opposite palm.

While Bobby focused on the movement of her spine as she bent forward back and forth to collect the glass, he heard her gasp and yelp suddenly. Her surprised cry rang out like she was attempting a high note. It was music for him. Yes, music was his heart and soul, more precious than gold…and with that little squeal, she was just like music.

In the same moment she cut herself, Bobby's right index finger stung underneath his bandage. Days before, he had slit it on the part of his guitar string that pointed out from the tuning knobs. Looking from his finger to her, he noticed that blood dripped from a deep gash on her own right index finger. She wrapped her left hand around her finger and stood. Bobby watched her skip away to the bathroom in the back.

He stood still, considering what had happened. Had he felt her pain in his own body in the very same moment she had been cut? He wasn't sure of it, but he certainly wanted to be. She was really the most beautiful thing he'd seen since he'd arrived in England. Maybe she was the most beautiful thing he'd ever seen in his life. He had tried for a few minutes to think of a woman more beautiful. He had actually gone down a list of the beautiful women he could recall. They didn't seem to compare to the waitress with the song-like squeal. Maybe it was just a matter of proximity. He couldn't reach out and touch Joan Baez or Carly Simon, but he would find his way to the waitress. He wanted her then and there.

Bobby stood in place, mesmerized by the little ache, pricking his finger several times that night to recall the sensation. It was a sign. He definitely believed in signs.

Over the next two days, Bobby did not mention the incident to his friends. He hid it in his heart, where it would be safe from opinion and doubt. He knew what Kyle would say.

He'd laugh and smack Bobby's shoulder. "Enough with the magic romance fairytales already," he'd say. "I swear, you wouldn't be wasting your time in a fantasy if you'd just hit the ball to homerun. Trust me."

Well, he definitely didn't trust most of what Kyle said. They're fundamental philosophies on sex were as far apart as love and lies. "Get in where you fit in" was Kyle's mantra, and he did so as often as he could, most times without remembrance of his bed partner's name or age. Bobby had safer rules to follow—when in doubt, hold out. Yet, rather than debate over philosophies with Kyle, Bobby decided to keep to himself his interest in the beautiful barmaid.

Over the next few days, he mused. He thought of the way her black eyebrows curved to frame her face like a heart. Her eyelashes were long and straight, casting a shadow near the top of her cheek when she had first looked down at the broken glass. He recalled the way she shifted through the crowd as she served drinks. The way she stretched her legs long and precisely, she had to be a dancer.

Actually, he had imagined her more to be an aspiring singer. Maybe she was a song-and-dance woman. The singer-waitress combination made sense to him. He thought of what her favorite songs were and what she would look like sitting next to him on a tour bus, resting her head on his shoulder. He wondered what her voice would sound like on a recording. Would she buzz like Yoko or swell like Cher?

Bobby decided that he would talk to her on their last scheduled performance at her bar. When he found her, he had followed proper form at first, employing small talk. As he followed her outside, he thought more logically. When finding The One, standard rules of engagement didn't apply, right?

So, he said what he meant. He asked her to marry him.

Bobby didn't need time to speculate when's or if's. Like music, Kindle was his instinctual desire, one of those things that made him believe that he was in the right place at the right time.

Bobby wouldn't realize the power of his instinct until he reached forty years old. It was then that he wrote the song "Instinct" for Ricky Stallion's solo album. It was never released as a single, but the critics called it a hidden diamond in a mountain of otherwise rough and forgettable songs.

For now, Bobby walked on with Kindle, sifting through lyrics in his head, searching for a line that would bring her back to Unrehearsed Kindle.

"So," Kindle said, as they turned onto his hotel's street, "all we have to do is destroy the papers we signed this morning. Where did you put them?"

"I don't have them."

"Who has them?" she probed, seemingly unable to lift her dropped jaw.

"The officiant has them."

"What?" Kindle squawked.

"When we first got there, you were talking to that girl—that lady—Hannah. I gave them to the officiant then. It was like a formality or something."

Kindle shook her head, baffled. "Maybe I'm insane for telling an insane man that he's insane, but Bobby, I think you're insane." She stopped to face him.

Bobby looked around, searching for a thought. "Or maybe you and me are, like, tone deaf to each other right now."

"What?"

"Maybe we're not understanding each other right now. You're mad at me, or whatever. But I asked you to marry me from the beginning. You never said no. Not once. Not even in front of the officiant. Not now. Not really." He walked onward.

"What is that supposed to mean?" she asked, scampering behind him.

"People do what they want if they can."

"Are you saying that I secretly wanted this? Is that your Freudian view? Where did you get your psychology degree? McDonald's?" Kindle gripped his upper arm. "Can't you just get the papers from the officiant?"

Bobby stopped again, smiling. "Say that again."

She looked up at him with knotted eyebrows, her expression half-exasperated, half-fascinated. "Say what again?"

He faked a British accent as they began to walk again. "Say, 'Can't you get them from him?'"

She grimaced.

Bobby bit his lip. "I love the way you say 'can't.' It's like you're saying 'aunt' with a C. It's pretty incredible."

Now, it was Kindle who bit her lip to stifle a smile. "Incredible? It's just the way I talk." She put on a Southern accent. "It's better than Yank speak. *Can't.* It's like you're saying aint with a K."

"I don't talk like that," Bobby laughed. "I don't spell like that either."

They faced each other in front of the hotel, underneath the solid gold archway that extended out from above the doors. Bobby toyed with the lint in his jeans pocket.

"What am I gonna do, Bobby?"

"Why do we have to do anything yet?"

"Because *this*, in case you didn't know, is the meaning of insanity."

Bobby reflected a moment, his chin raised upward, his eyes closed. He deliberated. "When we're performing sometimes, I like, mess up in front of the crowd. Like, seriously. Sometimes, I play a note for too long or the wrong chord or something. Sometimes it throws everything off. But sometimes, it, um, it makes the song sound better. It makes the whole performance better. You can't really plan for stuff like that. They're called happy accidents. Does that make sense? Do you get what I'm trying to say?"

She sighed "This isn't a stage."

"I don't think that's the point."

"Then what is?"

He shook his head, smiled, and crossed his arms, teetering back and forth on his heels and toes. "I could be, like, the best thing that ever happened to you. Live without regrets, right?" She opened her mouth to respond, but he continued. "You could've said no. You could've told the officiant that you didn't mean it." He dropped his gaze. "I mean, you could still change your mind or whatever."

"You are amazing in a very ridiculous kind of way. Do you realize that?"

He wasn't sure if he did realize that, but he did realize that she was no longer fuming. She might have been thirty seconds from a smile.

"Besides," she said, "living without regrets is something people say to avoid feeling stupid about their mistakes."

Bobby smiled. He had reached a dead-end for words. So, instead, he followed his impulse and opened his arms to hug Kindle. Like every great artist, rarely did his instinct fail him. Kindle settled her head into to his chest and he crossed his arms around her back, pressing his cheek against her hair. "Don't you worry 'bout a thing, Pretty Mama."

She patted his back listlessly. "Thank you, Stevie Wonder."

Bobby began to sing, his voice a solid tenor, his pitch more exact than with anything he himself had written. "Cause I'll be flying on my wings when you check me out."

"Those aren't the words." Kindle's stomach vibrated as she laughed. With her breast pressed against his chest, Bobby could feel her heartbeat. He tapped his finger against her shoulder, following its rhythm. He thought. Maybe she just needed time to catch the pace.

"So, I guess we're headed back to the Registry?" Bobby inquired softly.

"Yes. I just need a moment to take care of something inside."

****

Bobby was obviously unsure of why she had walked him to the hotel after the ceremony. He gazed at the ceiling and then narrowed his eyes at her as they strolled in.

"Do you have to work this morning?" he asked.

"No," Kindle responded, distrait. She looked around, searching for Holster. He must have run to the bathroom.

Bobby stared at her.

"Well, since we're here, you may as well visit your mates," she said.

"But I thought that we were going to take care of it."

Catching sight of Mr. Holster, Kindle nudged Bobby's shoulder, pushing him in the direction of the elevators. "Can you just go?" Her voice commanded, but her eyes pleaded. "Please. I'll be here when you return."

Bobby strode away but stopped suddenly.

"I'll be right here," Kindle said.

He walked into the open elevator, glancing at her briefly and then staring straight up as the doors closed.

Kindle took a quick look around before walking forward to Mr. Holster, her problem-solver.

He watched her blearily. "What's the matter, Kindle?"

"Mr. Holster, I think that I've ruined my life as of thirty minutes ago. I made a silly, silly mistake." She glanced at the elevator. "But at the same time, I'm not totally certain it was a mistake. Maybe it was just an accident."

"What does that mean exactly?"

She rested her fingers on her bottom lip. "It means that I'm a wife."

"A wife?" he asked, his voice raised. He smoothed his hair back to feign composure as a guest entered the hotel. "Who's your husband?"

Kindle dropped her head and raised it slowly, penitently.

"Room 205." Mr. Holster stood tight-lipped, grim. He laid his chalky hands on the desk. "Have you found love?"

Kindle stepped forward, laying her hand on the counter's gleaming mahogany. "It has supposedly found me."

Mr. Holster waved and greeted the elderly couple that headed for the elevator.

She tapped one of his wrinkled hands. He balked. She had hardly touched or been touched by him before.

"Kayanne warned me," he murmured.

Kindle pressed his other hand against the counter. "What?"

Mr. Holster slipped his hand from beneath hers. "You should go. Handle your affairs. This is your day off."

"What did my mum say?"

He smiled at the next guest.

"What did she say, William?"

It was her first time using his first name. He wasn't as shocked by her impudence as she was. He reproved her with a quiet, hard glance.

"Mr. Holster, she was my mother. You don't think that I deserve to know every bit of what she said?"

"What was between us was between us."

This was, in fact, true. In her last days in the hospital, Mr. Holster was there morning until evening. Kindle assumed that he had few friends. Maybe her mother was the only one, since his wife's death. In her last moments of clarity, her mother had requested that Kindle leave the room so that she could speak with Mr. Holster alone. Kindle struggled to listen at the door; her mother's voice no longer exceeded a whisper.

"I deserve to know," Kindle pressed.

Mr. Holster snatched a tissue from the desk and faced the closet door, wiping smudges off its handle. "Your mother worried about you. She knew you'd be lonely. She thought that you would throw your life away to a man. She feared that you would become her."

"What are you trying to say?" Kindle asked, folding her arms over her chest.

"Your father was no saint."

"I'm aware of that."

"She didn't want the same for you."

Kindle scraped her nail over the desk, attempting to inscribe a cross. Indignation surged through her veins, like sudden adrenaline. She was prepared to argue the impossible. "I haven't necessarily thrown my life away. I married. That's something that my mother never did."

He angled his face toward her. "You said with your own mouth that your life was ruined. I only agreed." He sighed. "Would you like me to give my approval instead?"

"No. But maybe you can find it in yourself to no longer see me as a child." Kindle breathed. She tried but failed to disguise the emotion in her voice. "I've taken care of myself without my mum for some time now. By myself. Does that not make me fully grown?"

When Mr. Holster looked into her eyes, Kindle saw something in his half-opened eyes that she hadn't seen since her mother died—sorrow. "You haven't grown up, Kindle. Circumstance will only grow you up if you let it." He walked to the other side of the desk, standing beside her. "The saying is proven true on you: youth is wasted on the young. You're floating. I'm sure he is too. A fine looking boy, but obviously as immature as they come. You won't understand until it all falls apart. The young at heart aren't built for marriage. It is the art of sacrifice."

She faced him. "All I do is sacrifice. Is it so wrong for me to have something—*someone*—for myself? My whole life, I've had nothing, If that isn't sacrifice, I don't know what is."

"You've sacrificed things. Never yourself."

"Life isn't one-size-fits-all." She swallowed down a wave of tears. "You can't really believe that you know everything that's right for *me*."

"Kindle, I've known you since you were a little girl," he said, composed. "I have no doubts about what's right for you."

Chapter Three

Past Time: 1964

For every stride her mother took, five-year-old Kindle took three gangly steps, hunching forward and swinging her right arm back and forth. Kayanne held Kindle's left hand firmly. As they hurried down the sidewalk, Kindle's face nearly thumped the back of her mother's waist. Kayanne stopped suddenly when they reached a particular Victorian house. The house was beige-paneled with green crisscrossing lines on all three stories. On the second level, six narrow, side-by-side windows sat directly in the middle of the house. For young Kindle, the house emitted nothing but intrigue. She took a step forward before Kayanne yanked her back. Looking up at her, Kindle realized that her mother was more mortified than intrigued by the house.

Mr. Holster stepped out of the front door, making his way through the two columns of manicured bushes to the sidewalk where they stood. So, this was Mr. Holster's house? If that was the case, Kindle couldn't help but to think her mother's mortification was a bit dramatic. Mr. Holster was quiet, if not amiable, and he always smelled like sugar cookies and cologne. Plus, he let Kindle take as many chocolate mints from the hotel desk as she wanted, even when she wasn't as obedient with him as with her mother. What more could a child ask for?

"Mr. Holster," Kayanne said.

"William," he corrected. Mr. Holster looked different, wearing a white polo shirt, khaki pants and penny loafers in place of his hotel uniform. He seemed taller, thinner.

"Yes, William. How are you?"

"I'm okay, Kayanne."

"How's Peter?"

"Peter? What's wrong with Peter?" Kindle wondered aloud, though she did not realize she had until her mother looked down at her with taut lips.

"He's well," replied Mr. Holster. "He hasn't awakened yet."

"Hasn't awakened? It's near noon." Kayanne glanced from side-to-side. "Do you think it would be better for me to come at a different time, when he's up and settled?" She passed her fingers over her bun and straightened out her long tan skirt. Kindle pressed her hand over her own flowered church skirt.

"This is the one year anniversary, Kayanne. I don't think he can handle getting up now. He needs a day or so to regroup."

Kayanne ran her hand under her chin and sighed. "I'm sorry, William. I don't know how to say how sorry I am. If I had known, I wouldn't—"

"It's okay. I wouldn't expect you to remember. I was never any good at counting days either. All is well. Peter will be fine."

"And what about you?"

Mr. Holster walked to the front door. They tailed him. "I'm in decent shape," he said.

When he opened the door, the aroma of the house overwhelmed Kindle. So this was why he smelled like cookies. He lived in a chocolate and vanilla emporium.

The color scheme matched the fragrance perfectly; everything was brown and beige. He took them to the living room, in the rear of the house, where the couch was light like a vanilla cupcake and looked as if it were made of plastic. The walls were ebony, tiny holes scattered all over them.

Mr. Holster held his hand out to the couch, and Kayanne sat. Kindle took a seat beside her at the edge, staring up at Mr. Holster.

"I'm sorry for the sparse furniture," he began. "When Elizabeth passed, Peter couldn't bear to have the furniture. Decorating was Elizabeth's passion." All three of them looked up toward the ceiling when they heard commotion upstairs, perhaps the sound of a waking fifteen-year-old, as if Peter had responded to the sound of his name. Mr. Holster blinked his eyes. Kindle noticed that his eyelashes were blonde. His hair was mostly white with traces of yellow—leaves changing colors in the winter.

Kayanne blinked her eyes slowly. "Once again, I'm terribly sorry."

"Thank you for your condolences, but you haven't any reason to be sorry. The only certainty in life is that we'll leave it." Holster stood next to a tall wooden table, leaning his arm against it and maneuvering a pack of cigarettes from his pocket. "What can I do for you, Kayanne?"

"Is there somewhere Kindle can go?"

Kindle begged Mr. Holster with her eyes, hoping against all hope that even in such a large house, there was no place for her to go.

She was sent upstairs to an empty room with the six narrow windows. After a few moments of sitting on the floor in silence, Kindle scaled her way along the wall back downstairs. She stopped short of the entrance to the living room and stood with her back in the corner, next to the arc where the living room opened.

"What do you mean?" Mr. Holster asked.

"I'm not afraid to die, William." Her mother's voice was brisk, professional. "Not at all. If this is what it is, then I'll go willingly. Maybe I can make up in penance what I've lost by sin."

"That's a good Catholic prayer. Although, I was sure you were an Anglican." He laughed shortly. "You haven't done anything so wrong that God would take your life. You had no way of knowing that the man would never marry you, that he would run away."

"Yes," Kayanne said, coughing exuberantly. Her coughs had grown louder and longer over the last few weeks. "You're

right about that. But I always had the choice to keep my legs
closed."

Mr. Holster paused. "Yes. We make mistakes. But there
would be no Kindle if it weren't for some poor choices. There's
usually some amount of good that comes with the bad, I think. I
nearly ruined twenty years of marriage, but Elizabeth forgave
me shortly before she died. There's always some good. We're
cut from the same cloth, Kayanne. We should both know this,
shouldn't we?" He paused once more. "How bad are the
symptoms?"

"Fevers. Rashes. Things I haven't had at any time in my
life, William. I've never been a sick woman. I've recalled
having only one cold bug my entire life. Only one. I never even
had morning sickness when carrying that little girl."

Kindle's heart beat fast.

"Sickness doesn't always equal death," said Mr. Holster.
"How did it start for Elizabeth?"

"You don't have cancer, Kayanne. Put it out of your
mind."

Unexpectedly, moist breath tickled Kindle's ear in a
drawling whisper. "What are you doing, little girl?"

Kindle sucked in her breath and spun around. Behind her
stood gangly, ginger-haired Peter Holster. Peter's mouth was
agape; his teeth slender, dull and crooked like his father's. He
was even dressed like his father—khaki pants and a polo shirt.
He wore white socks in place of shoes.

Kindle put her index fingers to her lips. "Quiet. They'll
hear you."

"Why are you here, little girl?"

Kindle turned her back to him, resuming her
eavesdropping.

"It's a result of stress," Mr. Holster continued. "You've
made yourself sick from the stresses of life. You need time to
yourself."

Peter stood up straight and placed his hands on Kindle's
shoulders as they quietly listened.

"How do you suppose that I do that?"

"I'll give you the time away from work."

"Work is the least of my responsibilities," Kayanne returned with a short, bitter laugh.

Mr. Holster exhaled. "Why don't you send her to a relative for a short time?"

She laughed again. "That's the reason that I came here. I don't have any relatives nearby and I would never send her across seas. But if this illness is communicable, I refuse to infect her. I came to you for that reason."

"I don't know, Kayanne," Mr. Holster replied. "This house may appear large, but for Peter, it will be very small with a little girl running around."

"I don't have any other options, William," said Kayanne, a subtle hint of exasperation in her voice. "I never wanted to impose on either you or Elizabeth. There were enough troubles in that area, as it were. I've been thankful for the groceries and the money and everything else you've given. I'm more thankful for that than you'll ever know." She paused. "But you did all of it out of the kindness of your heart, not per my request. This is the one thing that I'm asking you for. If it weren't for my child, I wouldn't ask."

Mr. Holster sighed. "Too many years I put you before my wife's wishes. Elizabeth saw the inordinate connection. I could never explain it to her." His voice dropped. "Maybe you were my soul mate."

"Maybe."

Kindle held her breath in the pause.

"But I've given you everything that I can," Mr. Holster continued. "Time, attention, counsel, money, all of it—even when my wife begged me to let you go, even when my wife became so jealous that she couldn't stand to be in the same room with me. Now that I'm left with Peter, I have to take into account his wishes. I owe him that."

"William, I'm sorry. You should know that you amaze me in every way, more than anyone else I've ever met. More than anyone. That includes John, you know. I always sent up prayers for your marriage. I don't want to put more weight upon you, but I need this as a last favor. I can't make my child sick." Kayanne took a deep breath. "I need you."

Peter squeezed Kindle's shoulders so tightly that she squirmed. She sucked in her breath to elude a squeal.

"Okay," Mr. Holster relented. "Okay. I will take her in. We'll have to clear out a room for her on the top story. When…when will she need to come?"

Peter released Kindle's shoulders and brushed past her, dashing to the center of the living room. His face was contorted and red as he stood before them, shaking. Kindle snaked her way from the entrance and stood beside him.

"No!" Peter contended, his pubescent voice crackling. "What the hell are you doing?"

"Peter," said William. "What are you doing?"

"She's not going to stay here with us. I won't let it happen. I'd rather let you bury me too than let you spit on my mum's memory, to act like she never existed. You can get rid of all of her furniture, but you'll never kill her memory. You can take down the pictures from the walls, but she still existed."

Kayanne stood. She pressed her hands against the sides of her face.

William stood up, unruffled. He stared at his son with static eyes. "No one wants to remove your mother's memory, Peter. I rid this house of those things for your sake. You know that Elizabeth would want us to take care of others."

"You never fooled me," Peter charged. "You could fool everyone else, but you could never fool me. I knew that you didn't love my mum. Not like I did. On the anniversary, you want to replace her with your mistress's child."

"Accuse me however you wish, Peter," Mr. Holster warned, "but don't you dare be disrespectful to a woman."

"I'm sorry. I'm really sorry," Kayanne burbled, grabbing hold of Kindle's upper arm. "We need to go." She pulled Kindle past both Mr. Holster and Peter, down the hallway to the front door. They stepped out into a haze of drizzle. Kayanne tucked Kindle's head into her side to shield her from the rain as they scurried down the sidewalk.

Kindle watched the drops of water wet the pavement. Her heart beat fast as she asked into her mother's side, "He's the one, isn't he?"

"What are you talking about?"

"Mr. Holster is my father, isn't he?"

"Are you a fool, child?" Kayanne stopped and reached down to pick Kindle up. Kindle wrapped her legs around her mother's waist as they hurried on. "You're not related to him. You should only wish that you were."

Chapter Four

Present Time…

While Kindle spoke to Mr. Holster two stories below, Bobby explained his present situation to his three band mates. Two of them lay on the bed closest to the window, while one lay sprawled out over the bed closest to the door where Bobby stood. They didn't sit up after the announcement.

"You've gotta be kidding me, Bobby," said Larry, The Dare's oldest member. "You're lying through your teeth." With his large angled ears, crooked nose and wafer-thin lips, the ongoing joke had been that his being drummer was for the best; that way, he would always sit at the back of the stage hardly seen, his hair and drumsticks flying back and forth to hide his face as he played.

"No, no Larry. It's the truth," Bobby responded. "I'm married."

"I knew you would be the one to do the stupid thing," said Kyle, shaking his head. He lay alone on his bed. "I knew one of us had to make a dumb-ass move. I said either I was gonna knock up one of these under-aged English girls or you were gonna run off with some British floozy. I knew it was gonna be you, though. I should have bet money on it. Fuck! I could have been rich."

If Bobby was known as the handsome one, his cousin Kyle was the cute one. His rosy cheeks, lustrous brown eyes,

glossy black hair and fair skin gave him the appearance of a
Chinese porcelain doll. The Manchester girls fawned over his
pretty features, not yet acquainted with his inward qualities.
"I swear to God, you're a retard," Kyle went on. "You
got married, dude? I should've known something was up. I
knew that you wouldn't get up at five in the morning just to
take a walk."

Larry rolled his eyes. "Well, the virgin prince's got a
wife now, so he'll probably wake up early every morning to
enjoy the delights of the flesh these days." Kyle and Larry
laughed and even Bobby smiled, suddenly warm by thought of
these so-called delights, which he had only mildly imagined
until this point.

Alex didn't laugh. He hardly ever laughed. Lead guitarist
and youngest member of The Dare, he was a self-proclaimed
hothead. He got his temper from his father, he said, and even
though the pot helped to calm him, it was necessary for him to
keep some of his rage in order to preserve punk essence. Alex
hardly employed the guitar skills he had cultivated over ten
years of playing, but he played simple power chords with
Angus Young fury. "Look, Carter, you're an asshole," he said.
"You really are. You have a wife now? Are you trying to ruin
everything?"

Bobby blinked his eyes. "What?"

Alex gritted his teeth. "Who the hell is she, Carter?"

"What does it matter?"

"Because if she's the girl you followed out the bar, what
do you think they're gonna say about us? I can read the
headlines now. Up-and-coming band The Dare lead singer
marries fucking wog. That's the word they use here, right?" He
looked around.

Kyle and Larry nodded.

"Cuz you know, that's all anyone will care about," Alex
continued, flipping over onto his stomach. "That means our so-
called 'sex symbol' is taken. Did you listen to anything Fred
said? Hell, I wouldn't call you a sex symbol. You're a lanky
asshole as far as I'm concerned, but if you're the one that gets
us an audience, then don't you think you should have thought
about that?"

Bobby frowned. "Look, I finally found someone I really want. Like, *really* want. What would you do if you found the right girl? Would you giver her up or do everything you possibly could to keep her?"

Kyle dug a misshapen cigarette out of his pocket. "I'd give her a rain-check until I got a record deal."

Larry scoffed. "Or live a couple days longer until I could find another love of my life. Come on, Bobby, how long have we been here? A few months? And you're in love? You've screwed this up royally."

"It's not like having a girlfriend," Kyle said. "It's not like *shagging* a girl. She's your wife. You got that? That means you've gotta take care of her."

"I know that," Bobby murmured, dropping his eyes.

"Really? Seriously? What if she wants to stay here? And then we get a deal that takes us out of this place. What're you gonna do?" Kyle blew out a whirl of smoke, a mesmerizing ghost that floated toward Bobby.

Larry propped himself up on his elbows. "Or what if she wants to have, like, ten babies? Catholics don't even believe in condoms, do they?" Kyle and Larry laughed again. Alex rolled his eyes and smirked. "What are you gonna do? You're looking at an uncertain future, dude."

"All futures are uncertain. You never know what's going to happen." Bobby smiled and spoke to the tune of Nat King Cole. "For all we know, this may only be a dream."

Alex sprang out of the bed, ambling toward Bobby. "Are you a fucking idiot? This isn't some wonderworld. So you know some black tunes. Who gives a fuck? I don't care if she's hot. I don't care if she's Helen of Troy. She's a complication and you know it."

Bobby looked away.

"I *know* you know it." Alex said. "Do you know this: you'll never be like her. And you should thank your lucky stars, dude. The whole world's open to you. But you married her. And now, the world just got a helluva lot smaller."

"Who do you expect me to marry? Somebody I don't love?"

"I'm not asking you to get married, dude." Alex snatched his jacket from the bed. "But you miss the point, like you always do. If that's all you've got, Bobby, then forget it. I quit. I'm done. "

"What the hell are you talking about, dude?" Larry said, staggering to his feet.

"I'm not gonna sit here and wait around for Ricky Stallion to ruin our lives. My dad and mom are already pissed that I've been here five months and haven't got a thing to show for it. I'm not staying here for this. I'm gone."

It was then that Alex walked out of the door and out of the group, taking only the guitar on his back. He said that he would make arrangements to get his belongings once he made it back to America. Back in Michigan, Alex joined a popular local band named The Arabs. The Arabs went on in music history as a one-hit wonder, forever remembered for how they made punk fans feel in the summer of '82. When he later began seeing The Dare and their new British lead guitarist in heavy rotation on MTV, Alex would try to capitalize on the fact that he was once The Dare's lead guitarist. The fact never got him the television interview he hoped for, but he was happy to at least flirt with women in bars who were intrigued by tidbits about Ricky Stallion and The Dare.

For Bobby, Alex's departure was a bit of a relief. Although Alex could play harder than the other guitarists, his riffs lacked real emotion. Emotion was indispensable.

When Alex slammed the door, Kyle made his way to Bobby, setting his hands upon Bobby's shoulders. "Motherfucker. Fucker's probably on his period or something. He'll be back." Kyle took a drag of his cigarette and blew another smoke ghost into Bobby's face. "There's no such thing as bad publicity in the business. That's what they say, anyway. But I don't care how much publicity you get, you and your missus aint gonna make your home here, Cuzzo"

"I know." Bobby shrugged and rubbed his inflamed eyes. "I think we're gonna try to reverse it or something."

"Whatever, dude. Don't try to eff up your little publicity stunt now." Kyle reached in front of the bed for Bobby's suitcase and shunted it into his chest. "May as well pack your stuff, man. This room was way too small for all of us anyway."

****

When Bobby returned to the lobby, he was staggered by Kindle's pressing elation. She smiled wide, hugged him and kissed his cheek, not inquiring about the suitcase in his right hand or the guitar case in his left. She grasped his wrist and carted him out of the hotel, giving a backward glance to the old manager.

Outside, she dropped his hand as they weaved through the swarm of people that packed the sidewalk. The cold wind blew Kindle's ponytail off her back into erratic swirls. Bobby slipped the rubber band off his hair, so that his strands blew over his face—a light protectant from the cold.

For a whole three blocks, Kindle said nothing. She folded her arms against her chest and held her mouth open in an O, perhaps trying and failing for words. Hardly blinking, she gazed intently at the sidewalk in front of them, as if looking into the future.

"What's going on?" Bobby asked, testing her clairvoyance. He stopped in front of a concrete building. "Are we going back to the Registry? This isn't the way, is it?"

"What were you going to tell everyone about this?" she asked. "What was your explanation going to be? 'Surprise, Mum, I married the nearest friendly neighborhood barmaid'?"

Bobby sniffled. "Not those words exactly." He began walking again.

Kindle caught up to him, wrapping her hand around his arm. "Are you serious? Are you really, truly serious about this disaster?"

"I am."

Bobby recognized now that they were close to her apartment. He pictured the inside of it, contemplating how much more like home it could feel than his hotel room. His hotel room was actually starting to make him feel a little queasy. He liked his bedroom floor without dried and hardened pizza cheese, grimy socks and crushed beer cans. He liked things the way his mother kept them. Larry, Kyle and Alex enjoyed the absence of their mothers—really, the absence of any order.

"A suitcase?" Kindle said when they had reached the gate in front of her apartment. "What is that for?"

"They kicked me out, Penelope," he replied, employing the sentiment of a long ranger. "Not out of the band... just out of the hotel room."

"Who the hell gets evicted from a hotel room, Bobby? Oh, please tell me you're not serious."

He pursed his lips, pushing his hair back from his face.

"What did you tell them?" Kindle huffed and waved her hands at his suitcase hysterically. "I hope you didn't lead them to believe this marriage was permanent. This will be over soon enough."

"How soon?" Bobby set his guitar and suitcase on the ground. "Why are we here?"

Kindle looked up at him fretting, not fuming. She stooped to the ground, crossed her arms over her knees, and buried her face into her arms. Her arched back rose and fell dramatically.

Bobby knelt down in front of her, reaching out to touch her back, but pulling his hand away when she suddenly sneezed and burrowed her head deeper into her arms.

"You know, I'm nobody to be afraid of," he offered. "I've never even been in a real fight. Not even when I was a little kid. You could probably beat me up, if you ever wanted to."

Kindle lifted her head slightly. The wrinkles from her coat were imprinted on her forehead. "What are you talking about?"

He swallowed. "I wouldn't hurt you. I could stay here, and I wouldn't harm you. I'm not a psycho or anything like that. I could even protect you, since you live alone."

She peeped up at him over her arms. "You just said that you're not a fighter."

"Only when it comes to what I really want." Bobby stood, extending his hand toward her. She didn't take it, but pressed her hands against the dirt to lift herself up. "Don't make

me leave, Kindle. Tomorrow, we'll take care of this. Today, let
me stay with you. Today, let me be married to you. See how
you feel about me tomorrow."

"I'll feel the same," she replied quickly.

"What can I do to change your mind? Just let me know.
I'll do that."

"I don't even know what to say to that."

Bobby looked up at the sun and squinted. "You are the
most beautiful—like, really, really beautiful—girl I've ever
seen. One in a billion. What would you do if you were me?
Wouldn't you want to be with you? You can understand.
Right?"

Kindle stared at him until finally their eyes met and she
thrust her key into the gate. "Let's go."

In the daytime, Bobby could fully see the condition of
her duplex. He followed her through the balding lawn, littered
with patches of dry dirt and browning grass. A couple yards of
wispy weeds led to a set of rickety, white stairs, each step
chipped down to the bare wood in the center. When Kindle
skipped one of the six steps, Bobby followed her example. The
screen door screeched like a wounded mouse when she flung it
open.

Inside her apartment, a thread of majestic, pale-yellow
light shone onto the white walls and wood floor. He blinked
quickly and surveyed the apartment. They stood in a tiny square
foyer in front of the door. Straight ahead, a short hall led to
what he presumed to be a bathroom on the left and a bedroom
on the right. Immediately left of the foyer was the kitchen, a
slender rectangle with an old, fallow stove and refrigerator
pressed against one wall and a sink against the other. Across
from the kitchen, the living room stood nearly empty. The
majestic stream of sunlight charged through its open window.
Left of the window, two steel fold-up chairs leaned against the
wall. In the corner, a stack of books rested atop a three-legged
wooden table near a tall silver lamp.

Kindle closed the door, the sound of the blowing wind
outside swiftly muted, as though the apartment were breathing a
quick sigh of relief. Her heeled feet clicked against the wood
floor as she walked forward two steps. "Be very careful about

the noise you make. The neighbors downstairs—they're poor, old and angry. That's a very mortal mix."

Bobby and Kindle stood motionless, as if it were both their first times seeing the room.

"So, um, you haven't got, like, furniture yet?" Bobby inquired, slowly, carefully.

"No, not yet," she said, mocking his cautious timbre.

"Sarcasm?"

Kindle pressed together her lips and proceeded down the hall to the bedroom. Bobby trailed behind, accidentally knocking his suitcase against a wall before entering the room. Inside, a flimsy mattress lay in the center of the floor. Directly across from the doorway, a long window stared back at him, its open blinds allowing full view of the noon sun. A small television set sat below it. Two tall stacks of books and a green vase were settled in the left corner. A wooden fan drooped lazily from the ceiling. Bobby wondered if it worked.

"I sold the furniture," Kindle said.

"Wow. So you just got rid of everything?"

"Yes. After my mum died."

"Your mom died?"

She smiled shortly. "Remind me to limit the amount of questions you're allowed per day."

He followed her as she walked to the kitchen. "Can I ask one more question?"

"Please do," she said, rummaging through the cabinets, apparently distracting herself from the conversation.

"Where will I sleep?"

Kindle stared into an empty cabinet. "There's enough room on the floor for you, Mr. Carter."

"Um, look," Bobby offered. He tucked his hair behind his ear. "I know this is all happening, like, real fast. But we are…" he hesitated. "…married or whatever. We can sleep in the same bed since this is all that we have. It's only one day."

Kindle smirked, shaking her head. "You think that I'm completely wacked, don't you? I'm not going to sleep with you. Your bed will be the floor of the living room."

"No, KJ You—"

"Kindle. My name's Kindle."

"Okay. Kindle. Kindle Jeanette Carter." Bobby smiled broadly.

"You're quite insistent for a man who will be single tomorrow."

"I'm just saying, you've got me all wrong. I'm not looking for...*that*."

Kindle looked through the last cabinet. It held a bottle of ketchup. "Sure, you're not," she teased.

He sniffled and wiped his nose. "I mean, it's not the only thing that I'm looking for."

The refrigerator moaned as Kindle turned and opened the door. Though the light was blown, enough sunlight shone through the living room window to make visible the single gallon of milk that sat in it.

Bobby ran his hands up and down his arms to warm himself. "So, uh, do you get a lot of guys looking for *that* from you or something?"

She turned toward him. "You know, I don't have any food. And I hate to be a bad house host. Not that I have houseguests often. Ever. So, I'm not really sure what to say for dinner," she said.

"It's not even lunch time yet."

"Well, I guess there's nothing for lunch or dinner. Or breakfast. Or anything, for that matter." She spoke informingly, unabashed.

Bobby glanced at her wrist. Maybe her skin clung to the bone for more reasons than appearance's sake. He was excited by the new opportunity. He had enough money in his left pocket alone to feed her for the rest of the day.

Bobby let Kindle choose where they would eat. She elected a deli two blocks away. The restaurant was a redbrick storefront with one window that wrapped around the entire building. Inside, white cedar chairs circled matching tables. The deli had the genial, yellow cadence of a coffee house he had once played in when The Dare first formed. Other than the cashier at the counter, the store was empty. Kindle ventured straight to the cashier, softly rattling off her order—a salami sandwich, no pickles, no onions, extra mayonnaise, toasted Italian bread, light vinegar. Bobby smiled.

They sat at a table close to the window, occupying the first few minutes with watching strangers walk by.

She finally turned her attention to him. "You're not hungry?"

"Not really. I ate this morning. Before I got you."

She smiled and began unwrapping her sandwich. "Oh the joys of being gotten."

He smiled back demurely.

"So what did you eat?" she inquired, bread clenched between her top and bottom teeth.

"A pop tart. And orange juice. And a banana."

"Pop tart?"

Bobby laughed, his eyes flickering up and down shyly. "That sounded a lot like poop tot."

She smirked, blotting the corners of her mouth with a napkin.

"They don't have Pop-Tarts here," he continued. "They're like, um, like a little square of fruit and sugar."

"Fruit and sugar squares?"

"Like a pastry."

"You brought them over from Canton? In Michigan, not Ohio."

He pressed his lips together in a smile. "I brought enough to last a long time."

"How'd you get on a plane with all of them?"

Bobby pushed his hair back with his palms. "Wasn't that hard." He was intrigued by her slow, polite chewing and how it must have spited her hunger. "I've eaten the same thing every morning before school since I was, like, twelve."

"Skimpy diet. How'd you get so tall in the first place?"

He thought carefully, then nodded. "I think it's just genes."

"So, then, you have fair genes."

"What do you mean?"

"You were blessed with the right DNA. If you actually think about it, you are of a special breed. I'm sure that you look at the crown of heads more than most other men do. That does make you quite unique."

"You mean that?" he asked, folding his hands between his knees and leaning forward.

Kindle nodded. She looked down once more at her sandwich. Bobby noted that her forehead was darker than her cheeks, more cinnamon than caramel. "I do," she said. "That'll be particularly useful when you decide to scheme your way into having our first child." She looked up with sparkling eyes.

Bobby traced his fingers around his lips, intending to smolder his smirk. "So, um, what about your genes? What genes do you have?"

Kindle sipped her tea and licked her lips. "What do you mean?"

"Well, you are black, right? And kinda white too? Something like that..."

"What?"

"Your skin. Your hair. Your hair is very long. Your skin is almost...I mean, it's not like mine, but it's not like...." Bobby looked around and then pointed at the ebony-skinned man in a white apron passing the window. "It's not like his either."

"So what does that mean?"

Bobby sniffled. "What I'm trying to say is that I've never seen someone like you before. Not in real life."

Kindle pushed her sandwich aside. "Can I make you aware of something? Maybe your parents live on a hundred thousand pounds a year and maybe you lived in a suburb. Maybe your only neighbors looked just like you. But your comment shows that you're scarcely aware of anything else, which is really a tragedy in in itself."

Bobby looked back out the window.

"Do you realize that my father was probably the color of *that* man. And my mum was a shade as light as yours. But I'm as black as you are white." Kindle lifted her chin and raised her eyebrows. She set her clasped hands in her lap. "I hope that doesn't completely unsettle you."

"I don't mean to offend you. I don't have any problem with Afro-Americans. Not at all."

"I'm not American. I'm not from Africa either. I'm English."

"I don't really know what to say," he said, bowing his head in surrender.

"Say nothing."

"What is it? What's so wrong?" he murmured. "You know, I'm not...I don't want to hurt your feelings."

Kindle lightly smiled and then snuffled. "Oh, you haven't. I was just considering my insanity for having done this with you."

"Having done what with me?"

She grabbed his wrist from the table and held it up, examining his hand. "You're so strange. And I'm equally so." She gathered the crumbs from her sandwich into a neat pile. "The lengths to which I would go..."

Bobby leaned forward, staring at her keenly. "What? What does that mean?

She dropped his hand on the table and patted it. "Nothing important. Are you ready to go?"

****

Kindle and Bobby walked back to the duplex together, but Bobby explained that he needed to gather some overnight items among other things. He promised to return that evening.

Shortly after sunset, Kindle headed to the bathroom—a cubicle fit for one, half the size of the hotel bathrooms. Inside, a cracked oval mirror rested atop the white sink stand. Next to it, the running toilet sounded, swishing and swirling over and over. The toilet's top had once fallen and cracked into three pieces. After attempting to piece the parts back together for a month, Kindle threw them away, unenthusiastically leaving the toilet's piping visible. The shower was in better condition than the toilet, though its floor had been garnished with sundry dark spots where the paint had been destroyed for as long as she and her mother had lived in the apartment. Kindle hadn't yet simultaneously afforded time and money to buy a shower curtain; she turned the showerhead to the side, so that when the water hit her, it wouldn't spray on the floor. In case that water did splash, she kept a faded pink towel on the ground.

Kindle undressed and folded her clothes, placing them on the sink stand. She took a look in the mirror, noting embarrassingly how her body had somehow become almost entirely womanly in the last two years since her mother passed.

She pouted, looking around at what had been a white bathroom at some point in time, probably several years before she and her mother had moved in. Maybe this apartment could have been fitting for Bobby when it was first constructed. Now, it certainly was not.

From the bold gleam of his hair to the design of his suitcase, Kindle had determined that Bobby hadn't any experience with this kind of thing. She imagined how well he had been coddled. He must have been dressed in such fine clothes as a child that his current consignment shop look was just rebellion. Sooner or later, he would realize that second-rate was really base. And then, he would leave.

Good thing that superficiality was of no interest to someone like Kindle. Good thing that she had agreed to Bobby's staying only one night as her roommate-husband.

Kindle exhaled slowly as she turned on the water in the shower. She stood under a skimpy waterfall, letting her palms fill with water to splash soap off her body.

Good thing that puerile ventures could most likely be retracted in a day's time with one trip to the Registry. Good thing that sudden surges of magnetism could be dimmed by the reality of indigence.

Kindle stepped out of the shower carefully and wrapped herself in a towel. Looking in the mirror, she sighed.

****

Bobby walked alone in the darkness. He found it strange the way that the Manchester streets were so flooded with people some evenings and how on nights like this, there was absolute silence, save the passing of a car from time to time.

He clutched a brown bag in his right arm, swinging his left arm back and forth as he strode. He enjoyed the way the cold ravished him. It did not ask questions. It took over everything, numbing toes, biting his face. Winter was his favorite season. Bobby remembered Christmas days past when he would neatly unwrap his Christmas gifts, while his mother and father sat side-by-side on the couch behind him. His father wore Christmas sweaters and smoked a large pipe. Bobby never understood why the winter holidays gave his father such a tremendous conversion of spirit.

Christmas was weeks passed, but the layer of snow blanketing the streets still called for reindeer and lighted trees. For the first time in the last couple weeks, Bobby missed home. It had been months since he'd seen his folks and several weeks since they'd talked on the phone. He remembered fondly his mother's excitement every time he called. He even kind of liked the way that his father talked to him now—deep and dour—like he could make Bobby into a man by talking to him like one.

Memories of his parents brought to the forefront the thought that he had been swiping away like a droning mosquito. At the deli, he had indulged himself in Kindle's polite chewing, her silky speech, the way the sun lighted her gold cheeks and cherry blossom lips. She wasn't pretty. Pretty was good for pictures, facsimiles of real life moments. Kindle was beautiful. Beautiful was when the sun illuminated a woman's face and hit it perfectly at every angle. That kind of thing couldn't be captured in pictures, but it was definitely more authentic than pin-up prettiness.

There at the deli, Bobby decided he would find a way to keep the marriage. Watching her was like putting his favorite song on repeat; he could see no end to his desire for it. He knew he'd have to keep the marriage under wraps until he was brave enough to bear his mother's long silence when she found out about Kindle. What Kindle was. What she was not. Some of which Bobby knew. Most of which he did not.

This wasn't to suggest that his parents discriminated against any type of person. They didn't really stand in defense of any type of person either. The Carter family was as insulated as a turtle beneath its shell. Bobby's father was to blame for that. He regularly refused dinner invitations from various other families at their church, at his work, in the neighborhood.

His mother had befriended several women, but not a single one that was what Kindle was. One Puerto Rican family had moved into the neighborhood within the last two years, but his mother hadn't reached out to them. Bobby himself hadn't reached out to the family either, but not out of disdain. His guitar had taken over his days and nights.

Yet, the truth still remained that Bobby had only found famous brown women attractive; the ones that wore afros or silk wigs. None like Kindle, who was somewhere between light and dark, coarse and straight. Maybe he was now explorer Bartolomeu Dias, looking upon a race unknown, unseen to virgin eyes, tasting for the first time the peculiar sweetness of caramel skin. Bobby anticipated Kindle's variety of beauty, but he had long since fallen in love with many other varieties. Mayfield. Gaye. Wonder. Stylistics. Redding. Hathaway. From them, he had found the meaning of true love in the blending of guitar, piano, moog, violin. From them, he inherited a kingdom without bounds.

Bobby considered these things before he turned the apartment doorknob. It resisted. He knocked lightly until Kindle yelled through the door.

"Who is it?"

"It's me, Kindle. It's Bobby."

She opened the door slightly and peeped out. She frowned.

"What's wrong?"

Kindle opened the door entirely for him and scurried to her bedroom, a doe galloping to safety. She wore a T-shirt through which he could see purple panties. He smiled.

Bobby stepped slowly into the bedroom where she sat on her mattress, Indian-style. Upon sight of him, she propped her knees up and covered them with her shirt.

"I got this for you." He hung the brown bag out before her. She eyed him guardedly before grabbing the bag and looking inside. She pulled out its contents one by one.

"So, I didn't know if you wanted to eat the same thing for lunch and dinner," Bobby continued, "but I didn't know what else you liked to eat yet, so I just got the same thing you ordered earlier today, plus a muffin, which is, like, dessert. It's a chocolate muffin. Like the same color of the man that passed by the window when we were there earlier."

"That's very thoughtful of you."

Bobby fingered his coat sleeve. "Chocolate's really good to me. I mean, I like it a lot."

Kindle began unwrapping her sandwich. "You should have brought me some milk to go with it. I like that well enough."

He grinned. "So, you need to sleep, huh?"

"Yes." She focused on her sandwich but pointed to the closet on the other side of the room. "There are sheets in there for you. And a blanket."

Bobby walked to the closet and opened it. Inside, a few outfits hung and on the floor, the sheets and blankets were folded. He picked them up carefully and turned back toward her. "Well, goodnight." He smiled to himself. "And, um, thought you should know—purple really suits you."

She looked up, wide-eyed, then peered back down at the slight gap between her knees. She smirked. "You're being naughty, aren't you?"

Bobby sucked on his top lip, half-smiling. He bowed his head once and winked before heading for the living room. He plugged the heater into the socket below the window and spread out three sheets on the floor. He pulled off his shoes and socks, lying down and spreading the quilted blanket over himself. His toes were left uncovered. He curled up to fit under the blanket and rested his head on the hard floor. He hadn't known to buy a pillow. Sleeping this uncomfortably would be motivation enough for Bobby to do all that he could to ensure that soon enough he could share a pillow with Kindle. He was sure it was possible. But for now, he would settle for purple dreams.

****

Kindle recognized that she had taken advantage of her mother's death. With her mum around, Kindle couldn't have cleaved to the first man that looked at her with unadulterated interest. If Kayanne found out about the impromptu wedding, she would have cursed in Patois. Kindle wouldn't have been able to interpret her words, but she would have extracted their meaning—"you're acting like a weak fool, Kindle; if it were

true love, you would have waited to test its durability." Forget
that the wedding was intended as a joke. Her mother would
have seen past that excuse. Kindle's own loneliness had duped
her.

"But you'll see," her mother would have said. "I see that
you're one of those girls who must learn the hard way. In case
you didn't know, one thing that all men are good at is leaving
when you need them most."

The times Kindle had questioned her mother about her
father's departure, Kayanne had quieted, narrowed her eyes and
said that grown-up business was not her business. She should
be a child for as long as she could. Childhood was the summer
of life. At the time, Kindle wondered if summer would ever
end.

Kindle emerged from the bathroom without taking a look
in the mirror, having mastered dressing perfectly in the dark.
She could even brush her teeth with the lights off. Energy had
to be preserved.

Before she reached the door, she stopped to glance at
Bobby as he slept. His body was a loose C-shape, his head
resting against his inner arm. A lock of hair fell across his face
but the rest was bound in a ponytail. The T-shirt he wore the
day before was a black puddle next to his arm. Kindle followed
the lines of his torso—the crisscrossing lines of his stomach
muscles and the dividing line of his sternum. Upon the upper
left side of his chest, he bore a patch of black-and-red ink—a
simple tattoo that she couldn't make out entirely from the
distance. She smiled, half-breathless, entirely intrigued.

For a pretty, suspended moment, she listened to the low
hum of his breath. When he began to stir, Kindle scuffled out
the door.

She walked through the dark morning, too agitated by her
thoughts to be irritated by the cold. She imagined that Bobby
was like a Christmas present, a life-sized doll, a genie. Kayanne
never believed in Christmas presents. They distracted from the
real meaning of Christmas. Kayanne had her theory on dolls as
well. Why invent stories for lifelike figures when real life had
enough troubles? As for genies, Kayanne didn't believe in gifts
that didn't have to be repaid. Everything in this life was just a

loan, even life itself. Don't expect anyone to give something for free. Kayanne intended to pay back Mr. Holster for everything she had borrowed. Kindle sighed. There was never any winning with her mother.

When Kindle arrived at the hotel, she spotted Mr. Holster aligning a picture on the wall. Still too indignant to greet him, she went straight to work, dragging her cart slowly from room to room. Coming upon room 205, her indignation was replaced with trepidation. The noise from the television blared behind the door. She knocked softly.

"Room service."

The door flew open. The man stared at her, his face hard and square, made more unseemly by his long, sloping jaw line.

"Room service," Kindle said quietly, looking over his shoulder at the other longhaired one lounging on the bed.

"Well, then service us," the lounging one said, laughing.

Kindle walked in and immediately began making up the bed closest to the door.

The lounging one lay flipping through channels.

The hard-faced one sat down beside him. "How's Bobby?"

She said nothing.

"I'm sorry. I don't mean to be rude. I'm Larry." He reached out his hand toward her.

Kindle stood in place.

He sucked his teeth. "Alright. I get it. You don't want to talk to us because this is all happening mega fast, huh?" Larry said. "But c'mon, how do you think we feel? It was just yesterday that we had four guys in our band and now we got three. Bobby C. doesn't seem to care one way or the other."

The other spoke. "Yeah. He's always been like that, in case you didn't know. Doesn't care much about anything." He flipped off the television. "I don't really see how you could know, since you guys have known each other for what, like, two days. But see, I've known that kid my whole life. He's always been as dense as he is today."

Kindle spread the blanket over the free bed and then stopped to look at them once more. "Dense?"

"Not dense exactly," Larry replied. "He's more…what would you call it?"

"I'd call it dense." The other one turned over on his back and folded his hands behind his head.

"Well, look, the guy's still like a brother," Larry said. "At least to me. He's not dense. I mean, he's more of a spaz."

"A spaz? Gentle. That's very gentle. " He shook his head.

"Come on, Kyle, he's your fucking cousin. You know he's not stupid. He's just on some kind of a trip all the time."

Kyle nodded and sniggered. "Okay, yeah—I get you, man. I get you."

"Get what?" Kindle moved her eyes back and forth between them. She circled her hand around her wrist.

"We're not talking African bush here." Kyle peered up at Kindle, spanning her body, as if assessing his cousin's choice. "No offense or anything. It's a phrase us white boys use for marijuana. But that's not what I'm talking about. Larry means that your new husband is always, like, on a romantic high or something. Bobby thinks there's this perfect love in the world and he'd put us all on the chopping block to get to it."

Larry bounced his legs up and down, shaking the floor beneath them. "Yeah. And it's not like he's purposely trying to sabotage our lives or something. He's not even, like, aware of how stupid his choices are."

"No offense again," said Kyle. "You aint the first girl that he's almost sold us out for."

"Yeah. There was this girl, Rebecca Lawrence."

Kyle sprung up to sitting position. "Dude, I almost forgot about Becky."

"I haven't," Larry laughed. "He swore she was his one and only true love. She begged to be our manager. She almost ruined The Dare."

"Until he found out she was cheating on him." Kyle shook Larry's shoulder. "Remember that, dude? He acted all suicidal for like a week or something."

"Dude, he didn't *find out* she was cheating. She *told* him she was cheating on him." Larry looked up at Kindle. "She said she was leaving him for another guy who had a band that she really wanted to manage."

Kyle stood. "Look here, don't you worry about cleaning the rest of this crap. I want to give you something."

Kindle stared at him, confused.

"Dude, don't look at me like that. I'm not giving you a gold necklace or something. Just a piece of advice, is all. Get out while you can. Bobby's on one of his highs right now. When it's all over, he'll drop you like a bad habit. Like, uh, like African bush."

They laughed monstrously and clapped their hands, reeling over, grasping their stomachs.

Kindle clenched her teeth, turning her back to them and grasping her cart handle. At the door, she felt Kyle at her back, grinding his hardened groin against her rear end. He held his hand against the door to keep her from leaving. "We've got rehearsal tomorrow night. Make sure he shows up, Missus Carter."

She smacked his locked arm. "If you don't move out of my way in two seconds or less, I can assure you that I will hit you in a spot where your future children will be born with headaches."

He stepped back, laughing. "No need to get hostile, sweetheart. It's my pleasure."

****

When Kindle stepped through the front door of her apartment, Bobby stood immediately in front of her.

"Kindle," he said.

"Bobby," she breathed.

"Guess what?"

"Why were you standing at the door?"

"I was waiting for you. I thought we were going to the Registry today."

"I don't want to talk about this right now." Kindle folded in her lips and brushed past him to her room, shutting the door behind herself. She exhaled once and began to cry, balancing herself against the wall. Her body vibrated as she tried muffling the sobs, but she couldn't quiet the hiccupping. She slid down the door to her bottom and hammered her head against her propped-up knees.

Bobby's voice sounded as if he mirrored her behind the door, bending down alongside her. "Well, um, guess what?"

Kindle ran her finger across her nose to wipe away the snot. She took a deep, quiet breath. "What? What is it?"

"My mom and dad sent me some money a few days back. I bought something for you today."

"I don't need a gift." She exhaled slowly to calm her shaking.

"I want you to see it. Will you open the door for me? Please."

She wiped her face, squashing her cheeks. "Not yet."

"Are you undressing?"

"No. I'm prostituting my body to the highest bidder."

"What?"

Kindle raised herself to her feet and opened the door.

Bobby was kneeling down with two lamps in his hands. They were bronze and tubular, with flat bases and ivory lampshades. He held them, their bases lying flat on his palm.

He stood up, still balancing the lamps. "Are you okay?"

"I'm fine."

"Your eyes don't say that."

"I'm well."

"You look like you're crying." Bobby set the lamps on the floor between their feet. He placed his hands on either sides of her cheeks and smeared the tears back to her temples, onto her hair, and down her ponytail. "Don't cry. I don't want you to be sad."

"Don't say that."

"Don't say what?"

"Don't say what you just said."

"Why?" he asked, twining his fingers through the curls in her ponytail. "I mean, I want to say that."

"You just get high off romantic idealism. Don't you?" She unraveled his fingers from her hair.

Bobby smiled and furrowed his eyebrows. "I hear that sometimes."

"You're still a child. You don't know what you want."
She stopped, truly questioning. "Do you?"
When his his eyes fell, her stomach was filled with
butterflies. She could hardly believe how beautiful he was as he
became thoughtful, sober. He was...precious, yet fitted in
stature and sure in his simple words.
"Children know what they want," he said. "It's adults
who don't, I think."
Kindle's gaze followed his. They held their conversation
with the floor.
"If you didn't want to be here with me, you wouldn't
be," he said. "Would you?"
"You're here with me, not the other way around. I belong
here."
"Why did you let me come in?"
"Because I'm stupid."
"I don't think so." He pulled her forward to him, hugging
her. He smelled like peaches and aftershave. "You seem pretty
smart, a lot smarter than me."
Kindle laughed low and short. "Not such a great feat."
Bobby smiled and his shoulders vibrated as if he were
holding in a laugh. "Kicks at my expense."
She looked up at him, her chin pressed against his chest.
"That could be a song title."
"I'd let you sing it, you know."
"But then I'd have to join your band."
"Definitely," Bobby said with a single nod.
As he ran his finger over her bottom lip, Kindle's mouth
parted. Shyly, she brought her lips inward, closing out his
finger, but tasting the saltiness it had left behind. She wondered
how saltiness could taste so sweet. She took a slight breath,
reclaiming her poise before she continued, "So your band
would be called Kindle and The Dare."
"No. It couldn't be called that. You'd have to make up a
name for yourself."
"Choose a name," Kindle pressed.
Bobby ran his thumb below her eye, wiping away a
remaining tear. "How about Ramona Mare and The Dare?"

"Ramona? Do I look like a Ramona? Sounds like a children's book."

"I like children's books."

Kindle put her fingertips together in front of her mouth. She exhaled. "So, are you going to stay another night?"

Chapter Five

Another night became a week. For Bobby, Kindle's silence on the marriage matter suggested that as long as he did not become a nuisance, his lease would be ever extended. Bobby provided for Kindle in every way he found useful, short of romantic rapture. He brought home food every day. He cleaned the bathroom once. He folded the clothes she had brought home from the launderette. He decided against purchasing the dozen roses from a floral shop he passed on the way home. Like a majestic ballad, this rhapsody had to progress slowly to its final love spell.

After rehearsal, Bobby was pretty sure that he knew why Kindle had cried briefly a week ago. When Kyle and Larry mentioned that Kindle visited their hotel room, they exchanged a glance before bursting into laughter. They didn't give up the details of the encounter, but Bobby knew that both of them could reduce Wonder Woman to tears. Not to mention their own scuffles. Larry and Kyle threw out insults and punches often and in equal quantity.

Bobby did not consider that The Dare had some fundamental relationship issues, nor did he press Kyle and Larry about what they said to Kindle; keeping the peace was the better choice. He tried only considering that one day soon, The Dare would play a show that would define the band and reach the attention of a record exec. He had no thought of which

record label would sign them, but rather, he envisioned The
Dare playing in a sweating arena and hearing his guitar riffs on
the radio one day. To get there, practice had to be relentless. He
pressed the band into seven hours of it that day. Every time
Larry stood up from his seat at the end of a set, Bobby looped
back to the first song, stressing the imminence of rehearsal with
every machine-gun strum of his guitar.

Bobby's desire for Kindle was growing quite imminent
too. He knew that it would take time to win her over
completely, but he also figured that, as with his music, he'd
have to put in good practice to get anywhere with her.

That evening after band practice, Bobby headed for
Rory's. Inside, the pub roared as usual, the band on stage
playing so hard and fast that Bobby couldn't make out a word
the singer said. However, when the song dropped with a
clashing of cymbals, he heard his name. Turning around, he
spotted Kyle sitting on the floor against a wall with beer bottles
at his feet. His accompanying wallflower was quite the show-
stopper—pixie-cut, pearl-blonde hair; burgundy cheeks and
lips; black leather pants and a matching vest tight enough to
pump her cleavage up to heights requiring a second glance.
With black-lined cat eyes, she looked up at Bobby.

Kyle waved him over and Bobby drew near, taking a seat
on the floor beside the girl, overtaken immediately by the
loudness of her perfume and the brassiness of her voice when
she said, "Lookie, lookie. What good deed have I done today to
warrant this kind of luck?"

Bobby leaned forward, taking a glance over at Kyle
before the girl steamrolled him back against the wall, quickly
pressing her mouth over his and trying to fondle his crotch with
ravenous hands. As Kyle bursted out in tipsy laughter, Bobby
reached for the girl's shoulders, pulling her back from himself.
He looked into her face. She was smiling simply, unfazed.

"It's how she greets everybody," said Kyle. He pressed
Betty back against the wall so that he could see Bobby. "Betty
Warner, meet my cousin Ricky Stallion. Ricky Stallion, meet
Betty Warner."

Betty reached for one of the bottles at Kyle's feet. She
took a sip and gargled with it before swallowing and reaching

out her hand to Bobby. "I'm Betty Warner, your savior who has yet to die on a cross." Her accent was acute, her words both slurred and broken

Kyle rolled his eyes. "Betty's caught a couple shows. She's the self-professed best damn promoter in the city. Says she can get The Dare into any club."

"Fuck me, if I can't," she said, faking indignation. She winked at Bobby. "Hell, fuck me, if I can. In fact, since I've already accosted you, I can only hope you have plans to rape me."

Bobby leaned forward, looking at his cousin. "Where did you get this girl from, Kyle?" he inquired, hoping she was too drunk to mind his rudeness.

"Oh, please, don't be offended by my forwardness," Betty intercepted. "All I'm saying is that I like strangers to pin me down and do push-ups over me. Is that a crime?"

A few feet away, a redhead sitting against the wall spewed out her drink, laughing uncontrollably. She scooted away from the girl next to her, joining their trio.

"The fuck?" Kyle breathed. He smirked at Betty. "You've got one fucked up sense of humor, Betty Warner. I swear to God, you're the strangest broad I've ever met."

"You're the most ornery American monkey *I've* ever met," she returned, grinning wide. "So we're equal."

Kyle smiled back. Bobby could see that her insult was cause for Kyle's immediate attraction. "Look at Bitch Betty with her sad insults."

The redhead crossed her legs, Yoga-style, looking once at Bobby before staring at Betty to see her response.

Betty leaned her head on Bobby's shoulder. "Bitch Betty. I like that name. It has a certain charm, doesn't it?" She rolled her head against his neck. "It's kind of snazzy. Like Ricky Stallion. Or like Kyle Ass Clown. Ha!Now, *that* name has super-hero intrigue."

Bobby shrugged his shoulders to roll her head off of him. He looked around, wondering where Kindle was.

"So, Ricky, I want to know about you," Betty continued. She backed away from the wall, turning so that she face him head-on. She held her hands in her lap. "What are your interests? Obviously, rock and roll. What about other recreational activities? Do you like Lucy in the Sky with Diamonds?"

"What?" said Bobby.

"LSD," the redhead laughed. "You know, Lennon's famous *acronym*."

"Oh, yeah. Well, I'm not into that," Bobby said, looking down, smiling but indifferent. He'd grown accustomed to strange times like these among the women Kyle found in clubs.

Betty nodded. "How's about other kinds of blow? Do you do that? Or what about orgasms? Do you like those much?"

The redhead laughed so loudly that she interrupted the music that had begun again. A group of people in front of them looked back.

Kyle snorted. "Betty, you obviously haven't got a clue."

Betty pouted. "What haven't I a clue about?" She looked Bobby over once before searching his face. She squealed suddenly and slapped her hand over her mouth. "Oh heavens! Please don't tell me you're suffering from a lengthy case of virginitis. Holy hell, my radar is defective. I never woulda guessed." She clapped her hands together. "Well, I do have a treatment for your ailment, that's for certain. Just let me know when you're ready to be cured."

The redhead's laughter erupted again until she nearly choked this time. After catching her breath, she spoke, slightly embarrassed. "It's stuffy in here, don't you think? Hot as hell, really. I'm sweating like a nasty girl." She reached inside her purse, pulling out a bottle of perfume. She sprayed her armpits, laughing.

"Why you gotta spray that nasty stuff, woman?" Betty complained. "It's disgusting."

"I think it smells fantastic," the girl replied. She pointed the bottle at Bobby, Kyle, and Betty, giving them each a squirt.

Bobby shook his head, irritated. He stood. "I gotta go, Kyle. I'll see you at practice tomorrow."

"Okay, dude." Kyle said. "Take care of yourself."

He looked down at his cousin. Despite his wanton ways, Bobby smiled. Kyle wasn't all bad, he supposed. If nothing else, he was loyal. "I'll be fine," Bobby said.

Actually, he'd be better than fine. He noticed Kindle walking toward the door. He followed after her, only looking back once when Betty hollered out, "I'll be your cure, baby. Call me when you need me."

He caught Betty's eye, breathing shortly before strolling out onto the street. He caught up quickly with Kindle, catching her by the arm.

"Hey," he said, as she turned to face him. "How are you? What's going on?"

"Nothing, really. Just glad to be off duty," she replied, looking up at him curiously before walking forward. "I know that's your brand of music, but it does become quite tiresome to the ears. And the brain."

"Yeah." Bobby said, looking down at her thin hands. They were reddening from the night air. "But, you know, performed by the right band, it can be totally killer."

He removed his right glove and took hold of her right hand, sliding her fingers into the glove. He balled up her left hand, covering it entirely with his right.

Her eyes fluttered as she looked ahead."So, what bands tickle your fancy, Stallion? Oh, let me guess. The Clash. The Ramones. The Sex Pistols."

"No," he said, looking also at the road, a path as promising as the Yellow Brick Road with her at his side. "Stevie Wonder. Pink Floyd. John Lennon. Lennon's my favorite though. I think he'll change the world, if you give him long enough. You can't get any better than that."

"So you're a lover of the living legends?"

He stopped as they turned down the darker street. "Well, yeah. If I had what they had, The Dare wouldn't ever worry about filling up shows."

She stood in front of him, turning her fist in his palm. "Well, you already have a fan of one, I'm sure."

"What do you mean?" he asked, backing up and leaning against the side wall of a brick flat.

She withdrew her hand from his. "I mean, you already have the obvious adoration of the little bird that used your shoulder as her head rest this evening. You know—the buxom blonde one at the pub. "

Oh. Her." He scratched his forehead, wondering how much Kindle had seen."Her name is Betty Warner. She's a music promoter or something. She's not, like, you know, anybody I'd be interested in." He reached forward, hooking his arm around her waist, closing the space between them. "Besides, I'm already kinda tied to somebody. Interest in another girl would be like eating when you're already full." Bobby smiled, closing his eyes and binging his face down to hers. The electricity was there, he was sure. The desire was present. But within seconds, she was not.

Bobby opened his eyes. Kindle was bent backward, bracing herself with the arm he held around her midsection, as though she were taking a slow dancer's dip. Looking down upon her face, he found her skin brighter than the copper moon.

He ushered her back up. "What did I do wrong? Do I need some kind of instruction or something?"

She looked around. "Proper preparations are needed. I'm sure you've heard of setting the mood, right? Man. Woman. Candle Light. A good meal. Fine wine—"

"Polka music," he interjected. "Dancing bears."

Obviously caught off guard, Kindle laughed loudly. She scrunched her eyes, smiling. "Leprechauns and fairies."

"Yeah. All of that." He nodded, then dropped his voice. "Or maybe we don't need all the trimmings. It doesn't have to be rehearsed, does it? Just needs to be the right time."

"Who says the right time is now?" she asked, running her hand over the sleeve of his leather jacket. "We've only known each other a grand total of two weeks, my faithful flatmate."

"Two weeks is fourteen days. That's—" he squinted his eyes, trying to calculate numbers in his head but to no avail "— a ton of hours. And right now, we're probably wasting seconds talking about something that's gonna happen eventually. We could just make it happen now."

"That's quite presumptuous of you."

He held his breath a second. "Why don't we just agree on something. Let's just agree now that I'm going to kiss you in sixty seconds." He looked down quickly at his wristwatch. "I'll be a gentleman about it. Or a sailor, if you want. Whatever you want, I'll be. Just as long as you give me your mouth for ten whole seconds."

"You really are a blokey bloke, aren't you?

"A what?" Bobby smiled, confused.

"A king of one-liners. A master of seduction. Glib. A snake charmer of words. Right terms for the right times, eh?"

He slid his back down slightly against the wall. "Oh, no. You've got me all wrong. I'm not that kind of guy. Not at all. I'm just..." he dropped his gaze briefly "...*smitten* or something."

Kindle's teeth sparkled as she laughed. "You've got such a deceitful shell, don't you? You're a romantic in gothic apparel. Why don't you write soul music?"

"Punk gets the job done faster." Bobby dropped his hand from her waist, flapping open one side of his jacket and looking at it. "I don't think my clothes are gothic. I just like dark colors." He looked back at his watch. "Fifteen seconds left before I kiss you though. You still have time to escape if you want."

"Oh, but you can't make me do anything I don't want. So, your threat is futile." She pressed her lips together, defiant.

He stared at his watch. "Ten seconds."

"You foolish, foolish boy."

"Seven, six..."

While he still counted, Kindle thrust herself against him, forcing him against the wall, her body heat engulfing him like a sauna. He felt the moist warmth of her breathing as she brought her face to his. She nestled both sides of his face in her hands and placed her lips gently on his. He swept her lips with his own, taking in her supple sweetness like the flesh of a tangerine. He engulfed her face with both hands, attempting to part her mouth with his lips. Yet, it wasn't long before he realized that she was determined to lead the kiss. She gave him long strokes of her lips followed by shorter brushes of her mouth, as if she were purposely leaving her sweet saliva on his lips, only to clear it away with the shorter kisses. He submitted to her style until his drive to lead was instantly increased by the tiny, feral moan that escaped her.

Bobby circled his arm around her midsection, turning them around once so that it was now he who pressed her against the wall, compelling her to submit to the speed and rhythm of his mouth. He removed his hand from her face, holding it against the wall to steady them. Kindle reached for the collar of his shirt, tangling it between her fingers, but soon, she pressed on his chest to mute their passion.

He lifted his face from hers. "Thank you," he said softly, breathing quickly as she moved away. He smirked. "Thank you, God."

****

The following afternoon, Bobby walked into rehearsal at the club where the band had played twice before. They would play at the venue the next day. The room smelled like old French fries.

"You're five minutes late," Kyle chided.

"I'm fifteen minutes early," said Bobby.

"But you're always twenty."

"I'm five minutes farther away," Bobby returned.

"Truth is," Larry said, taking a seat behind his drum set and twirling his drumstick between his fingers, "she's got you wide open."

Kyle and Bobby slung their instruments over their shoulders.

Bobby spoke with his pick clenched between his teeth. "Why do we have to talk about her?"

"Because," Kyle said, plugging his bass into the amp, "she changes the band's dynamic. You're always twenty minutes early for setup. It's like clockwork. Now, you're throwing the whole energy of the band off."

"But I'm still early."

"That's not the point," Larry said. He began tapping on the drum, casting that familiar spell on Bobby. "Point is that you're losing yourself."

"Maybe I'm finding myself," Bobby said absently. He began strumming to the beat. Kyle followed.

Rapt, Bobby began to sing.

Maybe I'm finding myself
Poor days done
Rich in her wealth
Maybe I finally won

"What the hell!" Larry yelled over the music, continuing to drum nonetheless. "Is every song gonna be a fucking fem-fest now? You're giving this punk thing a real literal meaning, dude. I'm still a man."

"Might as well let him sing," Kyle asserted, beating out a funky line on his bass. "I swear to God, he's pushing out hits like every week."

Bobby continued, closing his eyes.

Finally won you
I'll never lose
If you love me too
Just say you do
Say you love me too

Bobby named the song "Love Me Too."

The texture and tempo of the song did not match the sentiment, but at least the quick pace kept up with the rhythm of Bobby's heart. For him, that was all that mattered.

****

"Bobby, honey," his mother said. Bobby could hear her running water. It was almost seven o'clock in the U.S., which meant that his mother was doing dishes and his father was parked in his lazy boy watching Cronkite. Bobby was beginning to miss his mother... and Cronkite. And that's the way it was.

"Hey, Mom," he said, looping his finger through the payphone cord. "How's home?"

"Uneventful, honey." He could hear her heavy breathing and the stacking of dishes. "Dad and I really miss you. You know, he can't wait for you to come home."

"I know." Bobby looked around at the snow falling around the glass phone booth. People trudged through the layer of polluted snow on the sidewalks and crossed the slick black street with their heads down, trying to avoid the wind. Bobby was glad to be tucked away in the red-rimmed booth. It stood on the sidewalk in the city, beside a series of castle-like brown-brick buildings. From inside the booth, he watched cars slowly pass down the street. Though locked away in the booth, the cold chilled Bobby to the bone. The wind beat against the glass. At least in the booth, the snow could not wet his hair. He had forgotten his hat.

"Your father *does* miss you," his mother continued. "But what causes you to call, honey? Everything okay?"

"Yeah, Mom, everything's cool." He massaged his jawbone with the phone. "I mean, everything is fine. Me and the guys just finished rehearsal. We wrote two new songs."

"I'm so happy for you, sweetheart." She coughed. He knew she was waiting to hear the favor he would ask.

"Mom, I don't want you to worry about me. I know how you do."

"Always. But I'm learning."

Bobby drummed the phone stand with his knuckles. "I hate to ask, Mom, but, um, I really need your help. Again. See, I'm short on cash again and…"

"Short on cash, Bobby?" she whispered. Bobby could see her in his head. She was looking around to make sure his dad hadn't gotten up from the lazy boy. Not likely. "What happened to what I sent? I hope you're not being pressured there."

"What?"

"I know you remember the man who died a few years back. A black young man. He played the guitar."

Bobby squinted his eyes. "Jimi Hendrix?"

"Yes. Him. It's a very dangerous, not to mention expensive, habit and I don't—"

"No, Mom, I don't do drugs. I'd never do that. It's just that," he twisted his foot against the crunchy cement. "It's just that it's getting more expensive to live here. Added responsibilities and stuff."

"I thought you and your fellows were getting more opportunities."

"We are, but…I just…" He didn't want to lie to her. Lying always made his stomach queasy. "Could you just do it, Mom? I won't ask again. I mean, I'll try not to. But trust me, I'm doing the right thing. You know, I even go to Mass every Sunday and everything. I haven't missed one so far." He trusted that his mother would be happy to hear that.

Instead, she sighed. "Okay. But I worry about you. It's my motherly reflex to worry. I talked to Father Denneson the other day. He said he would pray for you too. And he read to me Luke Fifteen. Do you remember that, honey?"

"I think so."

"I just want you to know that you can come home whenever you like. We will always welcome you home."

Bobby didn't know how he felt about being compared to the prodigal son. "Yeah, Mom. It won't be so much longer. So, um, are you going to use Western Union again?"

"Yes, Bobby."

He hated how defeated she sounded. "Well, um, Mom, I'm really thankful."

"Of course." She stopped. She must have been checking for his father again. "But I need to know something. Where are you staying these days?"

His stomach dropped. "What do you mean?"

"Larry told me that you were no longer staying with them, that you had other ventures outside of theirs. Do you think it's really safe to live alone in a foreign place?"

"Well, it's not that foreign, Mom. I mean, America was owned by Britain once, right?"

"Bobby," she scolded.

"I'm sorry, Mom. I'm fine. I'm not being unsafe or anything."

"Well, do you have a number where I can reach you?"

He gave her the apartment number, not knowing what else he could do. "Well, Mom," Bobby hurried, "I love you. And I miss you. I miss Dad too."

Bobby envisioned her glowing smile and apple red lipstick. "Oh, we miss you too, my little chicken."

He hung up the phone, smiling at the remembrance of how he got the name "little chicken" the day his mother dressed him in a chicken suit for the Easter egg hunt when he was three years old.

****

Kindle and Bobby were married twenty-five days when The Dare played their first show of the year. Shortly after midnight, Kindle heard Bobby clamber into the dark foyer. She listened to him shuffle through the kitchen. After hearing a sudden clatter, she was tempted to investigate, but she lay still, unwilling to have him know that she had waited up for him.

The next morning, Kindle entered the kitchen with the intention of making a bowl of cereal. Upon opening the cabinet door, she found dishes stacked neatly one upon another. The bowls, plates, cups and saucers were lined neatly side-by-side. Each was snow-white with gold strip trim.

Kindle searched the kitchen drawers, like a child tearing through Christmas wrapping. She found gold spoons, forks, knives. Her lips parted in a smile and she shook her head, as contented as a young newlywed should be.

She stepped out of the kitchen, peeping at Bobby as he lay on the floor. His eyes were open. He quickly shut them, smirked, and turned over so that his back faced her. She beamed.

Kindle had resumed working at the pub three nights before Bobby had his first show. The beginning of the year was rather slow; there had yet to be a band as electric as The Dare. She missed them. She missed Ricky Stallion.

The day after Bobby brought the dishes, the sixteenth day of marriage, Kindle came home from work to another surprise.

She walked through the door to find her living room had been furnished. The living room set was queer looking—perhaps an ode to the psychedelic seventies—but it did officially make the living room livable. A long, furry couch was pressed against the wall beneath the window. A shorter couch was adjacent to it. Across from the shorter couch, a colossal chair sat against the wall, a stout glass table at its side. Bobby had placed the tubular lamps on the floor on either side of the table. In the center of it all was her favorite piece—a large, brown television.

The new items smelled artificially fresh, like they had been doused in detergent. She crept from entrance to the center of the room, in front of the furniture. A ray of light streamed out from under the closed bathroom door down the hall. She heard water run quickly on, then off.

Bobby stepped out of the bathroom into the living room, shaking water off of his hands. He stood next to her and rubbed his chin, grinning.

"What do you think?" he said, nearly laughing in excitement.

"It's purple."

"Electric purple, I think." Bobby looked down at her. "Purple is my new favorite color. It haunts me in my dreams."

Kindle's heart raced the second she recognized the allusion. "Electric purple," she repeated. She glanced down at the glass table, picking up the picture frame that sat upon it. "And this…this is a picture. Of whom? Did it come with the frame?"

"No, no. Those are my folks. My parents, I mean. Sometimes people say I look like my dad." He shrugged.

Kindle squinted her eyes and brought the picture closer to her face. "I guess I could see that." She dropped down in the large chair. It welcomed her kindly, its frayed cushions nearly swallowing her. "So, where did you get all of this? And the dishes?"

"The dishes, I bought from…from a place called Juliette's."

"Yes, I know the place."

Bobby nodded his head and put his hands in the back of his jeans. "And um, I got the furniture from a thrift store."

"A thrift store?"

His smile weakened. "Yes. I know it's kind of a strange color or something, but I thought you'd like it. Maybe."

Kindle lifted an eyebrow, crossed her legs, and wiggled her foot.

Bobby crept toward her. "And it's not that old, I don't think. It's clean. I sprayed it with a lot of cleaners and deodorizers. I'm probably almost high from all the fumes."

"How'd you get it all here?" she said, rotating her foot in circles.

"I had some help."

She raised her eyebrows.

Bobby pushed his hair from his face and pinched his nose. His gaze drifted through the room. "Larry and Kyle."

She was instantly shamed. No one had been inside since her mother. "Here? You brought them here?"

"I needed help."

Kindle poked out her bottom lip. "What did they say about this place?"

His gaze hit the floor; she was quelled by his embarrassment. "I don't think I should say."

"Very well, Bobby."

He smiled once more. "I almost cleared my savings account. Just for you."

"Do you think that was wise?"

"I, uh, I'm making more money now. Larger venues and stuff. And, uh, my mom is sending me more money."

Kindle paused, reflecting. "You haven't told her about me, have you?"

Bobby looked her in the eyes, despite her interrogation. "I haven't yet," he said softly, his lips barely moving.

"Do you *really* intend to tell her?"

"I know I'll have to one day. I just don't want to hurt her, you know?"

"You don't want to hurt her or you don't want to *disappoint* her?"

"I don't know what you mean?"

Kindle knotted her arms over her chest. "You don't want them to know about specific qualities I have?"

"Qualities?" He coughed. "Is this about you being Afro-American? I mean, English-American?" He shook his head. "Of color, I mean?"

"What *I* mean is non-white. Or poor. Or maybe orphaned. And what about my being a bastard?"

Bobby paused, then shook his head. "I don't think women can be bastards."

"What's the real reason you didn't tell her, Bobby?"

"The real reason?"

"Bobby, I'm your partner now, aren't I? You can tell me anything, can't you?" She scrunched her lips together, blinking her eyes sweetly.

"Sure. Yeah, I can." Bobby pushed his hair behind his ears with his palms. "I'm not ashamed of you or anything like that. It's just, like, my mom and me are kind of tight. So, I'm, uh, I'm just—what's the word? Treading lightly, I guess."

Kindle leaned back in the chair and closed her eyes, entangling her fingers in her lap. "I understand. My mum would be disapproving as well. Because our little affair occurred with such haste, but mostly because you're white." She laughed. "Or European-American. I mean American-American. Without color, if you will."

Kindle heard Bobby sniffle and she imagined his bashful grin. "So your parents wouldn't understand, either?"

"No, my mum wouldn't. Mr. Holster doesn't understand either."

"Holster? Like a gun? Who's that?"

"He's like a grandfather to me."

"Grandfather?"

"You're an amazing echo." Kindle opened her eyes to find him kneeling before her. "I don't know whether I'm fooling you or myself. Mr. Holster has just looked out for me a bit since my mum died. He's the older gentleman at the hotel."

"That guy with the grey hair?"

"I think it's more white, Mr. *Electric* Purple." Kindle smirked. "Mr. Holster hired me, as he told my mother he would if anything happened to her."

"Did your mom know something would happen to her?"

"She was sick for a long time. Unknowingly, though. I don't think she knew when she would die. She just took precautions. That's the kind of woman she was."

"Can I get a piece of your story?"

Kindle breathed deeply and grinned straightaway. "Ready for my sad story—the tale of death and destruction?" She sighed and began. "My mother and father were together for five years before I was born—that's what my mum said when I badgered her about it. My father didn't have a knack for fidelity, especially when my mum became pregnant. He was an artist type—singer or something. Much like yourself."

Bobby frowned.

"He was gone a couple months after I was born. My mother maintained herself well until I was four or five. That was when I was able to remember things. She got very sick: had rashes on her hands, had fevers, and things like that. She didn't want me to get sick, so she sent me to stay with her distant cousin in Sandwell. The lady was an evil old woman who put me to hard labor in washing dishes and mopping floors every day. Can't say I miss her." Kindle laughed hollowly.

Bobby smiled weakly.

"But she gave me back to my mum when she got better. My mum was well until I was about seventeen. At that point, she was sick a lot and becoming something like mentally impaired. When Mr. Holster finally insisted she go to the hospital, they diagnosed her. That was that."

"What did the doctors say?"

"Syphilis. Nasty woman's disease, right?" Kindle shook her head and faked a shudder. "It was too late by then. That's the nature of Syphilis untreated. There comes a point of no return. The disease had eaten at her aorta, among other things. Her brain had irreversible damage. She was pretty close to death."

"So what about your father?"

Kindle nodded. "Never formally met him. He came here once when I was fifteen or so. I heard his voice from inside the bedroom but never actually saw him. As for why he wasn't dead by then, I've got my own theory. He must have known he had it but hoped he hadn't given it to my mum. So he didn't tell her but got his own shot. I'm sure he's still around. That's the way of the world: the good die young and the wicked live frivolously."

Bobby looked down at the floor. "Did he give it to her after you were born?"

"If you're asking if I had it, then the answer is no. I didn't. She must have contracted it shortly after I was born." Kindle eyed him carefully.

He quickly glanced up at her and back down.

"It's for that reason that I've sworn off relations," she said breezily. "Even marital ones. The risk is too high. You can die a decent woman having had a single lover your whole life, as my mother did."

"So, you mean, you'll never do it? Even though, you might be, like—I mean, you *are*—married?" Bobby wrung his hands.

"Married to whom, Bobby?"

He looked up shyly.

"The answer is no. It's a promise I've made to myself."

"But what if the man is faithful? What if he's honorable?"

"I've never seen such a man."

"What about the Gun Holster guy?"

"Mr. Holster? Oh. Well, he's old. He's a different class of man," said Kindle.

Bobby paused, opening his mouth to speak and then stopping several times before he finally said, "I'm a good guy, Kindle."

"Mr. Holster don't seem to think so. He knows about our little adventure."

"I don't think he knows me."

Kindle leaned forward so that the tip of her nose nearly touched his. "And I don't know you either."

When Bobby spoke, his breath was sweet and cool upon Kindle's face. "I can tell you anything you wanna know."

"Alright, then," Kindle returned evenly. "I want to know the worst thing that you've ever done."

Bobby retreated his face from hers. "I'm not sure."

She moved her face towards his, closing the space. "Perhaps it's your lovely tattoo. I knew you were far more naughty than you let on."

He smiled, reaching for her hand and running it over his chest, allowing her to trace the location of his tattoo. "Just ink. Nothing to regret."

Kindle could hardly believe how crestfallen she was when he released her hand from his chest. She had instantly lost the steady thump of his heartbeat, the heat of his skin beneath his shirt, and the sturdiness of his flesh. Moreover, she was entirely surprised by how much she wanted to reclaim the sensations, so much that she nearly reached her hand back out for him, but refrained when she considered that he probably wasn't as lost in the simple gesture as she was. It was just a touch.

She dropped her hands in her lap. moving the conversation forward. "Then, what do you regret?"

"Oh, I don't know. Nothing too big." Bobby blinked and tucked his hair behind his ear again. "There was this time when I was seventeen and my dad and I got in a huge fight. I mean, I never fight with my dad, really. But he basically called me a jerk for defending my mom when he yelled at her for giving me money for a Fender."

"Fender?"

"A guitar."

Kindle nodded.

"I begged for it. He'd never get it. So she did. But you know, my dad's, like, ex-military. Really, uh…"

Kindle found endearing the thoughtful breath he took.

"…*stony*. So, he got mad at my mom and yelled."

"That's normal for ex-military?"

Bobby shrugged. "I don't know. Maybe. But it's not normal for him. He doesn't yell a lot in front of me. Just sometimes. He more, like, quietly disapproves of stuff."

"But that time, he yelled?"

"Yeah. He yelled. At her. He probably wanted to yell at me. But he doesn't; never has much. He never says anything real to me. Wish he had said something to me instead. Probably would have changed stuff."

"What did you do?" she asked, leaning forward on the edge of her seat.

"I overreacted, that's all."

"Did you strike him or something?"

"No, no. Nothing like that. I just raised my voice at him. In front of my mom."

"*That's* the worst thing that you've ever done?" Kindle laughed once and rocked back. "Oh, princess…"

Bobby laughed. "No. There's more to it. I told him that, uh, that me and my mom would be better off without him. And he just…he just left. For like a week or something. The day he came back, he had a seizure." His forehead wrinkled and his jaw tightened. "I watched him fall out of his chair, completely out of it. He was jerking and foaming at the mouth and all that kind of stuff. I just stood there watching him." He licked his lips, thoughtful. "My mom finally came in. She's the one who helped him."

"Do you think you wanted him to die?" She bounced her foot up and down until Bobby straddled it with his hand.

"I don't know " He paused. "Probably not. I love him and everything. He's my dad." He met her eyes and let loose her foot. "I'm sure I didn't want him to die. I just couldn've done better than what I did that day."

"At least you wanted him to live. That counts for something."

He nodded, remote.

Kindle lowered her eyes. "I wasn't as good as you were. Not long before my mum was very sick, I dreamt of what things would be like without her."

"Yeah?"

"Yes. I suppose I just wanted to know life without her. Because I believed that she protected me from life. And I wanted to live."

"Maybe you were right. About the protection thing. That's what parents are supposed to do, right?"

She visored her eyes with her hand. "I suppose so."

They sat silent. Kindle inhaled, holding his scent in her nostrils. He smelled like detergent, aftershave and shampoo. To her, that kind of combined scent had been the epitome of pampering. She hoped that it would become the smell of home.

Bobby took hold of her hand, pulling her toward him and wrapping her up in a hug. He rested his chin on the crook of her neck. "So, uh, what do you think of the furniture? I can't take it back."

"It's quite bizarre," Kindle laughed as her eyes watered. "It's us." She petted the side of his face. "Let me say that I'm sorry about what happened with you and your father. But I hope you realize that you can't blame yourself for things that happened when you were so young."

"Yeah." He burrowed his nose into her cheek. "It's okay. It's over now."

Chapter Six

Past Time: 1964

Seven-year-old Bobby understood that the problem with his fellow altar servers was that they didn't really think much of the Blessed Sacrament. The boys did what they were told, but their eyes were vacant.

Bobby, however, was sure of two things, if nothing else: first, Jesus was real. After his first Holy Communion, he told his mother that he was happy to finally see what God tasted like. Second, the Blessed Virgin was real too. Perfect mothers were pretty rare, but from his own experience, Bobby knew they existed.

Coming home after Mass every Sunday, Bobby's father reclined downstairs while Bobby laid his head on his mother's lap as she sat on her bed knitting. She stroked his head from time to time. Sometimes, he pretended to be asleep, just enjoying the way she caressed his back even when she thought he couldn't feel it.

One Sunday in September of '64, Bobby lay across the bed, his head resting on his mother's thigh. He looked out the window. The sun shined through the blue lace curtains and the nightstand radio played. Bobby was falling in love with "Unchained Melody." His mother didn't care for rock-and-roll; she preferred Sinatra. She had begun playing the radio for

Bobby after the day The Beatles invaded Ed Sullivan and he
stood in a trance in front of the television.

"Honey," his mother said, her voice as fluid as a love
song. "Are you still awake?"

"Yes," Bobby replied, turning his face over on her lap, so
that he spoke to her stomach. He watched her freckled arms
move steadily as she twined yarn around needles. .

She tilted his face up toward her, beholding him as if
newly acquainted with her only son's fresh face. "You're such a
beautiful little boy. You know that, don't you?"

He smiled. "I guess."

"And so smart too. You're the smartest little boy that I
know. You're our only baby for a reason. Another child would
have too much to live up to."

By this age, Bobby already knew otherwise. His father
had told him that his birth had been cause of his mother's
infertility. Another child being impossible, who else could live
up to Bobby's supposed glory? To his mother, he was perfect in
every way. She could see the van Gogh in his kindergarten
scribbling. She could follow the rhythm of his offbeat six-year-
old claps. She could envision the great cyclist in his first
uncoordinated tricycle strides.

Bobby had gradually become aware that perfection was
in the eye of the beholder. A few young boys misjudged his
wordlessness for wimpiness. Plus, Bobby's perpetually drippy
nose and complete disinterest in sports or super heroes made
him a pariah among most of the little boys. His nose stopped
dripping so much after he turned seven, but his chronic,
habitual sniff stayed with him. All that sniffing made him
suspicious to boys looking for anything to be suspicious about.
Back then, Kyle used to defend him. He once knocked out the
front tooth of one of the kids that called Bobby a butt sniffer.
Good thing it was a baby tooth. Better thing that he had a
cousin near his age to take up for him. His mother was right—
family was all you had sometimes.

Though some little boys judged him, most everyone else
adored him despite his quietness. With his green eyes and long
lashes, Bobby was instantly a hit among little girls and their
mothers. A child as respectful as Bobby—bowing at the Lord's

altar and in the presence of adults—was quiet but hardly overlooked.

"You can do anything, honey," his mother continued, as she set her knit work on the nightstand. "Do you realize that?"

"I think so," he said, yawning softly.

"Well, then, have you considered that maybe, just maybe, you will become a priest?"

"Hmmm?"

She brushed his hair back from his forehead. "A priest. You love God a lot, don't you, Chicken?"

"I think so."

"When little boys really love God, sometimes, they want to serve Jesus with all of their hearts, for their whole life. That's what priests do."

"Oh," Bobby replied, a soft yawn slipping out again.

"Father Nixon says that he will talk to you about it, if you want. Would you like something like that, Bobby? Would you like to have an audience with Father Nixon?"

"Carol."

Bobby and his mother both turned their heads swiftly toward the bedroom door, in the direction of the rumbling, robust voice. His father stepped in, towering, commanding. He still wore his church clothes, his attire crisp and trim like an army uniform. Though his black Oxford shoes were the epitome of gentleman, he walked hard in them, as though he wore military boots, unable to abandon his training from twenty-five years ago.

"Frank," she returned, patting Bobby's back as an indication for him to sit up. Bobby glanced up at his father. He looked into Bobby's eyes shortly and then looked back at his mother.

"Robert, excuse yourself," his father directed.

Bobby slid off the bed, stood up straight, placed his hands in his pocket, and walked out of the room unobtrusively. His father shut the door behind him. Bobby walked down the hall to his room, but after a moment, sidled back to his parents' bedroom door, pressing his ear against it.

"Obedience isn't something you're familiar with, is it, Carol?"

"It was only a question, Frank. Only a question," his mother responded softly, so softly that Bobby pressed his ear farther against the door.

"A question that you should have asked me first. Do you think that I gave him to you like some kind of gift? Do you think he belongs to you?"

Through the proceeding silence, Bobby swallowed nervously, hoping that they hadn't suspected his presence.

"Frank, please don't be upset. This isn't about who Bobby belongs to." She hesitated. "I think he belongs to God."

"Forget the fucking God excuse, Carol," his father shot out. "Do you remember what it took to get you a son? Ask your God how he felt about Sarah pressuring Abraham to be with Hagar. You think she could have said Ishmael belonged to her?"

"Why do we have to talk about that? It doesn't matter. It really doesn't," she said, her voice trembling now. Bobby's heart beat faster. He felt tears filling his own eyes and breathed quietly to control them. "I remember, Frank. I'll never forget. I don't think you'll ever let me forget, will you?"

"So you also see that he's a boy, not a little girl, right? That dream died when Robert was born. He's soft because of you."

"Soft?"

"Go ahead, Carol, completely emasculate him; make him a priest. That way, you can emasculate me too. Go ahead and cut off any chance of carrying my name forward."

His mother sniveled. "I would never try to do that to you. Never, ever. I love you, Frank."

"No. No, you don't. You love him. Or you say you do. But you'd much rather take away his manhood before he even reaches it."

Bobby could hear that his mother was sobbing, pushing words out through her cries. "I don't want that."

When his father began to yell, Bobby shuddered. "Grow the hell up, Carol! When will you stop crying over every small thing?"

"Frank, Bobby will—"

"I don't care if he hears. He's a man; let him handle himself like a man."

"He's only a little boy!"

His father's voice dropped and Bobby strained to hear him. "And I'm only your husband. Are you going to be more obedient to your husband or your son? Who did you make your vows to?"

"Oh, Frank—"

"Maybe you wanted to become a wife so you could be a mother. You want it that way; you can have it that way. I'll leave you with the one you're willing to obey. But when he goes to be a priest, you'll be all alone, won't you?"

His mother cried out. "Please, don't go, Frank. Don't go."

When Bobby heard the jingling of keys, he raced toward his bedroom door, but before he could enter, his father's iron hands clanked the back of his neck.

"What the hell did I tell you, Robert?" his father bellowed, pounding Bobby's face against the hall wall until his cheek was dimpled by a splinter in the wood paneling. "Are you hard of hearing or just plain rebellious? You'll learn discipline. There's no such thing as a man without discipline."

Bobby struggled for breath, gurgling and trying to push out feeble apologies. His father turned him around, backhanding him one good time, sending him to the carpeted floor, where the friction burned his face. Bobby could hear his mother cry out, but knew well enough that there was no use in her attempting to come to his rescue. It would only make things worse.

Bobby lay on the floor, his arms circled over his head until he heard his father march down the stairs and out the front door. It was then that he rose to his feet, pressing his hand over his throbbing cheek and wiping away his tears, determined not multiply his mother's pain with his own.

Slowly, he entered his mother's room and climbed on top of the bed, where she sat with her arms circled around her legs and her faced buried in her knees. Bobby circled his mother's back with his own arms, pressing his face against the crown of her head. In the midst of the dampness that his breath and her tearful sighs created, Bobby's mind began to run. He was sure that his father would be back later that evening; he wouldn't neglect family responsibility. Any meeting with Father Nixon would bring further discord. Bobby decided that he would not hold an audience with Father.

Paul McCartney's voice crooned from the radio, filling the room with The Beatles' "Yesterday." To Bobby, it was the only thing that made the moment half bearable. Over the next few months, he would listen to that song as much as he could.

Chapter Seven

Present Time....

February arrived faster than either Kindle or Bobby expected. They still had not tasted the physical delights of marriage, though most nights Bobby dreamed of sampling her every part like an hors d'oeuvre. Kindle grew more confident that she had become the center of Bobby's world. To be an object of desire was her childhood fantasy fulfilled. Though marital abstinence made nights long for Bobby, who could hear his wife breathing in her sleep through thin walls, he did not give up hope that he would know her beyond words and stories.

Even so, Kindle and Bobby were both well entertained with learning about one another. They were certainly undressing themselves, even if only proverbially. Bobby had come to know her silhouette well by mid-February. He was learning the sound and meaning of her sighs, whether they were contented, sad, tired, or discouraged. He knew that she took showers immediately after arriving home from work. It was a habit she rarely broke. He knew her joking flirtation and found himself often following his grin with, "You keep me coming, Penelope. You really do."

One evening, Kindle tried her hand at some soft jesting when he brought home sunflower seeds.

Kindle mused over how strange seeds were. She took one of the seeds from the pile Bobby had dumped into his hand. She cracked it open with her teeth, removing the seed and holding it in her mouth, bidding him to take it with his own. Bobby bent down, clamping his teeth over the sliver of seed that extended from her mouth. There, he could feel heat of her mouth as he slipped the seed from her mouth to his, clamping it between his back teeth before she kissed him. As with every time she lured him in, she backed away the moment his tongue made a bridge to the inside of her mouth.

"That's as much of your seed as I can receive at this time," she said, patting his chest, grinning in amusement.

He couldn't help smiling. She had learned her allure. She could have him any time she wanted him and for as long and as far as she was willing to travel. She had all the right ingredients for his arousal, and yet, the meat he craved brewed slowly. He didn't know when or if they would make it past fleeting kisses and benign touch to intertwined limbs and shared spirit, but for now, he was more than willing to play her game in the hope that it would be soon.

Even so, she was not all incitement and provocation. At times, she was a complete innocent. He had come to know her favorite games to play when she was a little girl. Hangman was her absolute favorite. Kindle liked equally showing off her vocabulary and guessing her opponent's word or phrase wrong for the sake of a good laugh.

Bobby realized that Kindle was smarter than any woman he ever thought he'd marry. She calculated three-digit operations in her head without error. She proffered historical facts from all around the world. The queen of Denmark was Margrethe II…Christmas Island was a territory of Australia…the world's deepest lake was Lake Baikal. She explained that she had read every book in that apartment and any others she had come across in her lifetime. Every single one. Her intellect was her pride and joy. Her speech was never broken, her facts never unproven.

Bobby found that Kindle loved to load him with the trivia on her life as well—from the time she'd poisoned a stray cat to the time when she had overheard a French couple talking about her in French; the French that she could speak was limited, but deceptively pretty and charming.

One night while she was taking a shower, Bobby discovered that she could sing. He pressed his ear against the bathroom door while she sang "Do-Re-Mi" from *The Sound of Music*. Her voice swelled like Karen Carpenter's, and like Julie Andrews herself, Kindle sang animatedly, her rich voice ringing out over several octaves. Her intonation, her precision, her vibrato were enchanting, so much that Bobby was only brought out of his rapture when he was startled by the opening of the bathroom door. The door bumped his ear. She smiled at him and walked to her bedroom. From that day onward, she sang loudly in the shower.

Along with her theatrical singing, Bobby began to take note that Kindle was a dramatic player on their domestic stage. She was somehow always aware of herself—her expressions, her phrasings, her movements. Maybe she presented herself the way she wanted to be perceived—as self-possessed, as royalty. Weird, Bobby thought, because she had only enough money to pay rent and one bag of groceries every couple weeks. But now, he took care of her.

In regards to taking care of her, he thought he did pretty well. He bought her more food than she could even eat. Her face became fuller and brighter. Her clothes fit more snugly, which gave him an even better view of her physical silhouette—her pinched-in waist, her Indian hips...and all the places his hands roamed in his dreams.

Bobby came to the realization that it had not been love at first sight, but his fondness for her was real and growing. He was coming to appreciate the gradual nature of love, how it came like the rising of the sun. Maybe love couldn't be traced to some singular moment, but everything Kindle did increased his feelings for her, like money added to the bank. Soon enough, he was sure he would look around to find that he was a ridiculously rich man.

The Dare's shows were increasing also. The money wasn't the best, but it was enough to live on without the constant help of his parents. Not to mention Ricky Stallion and his band were getting in newspapers. Fred promised that with a few more spectacular shows, they could have a deal in their hands.

****

On February thirteenth, The Dare was preparing for a show at Band on the Wall. The venue had been a jazz club, but punk had been introduced to it a few years back.

Three hours before the show began, the band—Bobby, Larry, Kyle, and. their stand-in guitarist Charles—checked out the spot. From the outside, Band on the Wall was a brown brick building with square windows layering each story. On the inside, it was larger than any place they had performed. With the right equipment setup, the space could fit three hundred people.

A small balcony jutted out over the doorway. To the left of the entrance, the broad stage extended out from the front wall. The stage stood as tall as Bobby's waist. Large multi-colored lights hung above it.

The band and Betty Warner stood in the middle of the floor, looking out over its expanse. Bobby looked up at the black cloth billowing over the high ceiling.

"So," said Betty, "what do you think? It's fab, isn't it?"

"For sure," Charles replied. "Gnarly." His eyes twinkled.

Larry stared at Betty with his lips parted but agreeing no less with a nod of his head.

Betty stood next to Bobby. He noticed then that she was somewhat tall for a woman, almost as tall as Charles, who was no giant, but taller than most of the women that approached Bobby after the shows.

"Thanks, Bitch Betty," Kyle said in mockery. "We, like, really appreciate all you've done."

Bobby laughed out loud when he realized that Kyle was speaking to her cleavage.

"What's so funny?" Betty asked, smiling, her pink gums bright against her burgundy lips.

"Nothing at all," Bobby responded. "Can you show us the prep room?"

"This way." Betty walked them across the room to a black door. As they followed behind her, she switched left and right, her hips like a hypnosis clock. They entered a plain, grey room. Two long mirrors rested against two of the walls and black shelf-space was built onto the others. A large black island stood in the middle of the room.

Bobby sauntered over to the counter. Paintbrushes, paint pallets, drawing boards and sketching pencils lay on top of it.

"Is this normally a dressing room?" he asked.

"No, Love. It's where I make the signs that we put on the outside. But it's your dressing room today."

"Really?"

She winked at him. "Yeah."

Bobby picked up one of the paintbrushes and felt the handle's ridged contour. "May I?"

"Have at it," she returned.

He chose a pencil and began sketching. The guys paid no attention. They stood before the mirrors, making faces at their reflections. Betty stood beside Bobby, watching him draw what became two sides of the inside of an apple. On the skin of one side, he drew a crescent shape representing a gleam. He smiled, realizing that he had drawn the gleam in the shape of one of Kindle's dimples. One side of the inner apple held two seeds on the inside and the other side bore the matching indents from the opposite's seeds.

"So you're a picture artist too? Thought you were just a singer," Betty commented.

He picked up a paint brush, dipped it in black paint, and swept it up and down the inner half of the apple that held the seeds. "Yeah. Just a hobby. It's not like music."

Betty leaned against the counter and rested her elbow against his side. "So what is music to you?"

He continued painting, breezily but with surety. "Music is my life."

With Betty staring so intently at his profile, Bobby began to detect her interest. "So, what's with the apple?" she asked.

He painted grey the seeds in the black half of the apple. "Maybe I'm just hungry."

Betty laughed and snorted. "I love apples. And I'm hungry too."

Bobby dipped another paintbrush in red paint. He dragged it across the skin of the apple. "Maybe you should eat."

"I hate eating alone."

He painted golden the apple's leaves. "Oh."

"He's married," Kyle interrupted. He was standing directly behind Betty.

Betty stood up straight and turned to face Kyle as Bobby began blowing on the wet paint.

"He's married?" she scoffed. "Where's the wedding ring?"

"Trust me on this one, Betty Warner. He's got an old lady waiting at home," Kyle returned. "I should know; I'm his cousin."

"Well, I didn't ask, so why tell?" Betty backed away to the door. "You lads need to get yourselves in order. I promised Simon that you would be a hit, so I don't have time for any crazy shenanigans or half-hearted guitaring." Betty waved at the band but winked at Bobby. "Bye, mates."

The band gathered together at the counter, encircling Bobby and the picture. They beheld the drawing with the intrigue of new parents at a bassinet. The depiction held more emotion than detail, but it was a mysteriously moving sight.

Kyle spoke. "You're a waste of a man, I tell you. Fucking waste."

****

During the performance that night, the crowd jumped, danced and screamed. Ricky Stallion was in full effect, imitating Mick Jagger as he trotted across the stage.

When they stepped of the stage, Bobby's sweat-drenched hair stuck to his cheeks and his shirt clung to his back. Kyle and Larry yelled, exuberant, as they entered the dressing room for their belongings.

Kyle smacked Bobby's back, laughing. "I swear to God, Bobby C., if you perform like that every night, we'll be millionaires next year."

Bobby smiled.

"And if you are, I will be right there with you. Time for you boys to bow down to Betty. I had a hand in this, you know." Betty dawdled in and shut the door. "Amazing. It really was."

She hugged Bobby, grabbing hold of the back of his sweaty grey shirt and twisting it between her fingers. She kissed the perspiration from his cheeks before releasing him.

She greeted the others. They rattled on and on about the performance, about Kyle's ability to pull a bass riff out of nowhere, about the girls that had noticed Larry even though he was in the very back. Bobby grabbed his drawing and began rolling it up.

"No, no, no," Betty cautioned. "Put a bag over it to keep it safe." She grabbed a huge brown grocery bag from one of the shelves on the wall and carefully placed the drawing inside. She handed it to him, starry-eyed. "For you, Love." She turned to the others. "So you men will be safe walking to your abodes?"

"Of course," Larry said. "Unless you want to come with us. You could keep us safe."

"No, Creeps. I plan on keeping myself pure tonight." Betty winked again at Bobby. "I'm Audi five thousand, Mates," she said, bounding out the door.

Kyle, Larry and Charles followed behind her. Drained, Bobby slumped down in the corner, dropping his hands lazily over his knees. He closed his eyes and reviewed the show in his head, recalling the vigor of the crowd and how it nourished his own energy. He smiled softly at the realization that the performance would not be the only high of the night. He had yet to see Kindle. He began to think that if The Dare performed consistently at this level of fame, he would be content in knowing that his wife awaited his arrival. He sighed, wholly satisfied.

With his eyes closed, Bobby began to fade into sleep, suddenly awakened by the dropping of his head against his shoulder. He stood, wiping his forehead with the back of his hand and grabbing his drawing from the counter. He sprinted out of the room, through the performance area and out the front door. The sharp cold stung his face.

"Finally coming out, mate?" Betty Warner swayed at his side.

Bobby furrowed his eyebrows.

She grinned, prodding his arm. "Gotta lock the doors before I can go home. I had to wait for you."

"Oh. Well, um, have a great night," he said, beginning the walk home.

Betty rushed to his side. "I have to go this way, too."

"Oh."

"Don't sound disappointed. That makes me feel like a cheap troll. Me don't like that."

"I don't mean it that way."

She patted his arm before curling her fingers around his bicep. "I'm glad. Because I'm only trying to be nice to you."

Bobby sniffled, following the cracks in the sidewalk with his eyes. "Thank you."

"So, mate, when did you get married?"

He sniffled again.

"Are you shy or something?" He opened his mouth to form a word, but she continued over him. "Of course, you're not. You're an entertainer. The Beatles couldn't have done it better themselves."

Bobby chewed his bottom lip. "You think?"

"For sure, I do. You'd make Lennon proud, if I does say so myself."

"Thank you."

"But I bet you're more like a Steven Tyler type, aren't you?" She pursed her lips and her eyes roamed his figure.

"I don't really know."

"Yes, that's what you are." Betty fussed with her hair. "Say, Bobby, where are you from?"

"The United States."

"That," she said, slipping her hand down his arm to his wrist, "I already know. Are you a California surfer boy? Or New York city slicker?"

"I'm from Michigan," said Bobby. He pushed his hands in his pockets, slipping off her hand.

"Sweet."

"Thanks."

After a moment's silence, she inquired, "So, you really married?"

He tucked his hair behind his ear, quiet.

"You don't have to tell me, Mate, but I hope your friends were joshing."

Bobby locked his fingers together and cracked his knuckles.

"Because you have other admirers, of both the A and R and blonde type," she said.

He couldn't help laughing.

"So, you aren't cold as ice?" Betty turned to face him and began walking backward, her hands shoved in the pockets of her black leather jacket. Her eyes glinted. "You have too much going for yourself to be tied down. What happens when you're ready to fly away? Recording companies are searching for free agents." She stopped as they reached the block down which he would turn. "And from what I've been hearing, you're on the cusp of stardom."

Bobby smiled bashfully, scrunching up his nose. "Seriously?"

"*Seriously*, seriously." Betty began walking backward again. When she stumbled suddenly, Bobby caught her arms. She thrust herself toward him until her chest grazed his.

"Great catch," Betty murmured.

Bobby searched her face, wondering if he could be attracted to her. He dropped her arms.

They continued walking in silence. Betty sucked in her lips, bumping arms with him and then smirking. When they turned the corner onto the street where he lived, Bobby asked, "Do you live on this street too?"

"No. I'm a little way from here. I figured you would enjoy my company."

"Oh."

"This is it? Moss Side?" she questioned, sizing up the apartment when they reached the gate. "Well, you'll be a rock star soon enough, rising from peasantry. You'll have a story to tell about pre-fame in the ghetto, now won't you?"

"Thank you." Bobby glanced at her but did not see her. He was entirely enchanted by the kaleidoscope of visions that played before him—a massive arena of cheering fans and a fleet of wild fans who chased behind The Dare's limo.

"So, might I come in?" she inquired, suspending his vision.

"I don't know about that, Betty."

She took his hand from his side and lifted it to her lips, planting a soft kiss upon it. Her saliva dampened his skin. He was briefly hot and then swiftly cold.

Betty placed his hand back at his side. "Don't worry, Ricky. Maybe you'll walk me home sometime. You're certainly welcomed inside my home."

"Look, Betty, I can't—"

"Let me assure you of something." She grabbed either side of his face, looking him in the eye with one eyebrow raised. "I'm the cure for you. So don't be so shy. You've got nothing to be afraid of. I can do a lot of good for you." She pulled his face toward hers and took his bottom lip between hers, kissing him gently. "This is the second kiss, Ricky. Remember—three time's a charm."

In an instant, Betty whirled around and skipped back up the sidewalk, escaping from view before he could fully gather the meaning of her words and what he would do about the kiss.

Chapter Eight

Past Time: 1973

As far as kisses went, Amy Meyer's didn't have the magic touch.

However, Amy Meyers' physical beauty was to her attractiveness as good lyrics were to a song—instantly recognizable but not the sum of the whole. Her skin was light but healthy, like the flesh of an apple. She kept her short, flaxen hair tucked behind her ear, though her long bangs frequently fell across her forehead. Her eyes were big and green, her nose keen, her heart-shaped lips like pink hydrangea. A small black mole right below the right side of her mouth made her beauty more of a rarity. Drawn as Bobby was by Amy's appearance, he realized that she had something extra that most girls lacked—vision.

Amy and Bobby were sixteen-years-old in the summer of '73. For the past three summers, they had enjoyed their days on Lake Ontario at his grandparents' and her uncle's lake houses. They had swum the lake together the first day their relatives introduced them and continued to every day each summer. On the first day they spent together, he liked that she wore a T-shirt over her swimsuit and long shorts for modesty's sake. That's what made her different than the girls he went to school with. She valued her wit over the size of her chest or the shape of her long legs. On top of being sharp and funny, unbridled energy emanated from her each time she smiled.

Plus, she was from New York City and far more cultured than Bobby. She knew about things that he paid no attention to—the private lives of stars, the best restaurants in the big city, the way to impress rich, sophisticated people. Bobby always laughed when Amy imitated the pretentious, big-city women. Of course, Amy had every opportunity to be just like those women, but she seemed to value life in its raw form. She liked bare-footed walks through lake trails, ice-cream outings, long games of monopoly, and most importantly, hours of uninterrupted radio play.

On top of it all, she had been the only one he had shared his secret with. He told her while they were canoeing the lake. She didn't freak out. Instead, she continued rowing the boat and said, "Well, at least she loves you more than most people's mothers do. That's all that matters, you know."

It was the best answer anyone could have given. It was the way he felt.

Amy was Bobby's first real girlfriend, even if she wasn't anything to write home about in terms of kisses . He didn't ask her out until June of 1973 when he arrived in Michigan for the first day of summer break. Having bought Amy a bouquet of white roses, Bobby showed up at her aunt and uncle's doorstep with a diffident smile and a guitar in his right hand. Her aunt welcomed him in, escorting him back to the veranda, where Amy sat cross-legged on the ground, her eyes closed, her face tilted up to the noon sun. Upon hearing them step onto the porch, Amy opened her eyes and jumped to her feet. She smiled boisterously, shaking in excitement as she threw her arms around his neck.

She kissed his cheek. "This is so far out. I thought you weren't gonna get here until tomorrow, Bobby."

Bobby looked her over when she stepped back. He loved the way her saliva sparkled on her teeth as she smiled. If he focused only on her smile, the little overbite that made her two front teeth poke out just enough to give her a practical beauty, he thought that she might be the most exquisite girl in a thousand-mile radius. He handed her one of the roses. "I just wanted to surprise you, you know? And you're surprised, so that's good."

"Of course, I'm surprised, Bobby C. You've made my whole day."

"I wanted to talk to you about something." He glanced briefly at her aunt and uncle. "Alone, maybe."

She looked over his shoulder at her aunt and uncle, who stood at the door. She skipped over to them and clasped her hands together in front of her. "Uncle Ted, Aunt Bess, can we be alone for a minute?"

They nodded, stepping inside of the house.

A better setting could not be had for Bobby's proposal. Amy already had a white flower tucked behind her ear and held the one white rose he had given her. He clasped the remaining eleven white roses in his hand. Two white wicker chairs faced each other in the middle of the veranda. A white beach towel was spread across the wooden floor. The wood of the veranda structure was painted white. Creamy daffodils stretched high from the green grass that surrounded the house.

Not to mention, she wore a white sleeveless button-up shirt tucked into her white shorts. Her hair was pulled into a loose ponytail at the nape of her neck. Her lips were cherry, as though she had just eaten a Popsicle. She was the embodiment of childhood, the embodiment of everything they were supposed to be growing out of—all of the small things Bobby feared letting go. Those days, his father had been lecturing him about the fact that drawing pretty pictures and playing a guitar for hours would not support him in the rapidly approaching future. Whatever that meant...

The only thing missing in this scene was Chicago's "Color My World" playing faintly in the background.—an amazing song, even though it was a little dated by then.

Bobby had a remedy for the lack of soundtrack.

"So you brought your guitar?" said Amy. "Is that the big secret? Are you a professional now?"

Bobby grinned. He handed her the rest of the roses as they walked to the veranda's flat white railing. She sat on the rail, grabbing hold of the column next to her to support herself.

She sat in the window between the columns, the lake scenery serving as the background to her portrait.

He strapped his guitar over his chest. "I don't think I'm a professional or anything like that. It's not like I get paid to do this or anything."

Amy nodded her head once, resolutely. "Not yet anyway. What? Are you going to play for me or something?"

"Well, um, I want to."

"Groovy, Bobby C."

"Groovy," he returned, trying the word out for the first time. He looked down at his guitar and strummed it once to evaluate tone. "I wrote something."

She raised her eyebrows. "Wrote something? Well, now you can't say that you're not a professional. You've got more going for you than any guitar player I know. You kind of look like James Taylor too."

"Do you like him?"

Amy rolled her eyes. "Is it possible for a girl not to like him? He's cute and plays the guitar like God. Nobody can do it like James Taylor." She smiled. "But you should do it like Bobby Carter. I'm sure Bobby Carter's got his own bag of tricks."

He smiled back. "Thanks."

Bobby surprised himself. Although he was short of breath from nervousness, the edginess quickly dissolved and playing became as satisfying as listening. His voice floated about the veranda, as if he were listening to himself through a speaker, singing his own words, hoping that he could somehow make the words fit the girl in front of him, although he was becoming certain that he had fallen more in love with living the dream of this moment than with her.

Back then, his voice took on the life of a crooner rather than a rocker as he sang out his chorus over acoustic strums:

I want to know, want to know, want to know
Will you take the time to relieve my sorrow
And we'll have fun in the sun tomorrow
But answer me before we lose time
Tell me, sweet sunshine, won't you be mine

He wasn't so proud of singing the words to her than when he first wrote them. Now, they seemed a bit…babyish. But Bobby was thrilled by the fact that by the end, she had clapped her hands to the beat through half the song.

When he finished, he pressed the guitar closer against himself, crisscrossing his arms over its body. She smiled.

"So," he said.

"So…what?" she responded, rubbing her hands together and swinging her legs back and forth, creating a measured beat as her feet hit the short columns below the horizontal rail.

"So…what do you say?"

"The song was totally awesome. You really are a professional, I think. That was like being at a concert."

"Thanks." He looked behind her at the field behind the veranda. "But I mean, what do you have to say about what I said…in the song, I mean?"

"I mean, the lyrics were decent too." Amy scrunched her eyebrows. "Do you want a cookie or something?"

Bobby laughed. "Well, I wrote the song for you. And I was hoping that you would answer the question."

"There was a question? I don't remember the lyrics so well now." She squeezed her eyes shut. "Give me a sec. I can remember. Hold on one sec." Her lips moved, as she tried recalling the lines. When she quietly recited the last line, she opened her eyes wide. "Are you asking me out? You want to be my boyfriend? Is that what you're saying here?"

He bit his lip, nodding.

"Goodness, goodness, goodness," she shouted, throwing her arms up, attempting to wiggle herself off the rail. She tumbled backwards, hitting the ground with a loud thud.

Bobby tore his guitar strap of his chest and placed it down tenderly over one of the wicker chairs, patting it as a dear friend before leaping over the rail to kneel down at Amy's side.

She lay on the ground, laughing and rolling as she held the back of her head and squinted at the beaming sun.

He scooped his hand under her back to help her to a sitting position.

"Are you alright, Amy?"

"Am I alright?" she shouted, laughing louder, her teeth glistening even more vibrantly in the sun. "Are you kidding me? I am so much more than alright." She clapped her hands together, brushing off the grass and dirt. "Do you realize that a superstar just played a song for me, asking me out? Do you realize that?" Amy hopped to her feet.

"Are you serious?" He stood up, patting dirt off his hands.

"Look, now, why would I lie? I think you're the best guitar player that I've ever met, Bobby. And you'll probably be famous one day, so I can tell everybody that the famous Bobby Carter was once my boyfriend. Can you believe that?" Amy stumbled over the small branch on the ground and fell into his arms, jumping up and down, grappling his wrists.

"You really think so? You really see that."

"Of course, I do, Bobby," she said, asserting her vision, the vision of his future. He loved the confidence with which she spoke about his destiny. "All you need is a stage name and you're going straight to the stars." She leaned her head toward her shoulder. "And you'd better watch out, Boyfriend Nuevo. The girlies are gonna be all over you like white on rice. Good thing I got you first." She kissed his mouth, pushing her lips on his with more force than he had ever gotten from the two other girls that had kissed him before.

When she finished, Bobby smiled, only softly aware of the passion in her kiss, as he mulled over stage names.

Spring

My beloved spoke, and said unto me, Rise up, my love,
my fair one, and come away.
For, lo, the winter is past, the rain is over and gone;
The flowers appear on the earth; the time of the singing
of birds is come
-Song of Solomon 2:10-12

Chapter Nine

Present Time...

Signs of spring surfaced by mid-March. It remained
frigid outside, but the temperature rose day by day. Rain clouds
loomed less frequently. Bobby began to believe that he was
now, in fact, in love. He was sure he had a real family with her.

Kindle had adopted a stray orange-and-white striped cat,
for whom she set out scraps of food and water. The cat had
never stepped inside the apartment, but he was often on the
porch lapping a bowl of water when Bobby came home from
rehearsal. One evening, he came pawing at the door as Bobby
and Kindle sat talking on the couch. It was then that Kindle
named the cat Kitty Wonder as homage to his favorite singer.
She said that besides Bobby and the cat, she hadn't known
anyone so eager to be near her. He laughed, then realizing that
Kindle and Kitty Wonder were officially his family. In that
moment, Moss Side became the capital of the world for him.

Although homesickness hadn't settled in, there was one
evening after a gig when Bobby felt that he would rather be
anywhere else than Moss Side. He hummed as he trotted along
the sidewalk toward the gate in front of the apartment. A slim
man stood at the gate, his arms perched between the bars. He
wore a dingy undershirt that made visible his crisp, toned ebony
arms. He smiled, chewing his gum and crossing his black-
sneakered feet.

"Who are you?" the guy said as Bobby approached the gate. The guy smelled like shaving cream.

"I'm, uh, I'm Bobby," Bobby said lowly, realizing that the man had no intention of moving from in front of the gate. Bobby stared at his dark arms.

"What are you doing here, Bobby? You here to rape and pillage our women?"

"Rape and pillage?" Bobby said slowly, although he hadn't meant to say it out loud. "No. That's not…I'm not…I live here."

"Which flat?" Ebony Arms asked. He asked so sternly that Bobby questioned for a moment whether he could be the landlord. He was sure the Ebony Arms was too young, younger than him even.

Bobby nodded his head at the flat straight ahead. He moved closer to the gate, hoping the man would move out of the way.

Instead, Ebony Arms pushed his hand against Bobby's chest. "That aint your flat, mate."

Bobby stepped back.

"I went to school with the girl that lives there." He paused, then nodded at the guitar case in Bobby's hand. "You play that much?"

Bobby rubbed the back of his hand across his nose. He was considering running the opposite direction and returning home when Ebony Arms was gone. "I'm in a band."

He nodded knowingly, like he was the lead singer of a band himself. "So you must have quite a few of those."

Bobby nodded. He wondered if he could run fast enough, even with the guitar in his hand. The man probably could tackle him. Bobby supposed he also had the option of knocking the guy in the stomach with his guitar case. In that case, he probably wouldn't be able to return home…ever.

"I play guitar too," Ebony Arms said. "Maybe you want to spare yours. I only got one." He reached for the case handle, crushing Bobby's hand beneath his own. "And that one got stolen."

Bobby quailed. He was wondering whether the man could have broken his fingers that easily. He'd never broken a

bone before, but he was sure this was the worst pain he'd ever
felt. The ache went cruising up his wrist to his arm. Still, he
refused to let go of the guitar. He wondered how long it would
take to play guitar again if his hand was broken. At least it was
his right hand; he'd still be able to move with ease up the fret
board with his left. Strumming didn't take as much
coordination. Fingerpicking might be a problem.

"Holding on tight, aren't we?" Ebony Arms asked. His
eyes were growing wider, his grip tighter. "Must be worth a
lot."

More than he knew. "Yeah." Bobby cleared his throat.
Clutching the handle tighter with his right hand, he reached for
his wallet in his back pocket with his left. He squeezed the
faded brown leather wallet, opening it to expose the three
hundred pounds he carried.

The man looked Bobby over and smiled. He dipped his
fingers in the wallet, gathering together the cash and putting it
in the back pocket of his jeans. He grinned, releasing his hold
and stepping to the side. He bowed at Bobby once. "Admission
granted."

Bobby walked quickly to the apartment, taking the stairs
three at a time. When he made it inside, the guitar case fell out
of his hand, crashing loudly to the ground. His hand throbbed.

Kindle sprang from the couch. She examined his
swelling fingers and knuckles. "What did you do?"

Bobby covered his right hand with his left, squeezing it
to hamper the pain. "Can I have some ice?"

She ran to her room and returned with a long white sock.
She filled the sock with ice cubes and pressed it against his
hand. "What happened to you, darling? Did you punch
someone?"

The pain was slightly nullified by the sound of "darling."
He almost smiled. As he headed for the couch and plopped
down. She sat beside him, pushing her toes beneath his thigh, as
she faced him and held the icepack against his hand. He turned
his face up to hers, kissing the tip of her nose, eliciting a
brighter smile than he had ever seen before.

When he explained to her what had happened, she
immediately recognized the boy that had robbed him as Rich

Ipinson, a neighbor she had graduated high school with. The
boy was really no threat, outside of being a petty thief.

"Wish I knew that," Bobby said with a sigh. "I didn't
know what he was gonna do, honestly. I didn't know it was like
that around here. Not really."

Kindle replied casually, "You did realize that you live in
the ghetto, didn't you?" She removed the pack and kissed his
middle knuckle. Bobby smiled.

So this was the ghetto? Well, he decided, there were
worse places than this, but right then, he couldn't really think of
any. Then again, he couldn't think of any place better if Kindle
weren't there.

It mattered a little less that he wasn't sleeping in the same
bed with his new wife. Bobby figured he was reaping
something of greater worth—familiarity. She no longer claimed
to not know him. In fact, whenever he joked with her, she
giggled and mused, "That's not true. I know you."

While Kindle was at work one evening, Bobby struggled
to hang the picture he had drawn over her bedroom window
without actually moving any of her belongings. In the middle of
his endeavor, Kindle arrived home and caught him. He stepped
back, knocking over a green vase. It clattered to the floor, a
light stream of dust escaping from it. Kindle looked concerned
at first but then smiled and left the room until he finished.

Mystery was still in her smile. Mystery still paraded all
about her, daring him to stand a little closer when she spoke, to
stay a little longer before leaving for rehearsal. She never
belched or excused herself for the bathroom around him. She
was steady in the keeping of her traditions—eating her cereal
with frozen milk chunks, washing her hands after every chore,
fastening her hair down with Bobbi pins before she slept. She
worked six days a week without change. She had her religion in
these things.

He also had his religion. Bobby continued going to
church every Sunday, leaving in the early morning and
returning while Kindle still slept. Attending Mass made him
feel as though he had paid his dues to God, who must have been
well aware of his avoidance of addressing some of the band's
misdeeds—the sex, the drugs…all the rock 'n roll excess.

Bobby knew better than to talk to Kyle about misdeeds. Kyle was mostly an atheist, except for the time when he had been arrested for drug possession and the time his dad threatened to kick him out of the house if he didn't find a job within thirty days. Larry had his hippie religion, which he took pretty seriously, considering that its basic doctrine was freeing the mind, body and soul through trips.

Instead of focusing on Larry and Kyle, Bobby focused on Kindle as his penance. He was genuinely concerned about her torpor. The hotel and pub were her work. He liked to think he was her play. There was little else in her life.

One morning in late March, Bobby sat next to Kindle on the couch before she had to leave for work. Outside of the window, lines of celestial blue and murky gray streaked the sky. Bobby slung his arm around her shoulder and covered his periodic yawns with his free hand. She held a cup of steaming tea in one hand and the remote control in the other. Of all the things that she insisted they pick up from the grocery store, tea was always on the top of the list. He laughed to himself. It was true—the British were fanatics for tea.

He ogled her as she brought the cup of tea to her lips.

"What?" she said, bringing the cup back down from her face. "Never seen a girl drink tea before?"

He smiled. "It's not that. I've just never had tea before myself."

"You've never had tea before?" she returned, her eyes widening.

Bobby held his knee against hers. "I haven't had a lot of things before, I guess."

"Well," she replied, responding to his intimation with a small voice, "since you've been so well-behaved, you may have some of my tea." She blew on the tea, bringing it forth to his lips and smiling amorously when he took a sip.

Bobby kissed her chin quickly and reached inside of his pocket, pulling out a worn piece of newspaper. He set the square clipping on her lap. "So, I was thinking about you and I found this. It's, like, an ad for a theater course. It was in one of those little daily newspapers things, you know. The class is like a month long or whatever. Not Broadway, but it's something."

He turned his attention to the television screen. "I want you to do it." He held back a grin. He liked the sound of his assertive voice.

Kindle stared at the clipping. "I can't really consider this."

"Why?"

"Theater isn't as easy as it looks." She used her index finger to casually buff her teeth. She turned her face from his.

"That's what the course is for, I think."

She shrugged, far removed. "I don't have the proper training."

"Not to, like, repeat myself, but I think that's what the course is for." He smiled

"With classes like these, it's good to have had some prior training."

"Well, I never trained at guitar. I'm self-taught."

"But you do realize that acting is totally different, don't you?"

"How do you mean?"

She shook her head. "Too many technical details to confront you with." She looked at him, her eyes relenting. She flipped to another channel. "Besides, there's no money for something like this. You have to save your money."

"*Our* money." Bobby pulled the remote from her hand, setting it on his opposite side. "I have the money. I mean, *we* have the money. How much is it anyway?"

"I don't know."

He brought the clipping up to his face, skimming it quietly.

Kindle revived the conversation abruptly. "Even if you could, I don't have time for it."

"What if you quit one of your jobs?" Bobby inquired with a yawn.

"I wouldn't do that."

The softness in her eyes fueled his campaign. "But you could. I could take care of the bills and stuff for a little while. And then, we'll see what happens from there. One day at a time—that's the best way to go about stuff."

"It's not practical. You're just a musician, Bobby. And I mean 'just' in the financial sense, not in offense of your art."

Bobby tucked his hair behind his ear. "I'll make it work," he announced. "We'll play two times a night if we have to. Plus, my mom is gonna send me, like, a grand for my birthday."

"That's in November."

"We could make it work till then."

"We'll see, I suppose."

Bobby considered this obvious relenting a definite success. The small victory crowned him with the confidence to address what he really wanted to.

When she stood, he grabbed hold of her hand and said, "We'll go to Mass. We'll ask God what He thinks about you joining the course."

Kindle looked at him as if she couldn't interpret this crazy talk. "I'm not a Catholic."

"Well, do you ever go to church?"

"Is this an inquisition? A crusade?"

He released her hand. "No. Not even close."

"The last church I went to was at my mum's funeral," she said. "But before that, we went often enough."

"So, do you want to come with me sometime?"

"Not particularly." She shrugged.

"Why?"

"There are other ways I can be with God."

"Like how?"

She rubbed her lips together. "Before you and I met, I went every Sunday to my mother's grave. I talked to her...and to God. I figure since she's already with God, I would have closer contact than being in a church."

Bobby hummed briefly. "Guess that's a way to look at it."

"I guess so."

Bobby reached for something, anything that would erase the idea that his crown of confidence came with no power. "So what if I go to your mother's grave with you? Will you go to church with me? I've never been to a grave before:"

"You've never been to a grave?"

"I don't know any dead people."

Kindle's eyes became static, as though she was staring into twilight.

Bobby tapped her thigh. "So, what do you say?"

"Say about what?" She nodded to herself. "I make no promises of attending Mass. But you're welcome to meet my mother. You can see exactly what kind of woman she was."

Chapter Ten

Past Time: 1974

Kindle lugged five full bags of groceries in one hand. With the other hand, she unlocked the front door, allowing for her mother to enter the apartment first.

Ten bags in her hands, Kayanne's muscles flexed as she lifted them to the counter. She clapped and rubbed her hands together, as if wiping away dirt.

Kindle set her bags on the foyer floor, closing the door.

"Bring them in here," her mother said.

Kindle hated this kind of provocation—her mother's habit of making commands right before she intended to perform them. Her mother's veiny, muscle-bound arm was reason enough for Kindle to never show her chagrin. Kindle had never assumed that fearing one's mother was normal, at least not for the girls outside of Moss Side. Girls within the ward must have known that hard times made for hard women. Kindle wondered at what age this hardness set in—she wanted to calculate how much time she had left to escape Moss Side before she cemented. The lily-white girls with red fingernail polish and petite penny-loafers that attended her school could not have known what it meant to be afraid of their mothers. They were foul-mouthed girls who looked the teachers over nonchalantly when reproved. No girl could act that way unless she was afraid of nothing.

Kindle waddled into the kitchen and set the grocery bags on the counter. Before her mother could utter a word, Kindle hustled to put the groceries away. Kindle snuck a glance at Kayanne while she scrubbed her hands at the sink.

"Perhaps you could say hi the next time that we see Georgia. Georgia is Kennedy's mum. Kennedy's my friend. A little bit. We see each other in school, anyway," Kindle rambled.

"Georgia's name is Mrs. Carrington to you." Kayanne ravaged through the pots and pans in the cabinet below the sink. "I don't have any reason to say hi to her if she hasn't greeted me."

Kindle rolled a can of green beans between her hands and turned around. Her mother's shoulders were broad, made even broader by the large wool sweater she wore. A couple inches taller than Kindle, Kayanne's head reached the overhanging light above the stove. Kayanne turned the stove knob with bony fingers, fingers shades darker than her vanilla face. Like Kindle, Kayanne's hair was scrunched together in a polished bun at the nape of her neck.

Kayanne chopped onions expertly. She did not dab her eyes. She moved quickly, she moved precisely. She was the queen of thirty-minute meals. In forty-five minutes, she would retire to bed. Thirty minutes after that, Kindle would quietly recline in the bed beside her mother. Kayanne couldn't tolerate interrupted sleep. Her days were too long to be a minute deprived of five hours of rest.

Kindle glanced over at the living room window. A gust of wind tousled the green lace curtains in front of the open window. The song of crickets blended with the crackle of the onions in the frying pan.

She looked at her mother once more. "Mum, you might do well to have more friends."

Kayanne sprinkled salt upon the ground beef in the skillet. "Are you advising me, child? Perhaps you should keep your head in places that it belongs. Like your books. That would do you well."

Kindle contained a sigh. Studying had not done her that well thus far. She was indeed a star student, but with Moss Side girls, teachers never spoke of the universities as a future option. All of her studying hadn't made her an attraction among her peers. It had made her near invisible. More than anything in the world, Kindle just wanted to be seen.

Kindle was born in Manchester. Between Years Five and Eight, Kayanne and Kindle took year-long stints in North Yorkshire, West Yorkshire, and then Merseyside. When they returned to Greater Manchester, Kindle was familiar with no one, save Mr. Holster.

She knew no one in her Year Nine classes. The kids had already formed their permanent friendship circles. Some of the teens were not from Moss Side, but the surrounding areas. Their parents were old hippie types with pounds to spare. These kids quarreled regularly and were well acquainted with physical altercations, but they seemed they stayed glued together for the sake of maintaining their esotericism.

However, most of the teens had grown up in Moss Side, well before drugs and gangs had emerged. The students had no fear or paranoia of one another. Their mothers were friends. Many of them were related in one way or another. Somehow, every person was another's cousin.

Not so for Kindle. Not only had she never met her half-aunt (she lived somewhere in Kingston), her grandparents had passed before she was born. A recent inventory of her life turned up that she spent most of her time with her mother, Mr. Holster and the girl named Kennedy who was something like a friend at school. In all of their years of struggle, Kindle had never felt so impoverished as she did when she realized that she didn't have one true friend.

Kindle picked up a lone crumb from the floor. "Don't you ever feel like you need anyone?"

"Who would I need, Kindle?" Kayanne challenged.

"Well, who would you want?" Kindle fixed her eyes on the gas flames swelling from the burner. She pretended to be mesmerized, in the case that her mother turned around.

Kayanne swung her spatula back and forth as if conducting an orchestra, before dropping it in the skillet. She rubbed her hands against the towel hanging from the oven handle. "Tame yourself, Kindle. I don't want to have to tame you."

Kindle put away the last can. She bundled together all of the plastic bags and held them against her chest. She breathed waveringly, instantly emotional. She deepened her voice to conceal her passion. "I don't think you understand."

Kayanne spun around. She picked up the spatula and pointed it at Kindle. "Don't understand what? What is there to understand? Please inform me, Ms. Smarty Smart."

Kindle decided that now, her mother was officially aged. Her light skin looked like cemented dough. Lines creased the corners of her eyes and her forehead. Her dark cherry lips had thinned out. Grey hairs stuck out from her bun and from the edges of her hairline.

Kindle crisscrossed her arms over her shoulders. "People are all different. They aren't all like you. Some people take your not speaking as an insult. Some people are social."

Kayanne knotted her arms over her chest. The food sizzled behind her. "What in all of earth and creation makes you think that you can tell me about people? You haven't the slightest clue about people." She turned back around to wave away the smoke over the food. "If you were as smart as you're pretending to be, then you would realize that."

The fizzle of the flames beneath the food, the clapping of her mother's feet on the kitchen floor as she walked back and forth from the refrigerator to the stove, the hooting of an owl outside—these were the only sounds to intersect the silence for the next few moments.

"I do know some things," Kindle said softly. "I know that you act very peculiar around people. People don't like strange people." She folded her hands together and knocked them back and forth against her thighs.

Kayanne picked up a potato from the counter and hurled it at Kindle. The potato thumped her shin. The shock of the action itself anesthetized the pain. Kindle blinked her eyes. Her mother had turned again to the stove and was driving the skillet back and forth agitatedly.

Kindle wiped a solitary tear from her cheek.

"Don't let your mouth write a check your butt can't cash. Just be quiet sometimes, Kindle."

Be quiet sometimes? Sometimes quiet. Always brewing over with contemplations, with intrigue. Never taken seriously. Well-spoken but hardly heard. That's what Kindle was.

As Kindle picked up the potato from the ground, she considered that weak arms were far better than a weak mind. What did she stand to lose for speaking her mind? Perhaps a fight. She would never gain respect through silence. The French Revolutionaries maintained many casualties but got what they wanted in the end, right? The peasantry had to rise at some time. Kindle's recent inventory of her life proved that she could be counted among peasantry.

"Some chances must be taken," said Kindle. "What if our flat burned down? Who would you call for help? Mr. Holster? I don't think he should be your only resource."

"Close it, little girl."

Kindle tapped her foot against the floor. "Have you ever thought that your attachment to Holster drove my father away? Why would anyone want to be around someone like you? You're not open at all. Only to Mr. Holster, and hardly that."

Kayanne snatched up the skillet and dropped it on the counter. It spun off the counter onto the floor, where the food flew in every direction, spurting onto Kindle's pant leg.

"You're not smart at all, are you?" said Kayanne, her hands shaking. "You're in Year Nine. You think you've figured out the way the world turns because of science class? You don't know who I was."

"So, you were someone else before my father left? You were someone else before you met Mr. Holster?"

Kayanne extended her neck, high and mighty. Cavalier, she looked at Kindle as though they quarreled over a shared lover. "I was someone else before you. And I'll be someone else after you."

"Is that what you're waiting for? Will my father come back once I'm gone? I could leave now if that's what you want." Kindle widened her eyes to halt the tenacious flow of tears. "That's what I want. I want to be gone."

Kayanne glanced at the clock above and looked back down at Kindle shortly. She left the kitchen silently. Kayanne did not have time for interruption, no tolerance for anything short of five hours of sleep. As Kindle stooped down to clean her dinner off the floor, she hoped that she was not beginning to hate her mother. She couldn't afford any further destitution.

Chapter Eleven

Present Time...

"**M**ummy. Meet Bobby. Bobby, meet my mum."

"It's nice to meet you," Bobby offered.

"You're acting shy. She was always straightforward and she liked straightforward people."

"Okay. So what should I say?"

Kindle knelt down in the grass and rubbed her hands over the letters and numbers carved in the granite. *Mother. 1940-1978.* She shook her head, considering that her mother's thirty-eight years were only defined by "Mother."

After Kayanne's death, Mr. Holster had suggested that Kindle begin visiting a gravesite to anchor her soul. He thought that it might help her to remember her past, what she was, where she came from.

Kindle gained none of this from visiting her mother here. Instead, she imagined her mother to be whatever she fancied. There'd be no exasperated bleating, no punishing silence. The graveyard proved the perfect setting for conversing with her mother.

The visits had become a ritual for Kindle. She dressed in the same long black dress and short black heels she had worn to the funeral. She wore her hair down and brought a dandelion from the front yard. She held up the one picture she had of Kayanne—a black-and-white photograph taken some time in the early Fifties. Posing before a grey background, Kayanne did not smile, her eyes did not speak. Her hair was long, a series of oily waves, and her pale eyes were only half-opened in the photograph.

"You should just talk to her," said Kindle. "She'll hear you. Tell her about yourself."

"Okay." Bobby knelt beside her and gazed keenly at the stone. "Well, hi, Missus Madden. I mean, Miss Madden. My name is Bobby. I mean, Robert Carter. I don't think you know yet, but I married your daughter."

Kindle shoved Bobby's shoulder. "Why'd you have to tell her that?"

"Maybe she'd want to know why I'm here." He faced the stone again. "I think it's a good thing because I really love her. It probably seems like it was all of sudden. It's working out though. I know Kindle didn't think it would. She was really worried about what you'd say. I don't know if you can see me, but I'm, like, white."

"Like white? Oh, Bobby…" She wrung her hands.

He picked up the dandelion Kindle had laid down and twirled it between his fingers. "But I definitely love her." Bobby patted Kindle's head and dangled his hand over her shoulder. "I haven't told my folks yet, so you're the first of our parents to know. I promise you, I'll take care of her. Just like you did. That's why I want to send her to acting school."

"She doesn't want to hear about this."

"You're her daughter."

"I need you to find a better point."

"What do you mean?"

"This isn't hard to figure out, Bobby."

Bobby looked up at the two trees that canopied the little plot. "How do you know that she hasn't changed her mind?"

"You're being silly." Kindle unwrapped his arm from her shoulders.

"I'm being serious. Maybe your mom didn't want you to do it because she couldn't help you do it. But now, I can. So maybe she's changed her mind."

"Not likely."

"If she really loved you, she'd want you to be happy."

Kindle placed her head on his shoulder. She could have lectured him about the myth of such simple love, but she refrained. "Do you consider yourself some kind of angel?"

He looked down at his scuffed black shoes. "How do I answer that?"

Kindle also stared at his shoes. A moment's silence passed before she conceded. "Okay, then, we'll have it your way. I'll do it."

Bobby nodded and twirled the dandelion once more through his fingers.

Why would she do it? Not because her mother would approve of it, even in her afterlife. Bobby's logic was infantile at best, too weak to convince her of anything different than what she already knew about Kayanne. Rather, Kindle took his offer because Bobby was becoming like the parent that she never had. Gentle. Kind. Affectionate. Loving. Believing. Present.

****

On late Saturday morning, Kindle enrolled in a month-long theater course. Bobby went with her to enroll. He stood next to her, tapping his fingers on the secretary's desk as the secretary discussed the details of the course with Kindle.

That same day, Kindle decided to tell Mr. Holster that she would no longer work for the hotel. She drew courage from Bobby's presence, trusting that Mr. Holster wouldn't react angrily in front of him.

They arrived at the hotel around noon. Outside the door, Kindle looked Bobby over, as satisfied as she was going to be with his attire. That morning, she had rummaged through his clothes and pulled out a brown T-shirt and faded brown jeans. She handed them to him and asked if he had anything to cover his hair with. He had a newsboy cap. It would have to do.

Kindle stood in place in front of the door.

"Are we going in?" Bobby asked.

"Aren't you going to open the door for me?"

He gave her a brief once-over and then smiled knowingly. "For sure." He swung open the door and followed behind her as she stepped inside.

Mr. Holster stood at the check-in desk, unmoved by their entrance. Bobby took his hat off and smoothed his hair down. He followed Kindle to the desk.

"Good afternoon," Mr. Holster said to Bobby.

"Hello, Mr. Holster," Kindle said.

"Ms. Hyrum," he returned.

Bobby looked down at the desk and traced his fingers in small circles over it.

"I have to tell you something," she said.

He shot a glance at Bobby. "Are these private matters?"

"It's okay. I just needed to tell you that…" She trailed off, hesitating. Her heart thumped and she swallowed. "…That I will not be working here any longer."

"What?" He gaped, wearing an expression of unbridled shock—squinted eyes and a clown frown. She felt strangely accomplished that she had been the one to provoke it.

"I'm going to pursue other ventures."

"Of what kind?"

"Mr. Holster, I've always wanted to do other things. There are so many things that I could do. And I'm going to do them now."

Through her short, breathy explanation, Mr. Holster had fixed his eyes on Bobby. Bobby's sparkling green eyes met Holster's puffy blue ones, like a stream trickling to the ocean. Kindle was troubled.

"This is your idea, sir?" Mr. Holster sizzled.

"Yeah. It's what Kindle really wants," Bobby said. Kindle felt embarrassed. Bobby had no command in his voice, not even a little. He almost sounded nonchalant.

"You advised her to quit her job? The source of her income?"

Bobby nodded.

"Why?" Holster's voice trembled, cold as ice.

"I think she needs time to chase her dream," he said, directing his eyes back to the desk. "It'd be killer for her. I mean, it would be awesome for her."

"And what will she do for money?"

Kindle hoped that Bobby would straighten his back, pull back his hair, deepen his voice.

Instead, he shrugged. "I work."

"What's your profession?"

"I'm a musician."

Mr. Holster shook his head.

Bobby looked back up at Mr. Holster with genuine confusion.

"Mr. Holster," Kindle began. She could find nothing more to say.

Bobby spoke. "I can take care of her. I will. I'm, like, her husband or whatever. That's what I'm supposed to do. That's what I'm gonna do."

Mr. Holster's face was fixed, his jaw set. "Husband? You're no husband. You're hardly even a man."

Bobby looked away from Holster, casting his stare to the ground. Kindle wanted to hug him, but Mr. Holster's glare subsumed the urge.

She pursed her lips and looked at Bobby. "Well, this is how it is, Mr. Holster. It's what I'm going to do because," Kindle peered up at Mr. Holster, "because we're both adults. And we're making a decision. So I hope you accept it, even if you can't support it."

"I have no choice, do I?" Mr. Holster wiped his hands together, as if he were dusting the matter off. "Do what you feel is best. But you should know that this is what you're mother feared the most."

"I won't live in her fear, Mr. Holster."

She caught his eyes quickly, saying goodbye in her heart and stepping away. Bobby walked to the door beside her. He lapsed behind when they reached the outside.

Kindle slowed her pace. "Mr. Holster is like my mother. He's ultra-protective. He doesn't know how to be free."

Bobby looked down, kicking the ground as he walked. The sun hit the crown of his head, sunlight bouncing off his gleaming hair.

"I hope he didn't offend you. He and mummy were a perfect pair, I suppose."

They continued in silence. Kindle could think of nothing to say. Bobby pushed his hands down in his pockets. She looped her arm through his, hoping he'd smile. He didn't.

When they reached the apartment gate, Kindle asked, "Why are you quiet? What's eating you?"

"Nothing," he returned, pushing through the gate and climbing the stairs three at a time.

Bobby stepped over a crouching Kitty Wonder before entering the apartment. He snatched his guitar from the couch, stuck it in the case and slung it over his back.

Kindle watched him from the front door. "Where are you going, Bobby?"

"Rehearsal's at two."

"It's only twelve forty-five."

"I know."

When Bobby reached for the doorknob, Kindle shunted his hand. "Why are you angry? I don't understand you."

Bobby rolled back his shoulders. He avoided her eyes. "It's nothing. Can I go please?"

"You don't have to lie. I know you, Bobby."

"I don't want to talk."

She stepped aside from the door and stomped to her room, muttering, "Have a killer time, Mr. Carter."

****

Kindle had actually thought about it before...thought about finding her way to Bobby in the middle of the night and unwrapping both of them, pretending as though she really knew how to be a sultry vixen. She had actually wanted to reward his perseverance with her love, but the feeling dissipated when he walked out the door that afternoon without a word. So, now, alone, she considered her options for payback. The options opened up quicker than she expected.

Carol Carter called for her son shortly after he left.

Kindle snatched up the phone. "Hello?"

"Yes. I'm looking for my son. Robert Carter. Maybe I don't have the right number." Her voice was a female version of Bobby's. The same lightness. The same inflections.

"Mrs. Carter?" Kindle smiled.

"Yes, it is. Who am I speaking with?"

****

The garage where The Dare rehearsed smelled like wood and exhaust. Bobby sneezed three times before striking his first chord, giving an inadvertent count-off to the first song.

The garage belonged to Fred's manager friend, Ian. Fred and Ian stood chatting on the far left.

Fred was short with cropped red hair, freckles and a Jell-O gut he tried tucking into his pants along with his polo shirt. Ian was his opposite. Ian's disheveled auburn hair was a long backdrop to his perfectly oval face. He had the kind of long, narrow features that were fit for a caricature. He stood tall and gangly, towering a good six inches over Fred.

During the entire rehearsal, Bobby sang with more morose than ever; each song fell behind tempo. The guys made faces of embellished confusion at him.

When the session ended, Fred called them over. Ian began rearranging lumber in the corner.

"Gentlemen, you're moving along pretty good. I like the new direction, but you gotta keep up the pace."

"Yeah, we will," Kyle said. He crossed his arms over his chest, glanced at Bobby and lifted his eyebrows. Bobby didn't flinch.

Fred chuckled, apparently amused by boy banter. "Good news, guys: Band on the Wall wants to have you back. I spoke with Betty Warner earlier today. She'd like to help market you. She wants to get together with you guys on a regular basis, see what she can offer you."

"No shit? Killer!" Kyle said.

Charles and Larry nodded.

"No way," Bobby mumbled.

Fred patted Bobby's shoulder, huddling him down. "Yeah, Bobby, I gotta say, it surprised me too. But the way you've been playing the last few shows, I can't say I blame her for wanting to get invested early."

Bobby dropped his head. "No. I mean, I don't want to meet with her."

"What?" asked Fred, his smile wilting.

"We can find somewhere else to play, can't we?"

"What do you call yourself doing?" Charles said, charging forward so that he stood nearly chest to chest with Bobby. "You realize you're piddling on all the chances we've got to make it, don't you?"

"What?" Bobby crossed his arms and looked Charles over with weak eyes.

Charles gripped Bobby's shirt so that it ripped at the shoulder seam.

Kyle jammed himself between them. "Hey, Charles, stay cool. You touch my cousin, I'll fuck you up." He faced Bobby and spanked his hand against Bobby's stomach. "What's up with you, man? What's your problem with Betty Warner?"

Bobby covered his mouth and cheek with his hand, his voice muffled when he replied, "I don't trust her."

"Why not?" Charles interjected.

"Because…because she's just in for a ride or something. I don't know." His voice tapered off.

"I think that's the point. Actually, I *know* that's the point," Larry said. "As long as she can get us from point A to point B, she's welcome for the ride."

Ian raised his voice from the corner of the garage. It bounded off the walls, like his was the voice of God. "Please pardon my intervening, Fred, but I suppose I should say something. If your lead man has an instinctual concern, then perhaps you should listen. I've worked with several bands, mates, and those who were lucky enough to have a member with instinct and smart enough to listen to it have always fared better than those without it."

Fred turned his eyes from Ian to the band. "Well, boys, it your choice. I'm just a guide. Make the decision. Take it or leave it."

"Take it," Larry nodded. "We drop Betty, she might stop us from ever playing at the Band on the Wall ever. You can tell she's one of those revenge girls."

"Second that," said Kyle.

"Yeah," Charles responded quietly, descending from anger.

Bobby didn't want to sound curt, so he hesitated before replying. "I don't wanna do it."

Fred shook his head and raised his hands, a sign of defeat. "Well, guys, three yeses and one no equals a no." He patted his stomach. "We don't have a runner-up venue yet, but we'll find something. May not make as much, but I'll try for it. Come on, guys, let's pack it up."

The guys bickered as they followed behind Fred.

Bobby wasn't yet inclined to move. Ian sauntered over to Bobby and settled his hand on his shoulder. "My good fellow, never be ashamed to follow your instinct. You'll be fine. With or without them. I can see that from a mile's distance."

"Oh," Bobby said. "Well, uh, I've got a question."

"I'm full of answers. I've been in this industry years, a lot longer than Fred even. Could you believe that?"

Bobby shrugged and half-smiled. "I just wanted to know if I could have those blocks of wood over there."

Ian turned to look behind himself at the large stack of wood in the corner. "Well, I suppose I don't need all of it."

****

Bobby took the bus home. He stood, holding on to the ceiling bar, jostled again and again by the bus's sudden stops. He couldn't focus on anything but keeping his balance. During his trek from bus stop to the duplex, he recited ten Hail Mary's and an Our Father with the hope that God would keep him from Kindle's wrath.

When he made it to the apartment door, he petted Kitty Wonder once on the head. The cat squinted his eyes before trotting away. Bobby crept through the door to find Kindle sitting cross-legged on the floor before the television. Its images played off of her crisp skin.

He took a seat on the floor beside her. "Pat Benatar," he said, nodding at the television.

"Yes," she said, unmoved.

Bobby nodded. With his finger, he traced one of her curls from the nape of her neck up to her ponytail. "I like her too."

"I didn't say I liked her," she said, nudging away his finger.

"Do you like me?"

"I haven't the energy to dislike you."

"But I put you in a bad mood, didn't I?"

She tapped at her mouth, faking a yawn. "You don't have that kind of power over me."

Bobby leaned back, supporting himself with his hands. "So what did you do today?"

"Not much of anything."

"Nothing exciting?"

Kindle slowly slanted her face toward him then back to the screen. "Aside from talking to Mummy Carter, no."

"What?"

She turned off the television and threw the remote control at the chair. It crashed to the ground and slid across the floor. "I talked to Carol Carter. Interesting thing, actually."

"Who? My mom? My mom called? What did you say to her?"

Kindle tapped her finger against her chin. "Let me think."

Bobby stood up, grappling for words.

"I told her my name, for one."

"Did she ask who you were?"

"Of course she did."

He pushed his knuckles over his lips. "What did you say?"

"Your love has set my soul on fire," Kindle sang along with Pat. She looked up at him innocently. "I told her the truth."

"What's the truth?" Bobby switched off the television with the toe of his sneaker.

"*You* know what the truth is, Bobby."

He paced behind the television set. "So, what did she say? Was she upset?"

Kindle turned the television back on and stood up with her hands behind her back. "Not as much as I'd expect. She freaked a bit, but all-in-all, she contained herself."

Bobby halted. "Freaked? Did she cry?"

"I couldn't really tell."

He took large steps toward her, like a hunter to an elusive prey. "Are you serious, Kindle? That's not, like…it just doesn't seem fair."

"Why isn't it fair?"

"Because she's *my* mom. You didn't give me a chance to tell her."

"But you told *my* mother yourself."

He scrunched his hair between his fingers. "That's not fair. Your mother is…"

"She's what? She's dead, right? So, in essence, she doesn't matter?"

"I didn't say that. You're saying that. I'd never say anything like that."

"You don't have to. You *insinuate*." She jabbed a finger at him.

His volume readily escalated. "I don't insinuate. I don't even know how to insinuate, Kindle. That's not the kind of person I am. That's not fair."

"That's not fair?" she snorted, curling up her top lip in disdain. "You're so immature."

How right she was. He was a boy, not a man. Only boys feared their parents this way. Only boys felt they could almost cry over news like this. Only boys couldn't figure a sensible way out of this kind of trouble.

Only little boys pointed their fingers at girls the way Bobby pointed at Kindle. "I'm immature? No, I think you're immature. You only told her because you were mad at me!"

"No, I didn't."

"Yes, you did."

"No, I didn't."

"Yes—"

"No. I. Didn't." She turned her back to him. "I didn't even tell her. It was a scare tactic, Bobby." Kindle settled back down on the floor, Yoga-style, her back perfectly erect.

Bobby stepped back, his mouth ajar. "What?"

"She called here and I told her that I was a hotel maid and that you were in band rehearsal. She said to leave you a message." Kindle produced a slip of paper from her jeans and flung it up toward him. It fluttered through the air and settled beside the television like a feather. "She loves you and your dad loves you. Your cousin Meredith is engaged now. Your grandmother and grandfather are in town visiting. She wants to know if you'll come back to see them."

Bobby stooped down to pick up the paper. "Why didn't you tell her?"

"I should have," she said weakly. "Really, I should have."

He leaned forward on his knees and kissed her forehead. She held him weakly.

"Thank you," Bobby whispered.

"I want you to tell her when this year ends. If we're still together, still living together, you have to tell her."

"We'll still be together."

"I have nothing to say about that," Kindle responded. "The thing I can say is that people only keep secrets when they're ashamed."

"Or when something is so special that they wanna keep it all to themselves, right?"

Kindle sighed. For the first time, a deep worry settled over her as she considered that like their psychedelic furniture, she was possibly a temporary arrangement.

Chapter Twelve

Kindle contemplated the meaning of destiny when she met the girl. Maybe it was a coincidence, but it felt a lot like fate when the young woman introduced herself on the first day of acting class.

Kindle walked into class and noted that she was one of only six students. There was a blonde woman, a brunette waif, a tall, skinny man who sported both grizzly facial hair and an oniony smell, and a thin red-head, who was noticeably taller than the other girls, like an awkward giraffe among ants. Another man, also lean and hairy, had long carrot curls that rippled down to his mid-back. The teacher was male—tall, thin and balding at the crown of his head. His name was Nigel Pearce.

His speech was rubbish, really. His lisp made deciphering his greeting near impossible. Kindle did determine that he wanted them each to sit in one of the grey chairs that formed a circle in the center of the room. With frequent waves of his hands, Nigel stood outside of the circle giving scattered details of what they would do—something about executing improv exercises, preparing for short plays and learning proper stage etiquette. He also warned that it would be an accelerated course. Kindle feared that if the course went as fast as he spoke, she might not be able to keep up. She wondered how he could teach a class about acting—a true art of communication—if he himself had trouble communicating.

As she pondered these things, Nigel suddenly spoke with absolute clarity. "I know that I have fooled many of you with such vernacular," he said. "It is my hope that my students also shall become masters of foolery. In which case, I will have done my job well. In thirty days, you will not become masters of theater, but I trust that you will understand the dynamics of metamorphosis, the art of becoming what you never thought possible. In thirty days, you will be stage actors. That is if and only if you take the necessary steps. Studying and homework also come with the territory. Of course, nothing can be achieved without hard work."

Next, Nigel afforded them the opportunity to introduce themselves.

The smelly man's name was Geoffrey Taylor. The other man introduced himself as Sylvester Reeves, but preferred simply Reeves. The Brunette was Holly Thomas. The redhead, Miriam Peterson.

The blonde puckered her maroon-stained lips as though she were kissing the heavens and then grinned broadly. "My name is Betty Warner."

****

In the late afternoon, after band practice, Bobby stood in the phone booth. He opted for the pay phone over the home phone, unwilling to take the chance of having Kindle spy on his conversation if she had made it home from acting class.

It was rainy, but at least it wasn't cold. The people outside scattered like ants seeking refuge. Bobby wore a clear raincoat and leaned against the phone booth's wet glass, leaving a ghost figure upon it.

"Grandma, I really want to come there to see you," he said. "I really do. But I can't."

"Why not?"

"Because I'm so busy here."

"I haven't seen you since Tampa. Do you know how long that's been?"

"Two years, Grandma. I know. And I'm really sorry." He drew circles on the glass with his index fingers.

"It's because of your father, isn't it?"

"No. No, Grandma, that's not why. I miss Dad. Really." Bobby cringed. He hated lying. He wished she hadn't picked up the phone.

"Are you certain?"

"Yes." He cringed again.

His grandmother huffed. "Well, then, I want to say that your grandfather and I are highly disappointed. We thought that you would have more family loyalty than this. Especially after we've offered to buy your plane ticket. I want to say it, but I won't. You're an adult man. Adult men must make their own decisions, mustn't they?"

A guilt trip intended to sound like detachment —typical Choice Carter. Holding conversations with his paternal grandmother made him realize that his father was callous for more reasons than World War II. Bobby wondered why he himself wasn't like that. The "step-on-your-feelings-for-any-reason" gene must have skipped his generation.

Grandma Choice hung up on him. At the sound of the dial tone, Bobby placed the phone back on the receiver. So much for talking to his mother like he had planned before Grandma Choice intercepted the call.

Bobby sighed as he walked through the apartment door later that day. The blinds were raised. They couldn't be let down since Kindle had broken them last week. The scene of grey clouds hovering over the rundown duplexes was like a photograph embedded into the center wall. Raindrops hung from the bare tree branches like diamond earrings.

Bobby wished Kindle were there. The rain couldn't keep her from acting class or her night job. She was probably on her way to the windowless bar. What he wouldn't give to be playing in a bar, to be playing anywhere. What he wouldn't give to be surrounded by people.

Bobby thought maybe this was the beginning of homesickness. Yet, when he thought of home, a yellow paneled house with a white picket fence in Canton, he changed his mind. He couldn't imagine being in Canton, where a man was supposed to be a man by his age, but wasn't until he had proper schooling and a job. Come to think, it was probably raining in Canton too. His dad was probably sleeping, snoring loudly, without regard to the rain.

Bobby did what only instinct could give him when shadows of dismay and a stormy night threatened hm. He picked up his guitar from against the chair and sat on the ground, laying its body over his thigh to a perfect fit.

He played the first full song that he had learned on the guitar when he was fourteen years old. He sang along with Don McClean in his heart, recalling a long, long time ago how the music used to make him feel….how it used to make him smile…how it felt when the music died…and when he bid bye-bye to Miss American Pie.

****

The Dare played a lackluster show the following evening. Mickey, the new replacement guitarist, failed to tune his guitar and missed two solos. Larry mutilated the drum licks that Bobby had helped create in their last rehearsal. Kyle's bass lines were bland and bleating. Bobby blamed their drag on the need for more rehearsal. The band blamed it on Bobby, who had shown up only ten minutes early to rehearsal that day.

After exiting the stage, Bobby had no intention of staying in the club. The gritty skyline art on the walls proved more dismal than inspired. The wall behind the stage was a mural of musicians who had passed in the last decade. The red-and-white checkered floor seemed to be an attempt at eccentric regality, but it only served to make Bobby dizzy.

The audience was atypically punk. The men wore designer clothes that they had shredded and patched at the arms and knees. The women paraded around in leather pants and loose T-shirts, having also drenched themselves in pearl necklaces and diamond bracelets. The small club was probably a playground for the elite, who attended private universities in the day and escaped to Bohemian paradise at night.

When Bobby reached the door, a slight hand delayed him, grabbing him by the elbow. He spun around to respond, the people behind him dispersing to dodge the guitar on his back.

The girl smiled at him and bowed primly. Her short black wig slid forward slightly. She grinned, re-positioning it. Her face was powder white. Her long black eyelashes extended out like claws. Her crimson lipstick and bustier perfected her guise; she blended in like an accessory in the room.

"Betty," Bobby breathed. "What are you doing here?"

Betty wove her fingers between his and used the bond to draw herself closer to him, smashing her chest against his. At his recoiling, she hugged him securely, trading her forwardness for tenderness.

"Phileo love, Ricky. Why are you so afraid of me?" she whispered in his ear before drawing back from him.

"I'm not. I just need to go. Like, now."

"Where are you going?"

"Nowhere, really." Bobby pushed the black door open and stepped outside. The city lights shrouded the starlight. Bobby exhaled.

"What do you mean, nowhere?" Betty inquired. She skipped beside him, her red bag bobbing against her thighs as she walked. "Everyone is headed somewhere. I like to think that you're headed in the direction of greatness."

"You don't have to say that, Betty. I'm okay."

"Affirmative. I suppose it'll be the last time that I ever pay you a compliment since you obviously don't know how to take one."

A biker zipped between them. Bobby stared at Betty as she laughed, apparently amused by the fact that she had barely avoided being swiped by the young biker. She slipped off her wig and twirled it on her index finger. Her blonde hair was slicked back, stiff.

As they journeyed, Betty spoke easily to five near-strangers, greeting men and women who she claimed to have met once or twice at a bar or at a restaurant or at a concert.

One young woman, also wearing a short wig and a bustier, clutched Betty's arm before they could pass her.

"Alex," the girl exclaimed. "What are you doing, Love? What's your business?"

Betty laughed. "I've got no business now. *He* aint my business, Madeline. He's just a friend. He might be a superstar one day. Then, I'll make him my business."

The two of them giggled. Bobby noticed that Madeline wasn't white. Perhaps she was of Middle Eastern descent, her skin the color of tumbleweed, her lips thick, the space underneath her eyes burnished brown. A coarse red scar the size of a penny protruded from her cheek.

"I haven't found anyone to make my business lately." Madeline moped, poking out her moist bottom lip.

Betty walked on. Bobby and Madeline tailed her.

"So, you spend your days and nights by your lonesome?" Betty teased.

Madeline put her hands behind her back. "I am a sad old woman, aren't I? Martin is out of commission. Could you believe that? I'm terribly depressed." She jutted her bottom lip out farther. Bobby cringed. He was agitated by her hyper-drama, the rapid speed with which she spoke and her sudden, sharp changes of expressions. He tried thinking of ways he could quietly lose them.

"Martin is in commission, Maddie. The band is doing very well these days. He probably hasn't got time for you anymore," said Betty.

"Martin who?" Bobby interjected softly. He looked away when Madeline glanced at him with a smirk.

"Martin Lewis. The Creatures Below." Betty explained. "You must know the band."

"He's married," Bobby stared at the grey warehouse across the street. "I mean, I heard Martin had a wife or something?"

"Maddie don't care about nothing like that. As easily as he was snatched up by the other bird, he can be taken up again." Betty looped her arm through Bobby's, towing him closer. Madeline dragged behind them. "Besides, they're not getting on very well anyway."

Bobby palmed his mouth for a moment, weakly shaking his head. "I've gotta go. I should go now. I don't want to be late."

"I thought we were heading in the direction of your destination?" Betty responded. She released his stiff arm. "Where's your destination, Ricky?"

"Your name's Ricky?" Madeline stepped on the back of his shoes as they walked. "You've got a beautiful name. I love it. You don't happen to have a wife, do you?"

With a chortle, Betty looked back quickly at Madeline. "You can't have him. I've already claimed him."

"I have to go." Bobby stopped in front of the club door. "I really have to go. I'm sorry."

Betty waved away his concerns with a flimsy hand. "Don't worry, Bobby. We don't do what you think. We're not slappers, per se. You might say that we're groupies, but I prefer 'aficionado.' I admire chaps with future plans. Rock 'n' roll boys are at the top of my list."

"Motivated musicians," Madeline submitted.

"Yes. Blokes with big dreams. Can you blame me for drawing to you? You fit the profile hand-in-glove. You might even be interesting if you open up a bit. You must know that already." She tapped her mouth. "Oops. I wasn't supposed to say that. I vowed that I'd never compliment you again."

"Where do you have to go, Ricky?" Madeline inquired, hardly waiting for Betty to finish.

"Inside." Bobby gaped at the two women. They semi-circled him in front of the club door. Their shadows loomed over him, taking over the entirety of the small square sidewalk entrance. Madeline's gaiety shook the shadows, as she waggled from side to side. She grinned and Bobby noted that her left front tooth was chipped. Betty did not smile, but she placed her hands on her hips and pursed her lips. Bobby imagined that Betty peered out of eagle eyes, while Madeline was a baby robin. He hadn't interest in either one. A dove waited for him inside.

"Don't worry, Ricky. We'll leave you on your Jack Jones. Let's go, Madeline." Betty circled her arm around Madeline's shoulders. Before they bounced away, Betty stuck her tongue out at Bobby. He couldn't tell whether she intended the gesture as flirtation or offense.

Inside, Bobby didn't see Kindle. Head down, he made his way to the bathroom, communing with black shoes rather than tipsy, overexcited punks. Urine coated the white-tiled bathroom floor. Bobby stood at a urinal with his index finger beneath his nose. The fluorescent lights highlighted and cast a fog over all that should be hidden—the graffiti'ed walls, the streaked mirrors, the mold that browed over the faucet knobs. He closed his eyes. Not until he heard a clank did he reopen them. He sighted a sixpence coin splashing through a runnel of water and urine. It had rolled from under the vacant stall closest to the end wall.

"Anybody in here?" His voice echoed. He stepped toward the stall, attempting to open the locked door. He crouched down, leaning his head to the side enough to peek under the door without flipping his hair through the puddles.

Bobby looked at Kindle, from her feet up to her simpering face. He furrowed his brows. She continued counting her tips briskly, her feet rooted on the toilet rim and her elbows fixed on her knees.

"You found me." She fanned herself with a paper bill before stuffing all of her money in her pocket. "What took you so long?"

Bobby stood up and tore a long train of paper towels from the dispenser. He spread them out on the floor in front of the stall and knelt.

"Will you come out?"

Kindle opened the door and stretched her hand out for his. Bobby enveloped her hand, lowering her to the ground.

"You've rolled out the red carpet for me. You shouldn't have. I already trudged through the mire to get to the toilet," she said.

"But why did you come in here? This is a rotten place for a girl to be."

She fluttered her eyes. "At least I got to hear you pee."

Feigning embarrassment, Bobby combed his hair over his face with his fingers, peeking through the gaps between the strands. Kindle gathered together one side of his hair and crimped it behind his ear. He drew his lips up into a smile on the visible side of his face.

Kindle laughed. "You are the two-face theater mask."
She creased the other side of his hair behind his ear.

He beamed.

"I'm in here because I grew weary of waiting for you. I
wanted to check how well I did for the day, but I didn't want
any robbers coming after me, so I came to the place where I
would be least suspected."

"But you were found."

"Amazing grace. How sweet the sound," Kindle sang
sweetly.

"That saved a wretch like me," Bobby sang, employing
Otis Redding vibrato.

Kindle clapped once, vibrating with laughter. "That
saved a wretch like me," she screeched.

"You sound so good," Bobby fawned in baritone. He
compressed his lips over hers, but instead of kissing her, he
blew through his closed mouth so that both of their lips
quavered.

"You've broken the rules," she said with a smile. "I alone
am allowed to initiate lip-to-lip contact."

Bobby shrugged. "A guy can abandon discipline
sometimes, right? Some things call for rebellion, I think." He
stared at her , blinking his eyes in disbelief. She had grown
more beautiful in a few months' time, he was sure—her lips
more ripe, her eyes more curious, the curve of her waist and
hips more pronounced. He was sure of one thing now, and he
couldn't keep it to himself. "I am going to make love to you,
Penelope Princess." He observed her eyes. They had widened
so that he was sure now that he had scared her. "Not, like, right
now in the bathroom. I just mean, one day I will. And I'll be a
gentleman." He laughed. "Or a sailor, if you want. Whatever
you want, I'll be. Just as long as you lend your whole self to me
for as long as we have."

She rubbed her lips together slowly. He knew now she
was neither afraid nor turned off, but rather, such anticipation
was on her face that if he didn't know her better, he would have
thought that she was ready to make good on his promise right
then. But instead, she said, "Your naughtiness resurfaces itself
once more. I'm intrigued. Maybe delighted."

They both laughed, their laughter resonating until it suddenly multiplied.

Stalking in languorously, Betty Warner made her way to Bobby and Kindle with her hands behind her back, continuing to laugh after Kindle had stopped. Betty donned the black wig once more and a set of black-framed sunglasses with purple-tinted lenses.

"Hello, Ricky Stallion," Betty heralded, angling her shoulders to wedge herself between Bobby and Kindle. She faced Kindle, her back skimming Bobby's chest.

"Hi," he mumbled, withdrawing two steps.

"Name?" Betty extended her hand to Kindle.

"Kindle." She shook Betty's hand slowly, casting a quick, intent eye over her.

"Lovely name. So, you're the trouble and strife, eh?"

Bobby's eyes widened.

Kindle licked her teeth. "Perhaps, I am."

"My name is Alex, Kindle. I'm just an aficionado. No worries." Betty turned and blinked at Bobby. "Ricky and his band are punk prodigies, in my mind."

"I see." Kindle's lips cemented and she clinched her jaw, searching Betty's face.

After a moment's silence, Betty flipped her head back, her mouth wide open, as if she were yawning. She lowered her face and grinned. "I didn't pay attention to the sign on the door. Men's bathroom. Who would've thunk it?"

"You're more than welcomed to exit now," said Kindle.

Betty puffed out her chest and swung her purse forward idly, barely missing Kindle. "Well, now that we've settled that, suppose I'll leave you two on your Jack Jones."

She trudged out, the imprint on the bottom of her shoe stamping the dirt on the floor.

Bobby toddled back to Kindle. "Mad?"

"At you or Little Alex?" Kindle rolled her eyes. "That girl looks familiar. I can't place her though. Those types are all around these places. Birds with no nests. I'm sure you get that quite often."

Bobby exhaled. "Not really. I don't know," he said absently.

"Don't know what?"

He paddled his stomach and stretched up his arms.

"Don't know who Jack Jones is. Is that, like, somebody famous here?"

Kindle tickled his armpit. "Out we go. I'm ready to go home. The smell of pee is bound to knock me out soon." She looped her arm through his, walking him to the door. "What's wrong? You seem like a lost child."

He laughed softly, opening the door for her. "Sometimes, I am a lost child, I guess."

Chapter Thirteen

Past Time: 1961

"**G**o run and tell the twins happy birthday," Bobby's
mother said as she pulled a hot cake pan out of the oven. "They
just pulled up."

She turned to Bobby, smiling. She picked him up from
green vinyl, where he sat drumming on a pot, and lifted him up
to the window above the stove, pushing apart the floral curtains.
Outside, Meredith and Kyle jumped out of the canary station
wagon.

Bobby's mother set him back on the floor. "Go tell
them," she said, patting his behind.

Bobby ran for the back door on the other end of the
kitchen, meeting the twins there. Meredith trotted past him,
holding her pink, plastic purse over her shoulder. She went to
his mother for a hug and kiss.

"Happy birthday," Bobby said.

"Look what I got," Kyle said. He held up a bright red ball
of Silly Putty.

When Bobby reached out to touch it, Kyle snatched his
hand back.

"Too slow," Kyle said, smirking.

Aunt Catherine stepped in behind Kyle, her face blocked
by the tower of stacked pans she held. She peered around them.
"Be nice," she said wearily.

"It's my birthday," Kyle said, crossing his arms with a pout.

Aunt Catherine toddled to the kitchen, quickly pecking her sister's cheek before directing her words back to Kyle. "Well, then act like a big boy. Seven-year-olds know how to share." She reached forward to pat her sister's back. "How are you, Carol?"

"Fantastic," Carol said, spreading white icing on the chocolate cake. "Did you get enough food, Catherine?"

"This is everything," Aunt Catherine said, panting as she set the stack of pans on the counter. "I swear to God, twin birthdays are the most expensive thing on earth. Thank your lucky stars Bobby wasn't a twin."

"Mommy," Meredith said, climbing onto one of the white vinyl chairs. She set her hands on the table, crossed her legs and flipped back her chocolate hair. She was as pretty-picturesque as a Block Walker doll.

Aunt Catherine glanced over at Bobby and Kyle as they sat on their knees near the bottom cabinets, toying with the Silly Putty. She clapped her hands. "Off your knees, Kyle. Now. Ruin those pants and I'll ruin you."

Kyle looked down at his orange corduroy pants and back up at his mother, unconcerned. He stuck his fingers through the putty.

"Mommy," Meredith repeated. She pouted, her face a replica of Kyle's. They both had the kind of turned-down ruby mouths and expressive black eyes that made their moping a theatrical show.

"I swear to God," Aunt Catherine said, huffing, "a day doesn't go by when I don't imagine what Richard would have done with these kids."

His mother nodded, scraping the last bit of icing from the large bowl.

"Get off your knees, Kyle. I'm not gonna tell you again," Aunt Catherine growled before setting her mouth in a hard line. "If I have to tell you again, I'm gonna knock all of your little teeth out."

Bobby shuddered. He drummed on the pot slowly, counting to the tune of the alphabet song.

"But it's my birthday," Kyle said, scowling back, matching his mother's rigidity.

"It's my birthday too," Meredith whined, sliding off of the chair. She dropped down to the floor beside the boys, completing a circle.

"Don't start with me too, Meredith," Aunt Catherine ordered. "Get up."

Meredith looked down at her orange corduroy dress and back up at her mother, flawlessly mimicking Kyle's indifference.

His mother dropped her spoon in the bowl and wrapped her arm around Aunt Catherine's shoulder. She comforted Aunt Catherine as though her baby sister were a little girl, petting her stiff auburn hair. His mother was noticeably older, lines creasing the corners of her eyes. Her hair was drawn up into a French Roll; Aunt Catherine's was flipped up near her chin and tucked behind her ears. Aunt Catherine wore a plum turtleneck and plaid skirt, while his mother wore a white shirt and tan skirt. His mother was brown-eyed, Aunt Catherine green-eyed. Bobby always thought of his mother as the moon and Aunt Catherine as the sun. Indeed, Aunt Catherine looked brighter than his mother, but get too close to her and you'd get burned.

"What are you doing?" Meredith probed, staring at Bobby, still whining.

Bobby beat the pot faster, now mimicking another song—The Marvelettes *Playboy.*

"Dammit, Meredith and Kyle! What did I just say?" Aunt Catherine exclaimed, slapping her hand against the counter.

His mother ushered Aunt Catherine down into one of the chairs. Bobby stared at Aunt Catherine's foot shaking beneath the table. He tried syncopating his pot tap with the steady clap of her shoe against the floor.

"Don't get so agitated, Honey," his mother said, squeezing Aunt Catherine's shoulder. "Kids will be kids."

Aunt Catherine shook her head and sighed. "You have no idea, Carol. If Richard were here, I swear to God, these kids wouldn't try my patience the way they do."

"I know, Honey. I know it's hard." She side-hugged Aunt Catherine.

"You have no way of really knowing, Carol," Aunt Catherine returned. "I swear to God, you don't ever want to know what it's like."

His mother set her hands in her lap, silent.

"Let me see it," Meredith now whined at Kyle, reaching for his Silly Putty and smacking his arm when he snatched it back.

Bobby continued to beat the pot, quieter this time, allowing his mother and aunt's whispers to become the lyrics to his song.

"You don't know how easy you and Frank have it," Aunt Catherine continued, bitter.

His mother rubbed her hands over the table. "Sometimes," she said slowly, "sometimes you just have to be thankful. I know you loved Richard. I know no one has come along that will match him. But I also know that without Richard's passing, we wouldn't have been blessed the way that we are." She dropped her eyes down at Bobby. Unaware that he had been staring, she darted her eyes back to Aunt Catherine. "If you need anything, Frank and I are here for you. That promise stood before. It still stands. It will always stand." His mother patted Aunt Catherine's hand and stood. Aunt Catherine joined her at the counter, stirring another batch of icing.

Meredith had continued to screech, demanding Kyle's putty. She reached across the circle, grabbing Kyle by his throat, pressing her girly claws into his neck. The toy fell out of his hands. At the same time Meredith reached for the Silly Putty, Kyle reached for Bobby's pot, lifting it high above his head and slapping it down against her face. Blood gushed from her nose and she screamed, sounding off an alarm so piercing that Bobby clapped his hands over his ears.

"What in heaven's name!" Aunt Catherine began before turning around. At first sight of the lines of blood streaking her daughter's face, she leapt to her. "What happened?" she cried, scooping Meredith up with one arm.

Kyle quietly pointed his finger at Bobby.

Aunt Catherine reached down for Bobby, binding his shirt collar together and jerking him against the cabinets. His head bobbed back and forth against the wood. "What the hell is wrong with you, Bobby?" she screamed. "Have you completely lost your mind?"

His mother dropped down to her knees, struggling to loosen Aunt Catherine's grip from his shirt. "Catherine, stop it! You're going to hurt him!"

Bobby wheezed. Kyle picked up his toy and backed away toward the stove.

"Catherine, please," his mother pleaded. "It was an accident. He's five years old. Let him go! You're going to hurt him!" She slapped at Aunt Catherine's hands. "You could kill him, Catherine! He can't handle this. He has slight asthma—just like you did when you were a little girl. Just like you did!"

As if she had been electro-shocked, Aunt Catherine stopped instantly, her hand falling limply from his collar. She looked down at Bobby, staring him in the face for the first time he could ever remember.

Aunt Catherine stood, still holding her hand down against Meredith's nose. "We have to go," she said. "Now. I'll call you later this evening."

Meredith's cry quieted to a whimper.

"We can still have the birthday party," his mother said, looking up at Aunt Catherine while pressing Bobby's head against her breast.

"Not today, Carol," she responded, walking toward the door. She stepped out, leaving the door open behind her.

"Sorry," Kyle offered somberly, handing Bobby the Silly Putty before following his mother and sister.

Chapter Fourteen

Present Time…

Before the start of Thursday's class, the group of acting
students sat in the circle of chairs waiting for Nigel Pearce to
arrive. Above the whispers, one voice could be heard distinctly.
"This little girl is overrated. What's her name again?"
Betty said rowdily, as if her tiny pink skirt and shredded tie-dye
T-shirt didn't gather enough attention. She raised her eyebrows,
puckered her lips and resettled a blue fisherman's hat on her
head, looking around the room with a lazy stare.
"I think her name is Candle," Geoffrey Taylor responded.
He crossed his legs toward Betty, his bony knees pointing
angularly through his black stretch pants.
Miriam Peterson yawned and glanced to her right, where
Geoffrey sat with his back to her. Betty faced him from the seat
beside his. Miriam returned to her conversation with Holly
Thomas at her left, leaning forward so that Betty faced her long,
wagging red ponytail and the jagged imprint of her spine
through her grey T-shirt.
Betty curled up the left side of her mouth, widening her
eyes defiantly at Miriam's back. "Her name isn't Candle,
Love," Betty continued, leaning in toward Geoffrey but raising
her volume. Holly wrinkled her eyebrows and Reeves lifted his
head from the script. "Something like Kindle. Whatever it is,

she aint my cup of tea." She crossed her legs and slouched over, looking Geoffrey in the eyes. "But could you blame Nigel for his kindness? There aren't many large parts for little woggies. Even Othello's wife was pale, wasn't she? I wouldn't lie to the girl if I were old Nigel. Oh well. It's horses for courses, I suppose."

Reeves stood up from the circle and sat in the corner with his script.

The chair on Kindle's left was now empty. At her right, Holly Thomas continued conversing with Miriam. Kindle caught Geoffrey's empty eyes as she looked up from her script.

"I see your case," Geoffrey offered blandly.

"My case is perfectly clear. This isn't the industry for that kind. We all have something in common." Betty skated her finger up Geoffrey's forearm and then her own. "Possibly she missed that. I'm sure she'll learn that she can't keep what she's not fit for. Acting parts are a lot like men—they ultimately go to the woman most fitting for the part."

Miriam rolled on her behind, spinning around to face Betty. Her eyes widened, her nose wrinkled in a sneer, her chest heaved. "You are beastly, aren't you? Where are you from? Liverpool? I've never heard anything so pitiful and rude in my life. Never."

Betty sat impassive, blinking her eyes once and raking her index finger through her mascara-clumped eyelashes. "Actually, my ties are in The East End."

Holly locked Miriam's wrist to prevent her from standing. Miriam smiled wryly, and Kindle noticed for the first time the small gap between her two front teeth. "East End?" said Miriam. "Why am I not surprised? Welcome to Manchester. Just so that you are aware, we don't talk like that here."

"So I take it that you don't believe in the truth. Well, I'm sorry. I didn't know that I was among a group of phonies." Betty clutched Geoffrey's upper arm and grinned. Geoffrey sighed, glanced quickly at Reeves and then back down at his lap.

"And I didn't know that I was in the company of a prat. Please forgive me," Miriam returned.

Reeves staggered to his feet and entered back in the circle, standing in the middle. He stood with his hands behind his back, perfectly erect, gallant. "Boys and girls, let's focus on other things. Like acting."

Betty removed her hat and tousled her hair. "I'm easy. If Miri has some issue with my words, let her speak." Dropping to her knees, Betty scooted over to Miriam. She tapped Miriam's lap once with her head before looking up at her with gumball eyes and a frown. "What exactly did I say wrong, my lady? Please help me improve myself."

Miriam pressed her palm against Betty's forehead. "There is a time and a place. And that time is not now. That place certainly isn't here, not amongst the racially-educated." She maneuvered her legs to the right so that she faced Holly entirely.

Betty stared at Miriam's profile, looking over her sharp nose and glossy, freckled cheeks.

"Get your own business, Betty," Miriam said. "And get off your knees. Save your drama for class. Maybe you would perform better then."

Betty stood, her tan knees white-rusted by the carpet. She nuzzled her hat onto her head "Oh, well, cor blimey!" she exclaimed, glancing at Kindle and smacking her hand over her mouth. "I had no idea you was there. Oh, but I was only pissing around. You've done an excellent job thus far. I'm wishing you the very best."

Geoffrey uncrossed and crossed his legs once more. He palmed his cheek.

Betty bowed, catching her hat in her hand when it slid from her head. She pressed the hat against her breasts. "I should take a trip to the Khazi before Nigel arrives, cupcakes. Save my seat, Geoffrey."

After Betty skipped out of the room, Kindle recognized that she was among a group of actors, a group of strangers that could acquaint with each other without the fear of irreparable offense. With this in mind, Kindle stood, making her way to Miriam and Holly.

She smiled and cleared her throat. After two-and-a-half weeks in the class, she had yet to know what her voice would sound like addressing another student. "Thank you very much," Kindle nodded.

Miriam crossed her arms. She eyed Kindle wearily. "Please don't thank me. I'm no one's savior. Not trying to be. I just haven't got time for cheeky monkeys, like that Betty. Maybe next time you'd save myself and the rest of us the stress if you would defend yourself. Just a thought."

Kindle roamed back to her seat, rubbing her tight throat. She was incensed. She would have said something to defend herself, if she hadn't been so fixated by Betty's voice. It was crackly and thin, like sandpaper colliding with brick. Kindle had heard the voice before, she was near positive. She must have misplaced the memory.

****

The entire third week of Kindle's acting course, Fred found no open venue where The Dare could perform. He promised that it would be the last vacation that the boys would have. Despite Bobby's unwillingness to meet with her, Betty Warner settled for convening with Fred, provided that Ricky ("and The Dare, if need be") would perform three shows at Band on the Wall the following week. It would be the first week in April.

Bobby accepted the performances without hesitation. Each day of their supposed vacation, he pushed The Dare through long rehearsals at the club, rejuvenated by quarter-note thoughts of his wife. Betty Warner visited every rehearsal, clapping wildly after each song.

While the band packed up after one rehearsal, Betty found her way to Bobby as he wound his amp cord around his hand. The outfit she wore that day was more revealing than any other—a purple miniskirt, fishnets, and a bedazzled black bra.

"Sticky Ricky," she said, standing in front of him with her hands behind her back. "How goes it?"

"It goes good," he responded, setting the wire in his open guitar case. "But I goes out," he continued, half-smiling. "Don't have time to talk, Betty."

"I suppose I should call you 'Slippery Ricky.' You're always finding a way to escape me. I'm beginning to get the sense you don't like me. Or maybe you're scared of me like the duck 'n geese."

Bobby knelt down to close his guitar case. "No idea what you're talking about." He walked to the steps that led down from the stage, following the rest of the band toward the door.

Betty skipped behind him, eventually speeding ahead of him to close and lock the door after Larry walked out. She stood against the door, silently announcing that he wouldn't make it outside without her permission.

He sat his guitar case down on the floor and crossed his arms over his chest. "What do you want from me, Betty?" His voice echoed, reverberating off the club walls. "I don't think I have anything to give you. I'm pretty sure I'm not the kind of guy you're looking for."

With the tip of her shoe, Betty tipped over the guitar case and stood on it's flat side, giving her the extra inches to look him directly in the eyes. She held his shoulders, steadying herself. "You don't know what I want, Ricky. If you did, you wouldn't question the validity of this attraction." Her eyes sparkled. "You would Adam and Eve it."

Her simpering face gave away the fact that she loved speaking a language he could hardly grasp. Yet, he was curious. "Adam and Eve it?" he inquired.

"Cockney rhyming slang, Love. 'Adam and Eve it' means 'believe it.' See how it works now?" She smiled brilliantly. Bobby couldn't help seeing a young Pattie Boyd in her. Peculiar. Blonde. Beautiful. "Isn't it interesting? I swear I'll let you go, if you play the rhyming game with me for a moment."

He pulled her hands from his shoulders and placed them at her sides. "I only have one minute."

"One minute is all I need, Slippery Ricky." She tapped his nose with her forefinger. "So, you heard me say, 'duck 'n geese.' What would you imagine that to be? I'll give you one guess at it. The duck 'n geese carry billy clubs here in England. In the States, they carry guns."

Bobby smiled, near proud that he had figured out the rhyme. "The police."

She nodded. "Actually, it means the fuckin' police. It makes for a more perfect rhyme."

He laughed, and when she laughed back, he instantly noticed the jiggling of her melon breasts. He looked past her toward the door.

Betty placed her little hand over his cheek, sweet but not as sexual as he had expected from the times she had touched him before. "Okay, Love, I have one more. What about the phrase, 'jam tart.' I suppose I should give you a clue on this one as well." She placed both of her hands over her left breast. "I love you with all of my jam tart." She caught his eyes, her expression serious.

"Heart," he replied quietly.

Jolly, she reached for his hands. "That is exactly it. Aye! You're my favorite person, Ricky. I tell you, I could bottle you up and use you for medicinal purposes." She moved his hands to her breasts, pressing his right hand down toward the middle part of her chest so that he could feel her heart beat. "There is something about you that I love very much. Your innocence, I think. I don't mind that you don't have the same experiences that I do. In fact, I love that about you. I've never met a rock star so lily-white pure." She removed his hands from her breasts, and to his own shame, he was briefly crestfallen. "But don't get me wrong. I want to be with you in the dirtiest way imaginable. With you, I certainly wouldn't mind a good Donald Duck."

He furrowed his brows.

"Donald Duck is my most favorite rhyming slang. It's the kind of lovemaking that starts with an F." Betty stepped down from his guitar case and turned toward the door. Bobby could hardly help tracing the thin line of her spine as she leaned down to unlock it. She opened the door, letting the sunlight into their dusty cave. "Be safe, Slippery Ricky. Until we meet again, Love."

He picked up his guitar case and stepped toward the door. Before he exited, she patted his back and quacked like a duck.

Despite the moral discomfort, Bobby got used to Betty hanging around, though he held the fear that Kindle would walk through the club door every day. He could never have her know that Betty was a pretty little appendage to their rehearsal. He couldn't even calculate the days that would set him back in his pursuit of Kindle.

At the end of his walk home from rehearsal each day, he skipped up the stairs of the duplex and stood outside of the apartment, biding the short time between anticipation and desire. Kitty Wonder now was comfortable enough with Bobby to paw at his feet. The gesture always made him smile.

Bloated with the excitement of each day, Kindle nearly pummeled him when he walked through the door. She drove him to the large chair and executed a giddy exposition of what she had learned each day. She brought stories about her fellow actors, who she claimed were marginally more experienced than her but radically less determined. She brought vamped explanations of simple acting terms. She brought souvenirs of her days—hand-made paper props.

She brought a smile to his face.

Bobby hadn't talked to his mother or father since he'd spoken with his grandmother. His unwillingness to see his grandparents probably unbraided much of his mother's support for the music thing. His father's opinion of this Manchester business was likely confirmed. Funny how one of Kindle's smiles could cover a thousand thoughts of Frank Carter's silent judgment.

Moreover, Bobby didn't have time to think about his father's disapproval. He stayed busy with a special project. He spent a couple hours a day on it, coming back from Ian's garage each day with the assurance that he was morphing into a rugged man, a real man. He hoped that Kindle wouldn't smell paint and wood on him.

March drew to a close and Kindle had yet to confess her love. She did say that she loved the way his hair smelled like peaches after he took a shower. She said that she loved the way that he looked at her sometimes. She said that she loved that he knew how to maintain a tidy home, even if he knew nothing about cooking.

Bobby found some way to slip in an "I love you" every day, sometimes twice a day when he thought it might encourage her to reciprocate. Who couldn't love a girl like Kindle? he wondered. When he watched her practice her soliloquies, he would hum softly, "My Kindle wants to be a superwoman...." Truly, she was a girl after his own heart.

Girls like this were one in a billion—girls who weren't willing to give themselves away in a single day.

In 1977, Bobby had asked brown-haired, grey-eyed Rachel Hartford to marry him. Not only had she said no, she had asked who he knew that married young if they hadn't killed the rabbit.

"Be free, babe," she said. "We have forever and a day. We can do other stuff, if you want. We don't have to be married to do that."

Bobby hated how Rachel talked to him like he was mentally retarded, like she could be his sex-educator or something. It was over for him the day she rejected his proposal, but he officially ended it the next week.

His friends questioned what kind of weirdo he was. What kind of guy only got to first base and left a girl waiting for him to hit a homerun? What was he waiting for?

At the time Bobby could only laugh lightly at the questions, unsure of how to put into words what he was waiting for, why girls like Rachel Hartford and Betty Warner weren't it. As he watched Kindle perform daily, he realized there was no longer any need to put into words what stood right before him.

****

A silver half-moon reflected a portrait of a cement building and a brick building onto the canal's shimmering water. At an angle, the grey cement structure faced the canal from nearly a mile away. Standing tall and regal, that building was the industrial pride of the city skyline. The other building was a rustic brick edifice, lodged only feet from the water. In fact, it looked as though it were floating upon the current, supported by the wild grass at its front. The building was stacked with several rows of windows, like eyes looking out over travelers.

Kindle and Bobby stared at the brick building from across the small channel of water. Behind them, a ratty walkway lined by a shabby metal fence led away from the canal. Several feet above the water, a thin stone slab aligned the edge of the channel. It was on this edge that Bobby and Kindle sat, their feet dangling just above the water.

The slow fall of rain wrinkled their reflection upon the water. The hood of Kindle's bright yellow raincoat covered her hair and irradiated her face. Her cheekbones glistened, her lips glimmered. The raindrops printed dark splotches on Bobby's grey sweatshirt and blue jeans. His white shoelaces wagged over the water.

"Do you think it's really gonna start pouring?" Bobby asked, slipping his damp hair behind his ear. He spewed sunflower seeds into the water; they blended in with the rain drops. "I never can tell the weather here."

Kindle locked her leg underneath his. Slowly extending her leg back and forth, her heavy heel knocked against the cement. "I haven't got the slightest idea," she said. "You should have brought a raincoat. I suggested it for a reason." Kindle rubbed her shoulder up his arm. "But I must say that that rain suits you very well. Your lips are maroon."

Bobby blew out a cold, smoky mist before their faces. "Pretty rad, huh?" He poured sunflower seeds into her hands. "I never really liked the rain. It's kind of depressing."

"It doesn't matter one way or the other to me." Kindle maneuvered a seed out of its shell with her teeth. "My mother died on a sunny day. The final gathering for her was on a rainy day. She died near this time of year. I think it was this day, actually." Spitting the shells in the water, she deliberated. "Weather's not really a good predictor of anything."

Bobby looked out over the channel. He wondered if he could penetrate the murky water with his eyes, if it was actually possible to see to the bottom. He couldn't see beyond the ripples on the surface of the water. He sighed, draping his arm over Kindle's shoulders.

"Would you like to know something creepy?" Kindle peeped up at him, like a baby bird previewing the outside world from its nest.

Bobby smiled.

"My mother isn't at the plot at the cemetery."

"I don't understand what you mean." Bobby cupped the back of her head and began fondling the coated nylon. "Where is she?"

Kindle pressed her hands against the cement, lifting herself to her feet. She patted her hands together, dispelling tiny pebbles from her palms. "She's here."

He cracked a shell with his teeth and threw into the water the handful of shells he had collected in his hand. He shook his head. "You mean, like supernatural?" Softly, he added, "I don't really believe in ghosts or anything like that."

"Nor do I. But if you don't know it already, cremations are far less expensive than purchasing a casket or gravestone, etcetera, etcetera."

Bobby tugged on her pants, settling her back down to the ground beside him. "Who do you visit at the gravesite then? Who is that person?"

She laughed artificially, loud and airy. She cracked the shell of a seed with her teeth, spitting the remains into the water. "Please don't make the story any stranger than it already is. The gravestone is my mother's. Or technically, it belongs to Mr. Holster, since he bought it. But no one lies beneath the stone."

Bobby stared at the water once more. The rain had lightened to a drizzle and the water was suddenly flat, without tide, without ripple, tiny images of the stars mirrored on it.

"There was only Mr. Holster and me. We were both at her bedside when she passed on. We didn't need a real funeral. We just had a gathering at a church with some others from the hotel. That's all, really." Kindle rocked from side to side. "You know, I had actually thought my father would have found out and that he would have attended. I don't know why I thought that." She laughed. "It's really strange."

"Yeah."

Kindle raised her eyebrows, as if expecting something more than simple agreement.

Bobby shuddered as a gust of cold wind swept through his damp hair. Kindle's hungry look made him uneasy. He didn't know what to say.

When he had returned from rehearsal earlier that evening,
she had moseyed over to him, grinning. She decided that she
wanted to take a walk to the Canal, to show Bobby a place
where he might find inspiration for a song. Exhausted as he
was, he followed her out the door. Along the way, Kindle had
looped her arm through his and do-sa-do'ed with him in the
middle of one of the wet streets. She had joked about how the
few prickly hairs that had grown from his chin since the last
time he had shaved made him a savage beast. She talked about
the fact that the hotel she and her mother used to work at was
formerly called The Dreamery and that before it was a hotel, it
was a cotton mill her grandfather once worked at. Bobby
watched her with a half-smile.

Neither disenchanted nor entirely intrigued by Kindle's
capriciousness, Bobby sat content for the first few minutes they
spent sitting in silence at the canal. He contemplated how water
might be used as a symbol and what simple lyrics he could
memorize, not having a pen and paper or his guitar.

Now, the tone had changed. From her voice, she sounded
neither entirely serious nor entirely joking. Maybe she wanted
to cry. Her voice sounded like she might suddenly burst into
tears, but her eyes did not water.

"So, you expected your father to be there. Why…why do
you think that you expected that?" he tried.

Kindle shook her head, biting the knuckle of her index
finger.

He gripped her wrist, dislodging her hand from her
mouth. "Is something, like, wrong?"

Before she fluttered her eyes, Bobby spotted the veil of
tears she flushed down. "Mr. Holster gave me her urn, Bobby. I
was supposed to keep it in my home. I do keep it there. It's that
green vase that you knocked over."

Bobby's rubbed the inner corner of his eye. "I'm sorry,"
he replied softly. "I didn't know. But I promise—nothing came
out but dust."

She laughed low. "I know. That's because on my way
home, I walked along this path and the urn fell in the grass.
That's where most of the ashes fell out." Kindle pointed at the
grass near the fence. "I tried to gather the ashes from the ground

to preserve as much as I could. Eventually, I just swept the ashes in the water with my feet. I dumped the remaining ashes in the water too. I got rid of all of it that day. I didn't even tell Mr. Holster. He probably thinks I keep my mother in my living room. It wasn't my idea to purchase the gravestone though. Mr. Holster purchased it because he said we needed some public memorial of her."

"That's really...*sad*. I don't understand," Bobby murmured. Placing the finished sunflower seed bag underneath his thigh, he leaned back on his hands.

"What is there to understand, really?"

"I guess I don't understand why you talk about your life like it's—"

"Like it's what?" She scooted closer to him, inspecting his face.

"Like it's not your own. Or maybe like it's not that important or something." Bobby pinched her hood at the crown of her head and drew it back. "My Aunt Catherine—that's Kyle's mom or whatever—she's always saying that if you can't own anything else, you may as well own your feelings. Kyle's pretty good at that."

"He's not necessarily my idol." She petted his fingers.

"Yeah." Bobby shrugged and folded in his lips. "But I guess you brought me here for some reason."

"I don't feel sad," Kindle said brazenly. She stood up and skipped over to the metal fence, gripping the crisscrossing wires as if she were a prisoner. "Not at all. It's not sadness that I feel."

"No?" Bobby observed Kindle from a distance. She had begun mining the dirt with her feet.

"No. It's probably more along the lines of anger. I was put in charge of a silly vase. If she kept more people around, we could have afforded a real funeral." Kindle's loose curls bobbed when she shook her head. "You know, my mum claimed to be so practical, but how practical is it to be alone all the time? She had contact with no family or friends. What did she expect to happen in the case of her death? Did she expect that her only child would be able to carry the burden? It's not at all responsible. Ill-preparation is to blame."

Ashamed of the fact that her sudden agitation had put him off, Bobby finally stood and scrambled to her side. "People never really get sick on purpose."

"People don't live alone by accident. The world is far too big to easily live in seclusion. Yet, somehow, she managed that."

"Seclusion can make you feel..." He paused affectedly. "It can make you feel lonely, right?"

Kindle tossed her hair up to the top of her head, leaving her neck exposed. She really was a swan. "I'm surprised you can pronounce that word. Lonely." She spun around. "I have a wonderful song line for you: *When the urn drops, the only thing you can own is your feelings. Lonely.*" She lifted her foot from the ground and held it against the fence. Her shoe had etched a zigzagged canyon in the mud. Mud drops flapped from the sides of her shoe. She spread her arms out over the fence coolly. "Have you ever felt so lonely that you talked to yourself to feel that someone would?"

"No. Not that I can remember." He rubbed his hands together in front of his thighs.

Bobby pondered how he could inject comfort in the following silence. He considered that he could try relating, recalling to her his own parental problems, how the last time he had seen his father, they'd had a fight over his so-called rock and roll foolishness, how his father had found the nerve to come to his and Kyle's apartment to call him a deadbeat before dashing his Fender against the wall, completely destroying it. Maybe he could explain to her that Kyle had been the one to call the ambulance when his father had had another seizure after Bobby couldn't keep himself from hemming the old man against the wall, his arm at his throat. Perhaps he could tell her that part of the reason he had left Canton for England was that if he had stayed, there might be no one left to save his father if they got into another argument.

Yet, Bobby realized that she didn't need to hear his past troubles. She needed a protector of her own. He could see in her a quaking volcano, intensifying with every second, until finally, he heard the sudden surge. She wheezed, curled over and sobbed vehemently. Bobby caressed her back, towing her forward so that her head huddled into his stomach.

Still hunched over with her arm wrapped around her stomach, Kindle pushed him back. "I don't need to be held."

They endured another moment of silence before she heaved a trembling sigh and cried once more. Knees wobbling and shoulders vibrating, she reached for Bobby, curling his sweatshirt between her fingers. She used him as levy to stand and wrapped her arms around him. With her head snuggled into his chest, her feet on the tips of his own, her hands folded together on the small of his back, Bobby breathed deeply. He was greater than a hunter, stronger than a fighter, more enduring than an athlete. He was a man capable of holding together a broken woman.

Bobby pressed her back. "Is this why I'm still here? Is this why you haven't made me leave yet?"

Kindle's shoulders suddenly drooped. She looked up at him, more innocent than a deserted child.

He nodded, completely and utterly in love with her innocence. He wanted to cover her more than anything in the whole wide world—now, with only his words, but someday soon, with his entire body. "Well, for me—for how I feel—I like being married to you." Bobby puckered his lips, shrugged and tickled her scalp with his fingertips. "It's better than sunflower seeds. It's better than thrift shops. Better than November last year, before I met you."

****

"What do you think of me, Kindle?"

Betty dropped down to the floor beside Kindle, her arms and shoulders juddering from the pound of her behind against the thin carpet. She brought her legs together meditative style, both feet resting on their opposite calf. Twirling her long, black wig braid around her hand, she chewed her gum raucously, a mist of saliva deploying with each gnaw. She pressed her arm against Kindle's as Kindle rolled her head around in circles.

"Do you hear what I say? What do you think of me?"
Betty repeated. She slanted her head, looking up at Kindle's
profile.

Betty and Kindle were tucked away in the corner of the
room waiting for Nigel to arrive. Kindle had planned to practice
the skit once more. She intended to impress outstandingly
Nigel, to wrestle his attention away from the other students. All
of the students stood on level ground this day. Even Betty could
not steal his attention with her appearance. She, like the rest,
was forced to wear a black leotard and black leggings.

With her index finger, Betty poked Kindle's bicep. "Aye.
Such tone. Such a lovely figure." She tenderly tangled her
fingers through Kindle's curls. "Such lovely hair. You are
different from us. In a way, maybe that makes you the bees
knees."

Kindle seized back her ponytail and flicked Betty's
fingers away with her own. "You made it apparent that you
don't like my kind."

Betty scrabbled through the fat, black shoulder bag at her
side and dug out a silver-wrapped piece of gum. She held it out
to Kindle in the palm of her hand. Kindle ogled the lines etched
in Betty's palm. She was caught off guard by the silkiness of
her skin when she slid the piece of gum from Betty's hand.
Kindle looked her over, fascinated by her features—the quiet
sparkle in her sleepy, princess eyes, the dramatic arc of her
waist, the striking angle of her cheekbones.

Betty bit the insides of her cheeks, further articulating the
exotic quality of her face. "I told you that I was only pissing
around. My best friend Maddie is a Paki." Betty laughed. "On
top of that, I'm a Northern Monkey. You can't take me too
seriously, Love."

Kindle arched her back, bending forward to stretch her
fingertips to the tips of her shoes. Betty scooted to the end of
Kindle's legs and offered her hands. "I'll help you."

Kindle gripped her hands, allowing Betty to gently
stretch her forward.

"I want to know what you think of me. I don't want to
make any unnecessary enemies. Besides, you're a lovely girl, I
think."

"Thank you," Kindle returned, pacing her breath, attempting to ease the strain on her ligaments. "You can loosen up. Please."

She pulled harder. "Maybe you and me will end up as friends."

Kindle squirmed. "Let me loose!"

"Oh dear. I'm sorry." Betty loosened her grip and released Kindle's hands with a motherly pat. She crawled back to her bag and wiggled out a pair of glasses. She pushed the black-framed glasses up her nose, peering at Kindle through purple lenses. "I'm sure that we will share many things in common. Obviously, we're both just aficionados of the fine arts, yeah?"

Kindle gaped.

****

By Friday, Bobby had seen Kindle only a few times during the week, and each time, only in passing. While she attended acting class during the day, Bobby and The Dare rehearsed. At night, he performed while she worked.

Bobby ended Friday's rehearsal early, beginning at ten in the morning and packing up to leave Ian's garage by one. He needed to make two trips to carry the lumber from Ian's house to the apartment.

When Bobby made it inside the apartment with the second set of wood, he placed it on the floor. Out of his coat pocket, he pulled a plastic bag full of nails, screws and a hammer.

He sectioned off the first two wood pieces.

He began to sing as he worked.

May I, May I…

****

"Go ahead and ask me," Betty said. "I know you want to."

The room was dark, save the seven candles Nigel had lit to add drama to each student's soliloquy. Miriam stood in the middle of the circle, pouring out her heart to the theme of *Hamlet.* Betty sat next to Kindle in the circle, whispering in her ear. She smelled like cherry bubble gum.

"Yes, I'm Alex from the bathroom," Betty went on. "Yes, I'm Ricky's aficionado. Yes, I am the one who got Ricky and his band the gigs at Band on the Wall. Yes, I've spent a lot of time with the band lately. Yes, yes, yes. Have I answered all of your questions?"

Miriam waved her arms, quoting lines about slings and arrows of fate.

"Have I answered them or not?" Betty repeated, loud enough for the class to hear her.

Miriam stopped mid-sentence and glowered at Betty. Betty simpered. Miriam rolled her eyes and returned to her lines.

"Answer me," Betty said, pressing her lips against Kindle's ear. "Please."

Kindle spoke through clenched teeth, staring at Miriam. "What is it that you want from me, Alex, Betty, or whatever you call yourself? If you want Bob—" she stopped, renegotiating how much she was willing to give. "If you want Ricky, then all I can tell you is to follow your heart. If it were really possible for you to have him, I'm sure you would have had him already."

Betty laughed. Miriam glowered again. From the front left corner of the room where he stood, Nigel put his index finger to his lips.

"You're the cat's meow, aren't you?" Betty whispered, crossing her legs toward Kindle. "You're so sure of yourself. I admire that about you."

Kindle glanced sharply at Betty.

"I just want a chance," Betty said, her volume rising marginally with each word. "There are far more women on the earth than men. That's the reason why each man should have a go with a variety of women before making his final decision. You got a chance to know Ricky, I presume. I just want a go." Betty crossed her arms. "Does he love you? Some married people don't love each other. That is, if you really are married. Ricky hasn't said one way or the other." She stopped, looked up once at Miriam before looking at Kindle again and dropping her voice. "Are you pregnant? Because if you are, then that's no reason to stay in a relationship. I just want a little chance with Ricky, just to see if we could get on good. I think that he may have slight feelings for me."

Betty's voice had moved up significantly from a whisper, cutting straight through the end of Miriam's soliloquy.

Miriam stomped over to Betty. "What is your problem?" she demanded. "You're like a wild beast,"

Betty smiled. "I'm so sorry. I didn't mean it. If it makes you feel better, you can talk during my entire monologue."

Nigel moved to the middle of the circle. "Please, let's try to get along. Betty, please keep quiet during the performances. Miriam, job well done."

Betty turned to Kindle immediately, as if Nigel's voice were as consequential as rustling leaves. "So, are you going to allow me a chance?" Betty asked.

Nigel coughed softly. "Let us see. Who will go next?" He pointed at Kindle. "Are you ready, dear? It's your turn now."

Kindle nodded and stood.

Betty circled her hand around Kindle's wrist. "You gonna give me a chance or aren't you?" She whispered. "It would only be nature's way."

Kindle wiggled her wrist away. "I'm sorry, *Betty*," she said, "but it's my turn now."

****

Bobby nailed down the last piece of wood, extra careful not to beat the nail into his finger. He couldn't have anything compromise his playing. He stepped back to look at the near-complete project. Couple more hours till show time. He hummed to himself, hammering the lyrics into his memory.

May I, May I...

****

That evening, Kindle walked through the city in sneakers a half-size too small. She curled her toes as she hurried along. Having only paid five pounds for them, she could manage the discomfort. The thrift store's pickings were slim, at best. From her first and only visit there, Kindle had also picked up the black-and-white spandex shirt and tattered black jeans that she wore. She had brushed her wet curls straight so that her hair covered her entire back like a cape.

Kindle entered the line that curled out from the building. The crowd here was more pierced and tattooed than the ones that visited her pub, especially the square-faced man with pink hair that stepped out of his place in line and tapped her shoulder.

"You look hot," he said. He wore a white shirt and a black leather jacket littered with silver stones. A silver nose ring looped over his nostril.

"Thank you," Kindle mumbled.

"Is this your debut here? Never seen you here before."

"I've never been here."

"I've seen you somewhere before though."

Kindle turned her back to him. "Doubtfully."

"Yes, I have. Waitress at Rory's, aren't you? I've been there a few times, you know."

"I see."

"You've seen these guys before, haven't you? Dudes are fucking tubular!" He began to shout, his voice carrying so that the whole line could hear him. "Hey, Dare Heads! We're gonna tear the place apart, aren't we?"

Some of the crowd ignored him, continuing with their chatter, but a great deal of them shouted back in agreement.

It was then that Kindle felt that her and Bobby's secret should be exposed.

She stood in front of the ticketholder. "I'm family of Bobby Carter."

"Who's Bobby Carter?" the ticketholder responded, counting his tickets.

She shook her head and paid silently.

Inside, Kindle found her way to the bar in the back, as she was accustomed to doing at her pub. Once there, she was lodged securely in the throng of punks.

When the band entered the stage, Kindle held her breath. Bobby's skin gleamed as he stood embracing his guitar, poised like a statue. The air conditioner above rippled through his hair. He did not attempt speaking over the crowd but counted off and began playing and singing. At first, hard and loud. The performance went on as a showcase of the colors he could create with his voice. Sometimes he sang with a screech—red and wild, neon with staccato. Other times with a mumble—cold and blue, persistent and melodic. No matter the tone, the crowd hung onto his every inflection, moving when he moved, slowing down when he slowed down.

His voice rang more mystic than she remembered. It was raspier but his tone richer. It was deeper and more deliberate. He moved as though having a love affair with his microphone stand and guitar, keeping in perfect tune with the audience. When the crowd cheered for more, he gave more with his voice, with his body. If they stood in quiet enchantment, he closed his eyes as though in a daydream. He avoided announcing songs, but rather, melded one song into the next. Was this how a virgin knew to make love?

In the four months since he left her pub, he had become something else, no longer just a musician but an entertainer.

Kindle stood on a metal bar at the bottom of the bar counter, raising herself up to see over the tall men in front of her.

The bar tender behind her yelled to her over the music. He was American. She had heard his accent all night long as he took orders. "In a trance, aren't you?"

Kindle looked back at him. "What did you say?"

"You look like you're hooked."

"They are very good," she said, at a loss.

"Better than good. Especially Ricky Stallion. You're going to see that guy on TV soon. Promise you that."

"Why do you say?"

The bar tender slapped a white rag over his shoulder. "Cuz you can't keep a band like that off the ground. Well, I don't know about the band, but the front guy's got it."

She nodded and faced the stage once more.

Bobby finally spoke to the crowd, his voice familiar, but floating, transcending the very small, very corporeal quality it took in the apartment "Hey. Hey. Hey, guys."

The audience continued whistling.

"Quiet for a minute, will ya?" he yelled.

They hushed.

He smiled, looking down at his guitar. "Thanks, guys, for everything. This is our last song for the night. I really hope you like it."

Kindle glanced around the room once before Bobby began plucking a simple melody. The drums entered and picked up the pace. The bass was a thumping heartbeat, a foreshadowing, a mystery.

It happened by accident
The desire you gave
The love I spent

It happened by accident
Sweet Child of November,
I never planned for it
But since we collide
I'm crying to come inside
Oh, May I, May I

It happened by accident
Like secret fate
It won't relent

It's never broken, never bent
One in a billion
Lottery of events

Run but never hide
Let me set your fear aside

Oh, May I, May I

The melody changed abruptly, bringing the song to its
bridge. It was the soundtrack of a daydream.

Baby,
I've loved you a thousand times in my head.
Satin sheets and a whisper
On our brand new bed

Baby,
I've loved you a million ways in my heart
Fireside, heat, an ember
The Kindle that sparks

He returned to the former melody, changing the musical
phrasings of his voice and guitar to press the song onward to its
climax.

It happened by accident
The desire you gave
The love I spent

Yeah, it happened by accident
But I live it on purpose
Loving you's my true intent

Cuz sweet dreams never die
I'm still crying to come inside
Oh, Baby, May I, May I

Bobby and Kyle stopped playing, leaving a single
marching drumbeat. Slowly, Bobby began to sing, his voice
growing louder with each syllable. Kyle sang a soft harmony,
repeating Bobby's words. Over and over again, they sang:

May I, May I

The song came down in a perfect decrescendo—one in which the audience stood silent at the end, mesmerized. What would punks do with a song like this?

To Kindle, it didn't matter. She knew what she would do. As the band left the stage and the crowd began to disband, Kindle pushed her way to the door through which the band disappeared. The door was locked.

A young woman walked up beside Kindle, barely taking notice of her as she inserted a key in the door. Her fire engine red hair fell like a curtain over either side of her face as she turned the key. She walked in, switching, the top of her thighs an appetizer for her nearly exposed behind in her black miniskirt. Kindle held the door before it closed entirely. She peeped through the slight crack.

****

"My dearest Ricky," Betty chimed. She whispered in Bobby's ear while veiling his eyes with one hand and caressing his back with the other.

Bobby dipped his head down, slipping her hand off his eyes. He angled his face at her and then looked back at the table. Today's wig was red, today's lipstick black.

Mickey, at first standing on the other side of the table, caught Bobby's eyes and then Betty's before he strolled over to the corner where Kyle and Larry packed up their instruments.

"I lose," she said, tugging on a lock of his hair. "I have to compliment you. You amazed them. But you don't amaze me. I already knew it was in you."

"Thanks, Betty."

She yanked his shoulder, spinning him around on the stool. "Do you mind having a look at me? I'm really not a troll."

"I know," Bobby responded. He inclined his knees away from her.

"If I tell you something intriguing, will you believe me?"

"I guess it depends on what it is." He slumped down, placing his elbow on the table and supporting his head in the palm of his hand.

"In my Alex days, I met someone very special. Someone you might be interested in."

"Alex days?

She gripped either side of his face so that he faced her. "Can you keep your mind on the point at hand? I know someone special. His name is Spencer. He's got a little label that you might be interested in. I could pass him a demo from your little band. It would be easy-peasy."

"What's the cost?" entered Kyle. He moved to the place where Mickey had first stood.

"Haven't you any business of your own?" Betty challenged. She winked at Kyle, grinning so that her pink gums and white teeth shone as bright as lightning against her black mouth.

"Don't you have anything better do than throw yourself at Prince Stallion?"

"Not particularly." She shooed him away, flapping her hand. Grabbing Bobby's face once more, she whispered, "There is only one small cost. Just one." She tapped her breast and out of her bustier fell a small silver packet. She caught it with her hand and held it up before his eyes, like a doggie treat. "It will hardly cost you."

Bobby blinked and looked over his shoulder. Kyle caught his eye, smiling. Turning back toward Betty, he wiped his hands together. "No offense or anything, I don't really see that happening."

Betty and Bobby both glanced sharply at the door as it gently clasped shut.

Betty wound her red hair over her shoulder. "Sounds like one of your groupies listening at the door." With an exaggerated pout, she clipped her heel against the floor. "Well, fiddlesticks!"

Bobby squeezed his lips together, trying to avoid a smile.

Betty grinned and pulled his sleeve. "You can laugh, Ricky. It's okay. No big deal. I'll get you sooner or later. But for now, we shall simply be mates." She blew a kiss at him as she marched toward the door.

"So when can we get you that demo tape?" Kyle yelled before she disappeared.

She spun around. "Certainly not now. Everything has its price. I'm sure I'll coax Mr. Stallion into paying up soon enough. He won't regret it." Betty glanced once at Bobby before closing the door behind her.

Bobby wiped the sweat from his brow and frowned.

****

When Bobby arrived home, Kindle wasn't there. He'd expected that they would arrive home at the same time, but it was better this way.

He reclined on the couch, sipping apple juice through a straw when she pushed through the front door.

"What happened to you?" he inquired, for lack of better words. He wanted to say she looked like a dream, but that was more trite than he wanted to chance.

"What a greeting." She took a seat on top of the television.

"No. No, I don't mean that in a bad way. You look like a, um, dream."

"Perhaps more like a nightmare. I know my getup is a bit gutter punkish."

"No, no. Like a fantasy. You look really, um, very beautiful. I mean that. Really." Bobby chewed the tip of his straw. "You wore that to work?"

"I did." Kindle looked down and then up again at him. She crossed her legs. "How was your night?"

"Killer, completely killer." He wagged his legs open and shut.

"Good for you."

"Well, what about yours? What about your day? What did Nigel say about your soliloquy thing? I haven't seen you in, like…" He counted on his fingers, then smiled. "Forever."

"Everything was lovely." Kindle stretched her arms up and stared at the ceiling, grinning. The imprint of her dimples made his stomach flutter. "He's recommending me for a local audition. Nobody else, though. That's what he said after I did a skit."

Setting his cup down, Bobby knelt before her and held his hand up. "Killer, Kindle. See. What'd I tell you? I knew it was gonna happen for you."

She clapped his hand. "Yes. You did say that." She yawned, stretching her arms again. "I know. Do you smell chemicals? Paint? Something like that?"

Bobby jutted out his bottom lip and shook his head. "Little bit. Maybe." He tickled her underarm. "Sleepy?"

She dropped her arms and squirmed, laughing softly. "I am. But we can stay up together. In fact, I'll sleep on the other couch. We'll have another slumber party."

"That's totally cool." He glanced at the floor.

Bobby watched her walk away. He had expected something to happen when she reached her room. He thought maybe he'd hear her shriek. Maybe hear her gasp. Maybe hear her shoes clamber against the floor as she ran to him. But he heard nothing. He walked to the room and stood behind Kindle.

Beside her, Bobby admired the bed that he had made with his own hands. The bed was made of wood paneled together evenly, polished and painted forest green. He had constructed a headboard with five strips of thick wood that he bounded together and rounded off. The mattress that once sat on the floor now lay between two wood panels. The sheets were fern, the comforter surprisingly downy. The room smelled of wood and paint, like a new house.

Kindle looked back at him, flummoxed.

"I made it." He wrapped his arms around himself.

She still wore her bewilderment with an open mouth. Maybe she was trying to decide what question she should ask first.

"It's love, I think," he said, answering the question of why. "This is what I feel like love makes me do."

Kindle gave him a short glance and walked to the bed, patting and rubbing it as if it were a petting zoo animal.

"I like the color green. I once heard that it means, like, newness." He walked to the bed and sat on the edge of it. It was as sturdy as it was when he first tested it out. He patted the space next to him. "Will you sit?"

Slowly, she took a seat on the bed smiling, obviously as impressed by its sturdiness as he had been. "I can't believe this," she said.

"Me neither. I didn't think I could do it."

Kindle chewed on her top lip. "You're too much, Mr. Stallion. Out of this world. How did you get here?"

"On my spaceship." He grinned.

"And you landed at my pub."

"And you hid me away in your house, like Bigfoot or something."

"People hide Bigfoot in their homes?"

"I guess I just made that up?"

She sat her legs up on the bed, sitting Indian-style. "Bobby, I have a something to tell you."

"Is it bad?"

"No."

"Tell me, then."

With a sly smile, she said, "I was at your show."

He smiled back quietly.

"Yes, I was there. And, yes, I know that the attire gives it away."

"I guess it does." He bounced backward on the bed, his head landing on the pillow, his hair outlining his shoulders. "That's so cool, man." He sat up again quickly. "What'd you think?"

She scrunched up her nose and shook her head.

"It sucked?"

"No." She smiled. "Not at all. You already must know how perfect you were."

He lay down again, pulling her with him by the wrist. Their heads shared the pillow. "So we're both making it. Now, I have to see you in a play or something. "

"You'll have to wait, my good fellow. It will take a lot of preparation before you will see me. You are stiff competition."

"I don't wanna be your competition," he said.

"Good. Because I'm relentless."

"Yeah? In that case, I give up."

Their eyes met before they broke out into laughter. They laughed louder and louder, tickled by one another's amplified laughter. Bobby cut short her last laugh, gently squeezing her chin and bringing his lips to hers. He kissed her slowly and rhythmically, without any thought except how it felt to have her hands pushing against his chest, as though she were signaling him not to come further. Yet, she followed the pace of his lips, the pattern of his mouth brushing over hers again and again in perfect time.

He kissed her until he was out of breath, until his lips were the same color hers had been, until he was sure he would suffocate if he did not stop.

"I know I broke the rules," he said with a single blink of his eyes. "Forgive me."

"You don't need my forgiveness," Kindle said, catching her breath. "Trust me."

"So that means I'm safe?"

"Don't think of it." She rose up slightly, bracing herself on her elbows. "I may have loved it."

Bobby braced himself on his elbow also. "That's good then, right?"

Kindle snaked his shirt between her fingers, staring at her hand and not him, as though she were commanding her fingers with her eyes. She lifted her face so that their noses brushed. He inhaled her warm, gently flowing breath. She finally gave in entirely, dipping her mouth over his long and resolutely. In that moment, they became two kids exploring the variety of a French kiss.

Bobby stopped abruptly. "You have a lot of power in your lips," he said. "Did you know that? I don't know if I can keep myself from you."

Kindle rubbed her lips together. "Who's telling you to?" She searched his eyes.

He raised his eyebrows. "Wow. Are you, like, serious?" She nodded.

Bobby sat all the way up, exhaling shakily. "Wow. Like, wow."

She sat up. "Now, get on with it, before the moment passes."

Bobby's soft laughter slipped out. Maybe joy had squeezed his insides. He looked her in the eyes one long time, silently asking one more time, "May I?" before reaching for her midsection, crumpling her shirt in between his fingers and gliding it up her body. He kissed her face and neck, struggling to unfix her bra until she reached behind herself, unfastening it for him. He backed away to look at her. The sight was better than he had dreamed, surreal really. The outline of her undergarment was tattooed on her shoulder, like a swirl of French vanilla against caramel. Again, his soft laughter slipped away from him.

Kindle pulled her long hair over her breasts. She looked like a picture of Eve in the Garden. "Are you okay?" she asked.

He nodded quickly. He did what he felt he should, crossing his arms over his body and lifting his shirt over his head. Kindle laughed.

"I know. Strange tattoo, right?" he said.

She nodded and smiled as he brought forth his lips to hers again. He recalled the place where he had mentally marked to kiss her, pressing both of his lips over her bottom lip— tasting it, nibbling it, savoring it—until Kindle pulled herself back to ask, "What does it mean? The tattoo, I mean."

Bobby picked up her hand and glided her fingers across his upper chest where the small Chinese letters had been printed a year ago by a bearded tattoo artist. The prickling of her fingertips shot electric bullets through his veins. He was near dizzy with the knowledge that it would really happen this evening.

"The word means 'love,'" he said.

"What did you know about love when you got it?" she whispered.

"Nothing," he whispered back. "Nothing at all."

At the time, he had only known that *Love* was his favorite Lennon song. Now, he only knew that true love was the only thing that he wanted to make. Thus, he leaned Kindle back so that her head rested on the pillow, before untying her shoes and taking them off one-by-one, setting them neatly on the floor. He watched her watching him intently as he peeled down her jeans.

He laughed again. "Purple."

She nodded. "It's the only color underwear my mum ever bought me, since purple was my favorite color when I was a little girl. Needless to say, I stuck with the tradition."

Amused, he traced the white trim, at the crease of her leg and pelvis. "Man, I love you," he said, pushing stray hairs back from her face. He was astonished by how easily love could be the guide of the inexperienced. He kissed and touched her expertly, as softly as he knew how, as much a gentleman as he could possibly be in light of his pulsing desire. Certainly, sailors weren't need for this night.

As he pressed his wet mouth over her neck like a ripened peach, she suddenly began to laugh. "To be so chaste, you certainly are very *aware*. I knew your naughtiness knew no bounds."

Bobby breathed a pensive laugh. "Pretty sure we haven't seen the half of my naughtiness." He placed his finger over lips. "No more laughing for now."

She nodded, and they both smiled softly before returning to the rhythm, the beat, the pace, the melody that would lead them through the rest of the night.

****

So close those eyes
You can close your eyes
We'll be fine
I don't have a love song
But I won't sing the blues anymore
Oh, but I can hear this song
And you will know this song
When I'm gone

Kindle fixed her eyes on Bobby as he hummed the song. "Those aren't the words, Mr. Stallion," she said with a mild laugh. Stallion—a perfectly fitting word for a man who would not give up on pleasure until she panted, sighed, and smiled with heavy lids. Who knew?

He smiled. "I know."

"So why are you singing them that way?"

"Because I'm not James Taylor. Nobody can do it like him."

Nobody can do it like you, she would have said. No one but you could fill up my life the way you have filled up my rooms, she would have continued. But to preserve the quiet simplicity of the moment, she only smiled.

Bobby and Kindle sat up at five in the morning, before the sun and after the moon. Bobby leaned against the headboard while Kindle sat in front of him. He had wrapped the green sheet tightly around her body, folding it inward at her chest to make a strapless dress of sorts. He had tossed the blanket over his lower body.

Bobby's eyes twinkled like diamonds in the dark.

"What does it mean?" Kindle asked.

"What does what mean?"

"The picture," she said, motioning towards the apple picture that hung on the wall. "I've always wondered."

He rubbed circles over his left eyelid. "Yeah. It's just what I was feeling at the time. I don't know."

"Is it like me and you? The two inner colors of the apple. Black and white."

"I didn't really think about it like that."

Kindle grazed her upper lip with her bottom teeth. "My place is with you," she announced.

Bobby closed his eyes, nodding.

"I thought about it, Bobby. I thought about it when you watched me rehearse a week ago, when I decided that it might be more than 'like' that I feel. You know, there are a million social divides that could keep soul mates apart. But you came here to England. To me. You crossed the dividing seas, didn't you?" She fit her fingers between his toes like a jigsaw. "Do you understand what I'm saying to you?"

"I think so," he responded softly. "But you know, like, the way I see it, love never really had a color. It's all black and white, really."

She smiled. "And so your picture really is lovely. What would you say? Killer, right?"

He leaned his head back and smiled, sniffed. "Thank you."

"Killer is a strange word for all things good, isn't it?"

"I never thought so. Not really."

Kindle reached forward to trace semi-circles on his shoulder. They showed up like red rainbows. "Have you ever really thought about it?"

"Yep, Kindle Carter. I have," he replied with a gentle smile.

"And?"

"I think it's like saying it's so great that it'll kill you. You'll just die." He leaned forward, closing his eyes and moving his lips from her right shoulder to the left, planting delicate kisses on each side. He looked up at her. "Like, uh, like how I feel being with you like this. Like I might die. Because life's not really supposed to be this good. Not really."

Summer

What is there to say about summer? It is the promise of love, the promise of the new sun, the deception of unfading beauty. It is the quiet season before the fall...

Chapter Fifteen

Summer was hot, especially for two young lovers.

Bobby's thoughts of Kindle could make for a thousand songs and not enough time to get them out. For Kindle, it made more intense her desire for embracing him and the stage and the entire world.

They began to wonder how many ways could they make love. They were two who had convinced themselves that they could truly *make* love out of pure desire. Lack of money could not prevent them from love. His mother's calls could not preclude it. A moment's argument couldn't counter it. Nothing could.

Nothing could make Bobby believe that Kindle wasn't the sweetest thing that ever was. Sweeter than Pop-Tarts. He had almost run out of those in the months he'd been in England. He got used to eating eggs and toast for breakfast, saving Pop-Tarts for special occasions. But he couldn't imagine getting used to not having her whenever he wanted. Bobby had never used a pet name for his former girlfriends—too embarrassed by the sound of "baby" or "sweetheart" coming out of his own mouth—but having decided that Kindle's love was the sweetest thing on earth, he got in the habit of calling her Sweetness.

When they were apart, he missed his Sweetness more times than he even wanted to admit. During shows, he often looked out over the crowd, hoping she had found some way to

skip out on work just to see him. There was actually one time
when she did. He noticed her in a back row, smiling up at him,
coltish.

In the middle of the last song of The Dare's set, Bobby
unstrapped his guitar from his chest and hopped down from the
stage. The drums, the bass, the lead guitar, and the audience
went on monstrously, despite his dropped vocals and rhythm
guitar. The crowd jumped around rowdily, like fish caught on a
line, as Bobby cut through them, slowly but purposefully,
bundling his arms and squeezing his shoulders together to avoid
brushing against anyone.

When he reached her, Bobby gave her a slow gander.
That day, of all days, she was entirely dazzling, like an Old
Hollywood dame. She wore her hair straight again, but the front
was waved, shaping her face exquisitely.

She smiled. "Don't you have a show to finish?"

"You're a show-stopper." He smiled, running his fingers
along the front of her hair. "Was that too corny?"

She reached for his face, drawing his ear down to her
lips. She nibbled at his earlobe briefly and whispered, "Terrible
song line but quire a sweet sentiment, Stallion."

"Thanks, Penelope P." Bobby slid his hands down her
side, then lowered them to her backside, enthralled by what a
work of art her body had become, pleasured by the fact that he
had been a part of making it that way.

"Naughty boy." "She pulled his hands back up to her
waist. "You've become quite the reckless character as of late."

He had to agree. Love was an opiate. Before, he wouldn't
have abandoned the stage until the show was finished. Before,
he wouldn't have left his guitar on stage for the band to look
after. Moreover, he would have never dreamt of letting his
hands publicly roam private territory, but the last few weeks
had brought on so many firsts that he was open to anything.

"Dance with me," Kindle said suddenly, as another band
took the stage and began immediately playing.

He smiled. That was a first he hadn't expected. "To this
kind of music? I don't know about that."

She looked around at the crowd. "It could be fun."

Bobby laughed out loud at the thought of Kindle abandoning what rhythm she did have to become a punk go-go-er. "You seriously want to?"

"Have some fun, Ricky Stallion." She pressed her hands against his pelvis. "I am quite aware of your rhythm technique. You can't hide it anymore."

They both burst out into laughter.

Bobby bent down to kiss her. "Okay. Make you a deal, if you want. I'll do it if I can choose the kind of dancing we do."

"What kind will that be?"

"Slow-dancing." He grinned. "My mom taught me. For prom."

"You want to slow-dance to *this*?"

He smirked. "Why not?" Taking hold of her hand, he led her to the middle of the crowd.

She held her free arm over her chest, protecting herself from wild, jerking arms. "I think we'll need some calmer music."

"I can handle that." He cleared his throat, setting his hands on her hips. "Baby, baby, baby," he sang over and over in her ear, creating their own slow melody in the midst of chaos. "Ba-a-a-by..."

"What fine lyrics," she laughed, moving to the tune of the music he made.

Bobby knew then that they were prince and princess, their love having bitten the universe in two and emerging from the divide, a domain all their own. It was a domain where nothing and no one else mattered. Bobby wished there was a way to express all that he felt. He wished he could sum up himself and give it all to her—his past, his present, his future. He wished there was a way to give her every hope and secret of his heart. It just seemed like words would never be enough to express it all.

"Do you ever get the feeling that you want to say a lot," he asked, looking down at her, "but you don't even know where to begin. Seems like there aren't enough words."

"That's what song lyrics are for. You can say it all in one line."

He nodded, knowing his attempt would be futile. "You can have anything you want from me. It's yours." He breathed. "That's all I really want to say."

He held her even closer, hoping to keep the punks from bumping into her with their sloppy movements. Though he tried keeping her untouched, a whirlpool of madness began. The group around them had begun to bump into each other, purposely inciting anarchy On the outer of edges of what was becoming a mosh pit, he spotted Betty. She smiled at him, blowing a kiss.

Immediately, Bobby bent down. "Hop up," he said, tapping Kindle's leg. "We need to go before it gets crazy."

She mounted his back quickly, and he stood, hurrying out the door, praying that Kindle had neither seen Betty nor Betty Kindle. It was better that Kindle found no need for jealousy and that Betty found no other entrance into his life.

All the way home, Bobby carried Kindle piggyback, strolling through the muggy black evening. She acted as his tour guide, pointing out the broken down buildings, identifying their special place in Manchester history. Without them, she had explained, there could be no room for the current artistic movement. She asserted that the old textile mills and the surrounding homes where the laborers lived were not rubbish. They supported and inspired the city's distinctiveness.

Perhaps Kindle was defending her own worth in light of her poverty. Bobby smiled and nodded the whole way, less excited by what she said than by the fact that she hadn't discovered that it was Betty Warner who had been the cause for their quick departure. Good thing Kindle wasn't a mind reader. She ate up his attentiveness.

When they entered the apartment, Kindle immediately tossed off her black shirt. "Holy Mother of God, it's hot."

Bobby smiled, snatching off his own shirt and pulling down his pants. "Careful. If you call on the Holy Mother of God, you should, like, ask for something."

"Forgive me, Father" she said, pulling off her own pants and underwear, facing him completely nude. "I forgot I was in the presence of clergy."

He grinned. taking off his last bit of clothing and lying on the floor, more comfortable nude with her than by himself. He enjoyed being seen by her, but more than that, he enjoyed seeing her as she lay down beside him, curling up at his side, resting her head on his arm.

They lay naked on the hardwood, watching the television, intermittently watching each other until they fell asleep. Yet, in the middle of the night, though still drunk with fatigue from rehearsal and the show, Bobby couldn't help skating his fingers down her stomach, up her chest, to the space between her breasts. She awakened immediately, looking him in the eyes. He pushed her hair from her face and scooped his hand underneath her back

She smiled softly, looking down at him. "What do you want from me?"

"I want to come in." He held her sides, positioning her to a perfect fit, breathing slowly at first, stunned again by the warm sensation of her inside. It was as though the sun shined inside of her, and they both glowed. "I want to stay inside," he murmured.

"Okay," she responded, nodding fervently.

"Alright," he breathed. He settled his hand on the back of her neck, pulling her down so that their noses touched and their rhythm became syncopated so that their bodies became like ocean waves, rising and falling with each other. He took special care to provoke her ever so gently until they reached the crest of the wave they had made. She did not shout or cry out, but but rather, she trembled and gushed, breathing Love's last breath, as Bobby held her face and brought her mouth to his. He kissed her, their lips meshing perfectly in their dampness. "I meant what I said earlier—" he whispered "—you can have anything you want from me."

Silent, she breathed softly into his mouth. Although he wanted to hear her say that she was his, he settled for the fact that her feelings were silent but palpable. He settled for the idea that maybe they would never explicitly say everything to one another but that there were other forms of expressions, ones in which they could speak deeply and celebrate each other at the same time.

Indeed, summer had arrived and each day seemed a cause for celebration.

****

"We don't celebrate The Fourth of July in England," Kindle said one late afternoon as they stood across from each other in their living room. She was practicing an Arthur Miller scene, hoping to sharpen her skills before her audition. Bobby read the lines of John Proctor. They were separated by the television set and the thin wall of sunlight that splashed through the living room window. An hour and a half had passed and she still wasn't satisfied with her performance. He thought her acting was perfect. She hadn't missed a single line and her accent was so convincing that he looked up from the book periodically to reconcile her face with the voice.

"I know you guys don't celebrate it here. But it's still the fourth day of July," Bobby replied.

"Yes, but it's not a holiday, so we have no need to celebrate it. In fact, it's like the anti-holiday here."

"But what if I just want to celebrate? Could we, like, take a short break from this?"

Kindle continued with her lines. "You are not open with me. You saw her with a crowd, you said. Now…"

Bobby read the next lines flatly and thus, caught an exasperated flash of Kindle's eyes.

She spoke her lines. "John, I am only—"

"I've never *not* celebrated the Fourth of July," Bobby said, bringing the script down from his eyes and tapping it against his leg. "So, I could take you out. It'd be like a real first date. I owe you one."

"Read the script, Bobby," Kindle commanded, her own accent in effect.

"Fine."

"Fine."

Bobby sang the lines opera-style. He stumbled over his last line. "Let you look sometimes for the goddess in me—" He chuckled. "I mean, 'goodness' in me and judge me not."

Kindle glared at him before reading the next lines with force.

He stared at her.

"Say your line," she demanded.

"It's still yours."

She crossed over to Bobby, standing with her arms folded against her chest before snatching the script from his hands. She looked it over, then bit the nail of her index finger. "So you were right. But you have to keep going anyway. You can't break the scene."

"Fine." Bobby pushed his hair back. "'Oh, Elizabeth, your justice would freeze beer.'"

"Do you have to sound like you're reading, Bobby?"

"Do I have to keep being this Proctor guy? He cheated on his wife, didn't he? I would never cheat on my wife."

She smirked, glancing at the floor.

"On top of that," Bobby said, "I don't drink beer or freeze beer or whatever. I don't think this character fits me."

Kindle tossed her head back. "So what do you want to do instead of this, Bobby?"

He touched her forehead with his and brought his lips close to hers.

Kindle clasped her hands together between their chests. "Too much of a good thing can be bad too. It makes you insensitive to the part of the world that suffers if you always get what you want."

"I don't get what you mean," he replied lazily, his lips brushing slowly against hers as he spoke.

"Fine then. I have an idea that will put you to work. You're going to write me another song, Bobby." She patted his chest and backed away.

Bobby grabbed hold of her wrist and brought it to his lips, kissing it softly. "Or you could write me a song instead."

****

Kindle thought she might be obsessed with Bobby. Was obsession following his every move? Was it finding bliss in the way he grabbed the neck of his guitar with one hand and tossed

himself back in the large chair? Was it adoring the way he
precisely balanced the guitar on his thigh, giving it such
attentive courtesy.

Bobby slid his hair behind his ear with his palm, rubbed
his eye, and began to tune his guitar. One side of his face was
made peach by the intruding sun. The sun painted the roots of
his hair chocolate.

Kindle attended her eyes to the blue-green vein that
rippled through the inward part of his upper arm. She chewed
on the nail of her thumb as she became once more fixated with
the smile lines around his mouth.

She had come to find that though he was a quiet man, he
was attentive and commanding with all things artistic—music
and love. He took his time loving her nearly every night,
pressing her firmly against their bed and provoking her gently
to release, in much the same way that he gripped his guitar,
making sounds come out of it more organic and beautiful than
she had ever heard.

Was she obsessed with him? Yes. But Kindle still had
mystique to preserve. She stood in place in the center of the
living room, pretending not to notice him.

Bobby patted his leg. At first, she thought he was
counting off the song until he did it again and looked up at her
with a smile. "Come here, Sweetness. Please."

Kindle strolled to him languidly, feigning dread. He took
hold of her wrist and set her on his thigh, her face brushing his
as she looked down and up again. His cheek was supple, as he
had shaved that morning. The peppermint scent of shaving
cream still danced off his skin. She couldn't help smiling.

"Can you play guitar like this?" she asked.

"I'm gonna try," he said. Bobby wrapped his arm around
her side to place his hand on the neck of his guitar.

Kindle leaned back and rotated her hips, making the
reach easier for him.

"Thanks," he said.

"So what will you play?"

Bobby shrugged. He began fingerpicking and looped
over and over an infectious melody. It sounded like a lullaby,
but the kind of lullaby Sarah Vaughn could make her own—

rich and dramatic at certain points. He looked up at her, as he balanced her legs on his knee. "So what are you gonna sing about?"

"I didn't know I'd be singing," she responded.

"Why don't you wanna sing about me?"

They laughed when he erred in his picking. He continued playing, fixing his eyes on the guitar.

"I don't want to sing another love song," Kindle said. "The airways are consumed with that."

"So, you wanna make a radio hit? Killer."

Kindle tickled the back of the guitar. "Of course, I do. But I will leave that field to you. However, if I do write a song, I would like it to be full of heart but not at all common."

"Then sing what's in your heart."

She tucked his hair behind his ear when it fell forward. "Well, that's a common saying, if I haven't heard one."

Bobby was silent, focused on his guitar, focused on the stroke of his right hand as he changed his picking to strumming. He commanded wood and wire, not as a conqueror but as a lover. She stared at his face for some time, hoping that he would look back and smile, but he did not. Kindle closed her eyes, rubbed her nose, patted her cheeks, trying her best to turn off her thoughts and feel the rhythm of her own heart. She counted off the beats of her heart and tried synching them with the beats of the guitar. After having waited several minutes for an opening—like waiting for a perfect entrance point into Double Dutch—she jumped in.

I missed you
But I wished you
Never come back

It's a matter of fact
You left me flat
Yeah, flat
On my baby back

Her voice elevated as she sang and it fell in perfect syncopation with the percussive beat he had added to his strums.

I missed you
But I resist you
Your disappearing act

It's a matter of fact
You put me on the rack
I know
You'll never come back

Kindle went on and on for so long that her throat grew raw and her mind empty of another rhyme. When she quieted, Bobby brought his playing to its proper end. She heard him gently prop his guitar up next to the chair. When she opened her eyes, he was staring at the wall.

"That was really good," he murmured.

Kindle passed the back of her hand over both eyes. "Thank you."

"What was it about? I mean, who was it about?"

She looked at him. His eyes were still fixed on the opposite wall.

"Only one of my parents is dead. But I have neither," she said.

Bobby patted her back, indicating that she should stand. He stood in front of her and covered her with his arms, embracing her shoulders with one arm and her midsection with the other. He burrowed his nose into her hair.

"I'm not depressed, so you don't have to console me," Kindle said.

"I know. But it's the Fourth of July. And you deserve fireworks. You know what I mean?"

"You're just saying that to divert my attention from the fact that you will steal my lyrics. But I keep a watchful eye."

Bobby backed away, but clutched her arms. "When you make me famous, I promise I'll mention you once or twice on stage. Promise."

Kindle laughed and wrestled her arms away. She slapped his face playfully and drew him in for another hug.

****

All was well for Independence Day, but truth be told, there was no real independence for Bobby when he was around Kindle. He could feel her in everything that he did. He thought of her in each stride.

He stood in front of her as evening began to fall. She sat on the couch reading lines silently, her lips moving but no sound coming out.

Kindle finally looked up at him and smiled. "Still have hopes of celebrating the anti-holiday, don't you?"

He sat beside her. "How'd you know?"

She ran her finger along his chin. "Something about that longing look in your eyes. And the fact that you have not picked up Little Otis." She alluded to his acoustic guitar, which he had name Otis when he first received it. The name was the first thing that came to his mind. He had always been inclined to do the first thing that came to his mind. It was instinct. That evening, he would learn that instinct had its own set of perils.

Bobby let instinct take over, speaking the first thing that came to mind. "What do you wanna do? We can do whatever you want."

"Whatever I want?"

"Sure. Yeah. Of course."

"Promise?"

"Promise."

Kindle smiled mischievously. He should have known she had nothing good in mind.

Within two hours of their agreement, Kindle and Bobby sat side-by-side at a tavern booth, surrounded by pictures of brews on the mahogany-tiled walls. The dim hanging lights above lit Kyle's and Larry's hair so that Bobby realized they both had not dyed their hair black in some months. Mickey's hair was indigo. In this light, Bobby could have sworn that Mickey's eyes were the exact same color as his hair.

Kindle had gotten just what she asked for. She had made it clear that if Bobby went back on his promise he wouldn't find a way back to her bed until much later notice. What choice did he really have?

To escape his own discomfort, Bobby focused on making connections between the little details of this scene. Bobby had ordered his burger medium, but saw no pink inside the meat. Kindle wore a pink T-shirt that he had brought home from the thrift store. She owned a pair of pink studded earrings that matched the shirt perfectly. The earrings were two of only five pieces of jewelry that she owned. There were five of them there. Five glasses of water sat on the table, one before each of them. There were two glasses of beer. One sat before Kyle and the other before Mickey. Kyle's drink still fizzed at the top, although he had drunk half of it. Every time he took a swig, he wiped his upper lip with the back of his hand and smiled at Kindle.

There were five of them at the table, but Bobby, Larry and Mickey were spectators. Kyle and Kindle exchanged little smiles at first. Both of them were equally sarcastic, but there was still a disparity. While Kindle could feign apathy, Bobby was near positive that Kyle really did have a heart of steel.

Kindle and Bobby had arrived at the tavern first and had waited a full hour before the band came. During the wait, Kindle's leg vibrated and she looked at the clock every few seconds. She did not smile when the guys entered, but rather, she stood, extending her hand. None of the guys shook it, but Larry and Mickey nodded at her. Kyle plopped down across from Kindle, eyeing her shiftily when she finally said a formal hello.

Larry had taken a seat across from Bobby, while Mickey had pulled up a chair at the end of the booth. In the beginning, the three of them tried making conversation about Ian Curtis's recent death. However, Kyle and Kindle had quickly transitioned from intermittently catching each other's gazes to locking stares. Kyle grazed his tongue over his teeth, his canines visible and sparkling. He was a beast preparing for battle.

"So, Kindle," Kyle began, leaning back and crossing his arms as the waiter refilled his glass of beer. "How are you enjoying our little Bobby?"

Kindle sliced her chicken in half. "Very well, Kyle. I certainly can't complain. But from your tone, it seems you have some complaint."

"No. I've got no complaints. I'm really happy. Totally stoked for my buddy." He downed a third of his beer. "My only problem is the lack of practicality."

"Oh, my dear Kyle, I would like to know what someone who shows up an hour late to a tavern that he lives five minutes from has to say about practicality. Please inform me."

Kyle belched loudly, then pressed his lips into a Cheshire cat grin. "You really wanna know?" He shook his head and took some more beer. "No. You can't really want to know."

"No, please, my good fellow, I would love to know. Absolutely," Kindle returned.

"Okay, sure, yeah. Alright. I'll tell you since you're ready to know." Kyle tossed his hair back and slid his finger around the rim of his glass. "It was about time that my cousin became a full grown man. I mean, we all know that he's had a bunch of girls, but he's never *had* one. That's them Catholic values for ya. Makes me proud to belong to the devil." He snickered. "Our little Prince Stallion needed to become a man. But I mean, practically speaking, he could have made that happen with someone other than…well, um…someone other than *you*."

Kindle compressed her lips, forming a thin smile. "You don't know me. In much of the same way that you know nothing of couth."

"Who needs couth when you got honesty? I know enough about you from just one look to make a good judgment. I'm sure you know what I'm getting at here, Ken-doll."

"If you're making a comment as close-minded as I think you are in the year nineteen-eighty, then your heart is as black as I suspected."

Bobby gulped loudly. Kindle cut her eyes at him.

Kyle drank the rest of his beer with bright eyes. Bobby could tell then that Kyle was attracted to her, as he was with any woman who gave him opposition. "Look here, Kindle, there's only one thing that's black at this table. I'll give you three guesses as to what it is, but I can guarantee you that Bobby will only need one. Maybe you'll need all three."

Larry laughed and Mickey twisted his lips to refrain from smiling.

Bobby's heart thudded, his anger rising. "Look, Kyle—"

"Don't," Kindle said, setting her hand over his forearm. "Let him say what he needs to say. I'd love to hear it."

Kyle belched again and exhaled. "I'm just talking about practicality. Bobby had every opportunity to have the snow bunny variety, but apparently, he really wanted a jungle bunny type."

Kindle stood swiftly and Kyle stood equally as fast, overpowering her attempt at intimidation with his two inches over her. He crossed his arms over his chest.

Larry stood. "Hey, Kyle, dude, let's get out of here."

Mickey glanced at Bobby and then stood.

"I mean, I'm not the one who wanted to be here in the first place," Kyle said. "But Bobby's *my* cousin, so I came here. It looks like Kindle's got something to say. So why don't you say it, Kindle?"

Kindle blinked her eyes and Bobby could tell that she was flushing down tears. She smiled and took a shaky breath after every few syllables. "I feel so sorry for Bobby. You're so far beneath him. For some reason, he thinks he needs you. He must think you're incapable of doing anything on your own."

"See, now, that's where you and me differ. You feel sorry for Bobby, but I don't at all. He got exactly what he wanted. In some ways, he might just be my hero. He got free housing and his own little servant, maid, *slave*—whatever you like to call yourself. You made him a man too, which I'm sure he's really thankful for." Kyle grinned at Bobby. "And to top it all off—this is the very best part—he didn't have to pay a dime for it. He didn't even have to put in any work, did he? If I had known you first, I would have gone for a deal like that." He lifted his empty glass to his lip. "I may have even bought you a drink first."

Bobby was hardly surprised when Kindle threw her water in Kyle's face, so that his hair matted down against his temple and his T-shirt clung to his arms and chest; however, Bobby was startled when she threw the glass against the wall. Larry and Kyle ducked to miss the glass bullet before it crashed, splitting into several large pieces.

Bobby stood up, dropped a wad of cash on the table and apologized softly to the waiter who had run to the scene. He ran behind Kindle as she flew out the tavern. Larry and Kyle's laughter was the last sound he heard before his exit.

Again, he wasn't surprised that Kindle had walked several yards ahead of him on the dark walk home, crossing streets without much notice of coming cars. He wasn't surprised that she had slammed the front door in his face when he caught up with her at the apartment. He wasn't the least surprised that she threw him a tiny blanket before she slammed the bedroom door.

However, Bobby was caught off guard when she yelled through the wall after three hours of silence. He had just begun toying with his guitar.

"You can't be serious!" she hollered.

Bobby stopped strumming and put his ear to the wall, like a telephone receiver. "What?"

"You actually find this a good time to mess around with your music. After what happened? You're off your trolley."

"I'm what?" Bobby shook his head. "I just...I...what did you want me to do?"

"Defend you wife's honor." She pounded the wall.

"I was trying." He sighed. "It's not simple. Kyle's my cousin. He has a lot of bad stuff going on inside of him. It's kinda hard to explain. He lost his dad when he was a baby. Sorta like you. Family is all you have sometimes. I think he, like, needs me, in a way."

"You do realize he doesn't care for you, right? He said that you were dense."

"What?"

"Are you listening, Bobby?" She huffed. "How could you let them say such horrible things to me? I don't understand you."

Bobby sighed, rubbing his eyes in circular motion. It had to be one in the morning. He preferred having their arguments in the daytime, when he had more energy to make up with her. "I mean, what am I supposed to say? I was gonna say something there, but you didn't want me to. Besides, I thought it was a bad idea to go in the first place."

"Are you saying this is my fault?" Her voice had dropped in pitch. Unlike all the other girls he knew who went into high-pitched hysterics, her voice always became deeper when she was riled. It was like darkness rapidly settling over sunshine. "Is that really what you're daring to say?"

"No. No way. I'd never say that."

"Of course you'd never *say* something like that. But the very dangerous part about you is what you fail to say. Even more than that, it's what you fail to understand."

"What are you saying?"

Kindle pushed out an exasperated sigh that could have moved him if he didn't recognize her gift for drama. "I'm saying that your friends don't want us together. Trying to balance me and them will result in nothing but confusion."

Bobby bit his lip, riding on their silence for a moment. "I've been doing okay since before today."

"No, *Prince Stallion*. You've been riding neutral the whole time. Unfortunately, you have come to the incline that will cause you to drive this situation in whatever direction you want it to go."

Bobby closed his eyes, backed his face away from the wall, and sat straight on the couch, his legs spread apart. He clasped his hands over his stomach.

He expected Kindle to continue. When she was sure she was right, there was usually no stopping her from reiterating how right she was. But this time, she was silent. Maybe this time she didn't know what to say. If so, Bobby knew they were both completely lost; he certainly had no idea how to remedy this. His heart dropped to his stomach for the first time since spring.

Kindle walked in the room and sat beside him. "What are you going to do, Bobby?"

He responded in a hoarse whisper. "I don't know."

Bobby could see Kindle through his peripheral. Looking at her head-on was too difficult, too much of a shame, too much of a gesture that he was ready to make a choice that he hoped to bypass.

When Kindle rubbed her ice-cold toes up his leg, he turned to face her. He smiled. Maybe the difficult conversation had come to an end before it had truly begun.

"Your feet are freezing," he said.

"But your heart is cold. You don't love me, do you?" Her voice was syrupy, like a begging child's. She wound her leg around his.

Bobby pulled her to him, hugging her tightly and kissing her temple before releasing her. "I love you more than my guitar, Sweetness. More than Manchester sunshine. More than Kyle and Larry."

Kindle climbed onto his lap and faced him, sitting Indian-style. "If that's so, then make me a promise."

"Okay," he replied, trepidation in his heart but no hesitation before his words.

"Promise me that if you have to choose between me and them, you will always choose me."

Bobby bowed his head. He placed his hands on her back to balance her. "Alright."

She grinned triumphantly and kissed him.

"But you have to make me a promise too, Kindle. You have to promise me that you'll never be the one to make me make that choice."

Kindle leaned back, bending her upper body over his knees. Her hair swept over his feet, her shirt sliding up her body. "I promise."

"Do you mean that?" Bobby asked. He pushed her T-shirt up farther so that it hung over her face when he tickled her bare stomach.

"Absolutely not." She struggled to pull her shirt back over her stomach, laughing.

As she wriggled, Bobby leaned forward and cupped the back of her head, bringing her up slightly. He pulled her shirt off the top of her head, tucking it between the couch cushions and kissing her softly.

"Well," he said, "I guess my promise doesn't count either."

She kissed him back. "You'd better hope that it does, Sailor."

They traded kisses back and forth until they toppled off the couch onto the floor. Bobby bundled her wrists together with his one hand, pulling her hands above her head and tickling her with his light kisses until heavy ones were in order from her neck to her navel. He tossed off his own shirt, pressing her against the ground with his chest. He shared himself with her until neither of them was sober enough to think about the validity of promises.

****

Even so, the summer made its own set of promises. It promised Bobby that The Dare would have more shows than usual. It promised Kindle that she had nothing else to worry about but one audition waiting for her in mid-August.

Nevertheless, the summer season seems to fade the fastest, and in England, it is easily forgotten by a rainy day.

It rained all day on the day of Kindle's audition. The sky was entirely grey. A raging wind shook the trees. It was a day completely ruffled by the rain. Kindle looked over the headboard, peering out their bedroom window. It looked as though their flat was drifting through a violent storm at sea.

Kindle sighed and hummed softly to herself. *Summertime, and the livin' is easy.*

"You okay?" Bobby asked groggily, one eye open, as he awoke.

Kindle sunk down beside him and pressed her cheek against his chest, slinging her arm over his stomach. She began to wonder if she stayed there just like that—completely covered by him, by the blanket, by love—it might be okay that her audition fell on a stormy day. It didn't have to be an omen.

"Wish it weren't raining," she murmured.

"You can't stop the rain. You just have to prepare for it."

She looked at Bobby strangely.

"I heard it somewhere. I can't remember where." He placed his hands behind his head. "But it'll be okay. You'll impress those guys. What do you call them anyway? Directors? Judges?"

"Do you really believe that?"

"Believe what? That you'll impress everybody? Totally. I do."

"I'm sorry to say that that only makes me feel incrementally better. I think I'm getting sick." She sat up, removing the blanket from her legs.

Bobby sat up also. He lifted his T-shirt, covering her head with it, teepeeing them inside the white cloud. "No way. Sickness is for losers. You're a winner, not a whiner."

"What are you talking about?"

"Do I have to make sense right now?"

"Your talk is bollocks."

"I don't think I know what you said."

"It means it don't make no sense," she replied, giving a laugh at her exaggerated Southern drawl. "Now, away from me."

"How bad would it be if I didn't take you seriously?" He grazed her neck with his lips.

Kindle roped his hair around her hand, pulling his face from her neck. "Determined to leave your love bites on me, aren't you? Branding me as though I belong to you, huh?"

"I thought you did."

She ducked out from beneath his shirt, re-entering the real world. "No more tomfoolery. You're a star already. It's my turn now."

****

"You are a sight for sore eyes, aren't you?"

Betty Warner stood at the door when Kindle entered the theater. Her cleavage spouted from her purple bustier like a vanilla heart. Her hair was tousled, pointing in several directions, but certainly designed that way for effect.

Betty placed in Kindle's hand a paper with the number five scribbled on it. "Give it your best try. Hold your cheeks in so that your face don't look so bloated."

Kindle looked at her blankly. "So you found a way to be here? Only to pass out numbers?"

"No need to be ornery, Love." Betty scribbled on the next sheet of paper she held. "Besides, that's not the extent of my job. I have pull behind the scenes too."

Kindle circled her hand around her wrist. She caught Betty's violet eyes. Betty's poor acting certainly didn't discount her anomalous beauty and a peculiar likeability that spiked through her crudeness.

"So why haven't you told him?" Betty said, scribbling on another piece of paper.

Kindle fanned her face with her number. "What are you talking about?"

"Why haven't you told Ricky that you and me are now friends? It's dangerous for married couples to keep secrets, isn't it? Least that's what my father used to say."

Kindle ran her hand down her neck, searching for a good lie. The truth would only work to Betty's advantage. She could not tell Betty that she feared an excited gleam in Bobby's eye at the mention of her name. Kindle wasn't so stupid as to forget that Bobby was just a man. Plus, Betty was a chameleon, which gave her a peculiar, but well-defined mystique. Kindle's was still in development.

"I haven't any reason to mention you, Betty," Kindle responded. "None whatsoever."

"Of course, of course." Betty ran her tongue over her teeth and rolled her eyes. "Best of luck to you, Number Five. I hope you get the part. But as we all know, acting parts—much like men—go to the most fitting woman."

Kindle rolled her eyes and turned on her heel, sauntering through the hall that led to the dark preparatory area behind the stage where several other girls were already assembled there, each wearing her hair in a ponytail, each rawboned, each wearing a black leotard and leggings. Three were blonde, two brunette, one a redhead. Kindle was dressed similarly, but her hips and backside were more pronounced, her hair in a high ponytail, long and curly. She wondered why she was there, why Nigel would believe that Stuart Daimler would see anything in her that fit his character.

"Are you okay?" the redhead with the tiny ponytail asked. Her eyelids were crinkled.

"I'm fine," Kindle replied, grasping her stomach.

The girl looked away and began talking with a group of blondes.

They stood behind a dark red curtain. Kindle heard the director call forward the first girl, Anne Price. One of the blondes disappeared through the curtain.

Kindle listened to Anne Price deliver her monologue. She felt irritated. Her stomach gurgled.

"Are you sure you're okay? The john is down the hall," the redhead tried once more.

"I'm well."

Anne Price finished and reappeared from behind the curtain. She smiled and bowed, while the other girls smiled and mimed their cheers.

Three more women auditioned before Kindle was called. She stepped slowly from behind the curtain, her shoes clapping against the stage before she stood still before the judges. The theater was large, filled with red seats that surrounded the stage. One man stood beside a seat on the balcony. The stage lights ran across the top, so bright that Kindle squinted, unable to make out the features of the men in the front.

She believed it was Stuart who spoke. "Begin when ready."

Dizziness trounced Kindle and her body sweltered. She clasped her stomach and slid her hand across the back of her neck to wipe away the sweat. Although she swallowed repeatedly, she could no longer hold down what she had been trying to back stage. As she opened her mouth to recite the first word of her monologue, she lurched forward and vomited on the stage.

****

At noon, Bobby sat on the couch strumming his guitar. He set the phone between his neck and collarbone.

"Little chicken."

"Hi, mom."

"Someone very important wants to speak to you."

"Who's that?"

Bobby heard her handling the phone.

"Hello?" he said.

"Robert."

Bobby sniffed. He stopped strumming. "Dad."

"Robert. How are you?"

"I'm cool. Just great, Dad."

"I haven't talked to you in some time."

"Yeah. How are you?"

His father sneezed. "I'm okay."

Bobby contemplated his next chord progression during what would have been a painful silence with anyone but his father.

Frank Carter sighed. "Well, I don't think I even have to tell you how much your mother misses you. I do too."

"Miss you guys too," Bobby said.

"So when are you going to come home to see your mother?"

Before he could reply, Kindle clamored through the door, her cheeks and eyes wet. She held her arms around herself.

"Robert?"

"Dad, I gotta, like, go," he stuttered.

Bobby hung up the phone and started for Kindle. She grabbed his shirt, drawing her face into his chest, crying so loudly that he didn't know if her sobs were real at first. He could feel her tears on his chest through his shirt, as though his own heart were crying.

"What's the matter, Sweetness?"

Kindle choked on her words. Bobby patted her back. She pulled away from him, galloping to the bathroom. He followed behind her, cringing at the sound of her vehement gagging and the proceeding splash of vomit in the toilet water.

He knelt behind her and rubbed her back as she brought her face up from the toilet bowl. "Are you okay? How'd you get sick? Did you eat something bad?"

Kindle shook her head.

Bobby petted her ponytail. "Did you get sick at the audition?"

She nodded.

"Wow."

"Wow?" She wiped the saliva glistening on her lips with the back of her hand. Her sobbing turned into sniffles. Her eyes were only half-opened as she slumped against the toilet seat, like a despairing drunk. "No, this is not a 'wow' moment. This is Sod's Law. Murphy's Law, what have you. It was bound to happen to me. I was destined to puke through my chance at stardom."

Bobby stared at the spot of olive green vomit on her forearm. "Why are you…I mean, I don't understand why you think it's all over or something."

"Why?" She straightened her back. "It *is* over. This is a sure sign of it."

Bobby reflected. He had glued her back together before. He could do it again. "You're gonna try again, right? What's the saying? It's like you gotta get back on the horse or whatever, right?"

"I've never ridden a horse, Bobby."

"You haven't? Wow. I mean, they're amazing to ride. My mom's dad had a ranch with a bunch of them." He offered his hand.

Kindle used it to pull herself to her feet. She plucked her toothbrush from the holder on the sink. "That's the difference between you and me. You've had horses; I've had feet. And they've failed me this time," she said.

Bobby stood. "What? No. See, I didn't own the horses or anything."

Kindle stared wearily at his reflection in the mirror.

"But I guess that's not the point," he said. "What I'm trying to say is that you weren't lucky this time, but you'll have better luck next time."

"There's no such thing as luck. Just preparation for chance."

As he opened his mouth to ponder the saying out loud, Kindle turned toward him and vomited on his bare feet.

****

Kindle did not stop vomiting that day. She vomited non-stop for two weeks. Her pub's manager sent her home three nights straight. On the third night, while Kindle lay nauseous on their bed, Bobby sought his mother.

Bobby explained that one of his friends had fallen ill.

"Boy or girl?" his mother asked.

"She's a girl, mom."

"Married?"

"Yeah, I think so."

She responded with a little laugh. "She's pregnant, Bobby."

"No, mom," Bobby said weakly. "I don't see…I don't really see how that could be. I don't think that's possible or anything."

"Must we revisit the birds and the bees?"

He smiled ruefully and looked to the ceiling, listening to Kindle vomit in the bathroom. His heart thumped in his chest.

That night, Bobby walked to the store and picked up a home pregnancy test. He asked the cashier about the test and how it worked. She recognized him from The Dare.

"So, you're Ricky Stallion. My name's Macy. You know, you're cuter close-up. Your hair's longer than when I first saw you."

"Thank you."

She inspected the test box, turning it over in her hand. "So you've knocked someone up? One of your groupies, huh?"

"No. It's just…for a friend." Bobby handed her the cash.

She placed the box in a paper bag. "You couldn't pay me to believe that."

****

Buying the test was not the hard part; handing it to Kindle over dinner was. They sat arm-to-arm on the couch balancing their plates over their legs, eating pancakes and eggs for dinner. It was the only thing he really knew how to cook.

Bobby reached in the paper bag and laid the box in her hand.

"What's your meaning?" she asked.

"You've been sick for a long time, that's all."

She sat her plate on the floor. "Then, you should have bought Ginger-ale."

"I don't think...I don't think that's the answer."

Kindle stood up and scowled at him before she marched to the bedroom. Bobby thought whether he should follow after her. He opened the box and read the directions, then carried them behind his back as he entered the bedroom. She lay on the bed, her eyes still.

Bobby sat beside her and laid the test device and directions by her arm. "It's gonna be okay."

"I know it is. I'm fine." She pushed the items away.

"Don't you just wanna see?"

Kindle turned onto her stomach. "Well, aren't you inspiring? Facing your fears head on. But *you* don't have anything to be afraid of."

"I'm not trying to be pushy."

"Of course you're not."

"I don't want you to feel pressure." Bobby looked away from her. He stared at the painting above their bed. Maybe it was prophetic. Maybe he shouldn't have drawn the seeds inside the apple.

"I don't want this," Kindle murmured.

Bobby knelt down by the bed and crawled his fingers up her back. "You never really know about stuff like this. Maybe, there's some kind of bright side. Maybe it's—I don't know—maybe it's not the worst thing that could ever happen."

"It is for me," she retorted, caving her back in to escape his fingers.

Bobby coughed.

Kindle flipped over. "Just give me the stupid little thing."

Bobby moved his face in and kissed her cheek. Kindle rose, jostling him out of her way as she headed to the bathroom with the test in her hand. Bobby sat on the bed as he listened to her urinate. He thought how strange it was that pee could determine if a baby existed. He began to think about what a baby would look like at this stage in a pregnancy, if there were a pregnancy. He considered the idea that one physical act could make a living thing. He wondered what life would be like if when shaking hands, a human being could be created. The world would be overpopulated. People would be new parents over and over again. Bobby couldn't even imagine being a parent once.

He tried calculating how many times he and Kindle had been together. He tried taking averages, multiplying, dividing and adding. Math was never his strong point. So, instead of relying on calculations, Bobby decided that if a baby had been conceived, he would feel it. His instinct would have let him know.

Bobby rubbed together his sweaty palms and ran his tongue around his dry mouth. He decided pregnancy was not in the realm of possibility.

Kindle entered the room with the test in her hand. She held it like a dishrag before dropping it on the floor on his side of the bed.

"What did it say?"

"I don't know," Kindle said with a shrug. "We can see in the morning."

"Why are we waiting?"

"Because I want to."

Kindle pushed Bobby onto his side of the bed and settled herself under the sheets. Bobby reached up to turn off the ceiling fan light. He reclined in the dark with his eyes open for two hours before he found sleep. In the middle of the night, he heard Kindle rise, pretending to be asleep as she took the test from the side of the bed and entered the bathroom. She came out slowly.

Bobby sat up in the bed, the headboard supporting his backbone. The light of the moon shining through the window lit her tears. He drew her to him with a wave of his hand. She came, climbing onto his legs, positioning herself in a ball and burying her head in his neck. Her tears rolled down his neck onto his shoulder.

"It's okay," he whispered. "It's gonna be okay. Everything is gonna be righteous. Cuz I love you. I'll take care of you…"

On and on he appealed until her weeping was quelled and he was sure that she was beginning to find sleep. It was then that he exhaled, giving consent to his own shameful tears—a reaction to his immediate consideration of whether rockstar and husband and father could be congruent in any way.

****

It was August 29th when they discovered they were with child. September 1st, the clinic doctor informed them that they had conceived approximately two months ago. Bobby wished that he could have determined the exact day of conception so he could recall if there was any difference in feeling than any of the other times.

Labor Day, being a holiday in the States, held the lingering undertone that he should be happy, that he should celebrate. He ignored the feeling. He didn't want to anger Kindle. She was still alternating between a stone mouth and trembling lips, between silent stares and weepy whispers. Bobby, however, was beginning to entertain himself with visions of their baby.

He pictured his three-year-old cousin Reese. Reese came out of the womb nearly bald, a light fuzz of golden hair layering the top of her head. Her eyes were ocean blue. The imprint of eyebrows was stamped on her forehead where the hair had not yet grown. Her lips were ruby, her skin sallow.

Bobby soon realized that his child probably wouldn't look like Reese. He tried gathering some images of exotic children. He imagined the child as one of the gold-skinned Indian children he had seen on a Christian Children's Foundation advertisement. Maybe the child wouldn't resemble Bobby at all.

Bobby began to wonder if his child not looking like him would be a bad thing. The child could be onyx-skinned, shimmering, brawny. He could grow up to look and sing and write music like Marvin Gaye or Curtis Mayfield. He'd be a pioneer.

He wondered what they would name the baby. Maybe John or Jacob or Julian. He wondered if those names would be appropriate for a little Indian child.

If Bobby thought about nothing but the child, he almost smiled. If there was no world but the one where Bobby loved Kindle and Kindle loved Bobby and Kindle and Bobby loved New Baby, Bobby was near certain that happiness was attainable. In that world, he had no other dreams than fatherhood and being a husband. In that world, Kindle could find some happiness in just being with him and Baby India. In that world, they would not have disappointed parents. Actually, Kindle already had no parents. In that world, Bobby's parents would have never existed.

Hiding a wife was a proven difficulty, but hiding a baby would be impossible. He could only imagine a screaming baby in the background when his mother called. He refused to tell a lie big enough to hide that. He could never move back to the U.S. He'd have to go into seclusion. He'd have to quit The Dare. With that thought, misery returned.

****

When Bobby arrived home from rehearsal on Labor Day in the late afternoon, Kindle still lay on her side in bed. She cried quietly, incrementally blowing her nose. She hadn't said anything in the past two days. She hadn't eaten. Bobby was concerned by it all but said nothing for fear of her wrath.

"Kindle." He lay down beside her, propping himself up on his side by his elbow, supporting his head with his hand. He rubbed her back with his free hand. She bowed her back to resist his touch. "You know, I love you, right? I've loved you just about every second I've known you. I love you more than Pop-Tarts. I love you more than Stevie Wonder. I love you more than summers on Lake Ontario."

Kindle muttered.

"What did you say?" he asked.

She turned over to face him. Her nose was wet and pink. He smiled; she reminded him of a puppy.

"I said that your love is a joke."

His smile faded. "What do you mean?"

"You don't know what love is."

"I don't?" he asked, his indignation not well forecasted in his voice.

"What is love, Bobby?"

He paused. "Love is like two dreamers dreaming the exact same dream."

"Oh, put it to rest."

"I'm sorry." He looked down. "I don't know how to explain love. I know it when I feel it."

"Did you know it when you felt it with Becky?"

"What?"

"Rebecca Lawrence. That's her name. That's what your mates said."

Bobby blinked his eyes before reclining flat on his back. "*That* girl? She was just a girl that I liked. A long time ago. Like, right after high school. I don't even remember her that well anymore. But why—"

"So how long will it be before you don't remember me anymore? Or have you forgotten me already? Maybe you never really knew me. Because how I feel doesn't matter at all to you, does it?"

He sighed. "Yeah, it matters to me. That's why I'm here."

Kindle sat up. Her face cast a shadow over his. "So you wouldn't be here for any other reason? It doesn't matter to you that you have a responsibility?"

"It does matter to me."

"You should start acting like it."

"Let's not fight. I don't want you to be mad."

She struck his shoulder with the flat side of her fist, springing him up like a jack-in-the-box. "You're what angers me. You're the cause of—"

"I didn't do anything to you," Bobby broke in. "Why are you acting like this?"

"I'm not the stupid little girl you thought I was. I'm not just someone to drop off your virginity to. But you are a very stupid little boy. Do you realize that? You're a child. Mr. Holster was right about that. You're not a man. You don't even know what a man looks like."

She raise her hand to strike him once more, but he caught her wrist, gripping it tightly until she finally lowered her arm. Bobby shook his head.

"Why are you shaking your head? I'm right, Bobby. You deserve to feel guilty. If I don't make you feel guilty, you'll just walk around like everything is well."

He shook his head again in simple resignation rather than rebellion. He stood, grabbing his jacket from the foot of the bed.

"Where in all of earth and creation do you have to go at a time like this, Bobby?"

"I don't know." He turned to the door. "I don't know."

"You're just going to leave me?" she cried.

He said nothing as he walked out the door.

Chapter Sixteen

Past Time: 1978

A fleet of raindrops made Lloyd Street slick and glossy. Lightning and thunder did not scare Kindle as much as they had when she was ten and clamping her pillow for protection. She was still young, but less afraid now. Plus, she was more enchanted by the city lights than by the darkness at home. Lights could not stay on without money, no matter what one's present situation may be, no matter how many different ways that situation was explained.

Rather than bury her hands in her coat pockets, eighteen-year-old Kindle drew her arms out of the sleeves and into the center of the coat, holding her arms at her sides. She laughed lowly, wondering if the other people on the sidewalk thought that she was armless. She began to imagine what they were thinking—that she had been born without arms or that she had succumbed to a flesh-eating virus that warranted the amputation of two of her limbs. How were they to know that she bundled her arms in her coat because her pockets had holes?

Kindle shrugged off her coat when she entered the club. She sat at one of the several round tables for two. A white haze filled the small, black room from where each of the four patrons smoked cigarettes. A yellow fog surrounded the five stage lights above. The black walls were filled in sporadically with brown bricks.

The jazz had already begun, the players on the stage performing a bland improvisation of "Little Ghetto Boy."

These players were not the ones. Three tall, pale ones played horns. Each wore his brown hair neatly cropped. The guitar player, plump and redheaded, sat in a chair, strumming his guitar languidly. A bald keyboardist stood at the back.

Kindle waited for the next act, discreetly wiping the perspiration from her armpits with the table napkins. In a way, it was strange that she perspired. She wore less clothing than she normally did—a black leather skirt that draped over her thin thighs and a baggy sleeveless turtleneck, so oversized that her white bra became visible if she lifted her arms from her sides. She had found the leftover clothes in the closet.

The air conditioner blew vigorously on that cool summer's evening. Two older couples sat in front of her to the left and to the right. Though she sat mid-way back in the small club, she was in the center of the room, unavoidable.

Kindle steadied a flyer on her lap, the tips of her shoes pointed perfectly perpendicular to the floor to prop up her legs. She stared at the paper until the music stopped and the second act appeared on this stage. This was the act. She dropped her sandaled feet flat against the floor. She straightened her back and lifted her chin. She didn't know which one he was, but she could figure it out.

Five guys strolled out from behind the black curtain at the back of the stage. A peanut-skinned man came out first, gripping a large instrument case at his side. He was heavy and tall, wearing a green vest, white T-shirt and black slacks. He pulled a trombone out of his case. Two others came out after him. They were brown-skinned, fit, taller but not intimidating. They were twins, one having brought on a trumpet and the other standing behind a keyboard. The man at the drum set was barely visible, but Kindle didn't care. He was of no interest.

The guitarist walked out onto the stage coolly. He was gangly, his hands appearing as if they could have touched his knees if he extended his arms fully. He was the most daring of the band with his black pants, black vest, bare chest and silver hoop earring. His skin was her tone— vivid, shiny on his forehead and yellow near his cheeks. He counted off their playing. Kindle watched closely as he switched chords and the muscle in his forearm bulged. He was the one.

Kindle paid no attention to the music. She only heard the crashing of the cymbals when she fell into deep thought.

The set came to an end, the crowd of four standing and clapping. When the band skipped down the stage steps, Kindle followed the guitarist to the door.

She grabbed his bare arm before he could step out onto the sidewalk. He looked down at her, bewildered, his eyes narrowed until they were slits. Quickly, he widened them and smirked, nodding his head as if she had spoken something that he understood well.

"Can I do something for you?" he intimated.

Kindle released his arm, drawing back from him and crossing her arms over her breasts, still attempting to hold her upper arms at her sides to avoid exposing her bra. "I need to speak with you. Here. At a table."

He raised his eyebrows. "Talk to me here? You want to talk here?"

"Yes, I do."

He gave her a short once-over. "Certainly."

Kindle cringed and swallowed. The man's shoes clapped steadily as he followed behind her, as though he kept a beat in everything he did. The man sat down across from her languorously, coolly. Too smoothly. She could have smacked him.

A waitress quickly tended to them, dropping a shot glass of brown liquid—was it whiskey?—before him. He smiled at her calculatingly, surveying her thoroughly.

"If we perform well, we get free drinks," he explained. "Not to boast, but the band had pissed plenty of nights away after our shows."

"I see," said Kindle.

"Would you like one? Getting a drink for a pretty girl like you—I'm not foolish enough to pass up the chance. I'd pay for it; wouldn't dare give to such a pretty face something that's cost me nothing."

"I don't want anything to drink." Kindle scratched the edge of the table.

"Don't want nothing to drink, eh?" He crossed his legs. "What is it that I can give to you?" He stared at her over the glass as he brought it to his lips.

The next band began to play. The singer sang crisp clear, imitating Otis Redding.

"Does the name Kayanne Madden mean a thing to you?" Kindle blurted.

The man uncrossed his legs. "What'd you say?"

"Kayanne Madden. You must know her."

"I do know the name. What does it matter to you? Are you some relation?"

Kindle pushed her hands under her thighs and leaned forward over the table, catching his eyes. "You act like you're surprised, as if you can't recognize me. I'm very aware of who you are, *John.* I'm very aware. My last name is Hyrum."

He drew in closer over the table, so that their faces nearly touched. "John? My name is not John, little woman."

Kindle snickered, hoping that he could see that she was as fiery as her name suggested. "But it is, Sir John." She dropped the flyer. It flittered to his side of the table. "I'm sure you can read. My mother wouldn't have given you a chance to begin with if you were both illiterate and an infidel."

He chuckled and took the last swig of his drink. "You're a smart little thing, aren't you?" He pressed the wrinkled paper against the table, running his hand over it, caressing it with his long fingers. "'John Hyrum on guitar.' You assume that's me. Unfortunately, my dear, this flyer was made a week prior to our show. John left three days ago."

Kindle drew back slowly, sliding the flyer to her side to give it another look. "Are you lying?"

"Don't have any reason to. John took off three days ago. He's been in the habit for some time now. Drug binges, is all." He shook his head. "So, I play what little guitar I can in his stead. My instrument is saxophone, little woman." He winked. "Although these hands are fit for guitar, among other things."

Kindle huffed, attempted a word and sighed again, looking up from the flyer into his eyes. "Don't lie to me."

"Got no reason to. I'm just the man who covers for him when he's gone, when he can't hold himself back from the dope."

"How do you know my mother?" she asked, barely allowing him a pause.

He laughed once more. "So, you're Kayanne Madden's daughter. I should have known it. Almost as pretty as she was." He smiled broadly, his molars and pink gums exposed. "More pretty than she was, if I'm allowed to say so."

"No, you're not allowed to say."

"Sensitive, are we?" He began quietly shredding the flyer into small pieces. "I've known John nearly thirty years, since we were little ones. I knew him before he met Kayanne." He chuckled, tilted his head to the side. "I remember when he met her. Shy and beautiful Kayanne. Naïve little Kayanne. Following him to every show. In love with him through every woman that he sampled. But if John ever loved anyone, he loved her." He took a cigarette and positioned it carefully between his lips. "The name is Sly Lavery, in case you wanted to know."

Kindle stared at all the tiny pieces of the flyer. They were like a heap of ashes in the center of the table. "So, *Sly*, did you realize that your very best friend had a daughter that he has neglected over the past eighteen years?"

Sly squinted, canopying the lighter's flame as he lit his cigarette. Insouciantly, he replied, "So, I suppose you are the daughter."

"Does it mean nothing?"

Sly sat his hand on the top of his crossed legs, inadvertently pointing his cigarette up at her. "What's it supposed to mean to me? I'm not your father. And I've got no excuses to make for him."

"But you could…you should have encouraged him to have something to do with his only child, don't you think, Sly?"

"You can call me Mr. Lavery. I'm old enough to be your father. Although I'm not your father." He rubbed his hand over his head, the cigarette trembling as he did. "Your father can't be convinced of doing anything he doesn't want to. Why do you think Kayanne allowed him to do whatever he wanted? He ruled his own life. No one was telling Johnny Boy what to do. Accept him or live without him. That's his slogan. Kayanne bought into that for a long time. I suppose that you, little one, are what changed Kayanne's acceptance. Children have a queer effect on your sex."

Kindle heaved a sigh. "So, you're saying he did not *want* to see me?"

"It aint rocket science, child. If he wanted to, he would have. Not as though he lived across the world. He's all around England, occasionally Manchester."

"Where is he now?"

Sly shrugged. "Never been a keeper of grown men. He'll find me when he's ready to play again. His story never changes."

The band pleaded for him to try a little tenderness…

Kindle felt that she would cry, so she spoke what little she could without tears falling from her eyes. "And so you say that he loved my mother?"

"Still loves her, I think. Tried to see her some years ago. But she wasn't taking him back. Says that she made him leave her apartment. Poor old bloke."

Still loved her? As if there was something left to love.

Poor old bloke? As if sympathy should be granted him.

"Goodbye," Kindle said, standing up, her knees weak.

"Where are you going? Perhaps I can take you there." His voiced dropped. "Perhaps I can take you somewhere."

The tear dangling from her eyelash cascaded down her cheek. She brushed it away violently. "Perhaps I could have my father. But more likely, I won't. Perhaps you have the same chance of taking me anywhere that I have of seeing my father tonight. Goodbye."

Chapter Seventeen

Present Time...

"The peace of Christ be with you."

"Peace be with you," Bobby echoed to the woman in front of him who chose to hug him instead of shake his hand. The woman must have worn the same perfume his mother did. It smelled like cherry blossom. She hugged him longer than anyone had at Mass.

Bobby sat in the dim church, hardly able to recognize what the priest said, despite the thousands of time he had listened to the liturgy. Only a few other people sat in the church for the weekday Mass, each person claiming an entire pew for herself. The church was nothing like anything he'd gone to in Canton. Its ceiling was umbrella-shaped, its walls concave, making the church an exquisite merry-go-round of crosses, flowers and paintings of Jesus, the Queen and the Apostles.

From the back, Bobby watched the priest prepare the Eucharist. He began considering if taking communion would be right. Kindle was angry with him. More than that, he was angry with her. Where was any communion in that?

A heat wave passed over him every time he thought of her words. He wasn't a man?

He had made it his business to be a man just for her.

Not just a man. A good man. Bobby avoided eye contact with the girls in the crowds who tried to get his attention while he played, even the really pretty ones. He threw away all the tiny pieces of paper with girls' numbers scrawled on them that he received in masses after the shows.

Bobby hadn't just made it his business to be a good man—he was a simple man, one who asked for nothing and expected very little. He would have loved for her to have created a pet name for him. He would have loved to have charge over anything in the apartment besides his own belongings. He would have loved for her to care for the house the way she had cared for his hotel room. Instead, she decided where everything in the apartment would be placed, what kind of food they would eat, the things they would watch on television…everything.

In light of the anger boiling under his skin, Bobby decided to forego communion. He went through the rest of the Mass, hoping that God might come down in some small way.

By the end, he had dared himself to talk to someone, anyone. When the priest and altar boy marched out, Bobby knelt at the pew quickly and followed behind the lady that had hugged him.

"Excuse me," he said to her as she walked out of the sanctuary into the hallway.

She turned to face him. She was short and wrinkled, pale and blue-eyed. She smiled at him.

"I was wondering…I was wondering if I could talk to you," said Bobby.

"Have we met, dear?" She pushed her purse up her shoulder, touching lightly her auburn hair.

"No, no. My name is Bobby. I just saw you and I thought…I don't really know what I thought. I don't know."

She looked him over. "Come with me," she said, taking him by the wrist.

Instantly warmed by her kindness, he followed behind her like a lost child. She led him to a mahogany bench beside a water fountain. They sat.

She crossed her legs, settling her hands in her lap. "What's the matter?"

He pursed his lips. "I don't know if I know how to explain it."

"You should try," she nodded, squeezing his hand.

Bobby's body began to cool. He hadn't met someone genuinely nice in a long time. "Are you married?"

"I was once upon a time," she said.

"What happened?"

"He passed. Three years ago."

"I'm sorry."

She smiled again. "This is not my therapy. I've had a lot of that already. What's your trouble, dear?"

"I'm married. I got married, like, seven months ago." He dropped his head. "Something like that."

"Congratulations."

Bobby sighed. "Yeah. Kindle—I mean, my wife, or whatever—is like, really beautiful and just kinda exactly what I want."

"That's always a good sign."

"But, uh, but now, she's having a baby."

The woman furrowed her brows.

"I mean, we both are. Together."

"Nervous some?"

"For sure," Bobby said. "But she's not happy. You know, it's like she blames me or something."

"Where is the need for blame?"

Bobby glanced at her hands as she held them in her lap. Her fingernail polish was the same color as her lipstick. "There is none, I guess. But we haven't known each other that long. And I just don't know…"

The woman raised her thin eyebrows. "Well, how long is not that long?"

"Eight months, maybe."

She leaned back. "How does your mum feel about this?"

Bobby felt his face get hot and hoped that he wasn't blushing. "She doesn't know."

"She doesn't know," the woman assessed. "Why doesn't she know?"

Bobby felt like he was in trouble. He tried to think of some other reason he hadn't told her besides her pending disappointment and his fear that she would tell his father. Both

of these facts made him sound like a boy and today, he was a
man, even if by perception alone.

"Well, I didn't get married by a priest," he said. "It was
at the Registry. And my wife's not Catholic. And, um, I mean,
there's just a lot of stuff that makes this kinda complicated."

"Complications," the woman mused. She patted his thigh.
"I'm going to tell you the truth. Is that okay?"

"I think so." He nodded slowly, looking at the floor
before meeting her eyes. He sighed, relieved. She didn't look
upset.

"You weren't thoroughly prepared for marriage," she
said.

"Well, yeah, yeah, I know that. I think."

"And you were a Catholic married outside of the Catholic
Church, which would mean that your marriage is invalid."

"Invalid?" He rubbed his right index finger. "Well, I
mean, I had the officiant say the Catholic vows."

"I'm sure you hadn't expected it to be that easy." She
lifted his chin with her fleshy fingers. "I am sure the marriage is
very much valid in your own eyes. But so I have found that
many things that felt valid—natural even—needed a proper
form to be sustained."

Bobby cleared his throat and clasped his hands together.
"I don't think I understand."

"Well, Bobby, puppy love is for the young. Really, it
doesn't last. It's not supposed to. It's replaced by something
much greater." She rubbed his knee and patted it resolutely.
"It's replaced by confidence and endurance. A marriage blessed
and valid in the eyes of God is one that has the opportunity to
endure. It stands on a rock more solid than even the vows that
we make. There is a reason for its proper form. Good intentions
are too weak to bind two people together for life. Young love is
deceptive enough to make you think so, isn't it? Now that
you've become a man, you must put away childish things." She
shielded his hands with her own. "And you *are* a man now, no
longer a boy. You could soon have a boy" —she chuckled and
dabbed her watery eye with a tissue— "or a girl of your own."

Bobby bowed his head, his eyes tracing the erratic lines in the ivory marble floor. "What am I supposed to do? I didn't know…"

She smiled. Her lips were so thin he could only see her teeth when she grinned. She tapped his arm. "You and your wife should go talk to a priest. He can help you make this right. You can have a real wedding."

"What if she—I mean, my wife—what if she won't come? What if she doesn't want to?"

"O ye of little faith. You haven't even tried yet."

****

"I'm sorry," Kindle said in the middle of the night. She rolled over and tapped Bobby's chest.

He had arrived home four hours ago and quietly climbed in the bed beside her. He was still reflecting in the dark on how being with Kindle felt sacred but somehow lacked validity.

She grabbed his T-shirt, pulling him closer to her and sliding her warm hand up his shirt to the center of his chest. "I'm sorry, Bobby."

He placed his hand over his shirt, covering her hand with his own. "Why?"

"My hormones are out of control right now." She breathed deeply. "But mostly, I said those things to you because I was afraid, Bobby. I don't want…" She sighed softly, trailing off.

He looked down at her. "Tell me."

"I don't want to become a person that I can't un-become. Children have that effect, you know."

He sighed. "Yeah."

Her voice was clouded by tears. "I don't want to lose my future. I don't want to lose you. I don't want to lose *myself*."

Bobby brought her free hand to her mouth and kissed it. "You definitely won't lose me. I don't know anything about kids. Not really. But I know that this baby is you and me. I don't think this baby can make you any less you."

She sighed again, pursing her lips.

He tried once more, proceeding cautiously. "What I'm trying to say is that I'll become someone else for this baby, if it means you can keep yourself." He abandoned caution, spilling forth his love. "I'll drop my future before I let you drop yours. You're gonna be a star, Sweetness. You're gonna shine brighter than the sun." He paused. "Maybe I'll be earthbound, but you're gonna soar. Trust me, Sweetness. I won't let you fail. I swear it."

Kindle pressed her lips against his neck, her speech dampened. "You're a good person. You're a better person than I am."

"I wouldn't say that."

"No, you wouldn't." She ran her hand over his head and loosened his hair from his ponytail. His hair fell over the pillow like a silk sheet. "When are you going to cut your hair?"

Bobby stared at the ceiling. "Do you want me to?"

"Not so much. It's lovely. What is your natural color?"

"Um, brown. Just, like, dark brown." He tugged on her hair tie and pulled it out so that her bun unraveled. He spread her curls out over her arms and chest. "You have beautiful hair," he said. "I wish my hair was like yours." He paused. "Can I ask you something?"

"Yes."

"Would our baby have hair like yours? Or like mine?"

Kindle took a deep breath. "I don't know, Bobby."

"Well, I don't mind either way. As long as it has hair, you know?"

"Is that your stance on racial equality?"

"No. Just how I feel." He brushed back the wispy curls at the edge of hair. "Hair is just really awesome. My dad's balding."

"Poor father," she giggled.

Kindle's short laugh was proceeded by a stark silence. He held his hand still over hers. She sighed.

Bobby finally spoke, sober. "Can I make you a promise?"

"I don't need any promises, Bob."

He laughed. "Bob?"

"That is strange, isn't it? The name of a used car salesman. Or an amateur swindler."

"My uncle used to call me that when I was little. My mom named me after him."

Kindle laughed hard and loud. Her hand grew even warmer against his chest.

Bobby smiled. "What? You couldn't imagine me as a Bob?"

"No. I couldn't imagine you as a used car sales man. Your hair would be like a young Paul McCartney's."

"I had hair like that one time. When I was like twelve. So, you can't laugh."

She laughed harder, her chest vibrating.

Bobby placed his hand on her neck and felt it vibration "Hey, I'm serious though; I do want to promise you something."

Kindle pulled his hand from her neck and stared at it. "You don't have to make me any promises."

"I want to though. I want to promise you that I will be here when you need me. I'm a good man, Kindle. I promise that. TCB, man. I promise that." He stopped. "Do people say TCB here?"

"I'm not so sure. I'm not really an expert on what people say."

"Well, taking care of business is what I'm about. I just want you to know."

"I trust you, Bobby."

"Thanks a lot, man." He cupped the back of her head and received her to himself with a gentle kiss. "Will you put your arms around me?"

Kindle wrapped her arms around his neck. He kissed her frontward and sideways, his mouth in perpetual motion over hers until he stopped suddenly. Between short breaths, he uttered, "If you had it to do all over again, would you marry me again?"

She twirled a strand of his hair around her finger. "You are very clever. You intoxicate me for the hard questions."

He smirked. "That wasn't really the plan."

"Of course it wasn't." She clawed her fingers down his chest. "Well, the answer is still yes. I would still marry you."

"Then, will you? Will you marry me again? We could do it right this time."

"Right?"

He pulled her hand out from beneath his shirt, clasping it and placing their locked hands on top of her stomach. "I don't mean right. I just mean different."

"If that's what you want."

He kissed her once more. "Yeah, that's what I want. Let's do it."

Kindle nodded. She pulled herself up, facing him and crossing her leg over his body so that she sat upon his chest. She bowed her face over his and kissed him.

He sighed, contented. "Yes, let's do it," he continued, amused by his double entendre as he reached for her thigh.

Everything was okay. At the very least, it would be okay some time soon. Bobby could finally fall asleep.

Autumn

With every good thing, change arrives
To the passing season we will lift our eyes
Then enters autumn with a sigh
Still, to summer, we must say our goodbyes

Chapter Eighteen

"I'm so stoked, man."

"Stoked is not even the word, dude."

"Then what's the word?"

"How the hell am I supposed to know?"

Bobby sat listening to Larry and Kyle yell across the hotel room. Kyle stood in the bathroom, flushing down a roach.

They hadn't changed the upkeep of the room since Bobby left. Piles of clothes still crowded the floor. The stench of men who cared for little else but a high and the next show engulfed the room. One of them had branded the nightstand with a cigarette. Bobby ran his finger across the burn methodically as he sat beside Larry on Kyle's bed.

It was late September and Kindle had a slight bump that the band still knew nothing about. They also didn't know about the little things that kept Bobby totally in love with Kindle.

Still largely infatuated by Kindle's British accent, Bobby tried imitating it sometimes when he sat alone in the living room. It seemed like every time he did, Kindle somehow managed to sneak in from the bedroom and catch him.

"I will need you to stop with this obsession with me," she would tease.

He always laughed, his face growing hot.

Each time they laughed together, Bobby became a little more comfortable with the idea that he'd have no other lover besides her. Other women grappled for his attention before, during and after every concert. But when he laughed with Kindle, he was always reminded that they had chemistry. He never wanted to forget that.

In early September, Mickey had been traded out for another guitarist named Tom. The band was set to play a gig at The Rainbow Theater. The venue, though quite a distance from Manchester, was well worth the travel. Pink Floyd had held shows there on a recent tour. The Ramones had recorded *It's Alive* there. Jimi Hendrix had set his guitar on fire on the theater stage.

The Dare wouldn't perform alone at The Rainbow Theater. They were scheduled to play a short set in between a dozen other local favorites. Even if The Dare was lost in the crowd of punks, Bobby was hoping to at least accumulate the residue of fame.

"You know who's gonna be there, right?" Kyle said. He stepped out of the bathroom.

"No," Bobby said absently.

"The one you let get away."

"What?"

"The infamous Betty Warner," Kyle said as if announcing that year's Grammy winner. "Dude, you might wanna stop putting her off. She's helping to organize this thing."

Bobby looked up. "What? She is?"

"No. I just made the whole thing up." Kyle rolled his eyes, laughed and sat beside Bobby. He smelled like pot. "Sorry to tell you, buddy, but she's got her busy little hands in everything." He stood again and stretched his arms. "That's why I invited her to our hole. I told her that you wanted to apologize to her for being such an ass."

"I never said that."

Larry interjected. "Obviously, dude. But the last thing we want is for blondie to turn our mikes off during the set. She's been complaining about you since you pushed her off at BOW."

Bobby stuttered. "So, when—"

The knock sounded on cue. Larry jumped up to open the door. Betty stood at the entrance, smiling.

She wore a Mohawk that looked as though her hair had been blown back and suspended mid-air. She wore all black and her hoop earrings were so big that they elongated her earlobes like an African tribal man.

"Ricky," she said, immediately walking to him. She loomed over him as he leaned his elbow against the nightstand. "Excited to see you."

"Yeah," Bobby responded, remote.

"How's your little world, Love?"

"Everything's cool, I guess." Bobby stood up, slipping toward the end of the bed—an awkward maneuver he used to avoid touching her breasts. He crossed over to Larry's bed.

"How's your wife Kindle?" Betty inquired loudly.

The three looked at her simultaneously.

"What?" Bobby breathed.

"How is she? How is the little stage star? Or has she given up acting?"

"What?"

Betty stepped toward him. "I didn't take her for your type. But horses for courses, I suppose. I guess I can't be so offended. I'm just not your kind of bird, am I?"

"What?" Bobby repeated.

"Are you playing dumb or do you think I am? I've got more smarts than your sex gives me credit for." She looked around the room, her eyes stopping at each of them. Kyle and Larry held their heads down in some peculiar reverence. Her smile made evident that she was entirely gratified by the way her presence turned men to boys. "How far along is she?" She raised a silencing hand. "And don't ask me how I know. It makes me feel stupid. I know a pregnant woman when I see one. Especially one who can't disguise her morning sickness during an audition."

The fuck?" Kyle said, incredulous.

Betty simpered and looked around at all three of them once more. "Children are really a blessing, aren't they? But you see, I really don't want to be responsible for promoting a band whose lead singer will soon be out of commission indefinitely." She pursed her lips. "'Spose we'll see what happens, won't we?"

Kyle and Larry both turned their attention toward Bobby.

****

When Bobby returned home, he had no appetite. He watched Kindle eat. Her appetite had picked up noticeably. As she devoured her chunky spaghetti, he wondered if she noticed that he had not touched a single bit of food on his plate.

Bobby stood beside her in the kitchen where she held her plate near her stomach and swirled spaghetti around her fork.

He couldn't figure out exactly why they had decided to stand and eat in the kitchen. Kindle talked about what she would have to do to audition for something, anything, once she had the baby. She wondered if she would have to lose a tremendous amount of weight.

Bobby stood balancing his full plate of spaghetti with one hand. He stared at it the entire time she talked.

"Are you going to eat, Robert?"

He looked up. "Robert? Why did you call me that?"

Kindle scraped her fork across her plate and shrugged. "I don't really know. But you're not here with me, are you?"

"I'm here. I'm okay."

"I don't think so." She placed her empty dish on the counter and gathered his plate from his hand, drawing a forkful of spaghetti from it before setting it on the counter. "What's your worry?"

"Nothing," he said quietly. "It's nothing."

"That's right. Go ahead and lie to me. You should know that I might not be interested in what you have to say once you decide you're ready to talk." She left the kitchen for the bathroom.

Bobby shook his head, washed off the dishes and headed to the couch. He tangled his hair into a ponytail, scooped up the guitar at his feet and rested it on his lap. He began strumming and singing, interpreting Zeppelin as best he could. He never thought he could do it justice. Except today—when it was exactly how he felt. He went through the lyrics, ending with the proclamation that he was about to lose his worried mind.

Bobby sat his guitar down and headed for the bathroom.

****

As soon as Kindle set her toothbrush back in the holder, Bobby was standing near her, leaning against the door with his arms crossed.

"Can I ask you something?"

She spat water in the sink. "What is it?"

"I just wanna know something."

Kindle stepped toward him so that the tips of their feet touched. "Just ask."

Bobby turned his face from hers. "Did you ever tell anyone about you and me? About us? I mean, about our marriage?"

"Why are you asking something like that?"

He rubbed his cheeks wearily. "I don't know."

"No. You know. What is it?"

"I went to see Kyle and Larry at the hotel."

"Okay."

"And they invited Betty Warner there. She's supposed to be a part of the planning stuff for the Rainbow Theater gig."

Kindle rolled her eyes, grunted and pushed past him to the living room, flopping down on the couch.

Bobby followed her and stood in front of the television. "It's just something she's doing. She's really into the music scene or something."

"So?"

"So, she knows that you and me are together." He paused. "Somehow she knows that. And I just want to know how."

"We're acquaintances, Robert."

Bobby crossed his arms. "What? Who? You and Betty? How? I mean, how do you know her?"

Kindle stood back up, capturing his shifty eyes. "You do remember my class, don't you? Betty was in it. And you should know that she was horrible and mean to me. Besides that, she wasn't any good. That's the reason Nigel didn't recommend her for an audition. She was probably angry and decided to find a way to make it to my audition. She assisted with it as some kind of a doorkeeper." For a second, she forgot the rest of her story. She could hardly believe how beautiful his flustered face was.

"Anyhow, I presume that she already knew we were together, given that *Alex* saw us in the bathroom together." Kindle raised her brows and fluttered her eyes.

"What do you mean?" Bobby asked, sounding now like a timid child.

Kindle flattened her hand against the center of his chest. "Trouble and strife is rhyming cockney slang for wife, dear. What did you actually think she meant by that?"

"I don't know." Bobby rubbed his eyes. "But you didn't even say yes. You said maybe or perhaps or something."

"When she asked me about you at the audition, I wasn't inclined to dispute the existence of our relationship. You are mine, aren't you?" She ended with a flash of her eyes and a taste of her own lips—a practice in the art of coquetry.

He looked away again. "Why did you do that?"

"Why wouldn't I do that?"

"Because…"

"Because of what? You sound embarrassed."

"I just want to know why you didn't tell me that you knew her."

"Do you inform me of everything you do? If you must know, I didn't tell you because I didn't want to bring her to your mind. Can you understand that?" Kindle put her hands to her hips. "Would you have told me Betty was at the hotel if it weren't for what she said? Don't pretend as though this was your only time seeing her. She told me about how regularly she interacts with you." She took a wobbly step backward. Her rounding belly had lately thrown her balance off.

Bobby held her elbow until she regained her balance.

She snatched herself away. "You know what makes this more pitiful? I've told you that she mistreated me and your only concern is why I didn't tell you that I've met her. You are crucially full of yourself."

"No, I'm not."

"Oh, but you are."

"No I'm not."

"*Yes*, you are."

He let out a short growl and covered his mouth.

"So, you're howling like a little wolf now? Your immaturity isn't endearing."

Bobby groaned. "I'm just tired."

"Tired of what?"

"Tired of fighting with you. Everything's like a fight with you now. I didn't grow up like that."

"Really? I recall you telling me stories of your parents' marital issues."

"Yeah, but my mom never gave my dad trouble. She was quiet. I just asked you a simple question."

"Nothing is ever as simple as you believe. You have an intention in everything. It gives you away."

"I don't have any intentions. I don't even know what that really means." He sighed. "I mean, I don't know what makes you say stuff like that."

"You're an idiot," Kindle decided, shaking her head with a patronizing smile.

"But you're cruel. You really are."

She gripped her stomach suddenly, hunching over.

"Are you okay? What's wrong?" he said, reaching for her once more.

Kindle glowered. "I think our baby is moving. If he or she could be called 'our baby.' Apparently, you don't want this baby or myself to belong to you."

"What?" Maybe he couldn't find any other word. He balled his fists.

"Just tell me the truth," Kindle said. "Say what you mean. Do you wish you were single again?"

Bobby hesitated. He pouted. "I'm just saying that in a business like—like the one I'm in—you just can't, like, tell everybody everything. It can cost a lot. Besides, Betty's doesn't mean anything to me. That's all I'm really trying to say."

"Well, unlike you," Kindle said, "I walk around every day with the evidence of what you're trying to hide. So, shall we trade? Because right now, I would much rather strap a guitar to my front than a baby."

"You're not even showing that much yet, Kindle."

She took another step forward, bidding intimidation. "Yes, you're right. But you try lying down and suddenly feeling the weight of something that's growing inside you that you didn't ask for. That's what it feels like every day for me. I can't breathe. I'm quite sure if you were in my position, you couldn't handle it."

"You don't get it," he breathed, backing away from her.

Kindle stepped forward once more, completely filling the space between them. "I am so sick of bearing the full weight of this. And for you to take that woman's side over mine…" She breathed to bring her voice back from tears. "You're selfish and you're really quite worthless in this whole baby endeavor."

"I can't believe that you would even say something like that to me, Kindle."

Kindle scowled. "Really? Have you so quickly forgotten my cruelty, Bobby?"

****

Kindle looked at him once coldly before stomping out of the room. Bobby kicked his foot against the couch. She never failed to reprimand him, never failed to remind him that she had the right to scold him.

Bobby reached for his guitar case. He left the apartment, slamming the door behind, nearly bowling over Kitty Wonder on his way down the steps.

Chapter Nineteen

The ride to London took no time at all. Bobby sat quietly on the passenger side while Fred steered the van. He alternated between pursing his lips, biting them and licking them—savoring the bitterness of yesterday's argument over and over. The scenery was a smear against the window as they drove down the highway. Bobby had no interest in the blathering of Kyle, Larry and Tom. As they bounced around the van, the band's equipment shook, Larry's cymbals crashing to the ground twice. They were single men, as voluble and careless as ten-year-olds.

Nothing was so loud as the showcase. In Bobby's opinion, all of the bands were equally awful. They played loud and fast, perhaps thinking they had captured the essence of punk music with power chords. They hadn't captured the essence of music at all, as far as Bobby was concerned.

As The Dare waited to go on stage, Betty entered backstage. With her black curly wig and maroon lipstick, she was an image of the Black Dahlia.

A few short greetings later, she took a seat in a chair beside Bobby, joining him in the lonely corner he had claimed for himself. She held two bottles of beer.

"What's your deal, Ricky? Has your woman upset you this fine day?"

Bobby leaned forward, placing his elbows on his thighs, dropping his eyes.

"You know, I'm not trying to be ugly. I wouldn't want you to be angry before hitting the stage. So, what can I do to help you? Have a drink." She held out the beer bottle in her hand.

"No. I'm not really in the mood for a drink."

"Of course you're not." She tapped his knee. "You don't drink, do you?"

"Not really."

Betty giggled and balanced the beer bottle against her knee. "I knew it. You are one of a kind." She sighed. "Marriage is dangerous for a star like you. You can't be so morose on stage. You have to forget about her."

Bobby glanced up at her wearily.

"At least for the time being." She nudged the beer top into his side. "Have some. It will help you relax."

Bobby lifted the bottle from her hand and peered at it closely. He snapped off the top, bringing the bottle to his lips. The drink burned going down, bitter in his mouth but its effects sweet. With one swig, he was revived, as though an electric jolt had charged down his esophagus.

"Now, that's better than anything, right? Told you I could be the treatment for your ailment."

Bobby looked at Betty again. He couldn't tell whether he was quickly inebriated or just spellbound by her persistence, but he did suddenly recognize Betty's strange charm. Maybe she was more than maquillage and theatrics.

"I know that it's terrible at first," she said. "But you grow to love it over time. It's what they call an acquired taste."

Bobby blinked. "What are you talking about?"

"The beer."

"Oh, yeah," he mumbled.

Betty crossed her legs toward him. "Yes." She searched the room before catching his eyes. She locked them with her own, so that everywhere her gaze moved, his eyes followed. It was hypnosis. "What do you think of me, Ricky?"

Bobby scratched his knees and shrugged. "I don't know."

"I'm not a bad girl. I'm not a phony either. Smart people like to call that kind of consistency of character integrity."

"Not sure I understand." Yet, for the first time, Bobby wanted to understand her.

She rubbed her bare shoulder against his. "I've never told anyone this. Maybe I just feel close to you. Maybe we're soul mates." Betty held out her hand until he shook it. "My name is Alexandria. Sometimes known as Alex. The name Alex passes for a bloke's name, yeah?"

"Yeah." Bobby took another swallow of the bitter remedy.

Betty struggled with removing her own bottle top. "There was a time when I could put that name down for anything and it would get me into places with powerful men."

Bobby clutched her bottle and snapped the top off.

She smiled, sliding off her wig and uncovering her slick damp hair. She tossed the wig at their feet. "My last name's Andrews. Alex Andrews is the son of Thomas Andrews. A talented bloke like you must know who he is."

"Yeah, I heard about him. Didn't know he had a son or whatever."

Betty wiped her mouth with the back of her hand, removing her lipstick to reveal her cotton candy pink lips. "Yeah, well, rich producers can have sons. I suggest that new artists don't."

Bobby stared at his empty bottle.

She plucked at the crusted mascara on her eyelashes. "Just my opinion. Anyway, the name Alex Andrews got me into some pretty wild parties. All I had to do was flash my ID at some naïve doorkeeper to get into all of these little social events. I've chatted up men at the top of the music industry ladder. I've enjoyed favors that I really shouldn't have."

Bobby rubbed his hand on his thigh.

"I knew it was wrong at the time," she said, taking hold of his hand, "but I wanted what I wanted. I had a need to feel like I was on top. What better way to get to the top than getting on top of the man on top." She giggled. "I'm sure you know what I mean."

Bobby looked away.

Betty pinched his cheek, looking him over with sprightly eyes. "I did make connections that come in handy from time to time. The truth is that I don't really *have* to work. Just a little visit to some of the *married* men I've met, and I could get just about anything I want. I used to bribe men without a second thought." She squeezed his hand. "I'm reformed now, Ricky. I'm Betty Warner now. That's my mum's name, you know. Thought it'd be good for something. My mum left me and my papa a long time ago."

"Oh."

She rocked side to side. "Well, the name was good for starting my new life. I suppose you could say that my mum gave birth to me twice. The second time around has been a lot better than the first, though. I keep everything decent for the most part. I work hard. I play sometimes. I go to church every so often. But I don't regret my past, Ricky. It was good for something. Both of my nyms were equally necessary."

"Yeah," Bobby said.

"The way I see it, you are Ricky on stage. You can be whoever else you're supposed to be outside of that. Use who you are on the stage to your advantage, Ricky. Forget about your little missus for now. Ricky Stallion is single and has the world to take on. Ricky has a job to do, favors to obtain, Love."

Betty kicked up her wig, catching it with her hands, and skipped to the other side of the room.

Bobby sniffed, staring at the bottle as though it could join his internal dialogue. He turned the bottle over. Two small drops hit the white floor.

He remembered one month ago when he stood with a mop in his hand, examining the vomit on the hard wood floor. It was erratic in shape, green, runny, ever expanding at his bare feet.

Bobby had seen throw-up before. Plenty of times. When Kyle and Larry partied hard at night, they usually spent their mornings hung over a toilet. Bobby used to hold back their hair from the toilet water, patting their backs and flushing the toilet. Vomit was nothing foreign.

But this vomit, Kindle's vomit, could not be flushed. She never found a way to make it to the toilet, even when he encouraged her to go when she first showed signs of queasiness. It always ended up that he was left cleaning vomit while she crawled back to bed. Every day, he cleaned.

That day one month ago, Bobby had become utterly fixated with her vomit, with its bumpiness, with its thickness in the center and wateriness around the edges. It spread so freely, thinning out but growing in size, showing no signs of stagnation. The doctor had said that morning sickness would end after the first trimester. The first trimester would end, but the last trimester would also end. A baby would crown. Bobby would cry tears of joy. Soon, he'd be wiping baby vomit off his shirts. Kindle would beg him to clean the other messes the baby made, while she took a break to nurse. He would agree, feeling like he could cry again, this time out of weariness.

Bobby flexed his legs, smearing the beer drops with his sneaker. At The Rainbow Theater, he would try his best to forget these things, everything outside of the stage.

"Betty," he said.

Betty had joined the band and Fred at the other end of the room. She nodded and laughed with Kyle.

Bobby raised his voice. "Betty."

She yelled back, "What's up?"

He held the bottle up and pointed at it with his middle finger. "Can I have another one? Please."

****

If being drunk was what he was on the stage, then so be it; the show was more excellent. Bobby took a chance that he wouldn't have ordinarily. They were only allowed three songs, but he began a fourth one on his own, strumming his electric guitar. Larry joined in on the drums, though he had never heard the song before. Bobby had written the song the night before, sitting alone on the couch. It was called "Mary Mae," for no other reason than it sounded good at the time and he already had written a song called "Kindle."

I'm a fool
You know I am

You are so cruel
I'm still your biggest fan

Don't need to say I love you
Wouldn't doubt you anyway
There's nothing I could do
What else could I say

Do you want me, Mary Mae
Do you want to have our baby

I'm a fool
You know I am
But you are too
I fall, you stand

Don't need you to yell at me
Couldn't hurt you anyway
Why couldn't you see
I'd never walk away

Do you want me, Mary Mae
Do you want to keep our baby

He repeated the lines again and again until Larry initiated the end with the slowing of his drum taps. The crowd stood rapt. Or maybe he was drunk.

"Thank you," he said softly into the microphone before disappearing off stage.

Fred stood behind the stage. His mouth was parted.

"What was that?" he asked.

Bobby sniffled. "I don't really know."

****

Bobby didn't return home until the next day. The band had stayed in London to sight-see. He enjoyed every minute of their adventure. He had almost forgotten how funny his friends really were.

Betty had, of course, solicited him for sex, even saying that she was much aroused by the way he handled his liquor.

"I was tempted to let your drunken self touch my Bristols again," she whispered to Bobby as the band walked along Downing Street.

"Bristols?"

"Bristol Cities," she laughed, looking down at her cleavage. "My pretty, squishy titties."

Bobby shook his head. "Not interested, Betty."

"But you are, Ricky," she replied. "I can tell. You just don't know it yet." Quickly, she grabbed his face and kissed his mouth. "That's the third kiss. I told you three time's a charm." She grinned and skipped up to the spot where Kyle stood staring at the Big Ben.

Bobby breathed, relieved to have her take interest in something else, but suddenly afraid of what this third kiss really meant.

Bobby abandoned his anger in London. Funny how time really was a cure for all ailments, even broken pride.

When he arrived at the apartment, Bobby found Kindle squatting on the ground before the television, picking at her fingernails. She did not acknowledge him when he drew near. Instead, she headed to the bathroom and shut the door.

Bobby knocked. "Are you ignoring me?"

"Not really."

He bit his nail, shifting his weight from one foot to the other. "When I was gone, I did some thinking."

"Well done. Would you like a prize?"

Bobby laughed. "I was thinking about our baby."

"Do you want to get rid of it?"

"Why would I wanna do something like that?"

"Inconvenience."

"Inconvenience? No. No way," Bobby said.

"So you were actually thinking of something other than yourself." He heard the sprinkle of her urine in the toilet water.

"Well, yes. I'm always thinking of you two," he said, raising his voice over the flush of the toilet.

Kindle ran the sink and opened the door.

Bobby continued. "I was thinking of a name for it."

"For *it*? For our *creature*?"

"For our baby."

She put her hands on her hips, her stomach appearing rounder than it ever had. Something was actually growing in there, like one of his mother's cakes puffing up in the oven. Bobby laughed aloud and smoothed his hand over her stomach.

Kindle tapped his hand away. "Not an exhibit."

"Sorry."

"What names have you come up with, Robert?"

"Well, I was thinking, you know, that we don't really know if it's a boy or a girl." He scratched the crown of his head and pushed his hair back.

"Okay."

"So then, um, we should pick a name that would fit a boy or a girl. But it'd have to be something totally rad. Nothing common, you know."

"Yes, I know."

"My grandma's name is Choice. I think that's a really, um, proper name, I guess. I mean, it has meaning. A boy or girl could have that name. And it would make the baby stand out."

"Are you serious? Choice? That's not really a name."

"It's my grandmother's name."

"Interesting." Kindle crowned her stomach with her hands.

"You don't like it?"

"I never said that," she said with a smirk.

Bobby rubbed his hands together. "Well, I want you to like it. I really do."

She walked past him to the bedroom. "I will have to think about it."

"Why? What's wrong with Choice?"

Kindle began folding the pile of clothes on the bed. "It sounds like a terribly rich name. It's for one of those types that look down upon the whole world."

Bobby stood in the doorway. "Well, yeah, kinda. But we will be rich one day, right? And I'll give you guys everything."

She looked up warily, but Bobby detected an emergent smile.

"You don't believe me?" he asked.

"I just want to know what you'll give us when all this happens for you."

Bobby grabbed an armful of clothes and sat on the floor beneath her. "It'll be everything you ever dreamed of. We won't just have one bed. We'll have as many as you want. They'll be in every room that you want. Eternal slumber." He paused. "Except you won't be dead or anything like that."

Kindle took her hair down from the ponytail on top of her head. It fell over her shoulders and down her back, so that she looked like an exotic medieval princess. She was a doll.

"What else?" she asked.

"Well, you want to do theater, right? The baby will probably like theater, too. So, I'll open up a theater for you guys. I'll hire the best directors in the world to put you in the best plays in the world."

She wiggled her foot against his thigh.

"Then, I'd buy you all the clothes you want. You'd never even have to ask. I'd just have a bunch of tailors sit at your feet. All you'd have to do is order them around."

Kindle smiled. "Why would you do all that?"

"Because I love you. It's what love makes me do."

"I think we've established that." She slid down the bed and he received her into his lap. She combed her fingers through his hair, binding it up on the top of his head and tying it together with the band she had taken out of her own hair. She kissed his cheek.

"So you're not mad at me, you know, for staying out all yesterday? Kyle and Larry and Tom—well, they wanted to stay." Bobby bit down on his lip. "And so did I, I guess."

"I'm not mad." She held back the loose strands of hair from his face and searched his eyes. "But back to your showering us with gifts; I want a mansion in Sussex."

"Which way is that?"

She grinned. "We'll buy you a map with all that money, Bobby."

"Cool." Bobby grazed her belly with his fingertips. "It's like a crystal ball."

She held her breath, her chest inflated. "Can you see the future in it?"

"I think I can." Bobby's eyes grew still.

"Are you okay?"

"I'm okay," he nodded.

"What are you thinking about?"

Bobby rolled back her shirt over her stomach. "I want to kiss you."

Kindle peered at her stomach. Bobby released her from his lap, setting her beside him. He stretched his body out on the floor beside her so that he lay on his stomach. Cradling both sides of her stomach with his hands, he kissed it—a gentle, soft kiss meant for his baby. The texture of her belly, the saltiness of her skin, the growing burliness of this bump they had made together, the sound of motion therein—it all brought tears to his eyes. He brushed them away quickly and sat up.

"What's wrong?" she asked.

He smiled. "Nothing really. I think I should tease you now."

"Oh, you silly boy…"

Bobby smiled wider. He bent her backwards until she lay on the floor with her knees up. Dividing her legs with his hands, he brought his face to her stomach and burrowed his nose and mouth in it. He blew on it suddenly, making a raucous noise that vibrated and tickled her. Kindle's laughter was raw, unrefined, unrehearsed. Bobby blew again and again until her wild laughter floated fluid through the air so that he breathed in her laughter and exhaled his own.

Interlude

Future Time: 1996

Choice could not sing. Even as a small child, she could
not follow precisely the melody of "Twinkle, Twinkle Little
Star." Although she could snap her fingers on beat, she didn't
have enough coordination for dance. To the surprise of her
family, she wasn't much interested in theater. The only time she
put on a show was when she needed to get herself out of
trouble. She could put on the kind of disoriented face that made
police officers send her home with a warning.

If not for her sweet little face and her pretty English
accent, Choice could have been a felon twice before—once for
theft by taking and once for theft by perception. Her handicap
kept her from any real punishment. What decent judge would
send a blind sixteen-year-old to jail?

Though Choice attracted enough sympathy to merit her
own brand of Hallmark cards, her cousin Peter never felt sorry
for her. He was the one person who believed in her wasted
potential. He thought of her as the ultimate con-woman, one
able to trick everybody except him into believing that her
blindness was a real handicap, instead of the factor that
sanctified her talent, her gift.

Peter discovered her gift one afternoon after school when
he barged into her room.

"I'm naked," Choice said lazily.

"No you're not," Peter returned. "You're a smart-ass is what you are."

"Well, if we insist on name-calling, then you, Peter, are an intrusive nuisance."

"How can I be intrusive in my own home?"

Choice heard him drawing nearer to the desk where she sat. He sat down on the bed behind her.

"What is it that I can do for you, Peter?" she asked, turning her face toward him and setting her arm over the sheet of paper in front of her. "Have I ruffled your wife's feathers again?"

"No," he replied. "I've actually come to see if I could find my Rolex in here. I'm hoping your fingers haven't become sticky again. Delphine says that she found her bracelet in your purse."

"Are you paying Delphine to assist me or to rat out every little thing I do? Which is it, Petey Pie?"

"Where's the watch, Choicey?" Peter asked flatly.

Choice laughed, shaking her head. She took off her sunglasses and pointed with them to the dresser on her left. "First drawer on the left."

She heard him rise from the bed.

"I took it to a pawn shop," she said, picking up her pencil once more. "They hardly offered me anything for it. It's not a real Rolex."

"Do you actually think I would keep a real Rolex anywhere near you?" asked Peter. He snapped the drawer shut. His feet rapped against the hard wood as he crept closer.

Choice spread her hands out over the paper. "What are you doing?"

Peter lifted her fingers up from the page, bending them backward. Her knuckles cracked.

"What in all of Earth and creation are you doing?" she shouted, lifting her hands from the paper to alleviate the pain.

He slipped the paper off her desk.

Choice settled her glasses back on her face. Most times, Peter acted more like an older brother than her keeper. Times like this, when he became snoopy—when he took the role of prison ward—she wanted to prick his rear end with her nail clipper file.

"What is this?" Peter asked. He sounded like he was pointing his finger at her.

Choice stood up, moving to her bed. She sat down and began removing her tennis shoes. "What does it look like, Petey?"

"It looks like the front cover of *Sobriety*."

She took her socks off and flung them at him. "Really, now?"

"Did you do this? How do you know what the picture looks like? How did you know how to do this?"

Choice pulled down her jeans, trying her best to provoke his departure.

He did not move. She knew he was ogling the picture.

"Do you have any more questions?" she asked, rubbing her hands up and down her bare thighs.

"Yes. Since when did you become an artist? And how on God's green earth do you know what Ricky Stallion looks like?"

Choice pulled her shirt over her head. She was ready to strip down to nothing—anything to get Peter to leave so she could finish her drawing. It had been keeping her busier than anything else as of late.

"I don't know, Peter," she said. "I will certainly let you know when I do."

Chapter Twenty

Present Time...

So it was that September also passed. Though it was cold again, Bobby and Kindle still had great warmth for one another. They tossed around more baby names, made up titles of movies Kindle would star in one day, imagined how they would furnish their first house, talked about Bobby's latest song ideas. They made love in between their musings.

The Dare's performance schedule increased, which increased revenue, which in turn, made it possible for Kindle to quit her job in order to get off her aching, expanding feet. Pregnancy wasn't hard otherwise, but it became increasingly lonely in October. Bobby played and rehearsed more than ever. She stayed home more than she ever had her entire life.

Kindle's life became a business divided into three projects: being with Bobby when she could, dreaming of being on stage one day and entertaining the baby in her stomach with songs and stories. When telling the baby stories about Bobby, Kindle realized that there was so much about him that she did not know. What school had he gone to as a child? How many aunts and uncles did he have? Who were his mates as an adolescent? Had he ever enjoyed anything outside of music and painting?

If she were to pass any of these answers on to their baby, wouldn't they need to spend more time together? Kindle could

have easily demanded more of Bobby's time, but she gave him
leniency, believing that he would truly give them all that he
promised. Eventually.

Eventually, he would have complete control over his own
time. He wouldn't have to depend so heavily on other people
for his success, especially Betty Warner. Nearly every day,
Bobby mentioned Betty, who had made herself the continual
way-maker for The Dare. Kindle tried stifling her irritation,
though it seeped through in a grimace from time to time.

Bobby hadn't yet mentioned her to his parents, or to his
manager. He would put his index finger to his lips to quiet her
when either called. She would roll her eyes, walk away and
think happy thoughts...the arrival of the baby, her return to
acting classes, the wedding in January. They planned to hold a
tiny ceremony in front of a priest this time. Bobby was insistent
on doing it at the Polish Church of Divine Mercy.

Kindle didn't really care where it took place, so long as
they were together. She bossed Bobby around less, as to ensure
that he didn't grow exasperated with her or their situation. The
night Bobby had spent away in London, Kindle was sure that he
had left for good. She had cried like a baby until she heard the
turning of the doorknob. She had quickly brushed away her
tears with her fingertips and turned on the television.

Nights were becoming most lonely. But by three in the
morning, Bobby was always there, wrapping his arms around
her as she pretended to sleep. Sometimes, he didn't wake till
eleven. Those times, she got to watch him. He always sweated
in his sleep, since he kept both space heaters in the room for her
sake. His cheeks were usually flustered and the perspiration on
his forehead matted his hair down against his skin. He slept
quietly despite the heat, his knees bending near his stomach to
keep his feet from dangling off the bed.

Bobby made it a habit to tell her about every show as
soon as he awoke, detailing all the little happy accidents that
made that particular show more killer than the last. There came
one instance on the last day of October when he could not wait
until the morning to tell her. He tapped her shoulder as he
leaned over her. He was still fully dressed, grinning.

"What is it?" she said with a yawn.

"Best news ever."

"You found a million pounds in a suitcase outside of our apartment?"

"Better than that. So much better than that." He extended his hand to her, helping her sit up.

"What happened?"

"We played. And the show was rad, man. I mean, they just keep getting better. Fred was there. Ian was there too."

"Ian?"

"He's this guy. I used his wood to build the bed." He shook his head, shaking away the question. "Fred sat us down. An Epic guy was at the Rainbow Theater before. Betty invited him or something."

Kindle clamped her bottom teeth on her top lip.

"The guy was, like, totally impressed. His name's Jude. Like, 'Hey Jude.'"

Kindle pressed his wrist. "Be still. You're shaking."

"He wants to meet with us. Can you believe it?"

"Of course, I can. Of course."

"This is like a dream."

She sighed slowly. "I know. You are excited, aren't you?"

Bobby leaned down and scooped her up into his arms. He swung her around, her face buried in his neck. She smelled the spice of liquor.

"Put me down, Bobby," she said.

He spun around and around, faster and faster.

"Put me down now," Kindle snapped.

He placed her carefully to the ground and rubbed her stomach. "Sorry."

"What have you had to drink?" she asked.

"What?"

"I can smell your breath."

Bobby took a step back, stumbling over a pile of folded clothes on the floor. "Just, um, just beer. It helps loosen me. I mean, sometimes."

"And who introduced this to you, Robert?"

"I'm not drunk or anything."

She sat on the edge of the bed. "Well, good."

"I'm not. I'm just happy. That's all. Just happy"

"I believe you."

"You don't seem happy for me," he said.

Kindle wrapped her arms round his waist, smashing her cheek against his chest. "I am happy for you. I'm extremely happy for you. When do you meet with the Epic man?"

"November fourth. Isn't it tripped out? What a birthday gift."

"Yes, it is."

He leaned down and kissed her vigorously. For the first time, she was dazed not by his touch, but rather, the smell of alcohol on his breath. She sighed, peering up at him and imitating a happy smile.

＊＊＊＊＊＊＊＊＊＊＊＊＊＊＊

The meeting with Jude was scheduled for noon. Kindle was still asleep when Bobby awoke that morning. Bobby had no idea how to present himself, who he should be for Jude. He wanted Kindle's reassurance that being himself was the right thing to do, but when he heard her sigh in her sleep, he decided not to disturb her.

Bobby picked out his black T-shirt with the word REAL written in white on it—the one he had made himself a year ago. He chose black jeans to match.

The whole band had gone with black jeans. When they arrived in his office, they took seats around a large oak table. Tall windows offered a birds-eye-view of the rainy city. Bobby looked around at the gold records scattered over the grey walls.

Fred sat twiddling his fingers over his burly belly. With his grey polyester suit and slicked back red hair, Fred looked like a cheesy pro-wrestler turned cheesy lawyer.

When Jude Black strolled into the room, Fred stood up to greet him, looking up a whole foot to catch his eyes. Jude looked over him with a well-mannered smile. The pro-wrestler turned lawyer thing probably wasn't so impressive to him. Jude himself wore his wispy, golden hair long and his white shirt only half-buttoned.

Jude extended his hand to each of them, grinning spryly when he grabbed Bobby's hand last.

He spoke casually of Epic's interest in them. Their talent was apparent, especially in "My Other Half." He and some other music wizard had discussed re-mixing it to bring it from a catchy tune to a radio hit. Turn up the snare hit, put an extra effect on the bass and guitar.

"I think the time has come for you guys," Jude said, pushing his hair back. "Enough of the local hero status. You play your cards right, you could be international demigods. I don't make promises, but the potential is there."

Jude tapped his knuckles on the table, watching Bobby carefully, as Larry and Kyle immediately began their rapid-fire questions. Bobby stared at the blue sapphire on Jude's middle finger.

When he finished answering Tom's single question, Jude directed his words to Bobby. "No questions?"

"No. Not really." He smiled respectfully. "But I'm stoked. Yeah. Totally stoked."

Jude leaned across the table, his hands clasped together. "Well, I have a question for you."

Bobby nodded. "Sure. Yeah."

"I've heard rumors. We have all heard rumors of your state of affairs right now."

"What do you mean?"

"It's come to my attention that you're a package deal. Do you understand what I'm saying?"

"I'm not sure."

"We're very guarded against package deals with young artists. I'm very well aware that no man wants to be lonely. Early in my career, I played around with the idea of becoming a package. The issue with becoming a package is that problems may arise with your—what shall we call it?—dependability." Jude looked from his blue sapphire to Bobby. "Do you understand what I'm saying now?"

"I think I do." Bobby looked from Jude to Kyle, all around the table, searching for a kind face. He looked once at Fred's placid face and realized that he knew about the marriage. He wondered which one of them had told him.

Jude smiled. "Maybe this is a time to think about making changes in your life. We're fully invested, but only if you are."

****

Fred drove Bobby home. He drowned out everything Fred said, focusing on each song on the radio, whether he liked the tune or not. There was something to be learned from even the worst song.

When Bobby arrived home, Kindle still lay sleeping. He knelt beside the bed and kissed her forehead.

"Happy birthday," she whispered.

"Thank you, Sweetness." He walked around to his side of the bed and lay down.

"How was your meeting?"

"Great," he murmured, sliding his hands behind his head.

"You don't look like it."

"Sorry," he said.

"Why are you sorry?"

"I don't know."

Kindle rubbed her hand across his cheek.

He recoiled.

"What's wrong?" she asked.

"Nothing."

"Don't lie." She propped herself up with her arms, looking down at his face, her hair falling like a curtain on either side of his face. She kissed him softly, her belly hard-pressed against his.

He lay still.

"What's the matter?" she probed.

"I don't know where to start."

"Start with honesty. How did your meeting really go?"

Bobby pushed her hair behind her ear, lifting her arms from beneath her and lowering her down on her back. "The meeting was good. And they're interested. Like, seriously."

"That's good. It's what you want, isn't it?"

"Yes."

"So why are you sulking?"

Bobby held his breath in his mouth, bloating his cheeks. He exhaled. "They don't want me to be married. That's all." Kindle crossed her hands over her belly, turning her attention to the ceiling. "I see."

"Yeah."

They balanced silence for so long that he thought she was asleep until she said, "I'm happy for you anyway. I'm sure it will all work out."

"Yeah."

****

The last thing Jude Black said at the meeting was that when The Dare was ready, Epic was ready to sign them. He also suggested that in the meantime, Bobby should consider what was in the best interest of all parties involved. While he was sure that Epic would sign the band, he could make no promise that they would release an album any time soon with Bobby's state of affairs being what it was.

Bobby had said nothing in return. He held his silence with everyone, even when Kyle and Larry asked him about before, after and during rehearsals.

"What's your fucking problem, dude?" Kyle had yelled during the middle of one rehearsal. He had stopped playing.

"What?" Bobby had murmured.

"I'm tired of your shit. I swear to God, you'd better make a fucking decision before I make it for you." Kyle snatched the bass strap from his chest and left the garage.

Bobby continued playing, focusing on how he could imitate the bass with his guitar.

In the three weeks between his birthday and hers, Kindle also became increasingly quiet. Their time together was severely reduced by his time on stage. Even in their moments alone, she did not speak, except to ask how the show was and if he had eaten.

Bobby refused to rehearse or play the show that Fred had scheduled for the same day as Kindle's birthday, to the response of The Dare's outright belligerence—Larry cracked his drumsticks and Kyle left rehearsal again.

The morning of her birthday, Bobby went to the store while she slept. When he returned, he hid the items he bought in the cabinet under the sink. He sat beside her watching television for the whole day in silence until the sun went down. She had fallen asleep by then, her feet resting in his lap.

Bobby bent over to kiss her feet before setting them on the couch and standing. He gathered the items he bought from under the sink and took them to the bedroom. He began sorting through them, setting out all twenty-one candles evenly throughout the room. Using a match to light one candle, he lit the others with that same candle. He set two Pop-Tarts over the bed and admired how he himself had written happy birthday on the pastries in tiny icing script. He pulled out of the bag a square radio and the tapes that he had bought for it, spreading them out in a semi-circle over the bed. Around them, he tossed sunflower seeds.

Returning to the living room, he tapped Kindle's shoulder. She shook her head, her eyes still shut.

"Let's go to bed," he whispered.

"I'm not sleepy anymore," she yawned.

Bobby held out his hand to her. She clasped it as he walked her to the bedroom.

He marveled at his own work. The light of the candles painted their large shadows on the wall. The song in the player made for a dream as Donny Hathaway tiptoed down a scale on the piano.

"Happy birthday," he said, ushering her down on the bed. Her instant veil of tears glowed in the candlelight. They were a remnant of raindrops after the coming of the sun.

"I love you." Bobby began to sing over her softly. "In a place where there's no race or rhyme. I love you for my wife. You're mine, all mine."

She stood up, smiling. "Those aren't the words."

"I know." He smiled. "But I do love you. That's why I made a song for you. I mean, that's why I'm playing *A Song For You*."

She laughed at first but transitioned quickly into a storm of tears, placing her hands over her face.

"What's the matter?" Bobby asked, pulling her hands from her face.

"Hormones."

"Pregnancy hormones," he said with a low titter. "I really love you. And you're twenty-one, you know. Happy times, man. I was pretty excited when I turned twenty-one. Now, I'm a geezer. Just wait till you turn twenty-three."

Kindle laughed. "You're twenty-four now, Bobby."

"Yep, I know. I'm glad you know too." When the song came to an end, he pushed rewind until the song began again.

"Your favorite song?"

"I don't have a favorite song," he said, nestling her in his arms. "But I like this one a whole lot."

"Yes, me too."

Bobby kissed her forehead. "January, last year, he died. Took me a long time to get over it. Couldn't believe it, you know?" He kissed the crown of her head. "But better stuff comes. For sure."

Kindle retreated from him and held out her hand. "Dance with me, Bobby."

He smiled. "You know now that my dancing kinda sucks."

"Can't do a little jig?" she teased. "Just hold on to me. I can lead this time." She spread her fingers, wiggling her hand at him.

Bobby clasped it and then set his hands on the small of her back. They both laughed at the way her belly served as resistance between them.

He moved against her slowly, kissing her again.

Water brewed in her eyes, her iris a fast-turning kaleidoscope.

"Hormones?"

"Not so much." Kindle ran her index finger along the rim of her eye. "I want you happy. That's what I really want. I want you to know that I will let you go. Wherever your dreams take you. I'll let you go there."

"I don't wanna go anywhere that I can't take you with me. I mean, anywhere you don't wanna go."

"I'm resilient."

He rubbed his cheek against her temple. "Resilient? You don't have to be that. I made you a promise. Remember TCB? I like to keep my promises."

Kindle rested her forehead against his chest, silent.

"Dude, I really hope that you believe me. I don't have any kind of real life without you."

"Me neither. I hope you believe me too."

He believed her. He believed her so deeply that he felt his heart breaking. Not knowing what else to do, he reached down on the bed for a pastry. "Have a poop tot, Kindle," he said. "For me. For us."

Her laughter lifted his spirits. It was almost better than music.

****

Days after Kindle's twenty-first birthday, Bobby sat on the ground Indian-style in front of the television. He tinkled with his guitar, while Kindle lie in bed for the night. A knock on the door interrupted his play. Dusting off his hands, he jumped up and bounded to the door.

"I'm sorry," said the man at the door. The man was tall, as tall as Bobby. He was chocolate-skinned and bald, save a remnant of curly white-and-black hair on the sides of his head. "I think I have the wrong apartment. I once knew someone that lived here."

The man was completely British, though maybe he could have passed for an older Isaac Hayes. He was dressed the way Bobby had always imagined an Englishman would be—black gloves, a black scarf and hat, a long black wool coat that nearly touched his ankles.

Bobby blinked. "Oh."

The man looked past Bobby. "What kind of guitar?"

"Martin." Bobby smiled, rubbing his hands up and down his arms to keep warm.

"I once had a Martin. Sold it." The man stretched his leg forward, brushing his hands together as he entered. He walked to the guitar and lifted it from the floor. "But I still play. I must always play. Must always find fun with toys." He hiked his foot up on the television and placed the guitar over his thigh. "We need our toys, don't we? There's no such thing as men—only little boys with adult responsibilities, right?"

Kindle appeared, stepping into the room in a large white T-shirt and Bobby's black shorts. She stood with her hands on either side of her lower back, glancing once at the stranger and then at Bobby as he stood still at the open door. The man plucked one of the strings, seemingly blind to Kindle's entrance.

He raised the guitar to his ear and plucked another string. He smiled, satisfied with its voice. "This is nice. Very nice. You picked it up before you left The States, yeah?"

Bobby nodded, diffident.

"What is your name?" Kindle asked, shooting Bobby another look before she stepped closer to the stranger.

"John."

"It's our pleasure," she responded, eyeing Bobby once more. "We never get strangers."

"That's good," John said absently. He directed his attention back to Bobby. "So, do you play around?"

Bobby shut the door and stood on the other side of John. He watched John finger the guitar, punching in the frets swiftly as he glided down the neck. His fingernails were sallow.

"I play for a band called The Dare," Bobby said.

"Good name. Good, strong name." John's eyes glistened as he peered up at Bobby and bended a string. "Better than anything I've ever been a part of."

"Oh."

Kindle crossed her arms.

"Well…" Bobby began faintly, intrigued by one of John's licks, by his musical fluency.

"We never had a sturdy band name. I tell people that's the reason we never made it big." He laughed. "Besides, the name Johnny Hyrum could never catch like Jimmy Hendrix."

Kindle slapped her hand down over John's, smashing his fingers against the fingerboard. "What is your name?"

The man furrowed his brows. "What is *your* name?"

Kindle closed her eyes and opened them slowly before charging to the bedroom.

"Excuse me, please," Bobby mumbled, sprinting past Johnny Hyrum.

At the entrance of the bedroom, Bobby watched Kindle tear through the pocket of a black coat she had lain out on the bed.

"Kindle," Bobby breathed.

Kindle spun around, a scowl shading her face. She pushed past Bobby back into the living room.

"Something wrong, young one?" John asked, kneeling down to set the guitar on the floor.

Kindle stood in front of John, looking down upon him as he stooped. Bobby cupped her shoulders. She released the photograph from her right hand and the black-and-white picture flittered to the ground, landing in the small space between her feet and John's knees.

John ran his index finger down the picture slowly. He coughed. "So, I guess you know who I am." He stared up at her, swabbing his nose with the back of his hand.

Kindle wriggled her shoulders, detaching Bobby's hands.

"Kindle?" Bobby and John murmured simultaneously.

"That's my name," she said. She stalked around John in a circle—a shark to her prey.

John rose, first lifting one of his thin legs and then placing his hands on his creaking knee to pull himself all the way up. He gabbled first to himself, wiped his lips and his mustache. He removed his scarf and coughed. "Where is she?"

Kindle reached for Bobby, grappling his wrist. Bobby sniffed once before he murmured, soft as summer wind, "She's not here."

John's face brightened, his eyes glimmering when he faced Bobby. "She's not here? I can still smell her here." He removed his hat, holding it out toward Bobby. "The two of you took over this place?"

"We didn't take it over. She left it for me," said Kindle.

John nodded. He moved to the large chair, touched its arm and fixed his eyes upon Bobby.

Bobby nodded once. John sat, his long legs propping up his bony knees so that they were angled up at the ceiling.

Kindle and Bobby stood a yard in front of him, side-by-side, arms crossed.

John pushed his hand up and down his thigh with the hand that held his hat. "How have you been? How has Kayanne been? I've been meaning to visit." He laid the scarf over the arm of the chair. "So many impediments. But I always intended to come, ever since Sly told me that you visited him at—oh, what's the name of the damned club?" He shook his head. "I can't remember, but Sly told me. He sure did. He bragged about how pretty you had become. He sure was right. You are as beautiful, as exceptional as you did when you first came out of the womb." He smiled and nodded, as though he were agreeing with the voices in his head. "I was there when you came out, you know."

While John continued to nod, Bobby began to nod—a contagion generated by nothing more than discomfort. Kindle also began to nod.

"I'm the father. Hers." John held out his hand. To Bobby, it looked like tree bark. "It's my pleasure, son."

Bobby stepped forward, clutching John's hand. Their hands—ebony upon ivory, wrinkled and smooth—were a picture of social harmony.

Kindle dashed to them, unfastening their hands.

Bobby lassoed her waist with his arm. Her violent breath inflated her ribs. He lowered his lips to her ear. "Careful."

John looked down, bobbing his hat up and down on his knee. "Kayanne will be a grandmother soon, I see. Where is…where is she?"

Kindle raked her fingernails into Bobby's left hand. He winced, less from the pain than from what she was asking of him with the gesture. She wanted him to be her voice, to speak for her.

"She's gone," Bobby said. "She passed away. Like, um, like a couple years ago. I don't know…"

The room was at first entirely still. Bobby was afraid to breathe.

John rose to his feet, his hat hitting the floor. He covered his mouth with his scarf. "Oh, my good Lord. My, my, my good

Lord." He shut his eyes and his brown cheeks shimmered as a tear tumbled down each side of his face.

In Bobby's head, he heard quivering strings. *How can you mend this broken man?*

If not for embarrassment, if not for fear, if not for Kindle standing at his front, Bobby would have reached for the old man and patted his feeble shoulders.

"Mourning time is over," Kindle announced brusquely. She disengaged Bobby's hands from her sides.

John sniveled, sucking in his snot.

"Did you hear what I said? If you're going to weep like a child, find some other place to do it," Kindle commanded.

Bobby quailed. He put his hands in his back pockets.

John looked down at Kindle, astonished. Bobby contemplated that for the first time, John was actually *seeing* his daughter. He looked her up and down, his eyes fermenting with tears once more. Bobby himself began to tear up. He breathed deeply.

John muttered. "Oh, hell. I am sorry for you. So sorry for you. So, so sorry for you."

"Why do you feel sorry for me? I'm not a victim. My mum is your victim," Kindle said. "She loved you. I never did."

"I know she did. I loved her too," John replied. Another tear paved its way down one of the rifts in his cheeks. He nodded. "I loved her."

"No." She smiled. "I'm very sure you didn't."

"You don't have the ability to gauge that, young one," John responded, his indignation rising.

"It's not very hard to figure out. It's very simple."

John knelt down, grabbed his hat from the ground and settled it on his head. "You're so young. There are so many impediments that you don't know about. They're just impediments." He tied the scarf around his neck and glanced quickly at Bobby. "You never expect them. If you did, you would prepare for them." His voice rumbled as he continued. "Kayanne knew that better than I did. Why do you think she'd never let me come back?"

"Don't blame her for your indiscretions."

"Who said anything of blame? I know my own wretchedness well enough. You don't reach my age without knowing a thing or two about yourself." He slapped his scarf against his leg. "I do blame Kayanne for one thing though. Just one. I blame her for keeping that William Holster around all the time. When you were born, looking so pale, so light-eyed—you looked nothing like me—what was I supposed to think? I really, really thought you were Holster's." John pinched his bottom lip. "I admit it. I left. I don't know what kind of man that makes me, but I did come back. When your mother showed me a picture, I was sure you were mine. You looked just like my baby sister. How was I supposed to know your features were going to change the way they did? But when I found out, I offered to take care of you. I offered for us to be a family. *She* rejected *me*. *She* made *me* leave. You tell me—what was I supposed to do?"

Kindle blinked. She swallowed, perhaps swallowing down hysteria, maybe dodging all of the emotions that swelled all at once. "It's better that you go, John. It's better that I never see you again."

"Speaking out of your emotions will get you nowhere. I've done it too many times," John replied. "Too many times. It's a damn shame what it will do to your life."

Kindle looked up once at Bobby.

Bobby coughed, his eyes dropping to John's shoes before meeting his face. "It's better that you go now."

****

Kindle showed no concern for John's appearance. She did not mention him after his valediction. In bed, Bobby clung to her hip the whole night, waiting for her to talk about. She did not. Still, Bobby didn't want to leave her, but it happened that the next day Fred called and said that it was imperative that Bobby take time out to meet with Ian. Fred wouldn't accept any more excuses.

Bobby arrived at Ian's house in the afternoon. They met in his dining room, sitting at a round glass table with children's toys scattered at their feet.

"Bobby,' Ian said, scratching his cheek with the sleeve of his wool grey sweater.

Bobby smiled. "Yep."

"I've been meaning to talk to you for some time now. This is a talk of priority."

Bobby shook his head. "I don't know if we need to have this talk."

Ian screwed his finger against the table, leaving a thick smudge upon it. Bobby studied the smear. "We must," said Ian. "Your future hangs in the balance. The future that has been offered to you is a near-miracle. If you're waiting for something better, you won't find it. This is it."

"I know."

Ian drummed his thighs with his knuckles. With his bare foot, he kicked away one of the toys beneath the table. "You don't know. If you're looking for a record company that will accept the state you're in, you won't find it." He kicked away another toy. "I wanted the same things you wanted—to be a superstar, a husband and a father simultaneously. Look around. Father and husband—that's what I am. But that's all. This is a business of sacrifice. Either sacrifice or you will be sacrificed. I thought you'd learned that already."

Bobby began to wonder if Ian's fingerprints could be seen in the smear.

"I *know* you've learned this already. You have to get your priorities straight. You've come to this country for one reason. That reason was not matrimony. That reason was music. It's not only unfair to yourself to carry on this way, but it's unfair to the young men that are here sacrificing with you. Give yourself a chance, son. Give yourself a chance to live your own life."

Bobby reached under the table, picking up a red fire truck. He traced his fingers over its ladder and placed it back on the ground. "What do you expect me to do?" he said quietly, still holding his conversation with the smudge on the table.

"Do the right thing for everyone, including yourself. You know what you must do."

Bobby nodded. "Yeah."

His confirmation was less an agreement than an admission to himself that even though he had no idea of what to do, something had to be done.

Chapter Twenty-One

Days after his talk with Ian, Bobby performed with The Dare at Band on the Wall again. He caught the eye of several people in the audience. They looked at him with such anticipation, as if he could grant to them anything in the world. He could only think of how it would feel to never perform again.

When he crawled into bed with Kindle that night, he lie down and fell into a deep, black sleep. He didn't dream but awoke at four in the morning, unable to find sleep again for the rest of the night.

Bobby stood up weakly and staggered to the living room, tossing himself down on the couch. A thousand thoughts competed for his attention, but one reigned over them all.

If he had no dreams or ambitions or anything else, fatherhood would fit him like a glove. Bobby was gentle at heart, patient, affectionate, emotionally available most of the time. If not for his ambition, he could be everything to his own child that his mother had been to him.

His mother had to be the best mother in the world. Maybe there was no one that loved a child the way she loved Bobby. At times, he wondered how much her devotion really meant in the scheme of things. Aunt Catherine was his real mother and had hardly spoken a soft word to him his entire life. Bobby was

Catherine's flesh and blood, but she could hardly keep her eyes on him for more than a few seconds.

By the time Bobby's mother resolved that she could not take another year without a child, her sister Catherine was still young and fertile—twenty-one years old, Bobby had calculated. Fertility was of more value in bringing Bobby into the world than love. Bobby had never been sure of how many times his father had slept with his Aunt Catherine, but he did know that his Uncle Richard had died a year after Kyle and Meredith were born and a year before Bobby was. Aunt Catherine, newly single, could play surrogate without the sin of double adultery. Maybe a man in her bed a few times and a child in her womb would ease her loneliness.

Bobby discovered the secret of his parentage when he was fifteen, during one of his parents' fights. He found out everything through their fights—their financial standing, his mother's sexual habits, his father's hatred of any kind of disorder. During one of their fights, Bobby had found out that his dad thought he was gay and that his obsession with the guitar was just a way to avoid women. The "damned thing" was getting in the way of him ever having a girlfriend.

Bobby's parents didn't know he was home early from school as they went back and forth about Bobby and the "damned instrument." It was the first time he heard his mother refuse to back down. She was crying but insisting again and again that she was only fostering the musical gift that she saw in Bobby. His father finally growled so loud that his mother could not yell over him. He threatened to take Bobby away from her. He had every right to take Bobby if he wanted. What rights did Carol have? Bobby was not hers. He was Catherine's.

During the course of the argument, his parents had gone through the why's and the how's. Two tubular pregnancies had rendered Carol infertile. She begged for a baby, offering her sister as a surrogate. Frank had agreed to appease her.

"Only to make you happy," his father had yelled. "Always to make you happy."

It never became clear in the course of the argument why Catherine had agreed to the arrangement. However, the arrangement had worked. Carol got to raise her nephew as her son. Carol and Frank took care of Catherine's financial needs until she finally remarried. Catherine kept her distance, steering clear of the danger of any emotional attachment to the child. Carol blamed Frank for putting the divide between Catherine and Bobby. Why had Frank found the need to keep reiterating to Catherine that she mustn't ever get attached to Bobby?

"You made her afraid to love him. You made her hate him. You made it seem like she didn't have any other choice," Bobby's mother had cried.

To Bobby's father, the situation was like a "damned soap opera." To Bobby's father, Bobby's mother had created this situation and this was the reason why her life would never be the way she dreamed.

To Bobby, the secret was so bizarre that he couldn't find any way to introduce it into conversation. He didn't even want to ask his mother if he had heard right. He was embarrassed by the secret. He was saddened by it. He was angered by it. He was intrigued by it.

Bobby never asked his mother if she knew that he knew. It didn't matter who knew. It really didn't matter at all. Nothing mattered but mastering songs. He also figured that getting a girlfriend would be a good idea; he was getting older. Playing music and finding a girlfriend—he could do those things. Those things were enough without having to consider what the exposed truth would do to his family.

Now, as Bobby sat on the couch considering fatherhood, he realized that his life would be more than music and women. He couldn't see how that would be possible.

His real mother had given him away to her sister as a gift. He could never imagine giving his half-brother Kyle his child; not as a gift, not as a way to avoid responsibility. There was no way out of this.

Bobby hung his head, hating himself for wanting a way out. Still, in his heart of hearts, he knew that he would give just about anything for an escape.

Tears fell down Bobby's cheeks, hanging on to his jaw and chin. He flipped on the television and tuned to a news broadcast, setting the remote control on the couch beside him.

As he began wiping the tears from his chin, Bobby heard the announcement. At first, he didn't understand it. It was like the newscaster spoke a different language. He changed the channel and when the other news anchor made the same announcement, he understood it for certain.

Bobby looked back down at the remote control, his lonely companion. As he listened to the report, he let his heavy head fall back against the wall. The wall pulsed as he knocked his head against it over and over.

Kindle entered the room. She sat beside him, setting her hand on his thigh. "What's the matter, Bobby?" She wedged her other hand between his head and the wall. "You're going to hurt yourself."

"I'm okay." Bobby cracked the knuckle of his index finger with his thumb. "John Lennon is dead. Somebody killed him."

Chapter Twenty-Two

The whole apartment mourned the loss of John Lennon.
Both space heaters' dials broke so that they could only be
turned up to their middle degree. The hot water heater gave out
as well. Kindle stood in the kitchen every day boiling water to
bathe herself. Bobby seemed unaware of the cold. He took cold
showers and walked about barefooted, coldness in his eyes. He
did not press his body against Kindle when he slept at night. He
was completely quiet the week following Lennon's death.

Prior to that week, Kindle had believed that she really
knew Bobby. She could read his moods and gestures, even if
she didn't know the first car that he ever owned or the name of
his first grade teacher. She had memorized every birthmark,
every scar, every ticklish spot. She knew the familiar smell of
his breath, the salty taste of his mouth and the porcelain texture
of his legs and forearms. She understood his initial shyness with
strangers and his ultimate fear of failure. What she could not
understand now was why Lennon's death had changed him the
way it had. For the first time, Kindle found Bobby more bizarre
than unique.

A week to the day after Lennon's assassination, Bobby
came home at four in the morning. He looked at Kindle in the
dark, standing at the foot of the bed.

"You're late," she said. "I worried about you."

"I know," Bobby sighed.

After a week of silence, his voice was cold but lovely, like snowfall. She was a child waiting for the snow, no matter how bitter the cold was.

"Lennon's dead," he said. "I didn't expect it, you know. I really didn't."

"You told me he was one of your favorites," she said, pulling herself up to sitting position.

"Yeah. He changed the meaning of music, in a way." He paused. "I love music."

"I know."

Tears fell down his cheeks. He sniffled, his pink nostrils quivering. "Yeah, I know you know. I started to think. I really started to think."

Kindle swallowed. "What did you think about?"

"Why I love music. How much I love it. How I always dreamed of it, dreamed of doing it big time."

"I know." Her heart beat faster.

Bobby covered his eyes with the back of his hand. "I don't know if I can live without it."

Kindle gulped, pressing her fingertips on the bulging baby in her stomach. "What do you mean?"

"I just don't know if I can."

Winter

Winter brought us here
How did I expect to keep you near?
With all of your cold and all of my fear
How could I expect to keep you near?

Chapter Twenty-Three

The next ten days were Kindle's to be silent and unmoved. She avoided Bobby's kisses, his advances, his everything.

She turned over in her head whether it was possible to hold a man back from a decision he had already made in his heart. On Christmas Eve, Kindle decided that she should see her mother.

Beneath dark clouds, she knelt beside the tombstone. She wore black scrubs, no longer able to fit into her black dress. Kindle spread brown leaves over the stone; the dandelions had died with the arrival of winter.

"Mummy," she said. "I don't know how to ask you this. I'm afraid of what you would say. But I need to know what you would say." She held her breath for a beat. "What should I do about Bobby?"

The wind blew, striking her face brashly, stinging her eyes.

Kindle swallowed. "I love him. I've found love. And he loves me. I'm sure of that. But I still need to know what you would do if you were me."

The wind carried waves of rain drizzle that began to wet her face.

"Bobby's not like my father. He knows how to love. He really does. He's always taken care of me. I love him so much for that. I love him for everything he is. He's nothing like John."

The clouds grumbled and the rain came down suddenly in a torrent. It poured upon her head and down her back. She went from cold to freezing, shaking, trembling.

Kindle looked down at the smooth stone that proposed to hold the summary of her mother's life. *Mother.* Behind that title was a woman full of truth, struck harshly and diseased by the reality of life and love. The answer to Kindle's question was clear in the life and death of Kayanne Madden. Mother. Not wife. Not intellectual. Not dreamer. Only Mother. The woman who had told her again and again that luck did not exist. One could only prepare for chance.

The reality of what the chances really were brought tears to Kindle's eyes. Her sobs overtook her so that she could not stand. She rubbed her hands across the pitiful, scanty grass, hoping that something would hold her and save her. Yet, she knew that nothing could.

****

For Kindle, Christmas day almost promised to be as somber as Christmas Eve when she awoke. The clouds were still dark. Bobby was already awake, sitting up with his hands clasped together over his legs. He was frowning.

Kindle sat up.

"Merry Christmas," she said, laying her head on his shoulder.

"Merry Christmas, Kindle." Bobby looked down at her and smiled.

"Merry Christmas, Ricky Stallion."

"Merry Christmas, Penelope Princess."

They both laughed shyly.

"Are you mad at me for, like, not talking and stuff before?" he asked.

"Not at all." She kissed his cheek. His skin was as soft and sweet as the inside of a marshmallow. She knew she would long for the feel of his skin on lonelier days.

"Man, that's a relief. Because I wanted to give you something. It's a Christmas present." Bobby covered her eyes with his hand and shuffled the pillows. "Open your eyes."

"I can't. You have your hand over them." She laughed.

Bobby spread his fingers. Between them, she could see the diamond ring he dangled before her face.

Kindle pushed his hand from her eyes and the ring fell from his finger. She received it in her cupped hands like rain from the sky. She brought the ring close to her eyes.

"My mom sent me that grand I told you about," he said. "She promised she would. And I promised you. I love you."

****

Kindle wore the ring and that's what Bobby wanted. But it did not make up for the fact that he had lied. It didn't make up for the fact that he had planned to lie. This had to be a mortal sin, worthy of numerous confessions.

As an Epic artist, Bobby received a cash advance. Therefore, it wasn't much of a sacrifice to buy the ring, but it did make for having to create a fitting lie before he could tell Kindle what he had really done.

Bobby figured that he would have to eventually sanction a secret-telling day. He'd have to tell his parents that he was married. He'd have to tell his parents and Epic Records that he had a baby. He'd have to tell Kindle that he had been signed to Epic under the pretense that he had been granted an annulment. At some point, he would have to tell Epic that he had fooled them to get the deal.

As Bobby sat on the couch Christmas night pondering the order of his confessions, Kindle entered the room and sat beside him. She pulled her fingers through his hair with the hand that bore the ring.

"You love me, don't you?" she said.

"Always have." He rotated the ring around her finger.

"Then, I have to thank you. It would only be right."

"No," he replied, shaking his head. "Getting the ring was the right thing to do."

Kindle shook her head and brushed away tears from her eyes. Her voice resonated, as if she were singing a song. "You have been a good man. A better husband than I've been a wife. I needed to say thank you."

"You're welcome, I guess," he responded softly with a gentle smile.

She pressed her hand against his shoulder. "That's not all. I just needed to say that I thank you for playing pretend with me."

Bobby dabbed at the tear on her eyelash with his thumb and streaked it down her cheek to her chin. "How'd I do that?"

She blew her nose on his sleeve and laughed. "I lived my childhood fantasy of being someone else's fantasy through you. I gained a mystique through you."

"A mystique," he said, puzzled.

"I've never had a boyfriend or lover before, you know. It just so happened that in testing out my mystique on you, I fell crazy in love."

He smiled.

"And you made me feel very, very beautiful," she continued. "I'm sure I couldn't have felt that way without you."

"But you are really beautiful to me. That's not a fantasy. Having you is my fantasy, though." He smiled again, faintly.

"Thank you." Kindle looked away. "But I am kind of a mistress to you, aren't I?"

"What?"

She laughed again and rolled her eyes, squeezing them shut before large teardrops rolled down her cheeks. "You were committed before me."

"No. You're my first, Kindle. Very first." Bobby frowned. "What kind of conversation are we, like, having?"

"I saw you with your first love the very first time you played at Rory's. Her name was music. That was your commitment before me, Bobby. I can't make you decide between her and me. I wouldn't do that. I love you too much to do that." She looked down at her ring. "Marriage is the art of sacrifice, isn't it?

They glanced at the door as Kitty Wonder began to purr outside.

"I'm going to be the one to sacrifice for you, Bobby. I'm just saying…" She closed her eyes tight. Bobby realized now that she was at a cliff, refusing to look at the ground below. "I'm saying that my father never really loved my mother."

Bobby furrowed his brows.

"If my father had loved my mother, he would have sacrificed for her, given everything for her. He wouldn't have just taken until she had nothing left to give." Answering the voice in Bobby's head, Kindle deliberated, "And I don't care what John says concerning the matter."

Bobby pursed his lips.

"But I've decided that my mother was loved. Holster loved my mother. He gave up more for her than anyone. He nearly gave up his marriage for her." She shook her head. "It's not important for me to get into that. I just think that sometimes what you're willing to give up gives weight and substance to your love. Sacrifice weighs more than kind words." Kindle exhaled. "You need to…you need to go to Epic. Make something epic of yourself. I hope you understand what I'm saying to you."

Bobby thought he might cry, both exuberant and shamed. Had he been waiting for her to say those words? He shook his head. "I don't think I can do that."

Kindle laughed. "You're worried about our baby? Our happy accident? Our Choice?"

He laughed and exhaled shakily. "Yes. And you, Kindle. I've loved you too long to stop now."

"You and your lines—I will certainly miss that." She smiled. "Stop your worrying. We'll be fine. Promise you that. Mr. Holster will have me back. This I know. And I will find help and even more work soon. You have no need to worry about my safety. Kitty Wonder will be here. He'll be like a guard cat."

Bobby smiled first, but then covered his face and heaved a quaking sigh before his tears began to fall. Kindle watched him, motionless.

"No, Kindle," he said, wiping his nose with the back of his hand. "No way. I'm not abandoning my family. Maybe we should just, like, agree on something. Compromise, you know?

That's what married people do, right?" He rubbed his index finger and thumb along the line of his chin and jaw, thoughtful. "So, maybe I could go—for now. But I'll still be able to take care of you. Even if it's from a distance for right now. Wherever I am, I'll come see you. All the time. I'll see the baby. I'll be here when the baby's born, for sure. We'll keep things quiet for now. Then we'll come back together. It'll be like Larry's dad. He's a traveling business guy. He travels, but he's home a lot too." He looked her in the eyes, searching for some sign that she believed in him. "I'll make sure you have everything. Mansion in that sex place."

She laughed. "Mansion in Sussex."

"Yeah, that place. You gotta know that it's gonna be you and me forever, Kindle. TCB, man. TCB."

"Please don't say that again."

"Why?"

"Because it's starting to sound odd. And a little outdated. It's almost nineteen eighty-one now."

They laughed shortly.

Bobby snuggled his nose into her cheek. "I'm not a liar. You gotta know that I'll do what I say. I love you, Kindle. Love you more than anything else. More than painting. More than Christmas…"

"Less than music." She patted his cheek limply.

Bobby buried his gaze in his lap. "Kindle…"

"It's okay, Bobby. I didn't mean it."

He placed his hand on the back of her neck, pulling her forward to kiss her forehead. "I love you, Kindle. You believe me, don't you?"

Kindle chewed her lip, a tear tumbling over her lips as she nodded. Bobby folded her in his arms as she covered her face. She stayed in his arms briefly but soon retreated to their bedroom, overcome.

Bobby wiped the tears resting on his eyelashes. He could not be sure of what the moment meant. He could not be sure of what tomorrow meant. It was then that he realized that he had not known the next step he would take throughout any of the past twelve months. Instinct had brought him this far; uncertainty would lead him home.

Bobby took the phone from the floor and set it in his lap. He turned the numbers on the rotary.

"Hi, mom."

"Bobby, honey, how are you?"

"I'm okay."

"What's wrong?" she asked.

"Nothing at all. I just needed to tell you something."

"I'm here. I'm listening."

"I'm coming home. Next week. Everything kinda fell into place. We got the deal we were looking for." He twisted the phone cord around his finger. "And, um, I think I have some other stuff to tell you too. When I get there. I will tell you when I get there."

"Oh, honey. This is amazing. Your father will be so glad. He's going to be so excited. Oh, my little chicken..."

Kindle crept into the room. Watching her stand with a worn piece of tissue in her hand, tears wetting her face and a perfectly rounded belly, Bobby couldn't have felt more like a little chicken.

****

A little over a week later, Bobby Carter rode to the airport, crying in his heart while Kyle, Larry and Tom laughed out loud. Rain trickled down the windows. The radio played as Fred drove. Roberta Flack was on the airway, bidding him farewell to Manchester, singing to him over and over, "do what you gotta do." But Bobby hummed his own chorus.

Told you I want you
You only laughed
Slice it any way you choose
You're my other half

Bobby fluttered back tears as they pulled up to the airport. He twiddled his thumbs, biting his lip until it bled.

Bobby had no idea of what he would face, of what was to come. He had no idea that his father would die the next year on the same day that Cronkite went off the air. He didn't know that

Kindle's water would break prematurely while she stood in the middle of Mr. Holster's kitchen floor, three weeks from the day of Bobby's departure. He had no idea of the brick walls he would face in trying to get back to his wife and child, in attempting to fulfill his promise.

Bobby had no idea of the ways Ricky Stallion would change him afterward. He had no way to forecast the alcoholism that would ravish him in the years to come. He could not predict the decade of short-lived stints in rehab for his heroin addiction. He had no prophetic vision of the women Ricky Stallion would sleep with on his tour buses and in hotel rooms, when loneliness accosted him in the worst way. He didn't know that Betty Warner would be among the women with whom he'd lay, ultimately making good on her promise that three times—three kisses—was a charm. He didn't see that he would become a father to three other children, each of them making him feel that he had made a miserable mistake rather than a happy accident. The many impediments that kept Bobby from Kindle and Choice could be detailed, but all that mattered in the end was that he could not keep his word. As much as he had believed that he was capable of keeping his promise, the impediments were as real as John Hyrum had said. But for now, he could see none of them

All he could see was Kindle. All he could see was that he walked away with a Choice.

****

Time changed, but the house had not. Still looming. Still mysterious. Still beckoning.

When Mr. Holster opened the door to let Kindle in, she noted that the smell had not changed. Maybe she had not changed. She was yet a child, gazing at the high ceilings in awe, hoping that he might offer her a cookie, a chocolate mint.

They stood in the dim foyer. Kindle folded hands together in front of thighs. Holster observed her keenly.

She cleared her throat. "Did you ever try your hand at redecorating?"

"No." Mr. Holster crossed his arms. "My wife is dead. That was her passion."

"Peter's gone too," Kindle added softly.

"Yes, he is gone. To Japan, now. He's done well for himself."

Kindle nodded. "I hope you're not lonely."

"Sometimes, I am. Today, I'm okay."

"Me too." Kindle paused. "But yesterday, I was broken apart. As of yesterday, Bobby has been gone a week. As of today, I've decided what is best."

He nodded. "You've become a woman. Maybe your husband needs more time to become a man."

"Yes." She nodded back. "Maybe, this time, you won't have to turn me away."

Mr. Holster looked upon her with unreserved compassion, as only a father could. Did he somehow know that when she told Bobby he was free to go, she had hoped that he would not accept her offer? Did he know that she had waited every day, expecting him to come through the door apologizing for ever considering leaving? Mr. Holster looked at her so tenderly that Kindle was sure he must have had some idea.

For a moment, Kindle thought Mr. Holster might smile. Instead, he reached for the bag she clutched in her right hand. "Come this way."

Epilogue

Future Time: 2010

Sometimes the radio station played music from the nineties, from Choice's adolescent years. Sometimes the music would wake her, sometimes not. This morning, she was not awakened by Blind Melon, Boys II Men, Michael Jackson, or Madonna but by a knock at her door.

Choice yanked the robe from the foot of the bed and wrapped it around herself.

"Answer it, Delphine," Choice mumbled.

Heavy-footed Delphine rose from her own bed in the far corner and trudged to the door. Choice sat up, lined her back with the headboard and crossed her feet.

Delphine plodded back. She gripped Choice's ankle. "You need to get up. Seriously."

"Who is it?"

Delphine squeezed tighter. "Get up."

Choice clutched Delphine's wrist, using it to raise herself to her feet. She clasped the steel walking stick near her bed with one hand and grappled for her glasses. Delphine placed them in her hand. Choice counted their steps as they walked.

She tapped the open door with her stick. "What's up?"

She heard breathing. Slow, steady breathing. Focused breathing. She heard fright.

"This is Ricky Stallion," said Delphine softly, rapping her fingernails against Choice's walking stick.

"What?"

"Hi," the man said. His voice was smooth like honey but light as powder.

Choice tugged on her ear lobe. "Ricky Stallion?"

The man sniffled. "Yeah."

"Fraud," she whispered to Delphine. She turned back to the man. "I don't deal with impersonators that suppose they will take advantage of my impairment. I've got nothing to give you."

"I think it's him," Delphine said. "I really do. Looks just like him. They wouldn't let any ol' person up here, Choicey."

"Ricky Stallion, eh?" Choice hummed before knocking the man's shin with her stick. "Why are you at my door?"

"I don't know." He exhaled. "I'm Ricky Stallion. I mean, I'm Bobby Carter. I think, maybe, that I'm…" He trailed off, hesitating. "Maybe I'm your father."

A Blind Choice: Chapter Two Excerpt

Bobby sat across from Lissette in a booth at his favorite restaurant in Canton—a bright-light tavern where people ate fries with their hands instead of forks and were either too young, too old, or too preoccupied with their busy children to appreciate Ricky Stallion. He had never been blinded by a camera flash there, not until today, when a teenage boy stopped outside of the window and excitedly waved his girlfriend over to snap the shot. Lisette smiled for it. Bobby winced.

"What's up, Bobby?" began Lissette. She held a compact, blotting her lips, smearing plum lip gloss evenly over her lips. Certainly she believed the camera had flashed for her, the passers likely mistaking her for Catherine Zeta-Jones. Bobby could see a basic physical resemblance—shiny dark hair, shiny dark eyes, shiny lips—but he was pretty sure Catherine Zeta's beauty wasn't as specious as Lissette's. Could there be anything less beautiful than a woman made rich from her reproductive abilities?

Bobby smoothed his hands over his jeans and stared at his fizzing glass of Coca-Cola. "I have something important to say."

"Well, I figured." She tucked her compact back into her bite-size, pearl purse, shaking her head, proudly reproving. "Geez, Bobby, don't tell me that you're hooked again."

"No," He took a fry and twisted it between his
fingers. "Nothing like that."

"Then what is it?" Lissette sighed loudly, so loudly that
the kids in the booth across from them turned to face her. She
smiled tightly, offering them a starchy wave. "Celeste is really,
really freaking out about you. You know, she said you've been
out of this world lately. She may be technically grown, but she
still needs a father."

"Yeah," Bobby replied, looking down at the edge of the
table where Lisette braced her finely manicured hands. He
remembered when her fingers were bony and her fingernails
short from excessive biting. She had once been young flesh and
blood, instead of stiff, middle-aged bone and joint. There had
actually been a time when he could stand to be around her for
days on end. She'd even made him laugh a few times before,
when she was still pregnant with Celeste.

Bobby leaned back and dropped his fry, rubbing the salt
and grease on his pant leg. "And by the way, not everything has
to do with drugs."

"But mostly everything," Lisette returned. "If this isn't
about drugs or Celeste, then why have I come here? I don't
frequent Canton. I don't really know why you insist on being
here yourself. I don't get you, Bobby."

And he didn't get why she insisted on worshiping gods of
lesser things, but he couldn't say that. He could only
confess. "I have a kid."

She looked around once before rolling her eyes. God
forbid that anyone should know what a sass she was. "I know
that already."

"I'm not talking about Martin."

She sighed again, leaning back cross-armed. "Oh, geez,
give me a break, Bobby. Don't you think you're a little old to
be fathering children? You're old enough to be a grandfather."

Bobby pursed his lips, flattening a proud grin. "Well, this
might make you happy then. She's twenty-nine years old."

Lisette fluttered her eyes. "Excuse me."

"Yep," Bobby nodded.

"Is this some kind of joke? Because I'm not laughing,
Bobby. I'm not laughing at all."

"I'm not that great at telling jokes, Lisette."
She folded and refolded her napkin, exhaling evenly.
"What's your deal, Bobby? What's going on with you?"
"Her name's Choice," he said. "That's her name."
She coughed over her glass, ripples jumping through the
water as if an earthquake had shaken the
ground. "Choice? What kind of name is that?"
'My grandmother's name." He knew that she didn't
know that. He knew that she knew nothing about him. But she
had, at a certain time, promised that she was in love with
him. And now, she claimed that her impudence was a
consequence of unrequited love.
"I need you to explain this to me because I really..." she
blinked once "...*really* don't get it."
"Her name is Choice Madden."
"Ay bendito," Lissette breathed, fluttering her eyes faster
at the slip of Spanish. God forbid anyone discover that she was
Lisette from the Block, that she came from Spanish Harlem.
"Choice Madden? Choice Madden? Do you even realize who
the hell that is?"
"Of course, I do."
"She's black, Bobby." She lowered her voice, leaning
forward. "She's African-American. How does that even make
sense to you?"
He smiled slyly. "She's English-American. And she's
mine, Lisette. I promise you that." He stared at his cola. It was
flat. "But I've got some time to make up for, dreams to
remember."

For more information about author Evan Tyler and *A Blind Choice*, the sequel *to A Happy Accident*, visit www.eptyler.com

Follow Evan on Twitter: @epicevantyler
On Facebook: www.facebook.com/epicevantyler

Made in the USA
Charleston, SC
24 January 2014